PRAISE FOR *ALL THEY ASK IS EVERYTHING*

"*All They Ask Is Everything* has everything—a compelling plotline and a cast of perfectly crafted, flawed characters, each certain they're the best mother for two bewildered little girls. It's a roller-coaster ride through the intense emotions motherhood brings—complete love and joy one moment, frustration and overwhelm the next. I was hooked from the very first page."

—Kitty Johnson, bestselling author of *Five Winters*

"A wise, thought-provoking novel about motherhood and whether having it all is even the right aspiration. Hadley Leggett delivers a poignant tale about what it means to be a mother in all its messiness and complexity. *All They Ask Is Everything* will have you rooting for three women who will make you appreciate your own village."

—Nancy Johnson, author of *The Kindest Lie*

"Equal parts tenderhearted and whip-smart, *All They Ask Is Everything* paints an unflinchingly honest portrait of modern motherhood. Leggett's deeply empathetic storytelling hooked me from the start and left me aching for her characters and the painful choices each faces. This stellar and moving debut is a must-read for anyone who's ever questioned what it means to be a 'good' mother."

—Lauren Parvizi, author of *La Vie, According to Rose*

"Honest and compassionate, Hadley Leggett's story gives voice to the complex struggles of motherhood, in all its raw and flawed beauty."

—Robin Yeatman, author of *Bookworm*

"With nuance and empathy, Hadley Leggett untangles what appears to be an impossible knot of a custody battle between three possible caregivers. I read with my heart in my throat, unsure who to root for at any given moment, and somehow rooting for them all. *All They Ask Is Everything* has everything you *could* ask for: fully drawn characters, a twisty plot that will force you to leave your judgment at the door, an exploration of the demands and sacrifices intrinsic to motherhood, even a romantic thread and, above all, the highest stakes—the well-being of two lovable little girls at the center of it all. A life-affirming and expertly crafted tale of motherhood, loss, and impossible choices that, despite the heavy themes, is full of hope and heart."

—Amy Neff, author of *The Days I Loved You Most*

"An honest and tender exploration of the demands of motherhood and the devastation that can ensue without proper support. Leggett writes with compassion as she takes the reader through multiple perspectives of a complex situation. Perfect for fans of Kate Hewitt!"

—Charlene Carr, author of *Hold My Girl*

All They
Ask Is
EVERYTHING

All They Ask Is EVERYTHING

A Novel

HADLEY LEGGETT

LAKE UNION
PUBLISHING

For every mother who worries she's not enough

One

NOTICE OF DEFAULT, screamed the bold black letters.

Hannah wanted to yell right back. She'd called the bank twice already, told them she didn't have the money yet. They'd granted her a deferment until December, so why were they still mailing notices?

Crumpling the pink trifold and tossing it aside, Hannah dug through the rest of the stack on the dining room table: two delinquent medical bills from Ivy's broken arm last spring, a threatening letter from the electric company, and three catalogs filled with pictures of cozy families in matching snowflake pajamas. Hannah picked up the first one, its cover taunting her with glossy smiles and a spotless living room. She ripped it in half. There. No more joyous, beaming dad. She used to take these kinds of photos for a living, so she knew better than anyone—under the right lighting, any family could look happy.

Piles of laundry notwithstanding, she and her girls *were* happy. The pills helped, and thanks to a sleepless night of internet research, Hannah had a new plan to solve their money troubles. Once she finished painting the Whidbey cabin, she'd fix the deed transfer to reflect her dad's true wishes. Then she could sell the property and pay off all those overdue bills, including her unpaid mortgage. By the time her mother found out, it wouldn't matter anymore.

Hannah added a flyer for grief counseling to the recycle pile. Why did they keep sending this garbage? She glanced up, startled by a golden light peeking through the miniblinds. For weeks the skies had been dumping on Seattle, a steady drizzle that seeped into your bones and drenched you from the inside out. But now, when she rushed to the window and yanked on the cord, the first streaks of dawn illuminated a cloudless sky. She wanted to whoop for joy. *Yes,* the weather promised, *this time your plan will work.*

Belting out Johnny Nash's "I Can See Clearly Now"—finally, finally the rain was gone—Hannah dashed upstairs and paced the hallway in front of the girls' bedroom. When she couldn't wait any longer, she burst through the door, only to run smack into a web of old sheets and towels tied around bedposts and clipped onto desk chairs. Two clothespins popped off, sending a threadbare quilt sagging to the floor. She grinned. Her girls were nothing if not industrious.

After repinning the blanket—Wren would never forgive her for compromising the structural integrity of the fort—Hannah peeled back the girls' covers to find three-year-old Ivy curled like a glowworm against her big sister's chest. For a moment Hannah imagined snuggling in beside them, drinking in the comfort of their sleepy scent. No, she felt too jittery to lie down. Placing a hand on each of their bellies, she began to tickle them awake.

Wren opened her eyes first, a look of confusion crossing her sleep-lined face. "Mommy?" She sat up, blinking. "You never wake up first."

Technically, Hannah hadn't woken up at all, because she'd never managed to fall asleep. Sleep no longer felt necessary, now that those chunky green capsules had worked their magic. "Today is special. We're celebrating."

"Celebrating what?" A crease appeared between Wren's brows.

Hannah touched a fingertip to her seven-year-old's forehead, smoothing away the wrinkle. "Celebrating that Mommy's all better and the sun came out."

They'd start with breakfast. No more letting Wren pour dry cereal into a bowl for her sister; this morning Hannah would make pancakes, steaming hot and golden, slathered with butter and syrup. She'd be the good kind of mom, the kind who stayed cheerful no matter how much her head ached or the girls bickered, who listened to every rambling story, played endless rounds of princess-mermaid-fairies, and kissed their tears away. The kind of mother she'd never had but desperately wanted to be for her daughters.

Ivy was still asleep, so Hannah tickled more, pressing fingers into soft, sweet flesh until her second daughter's eyes flew open. At the word *pancakes*, Ivy broke into a dimpled smile.

"Up and out to the grocery store," Hannah said, "and don't bother changing clothes. It's a perfect day to stay in jammies." Following her own advice, she twisted her long tangled blonde hair into a clip and pulled a sweatshirt over her tie-dye pajamas, a long-ago gag gift from Alex that had somehow morphed into a wardrobe staple.

She bustled her daughters into the gray station wagon, crossing her fingers it would start. Car maintenance was another of Alex's responsibilities she couldn't bring herself to tackle. But the engine roared to life, and she flew through the sleepy streets of their neighborhood, a gentrifying mix of peeling paint and chic, boxy remodels. Too high on sunshine to slow down.

As Hannah pulled into the empty Safeway parking lot, silence filled the car. She glanced into the rearview mirror and laughed: both girls had fallen back asleep. Of course they had, poor dears—she'd let them stay up half the night building a LEGO castle. One of these days she'd set some boundaries again, start using words like *manners* and *schedule*. But the girls had lost so much in the past two years; every no felt like another piece of their girlhood ripped away. Besides, letting them stay up meant less time for Hannah to wander the house alone, startling at every creak and echo.

For the second time that morning, she admired her sleeping ragamuffins: Wren's shoes were on the wrong feet, pulled over the fleece footies of her pajamas, and Ivy's matted curls circled her head like a dirty-blonde halo. Sunlight danced across their cheeks, and Hannah was seized by an unexpected longing for her camera.

Not the one on her phone, but her real camera, the Nikon SLR that had once been both her passion and her main source of income. She'd even won a hefty prize for her portraits—$2,500 and enough media exposure to launch a real career. But that was back when she was young and silly and cared about nonsense like the International Color Awards. These days her "first baby" collected dust at the top of a closet, hardly worth the shelf space it stole from stacks of Pull-Ups and outgrown onesies.

Hannah scanned the nearly empty parking lot. She couldn't immortalize the moment on film, but what would it hurt, just this once, to let them sleep while she ran in for a box of pancake mix? Ivy always woke up angry from naps, and dragging her screaming through the grocery store would hardly feel like a celebration. Hannah cracked the windows, then felt the chilly breeze and rolled them back up. The girls would be fine. The car would stay warm enough in the sunshine, and she'd be gone five, six minutes, tops.

Halfway across the lot, she turned around and locked the door again. The Volvo offered a reassuring beep.

—⁓—

Inside the store, Hannah fought the temptation to stop and admire pumpkin displays and towers of autumn produce glistening under the too-bright fluorescent lights. She wasn't here to browse seven kinds of apples. Pancake mix. Just pancake mix.

But strolling down aisle six toward baking, she spotted a row of red-and-white plaid lids—Bonne Maman strawberry jam—and all those jars sent her mind sailing back through time, into the tiny apartment she'd shared with Alex after college. He leaned against the peeling laminate counter of their pea green kitchen, spreading a thick layer of strawberry

4

goo on something white and starchy. A saltine cracker, or—no—a crepe. He scraped the edge of his butter knife to get every sweet, sticky morsel and then licked it anyway, just to be sure.

Of course. For a celebration like this, Alex wouldn't have made pancakes, he would have gone all out: crepes with strawberry jam and whipped cream and chocolate drizzle, that's what they needed.

Hannah pulled out her phone to do a quick search and groaned: only 379 million recipes for crepes, shouldn't take long to sort through. She scrolled down the top results and punched one labeled "light and fluffy." First ingredient: one and one-third cups flour. Marching into the next aisle, she was greeted by a wall of flours. Were the extra three grams of fiber from whole wheat worth the heavier texture? "Live a little, Hannah," she said out loud, and heaved a bag of all-purpose unbleached into her cart before waltzing over to the candy aisle for squares of dark chocolate.

Once or twice her daughters came to mind, and she imagined them waking up in the car, wondering where Mama had gone and why they were still strapped into their booster seats. But Wren could take care of Ivy for a few more minutes. Hannah pictured a picnic in the backyard later that morning, the three of them curled on a checkered blanket, nibbling on Daddy's chocolate-strawberry crepes. The girls would understand.

By the time she made her way to self-checkout, her cart was full. Too full. She'd promised herself not to break out the last credit card. But as she considered putting back the organic strawberries, Hannah noticed a white-haired lady behind her, breathing heavily and leaning against a display of candy bars and spearmint gum. A shopping basket filled with half a dozen Lean Cuisine dinners swung precariously from her wrist.

"Are you all right?" Hannah asked. The basket slipped, and Hannah leaped forward, snatching it before the frozen meals toppled to the ground. The woman turned two shades paler and swayed on her feet. Good Lord, was she having a heart attack right here in the store? "Let's just sit you down." Hannah held the woman gently under the armpits and lowered her to the checkered linoleum. "I should call a doctor."

The woman shook her head. "No need to fuss, it'll pass in a moment. Go on with your shopping." Her voice came out raspy, strangled.

Hannah desperately needed to get back to the girls, but she wasn't about to leave a sick old lady on the floor of the checkout aisle. "I'll find a manager."

As she raced through the empty store, Hannah cursed lane after lane of self-checkout—where were all the employees? Finally she found a produce stocker with flaming-red hair and adolescent acne. "I need your help. This woman up front, she's about to pass out, and I can't stay with her. Honestly, I shouldn't be here at all, I left my girls in the car, and they'll wake up any minute." The vegetable guy froze, a box of cucumbers held in midair and his mouth a bewildered O. Hannah grabbed his arm and dragged him back to checkout.

The woman's color had returned, and she tried to wave them away. Ignoring Hannah's outstretched hand, she struggled to her feet. "Just a little episode of A-fib, happens all the time. I'm fine now."

The kid from produce still looked worried. "Shouldn't we call an ambulance?"

Hannah yanked out her phone, ready to dial 911. "They always say heart attacks in women are a silent killer. Plus, she's sweating, and I'm pretty sure that's a sign, I read all about it in—" Hannah stopped, realizing they were both staring at her. Why weren't they listening?

The woman turned back to the vegetable guy, steadying herself against the shelf of gum. "Heavens, no. Don't need an ambulance. Maybe a sip of water, though."

"Right." The boy nodded with his whole body, hungry for a plan. He pointed at Hannah. "You stay with her; we've got cups in the employee bathroom." He bounded away before she could explain that no, really—she really, *really* had to get back to her car.

Each second felt like an eon as she waited for their redheaded hero to return. Finally he reappeared, walking ever so slowly, a paper cone filled with water balanced in each hand. Confident her new friend would be well cared for, Hannah returned to scanning her groceries, feeling a bit faint herself. She sighed with relief when the credit card went through, but didn't bother to bag the groceries, just tossed them in the cart and rushed out to the parking lot.

Hannah squinted toward the Volvo, temporarily blinded by a ray of sunlight glinting through the trees. Was that a car blocking her in? A *police* car? The produce kid must have called for help after all. She walked faster, and the cart rattled along in front, knocking together butter and flour and jars of strawberry jam. For a moment, she worried the eggs would break, until she saw two cops standing next to the Volvo, arms crossed. With a shove, Hannah abandoned her cart and sprinted across the lot.

"My girls—" Her feet crunched on broken glass. "What happened? Where are—" Hannah's stomach dropped: a jagged hole now decorated her passenger window. Terrible scenarios tumbled through her mind, car thieves and kidnappers and pedophiles. She lunged toward the car, but the male officer stepped forward, blocking her path.

"You're the mom?" The cop towered above her, a heavy black holster dangling from his belt. He made *mom* sound synonymous with *criminal.*

"What happened?" she asked again, gasping for air. "Are they okay?" She craned her neck to try to make out her daughters in the back seat but couldn't see anything through the grime caked on the rear windows.

"Your kids are safe," the policeman said. "Thanks to Olivia here."

Hannah hadn't noticed the small crowd of onlookers gathered behind her car, but now a perky brunette in spandex and sneakers stepped forward. "I heard a kid crying inside the car. When I saw they were locked in there with no parent in sight, I called 911."

Wait. Now Hannah was thoroughly confused. The police were the ones who'd broken the window? At least it hadn't been a kidnapper.

"Cars can heat up in minutes," the woman continued, her ponytail bobbing as she talked. "And didn't you see the forecast? Supposed to be the hottest November day in a decade, up to seventy degrees."

"Seriously?" Hannah crossed her arms in front of her chest. Sure, it was sunny, but the temperature could hardly be called warm. Besides, if the girls got too hot, Wren was perfectly capable of cracking open the door.

A man stepped forward and slung a protective arm around the woman's shoulders. "The little one looked terrified," he said, a touch of indignance in his voice. "We couldn't imagine why anyone would leave such a little kid alone." He placed a casual hand on his partner's belly, which Hannah now realized was round and hard beneath her workout tee. Of course. No parents could be more perfect—or more anxious—than those still expecting. She imagined this couple wandering the aisles of Buy Buy Baby, loading their cart with infant breathing monitors and slip-proof kneepads by the dozen.

"Anyhow, you're lucky I've started keeping *this* on my key chain." The husband held up what looked like a fancy pocketknife. "One punch and the glass shatters. It's got a seat belt cutter too. Safety first, right?"

An angry buzzing filled Hannah's ears. Why hadn't these absurd people simply asked Wren to unlock the door? Now she'd have to pay for a new window on top of everything else. "Just tell me where my girls are," she said, turning to glare at the cop.

"We're going to have to ask you some questions, ma'am." He pulled a notepad and pen from his pocket. "What's your name?"

"Hannah. Hannah Sawyer." She took a step toward him, fists clenched at her sides. "But I'm not telling you anything else until I know where my girls—"

"Mommy!"

Hannah whipped around at the sound of Wren's voice. There she was, leaning out the front window of the police SUV, grinning and clutching a stuffed panda Hannah had never seen before. Wren waved the bear's fuzzy paw and pretended to make it honk the horn. Hannah glimpsed a blur of blonde in the passenger seat and finally exhaled. Her daughters were in a police car, but they were smiling. This was all a big misunderstanding.

"Cops these days give out teddy bears?" Hannah flashed the officer her most charming grin, but his dark eyes looked the opposite of friendly. He introduced himself as Officer Perry and asked again for her name.

"I told you, it's Hannah. But come on, the girls were asleep and I only ran in for a moment, because we're celebrating today and the girls wanted pancakes. Then I got the idea for crepes, but there were so many ingredients, and this woman was having a heart attack—"

"Wait, what? Slow down or I can't understand you. Your name?"

"Hannah Sawyer."

His tanned face remained disturbingly blank, so she said it yet again, louder this time, enunciating each syllable as if she were talking to a child. But his frown didn't budge, and a bubble of panic rose in her throat.

"Okay, ma'am," he said, shaking his head and scribbling something on his notepad. "Why did you leave your kids in the car?"

"I told you. The girls wanted pancakes, and they fell asleep on the way—never wake a sleeping baby, right? But we're celebrating today, so pancakes from a box won't do, of course we need crepes." Hannah's thoughts cartwheeled over one another, each word slurring into the next, but she couldn't slow down. "Then I couldn't find the whipped cream, Ivy loves this one brand of whipped cream—"

"Lady, I can't understand a word you're saying." Officer Perry raised his voice to cut her off. "You left your children in the car, alone, for over thirty minutes."

Fanning her face, Hannah opened her mouth to reply, but her mind went blank. The once cheerful sunshine now felt oppressive, and for a second, all she could think about was the itchy, sweat-soaked pajama top stuck against her skin. Those damn pills made it possible to get out of bed in the morning but also made her heart race and her brain foggy.

Hannah took another step forward. She needed to feel the solid weight of Ivy in her arms, to hold Wren's hand and tell her everything would be okay. But the second officer blocked her path, leaning over to whisper in Perry's ear. His frown deepened.

"We're going to need you to come down to the station." His voice boomed from all directions. Hannah covered her ears and lunged again for the SUV. Perry grabbed her upper arm.

"My girls," Hannah gasped, trying to shake him off. "Just let me get my girls."

"No, ma'am, your daughters need to come with us." Perry's hand tightened around her bicep, and her mind flashed to Wren's favorite boa constrictor at the zoo, its thick muscular body squeezing helpless prey. She managed to wrestle away, but her elbow collided with the officer's groin. He yelped.

With a swift twist of her arm, Perry spun Hannah around and pinned her face first against the side of the Volvo. Her cheekbone crashed against the edge of the car's roof, sending pain searing through her temple. She squeezed her eyes shut. *Do not cry, do not cry, do not cry.* If the girls were watching, she didn't want them to see her tears.

"Calm down, miss." The officer's voice was flat. "We're only trying to help."

Hannah could hear him fiddling with something in his pocket even as he held tight to her wrists. She knew she should stop struggling, but her muscles didn't seem to be listening to her brain. Twisting around to see the girls one more time, she caught a gleam of metal.

Two

Julie hesitated outside the children's store, drawn by the lure of miniature socks and cotton onesies and fleece sweatshirts with teddy bear ears. On her way home from work, she'd stopped at the pharmacy next door to grab some toothpaste, but now she couldn't help herself. Despite the box of baby clothes packed away in her closet, tags still attached, she wanted to buy something new. To celebrate.

Because this time she was becoming a mother without needing to calculate HCG levels or monitor cramps or pray for a heartbeat to show up on the scan—this time her baby-to-be was already two months old. With a deep breath, she pushed open the glass door, heavier than expected. An electronic chime announced her arrival to the saleslady, who smiled from behind a tower of miniature turquoise shoes.

Two months old, the caseworker had said, but still about the size of a newborn. Julie had asked if he was a preemie, but no: "It just happens sometimes, with neglect." The words sent a familiar wash of acid up Julie's throat. Somehow women not yet ready for motherhood gave birth to healthy infants, while others who'd been prepping for years couldn't stay pregnant. Now Julie pulled out her phone and studied the photo again: the pink and blue stripes on the hospital blanket were crisp and clear, but no matter how much she zoomed in, the baby's face stayed blurry. It didn't matter; she could see his lovely dark curls and his tiny clenched fist, and she didn't care if he was cute or not. Walking over to a rack labeled "Newborn," she fingered the fleecy fabrics. This baby deserved something all his own, untainted by her memories of loss.

She picked out a pair of sky blue overalls, styled like denim but made of soft stretchy cotton. A bright-red airplane decorated the front pocket. To go underneath, she chose a yellow onesie that said MAMA'S BOY in sparkly black letters. For now, at least, this boy would have two mamas. Over and over during her foster care training, the instructors had stressed that reunification with the biological family was the ultimate goal. But Rhonda knew Julie's history—they'd bonded a bit during training—and the social worker had promised to send her some cases where the chance of eventual adoption seemed high.

I can handle giving them back, Julie had promised, first to herself and then to her family, and then to the caseworkers with their kind, concerned expressions. She couldn't afford a private adoption, and no one would pick a single mother to raise their baby, not with stacks and stacks of profile books featuring loving couples to choose from. Of course, Julie would cry if a baby went back to their original family—but those wouldn't be purely selfish tears; they'd be mixed with an altruistic joy for the other mother reuniting with her child. A completely different sort of grief than losing a baby in utero. And eventually, she'd meet the child who needed her not just for a few months but for a lifetime.

Now, as Julie fished inside her wallet for her credit card, her phone vibrated, sending a trail of goose bumps along her forearms. *Cascadia Family Services.* She fumbled with the phone and almost dropped it. "Sorry, I have to take this," she said to the saleslady. "Be right back."

She dumped the overalls on the counter, raced out of the store, and nearly collided with the swollen belly of another mama-to-be as she punched the talk button on her phone. "Rhonda, did the paperwork go through?"

The voice on the other end sounded too quiet, too gentle.

"It's Samantha. Sorry, but plans for your case have changed . . ." Samantha explained how the paternity test had revealed a different father than expected, also an addict but with an extended family in the suburbs who wanted to raise the baby. "We so appreciate your flexibility," Samantha said, as if Julie had any choice in the matter. "And I'm going to bump you right to the top of the list for future cases. You'll be the first one we call." In an instant, Julie found herself back in a familiar purgatory, where once again she'd be waiting and waiting for the phone to ring. But this baby's family would've turned up eventually—maybe it was better she didn't have the chance to get attached.

After hanging up, she couldn't bring herself to go back inside and explain to the saleslady why she no longer needed fake-denim overalls with an embroidered airplane. Instead she circled the outdoor mall, letting the November wind cool her burning cheeks. For once she was glad she didn't have a partner, no one she needed to disappoint with the news. She could call her mother, of course, but the sympathy in her voice would trigger tears Julie didn't want. And if she called Anitha, she'd get an earful for walking out last night on the blind date her best friend had set up for her.

Julie had tried to give the date a chance. She'd curled her cropped brown hair and painted her chewed-off nails and worn the high-waisted jeans meant to make her short legs look longer. But she'd barely made it through the artichoke dip before the guy's extended monologue became unbearable—she simply didn't care about his big-shot tech job, modern downtown loft, or well-connected socialite friends. Feigning a family emergency, she'd escaped to the comfort of her own couch and reruns of *The Office*. Maybe her bad behavior would finally teach Anitha to stop meddling in her love life. After Seth, Julie was done with men. Motherhood was what she'd always wanted, and at thirty-five years old, with a stable job and a two-bedroom town house, she saw no point in waiting around for another unreliable Prince Charming.

Suddenly craving a chocolate croissant, Julie slowed to a stop in front of a mom-and-pop bakery. It was past dinnertime, but this was another perk of living alone: no one to criticize your food choices. She parked herself at a table by the window and nibbled her pastry, letting her disappointment dissolve in flakes of butter and sugar. Then *Cascadia*

Family Services flashed across her phone screen again, and she almost choked. Maybe there had been a mistake; maybe she was getting a baby after all.

This time, Rhonda's gravelly voice filled her ear. "Heard what happened with your case, and I'm sorry. But I've got the perfect distraction while you're waiting for another baby." She sounded uncharacteristically chipper. "We took two little girls into emergency custody this morning, and they need a place to stay, just for a night or two."

Julie didn't know how to respond. This scenario was not at all what they'd discussed during her intent-to-foster interview. "How old?" she managed to ask, already trying to think of a delicate way to say no. Neglected babies were one thing—too young to remember the trauma they'd endured. But older children would remember everything, and they might not want to be taken from their parents. Older children might hate even the idea of a foster mother.

"Seven and three," Rhonda said. "Real sweet. New to care, no known issues."

"I'd love to help, but I'm not sure—"

"This is confidential." Rhonda lowered her voice. "But they were found by themselves in a parked car. The girls are traumatized and really just need a place to sleep for the night."

Only last week Julie had read a news story about how dozens of children died in hot cars every year, how parents forgot their sleeping kids and committed this unthinkable mistake. Apparently, on a sunny day like today, it didn't even have to be that hot—kids had died even in seventy-degree weather. Now the scene played out in her mind: two small girls strapped into booster seats in the back of a beat-up sedan, the air getting hotter and stuffier by the minute as they cried out for a woman who never returned.

"I know it's not the foster situation you're looking for," Rhonda continued, "but you're licensed for up to age seven. I wouldn't ask except we've got a real shortage of homes right now—"

"I'll take them." The words popped out before Julie had thought them through, but once she'd spoken, she knew she'd made the right choice. There would be opportunities down the road for a baby, and in the meantime, she could help these two children in need.

"Oh, thank goodness." Rhonda sounded surprised, as if she hadn't expected her plea to work. "When can I bring them over?"

Julie checked her watch. Friday traffic on Montlake could be a beast. "I can be home in forty minutes."

"Perfect," Rhonda said. "And I mean it, they're really sweet. You're going to love them."

—m—

Julie spent the drive home obsessing over how she'd forgotten to clean the tub last weekend and didn't want to bring kids home to a dirty bathroom. By the time she pulled into the parking lot of her complex, an ancient silver Jetta was already parked in the visitor space, with the ample backside of a cornflower blue pantsuit sticking out the rear door. Rhonda stood up and waved her over. "Can't thank you enough—their next option was going home with me tonight." She grabbed Julie's hand in a quick, efficient squeeze, and then motioned to the back seat. "Meet Wren and Ivy."

Two pairs of round blue eyes stared back, one face pink and tear streaked, the other stony white and defiant. Both girls wore stained pajamas, and Julie wondered how long it had been since someone brushed their hair—the little one's honey-blonde curls were a ball of frizz. As she said hello, Julie cringed at the sound of her own voice, singsongy and overcheerful. She tried again, remembering her training: connect over something specific. "Hey, those are cute bears you've got. Do they have names?"

The older girl tossed her panda on the floorboard and stomped on it.

Rhonda shrugged. "They're from the emergency responders. I don't think Wren wants hers anymore."

Of course she didn't. Getting left in a car and then taken into custody by child protective services must've been traumatizing, and Julie tried to think of something comforting to say. Instead, she just stood there, feeling useless, until Rhonda unbuckled Ivy and handed her over. The three-year-old wrapped her chubby limbs around Julie's neck, clinging like a starfish to a rock.

"Hi, little one." Julie breathed in the sticky-sweet scent of apple juice mixed with Play-Doh and cheese crackers, and thought of her four-year-old nephew.

"Remember, don't get attached," Rhonda whispered in Julie's ear. "There's a shelter care hearing on Monday, and we're looking for relatives."

Ushering Rhonda and the girls inside, Julie repeated *Don't get attached* like a mantra. She'd hoped for a baby, but now that she saw these scared little girls, she desperately wanted to bond with them, get to know them, cheer them up after the hellish day they'd just endured. Already she could feel her thoughts spooling into the future, jumping six steps ahead to baking cookies and braiding hair and planning play-dates with her nephews. Take it slow, she reminded herself. You're a stranger to them.

They'd hardly made it through the door when Julie's giant orange cat sauntered over, flopped to the floor in front of Wren's feet, and rolled onto his back, a rug of cotton candy fluff. Wren let out a tiny squeak, the first sound she'd made since getting out of the car. Gingerly, she stretched out her hand, letting the cat sniff first her fingers and then her face. He licked her nose.

"Ouch." A half smile snuck across Wren's face. "He's got a scratchy tongue."

"That's Popsicle. I think he's trying to give you a bath. Want to help me feed him?"

Julie set Ivy on the floor, and each girl dumped a scoop of kibble into the cat bowl—twice his usual portion, but it seemed only fair to reward the fifteen-pound icebreaker for his efforts.

"Popsicle's a funny name for a cat," Wren said, watching him scarf down his food.

Julie smiled, glad to have a story to tell. "The first night I brought him home, he followed me everywhere. Couldn't take a step without tripping on him. Then I was microwaving my dinner in the kitchen and realized he was gone. I opened every cupboard and drawer, searched the whole apartment, until finally I checked the freezer. There he was, shivering on the bottom shelf. Like a popsicle."

Ivy giggled, but Rhonda drummed her manicured fingernails against the countertop. "It's late. Sign these forms, and I'll let you get these munchkins off to bed." She handed Julie a thick stack of papers. "Got everything you need?"

Julie had prepped for toddlers as well as babies, buying every item on the recommended supply list. She had toothbrushes, picture books, and stuffed animals at the ready, and she'd even downloaded lullabies in case her future children had trouble falling asleep. Now she squinted at the girls, trying to guess their sizes. "I've definitely got pajamas that will fit Ivy, and I have a bag of hand-me-downs from my nephews. Something in there should work for Wren." But now she leafed through the paperwork and stopped short. "Um, Rhonda—there doesn't seem to be a medical consent form here."

Pursing her lips, the social worker motioned for Julie to hand back the forms. She thumbed through them slowly, then shook her head. "I'll email you one first thing tomorrow morning."

Julie panicked for a moment, remembering that she'd been instructed never to take a child without all the paperwork in hand. Once Rhonda walked out the door, she'd be legally responsible for these girls. But what could she do—refuse to help a pair of exhausted, traumatized children just because the social worker forgot to bring a form?

"Okay. I guess emailing it tomorrow will be fine. Thanks. But . . ." She motioned for Rhonda to follow her into the hall. "What do I say if they ask about their mom?"

Rhonda put one arm, then the other, into her wool coat. "Don't say much. Tell them she's not feeling well, and that you'll keep them safe until she can take care of them again. I'll call in the morning when I have more details."

Julie fought the urge to ask more questions, just to get Rhonda to stay, but once the door clicked shut, her confidence returned. Back in her substitute-teaching days, she'd wrangled an entire classroom of fifth graders for three months while their teacher was on maternity leave—taking care of two little girls had to be easier than that.

—⁓—

"No thanks," Wren said, when Julie handed her a clean pair of pajamas. "I'm fine in these."

Julie frowned. Something like orange juice, or maybe paint, was splotched down the front of Wren's pajama top, and the cuffs were tinged gray. She didn't want to think about what the bottom of her footies must look like.

"Actually, what about a bath?" Julie asked. "I've got some pink bubbles that smell like watermelon."

Wren flinched as if she'd threatened violence.

"Don't you guys take baths before bed?"

Wren shook her head.

"What's your usual routine? Bedtime stories? Songs?"

"I'm not tired," Wren said, sinking into a chair beside the twin beds in the guest room. "I'll just sit here with Ivy and wait for my mom."

Julie raised her eyebrows. "It's almost ten. Way past your bedtime, I'm sure."

"We don't have a bedtime." Wren crossed her arms in front of her chest. "We just go to sleep . . . like, whenever we get tired."

"Well, at my house we have a bedtime." Julie's words came out louder than she intended; without meaning to, she'd switched into teacher voice. She tried again, softer. "I mean, sleep is important. And you have to set a good example for your sister." The three-year-old had curled into a ball on top of her comforter, eyelids fluttering closed.

"Ivy sleeps no matter what," Wren said, not moving from her spot in the chair. "And my mom's gonna be here any minute. The police people said they just had to ask her some questions." Wren's voice wavered on the last word, and Julie wished she could wrap her arms around this stubborn little girl and hug her tight. So their mom had returned to the car, but the police were involved. Drugs? Theft? Domestic abuse?

"She didn't mean to leave us in the car." Wren stuck out her chin as if daring anyone to disagree.

Julie's head filled with a hundred questions, but she kept her voice light. "Of course she didn't. But Rhonda said you're here for the night, so let's at least brush your teeth. C'mon, I'll get you a toothbrush."

A reluctant Wren followed Julie down the hall, only to stop halfway and stare at the framed poster on the wall, a collage of comic book covers featuring all-female protagonists from Catwoman to the Black Canary.

Julie grinned. "You like superheroes?" She'd planned to read the girls Dr. Seuss, but now she had a better idea. "Let me show you something." Leading Wren into the main bedroom, she motioned to an enormous bookshelf filled with comic books dating back to her own childhood. The seven-year-old sucked in her breath.

"Want to pick out a bedtime story?" Julie asked.

Wren traced her finger along the spines and whispered something too quiet for Julie to hear.

"Sorry, didn't catch that."

She looked at her feet, then finally up at Julie. "I asked if you had any Batgirl."

Julie clapped her hands together and tried not to squeal: talk about connecting over specifics. "Sure, I've got Batgirl; I've got everyone.

Superheroes are kind of my thing." She chose a binder labeled **DC COMICS: 1999–2000**. After flipping through the pages, she pulled an issue from its plastic sleeve and handed it to Wren. "If you've read the newest series, you know Batgirl as Barbara Gordon, but I still prefer Cassandra Cain."

Wren held the comic book by its edges, like it was almost too precious to touch. "I've never read any of them, but I've got a Batgirl doll my dad gave me when I was a baby."

Her dad. Right. Rhonda hadn't mentioned anything about a dad. Julie tried not to sound too curious. "Where's your dad now?"

Ignoring her, Wren kept silently turning pages.

"Did Rhonda call your dad?"

Wren finally looked up, and her eyes flashed. "She can't. He's dead."

Julie's heart cracked a little more. These poor girls. And she was only making it worse with her prying questions. She pointed at the comic. "Want me to read you that? It's the first issue."

For a moment Wren looked hopeful, then shook her head. "I should go to bed." As she handed over *Batgirl: Volume One*, the stony mask returned.

—ɯ—

For someone who claimed she wasn't tired, Wren's eyes closed awfully fast after her head hit the pillow. Julie sat watching the girls breathe for half an hour before going downstairs to lock the door and switch off the lights. But just as she slipped under her own covers, Ivy began to cry: deep, racking sobs that filled the house. "Mama," she wailed. "Maamaaa!"

Julie raced down the hall to the girls' room and yanked the covers off Ivy's bed. Empty. For a frantic second, she thought Ivy had disappeared, which didn't make sense because her wails still filled the room. Then Julie's eyes adjusted to the dark, and she spotted the screaming toddler sitting upright in her sister's bed. Scooping her up, Julie realized

Ivy's pajamas were soaked, as were the sheets and comforter and even Wren, sound asleep despite the racket.

"Shh, it's okay." Julie rocked Ivy back and forth, trying not to think about the pee no doubt seeping into her own nightshirt. She chided herself; why hadn't she thought to put Ivy in a diaper before bed? Rookie mistake. She peeled off the wet pajamas and found a Pull-Up in the closet, thankful again for the recommended supply list. Changing the sheets would risk waking Wren, so she covered the wet spot with old towels and hoped the mattress protector would do its job.

Ivy's tears subsided once she was in dry clothes, but as soon as Julie laid her back down, she screamed again. Who could blame her? The little sprite had been through probably the worst day of her short life.

Julie wrapped Ivy in a blanket and headed for the living room. DSHS had made its position on bed-sharing abundantly clear, but they'd said nothing against cuddling a child on the couch. After approximately 127 rounds of "Baa, Baa, Black Sheep," Ivy's whimpers stopped, her body going limp and heavy against Julie's chest.

Brushing a curl of sweaty hair off Ivy's forehead, Julie admired her improbably long eyelashes and tiny mushroom of a nose. Her sandy-brown eyebrows grew together ever so slightly in the middle, giving her a worried look even in sleep. Julie's right arm was going numb and her bladder was painfully full, but she didn't want to move.

According to Abbott family lore, Julie had been desperate for babies since she was practically a baby herself. She idolized her own mom, who'd always been available for baking scones and building cardboard castles and hiking around the city—a beacon of comfort in a world that wasn't always kind to pudgy, plain-faced little girls. For a while, young Julie flaunted her maternal ambitions, pushing baby dolls in strollers and wearing baby dolls in front packs everywhere she went.

Then came circle time in second grade: Tommy Veeter had just revealed his cowboy aspirations, and Sarah Smith said she wanted to be a princess. But when Julie raised her hand and told the teacher she wanted to be a mom when she grew up, the teacher laughed. "Sure, but what *else* do you want to be?"

At the time, Julie's round freckled face turned brighter than her Pink Panther lunch box, and she refused to raise her hand for a week. But as an adult, she understood. You couldn't study or train to be a mom; motherhood was supposed to happen in the background while you pursued other, more culturally acceptable dreams. The problem was, Julie had never been quite sure what those other dreams were. Maybe that's why she'd stayed with Seth for so long, ignoring all the warning signs.

Now, cuddling Ivy close, Julie felt the rush of affection she remembered from her baby doll days, and wondered if mothers of newborns felt this same mix of awe, pride, and fear. She fingered the silver pendants around her neck—three tiny forget-me-nots, each with a different birthstone. For a moment, her eyes stung. Taking a deep breath, she refocused on Ivy's smooth cheek. *These girls need you,* Julie reminded herself. Once again, she pictured them strapped into their car seats, alone and scared, waiting to be rescued by the police. With a shudder, she hugged Ivy tighter against her chest.

Three

If Hannah's hands hadn't been cuffed behind her back, she would have pinched herself. In the span of less than an hour, she'd somehow gone from planning a celebratory picnic breakfast to bumping along in the back of a police van. Now, as sunlight blazed through the shatterproof glass and beads of sweat pooled on her brow, she fought the urge to bang her head against the window.

Had she just assaulted a police officer? No, he was the one who'd slammed her face against the side of her own car—that was the assault. The word bounced around in Hannah's head until it stopped making sense. *Assault, assault, assault.* Wait, salt. Did she remember to buy salt? Did you even need salt for crepes? Crap, she'd left all those groceries in the parking lot. And her daughters—what the hell just happened?

By the time Officer Perry herded her out of the back seat and in through the metal doors of the King County Correctional Facility, Hannah burned with alternating shame and outrage. Ever since Alex had died, the one and only thing she cared about was her daughters— how could she have been so stupid to leave them in the car? At the same time, the whole situation felt preposterous. Clearly she'd taken too long in the grocery store, but she'd been helping an old lady, for God's sake. And her girls hadn't been in danger, not until the eager-beaver baby daddy showed up with his window puncher. "Child endangerment" was a gross exaggeration.

As the corrections officer led her down a long whitewashed hallway, Hannah couldn't help but remember the afternoons she'd spent in another jail, under very different circumstances. Back when she'd worked as a freelancer for *Chicago Today*, long before the girls were born, she'd done an extended shoot at Cook County, photographing inmates to accompany an essay on prison overcrowding. "Life of an Inmate" was filled with raw, stark images—a line of female detainees crouched against a stained concrete wall; men gathered behind layers of barbed wire fences; crumbling underground tunnels leading prisoners from one nowhere to another.

After those shoots, she'd come home and collapse into Alex's arms, overwhelmed by all the unfairness and cruelty inherent in the so-called justice system. "I'm proud of you for wanting to help," Alex would say, tucking a strand of blonde hair behind her ear. "But you've got to bear witness to the misery without taking it on, or you'll burn out altogether." Hannah had never been good at shutting out other people's pain. What was the point of art, if not to confront injustice? But now all that secondhand anguish felt hollow. Visiting a jail was nothing like getting booked yourself.

The corrections officer was kind, at least. He kept asking if she could please place her hands against the wall for a pat-down or if she wouldn't mind pressing each finger onto the glass square for prints. They both knew she didn't have a choice, but she appreciated the gesture.

"Don't worry," he said again. "We'll get you processed quick as we can, and get you over to medical." Hannah wasn't sure how a visit with the jail nurse would speed things up, but Officer Perry had said the same before he disappeared: "You're lucky it's Friday—the doctor is here all day."

Hannah couldn't care less about seeing a doctor. All she wanted was to find her daughters, hug them and kiss them and try to erase the trauma of this unbelievable day. So far, all anyone would tell her was that the girls had been assigned a social worker from CPS, who'd be in touch shortly.

"Any relatives you can call?" the corrections officer asked. "Somebody to pick them up?"

For one brief second, Hannah considered contacting her mother. No. Not a chance. She'd never trust her daughters with the woman whose negligence had killed her father. Besides, Elaine was two thousand miles away in Chicago, and surely Hannah could get out of jail before her mother had time to fly across the country. If Elaine even cared enough to help. They hadn't spoken in over a year, and if she saw Hannah's name on the caller ID, she might just block the call.

Hannah racked her brain for a friend to take the girls but came up blank. When they'd lived in Chicago, her social circle had been filled with fellow photographers and designers and visual artists of all stripes. But now the only people she knew were moms from library story time or women she'd bumped into at the park. And since Alex's accident, she'd kept her distance from the other moms. No one knew what to say to her anymore, and no matter how hard she tried, she couldn't muster an opinion about ballet versus karate lessons, or the dangers of BPA in sippy cups. Gradually the casseroles, condolence notes, and *just checking in* phone calls died away, leaving a lonely but preferable silence.

"No relatives," Hannah said, blinking back tears.

"Don't you worry." The corrections officer patted her hand. "We'll get you right on over to medical."

Hannah wanted to scream. They'd taken her mug shot, her fingerprints, and all her belongings, not to mention every scrap of her dignity. Couldn't they let her post bail already so she could go rescue her kids? If only her dad were still alive, or if Alex's parents hadn't died when he was in college. Or better yet, if Alex himself could swoop in and save his daughters.

But that was Hannah's fault, too, wasn't it? Her brain settled into its familiar groove of self-blame, a river of what-ifs and why-didn't-yous. She picked at a blister on her thumb, one she'd gotten from stapling down new carpet at the Whidbey cottage. Digging her nail into the bubble of swollen flesh, Hannah was momentarily distracted by the pain coursing down her hand. When the vesicle finally popped, the resulting ooze gave her two fleeting seconds of calm. She squeezed her eyes closed, wishing she were covered in blisters.

—⁊⁊—

Hours later, Hannah was ushered into a drab, unfriendly exam room, featuring the same concrete floor and cinder block walls as the rest of the intake ward. A short balding man in a long white coat bustled in after her, clucking his tongue.

"First-time offender, huh? I hear we need to get you routed through mental health court. I can help with that."

Hannah blinked. Mental health court?

"Your tox screen came back positive for amphetamines. Want to tell me what's been going on?"

Hannah felt like a hammer had fallen from the ceiling and landed thwack in the middle of her skull. She leaped up from the exam table, shaking her head. "No way. I'm not on drugs, I don't even drink much, or at least I didn't before—"

The doctor held up his hand. "It's okay, you can be honest. If you're willing to do rehab, documented substance abuse could get things moving faster."

"No, I'm serious. I'm not on drugs." Hannah was close to tears, but she sank back down. The paper covering on the exam table crinkled beneath her tie-dye pajama bottoms. Why hadn't she at least put on jeans? "I get it, I made a mistake. I shouldn't have left my girls napping in the shade for a few minutes. But isn't there a Good Samaritan law or something? I was trying to help this old lady with a heart condition." The doctor looked bored, as if he'd heard it all before. "Anyway, I swear—I'm not on drugs."

He searched her face for a moment, then flipped through her paperwork again. "Sure you're not on any meds, then? Sometimes there's a cross-reaction."

Hannah froze. The pills, of course. Whatever antidepressant she'd been taking was now popping up on the drug screen. But Hannah hesitated to tell the doctor—the last thing she wanted to do was get her sweet, well-intentioned neighbor in trouble.

"I'm on—something—for depression."

He frowned, riffling through papers again. "What's your doctor's name? We'll call over and get a copy of your records."

Hannah swallowed. She hadn't been to a doctor for years, and there'd be no record of the pills she'd taken. She'd gotten them from Mrs. Li, the elderly neighbor who'd come barging through her bedroom door one afternoon in mid-October.

"Time to get up," Mrs. Li had said, yanking the covers off Hannah's curled form, switching on lamps and opening curtains. "Your girls need their mama." Her voice was a gusty wind, blowing purpose and efficiency into the stagnant room. Hannah squinted at the unfamiliar light. Ever since her dad's funeral, she'd been trapped in a cloud of numbness. Over the last few months, she'd spiraled so low, she could hardly speak a full sentence or drag herself out of bed. But now the unexpected appearance of this tiny bustling stranger snapped her into the present moment.

"Who are you?" Hannah screeched. "What are you doing in my house?"

"Just what any good neighbor would do. Your girls have been playing in my yard, alone, for an entire week now. You're going to lose them if you don't get out of that bed." Mrs. Li handed Hannah a glass of water, along with a prescription bottle filled with bright-green capsules. "These worked for me, after my son died last year. But I'm fine now, so you take them. Two a day, with water, and you'll feel better in a few weeks. Let me know if you need a refill."

Hannah eyed the label, over which someone had carefully printed in thick Sharpie: **MOOD PILLS**. She'd always been suspicious of antidepressants, scared that taking a drug to change her mental state meant her thoughts and feelings—her whole self—amounted to nothing more than a bunch of brain cells firing off chemicals. Out of courtesy, she accepted the bottle, never expecting to take the pills.

But two days later she'd found herself back under the covers, pulled from half sleep by a soft knock at the bedroom door. "Mom . . . ?" Wren's voice sounded tentative. "We're out of Ivy's cereal again. If you give me some money, maybe I can walk to the store?"

Hot shame flooded Hannah's chest. She threw off the comforter, sat up, and held out her arms. Sweet, dear, responsible Wren—only seven, yet taking on all the grown-up tasks of a mother. But Wren shook her head, hovering by the door.

Hannah groaned and climbed out of bed. This couldn't go on. Dragging herself to the bathroom, she eyed the orange bottle by the sink. As much as she hated taking medicine, avoided even Tylenol if she could help it, Mrs. Li was right: the girls had no one else. She'd lost her health insurance and couldn't afford a doctor. But these pills were free, and maybe they'd help. Before she had time to change her mind, she unscrewed the cap and gulped one down.

Now, weeks later, only a few capsules still rattled in the bottle. No matter—Hannah didn't need them anymore. Color had returned to her world, and ideas zipped through her brain. A few times, she caught Wren staring at her with wide, concerned blue eyes. But mostly the girls were thrilled with their new mom, the one who bought art supplies and let them splatter paint the living room, dug up the whole front lawn for a flower garden, and stayed up all night sewing Halloween costumes. Except now this brand-new supermom had lost her children. Hannah's stomach clenched as the nightmare hit her again: she had no idea where the police had taken Wren and Ivy.

"Even the name of a clinic works," the doctor said, tapping a pen against his clipboard. "We can look up the telephone number. The faster we get your records, the faster we can get you in front of a judge. And a judge is the only one who can route this through mental health court."

"I can't wait for a judge." Hannah's voice wobbled. "I need to post bail now and go pick up my daughters."

The doctor shook his head. "You're not going anywhere until after your arraignment. Not when your misdemeanor charge involves child endangerment." Hannah groaned and buried her face in her hands. All those nights at the dinner table, with her mother droning on about court cases—and still she had only the vaguest idea what an arraignment was. "But let me explain how our program works," the doctor continued.

Peering through her fingers, Hannah watched his hands wave with enthusiasm. By signing up for rehab or psych services, along with two years of probation, defendants with mental health disorders could get their charges dismissed. Exactly the kind of program Hannah and her team had advocated for, back when they'd worked on "Life of an Inmate." She'd just never expected to be offered such a program herself.

As the doctor waxed philosophical about reducing pressure on the criminal justice system, Hannah felt a brief surge of hope. Maybe he'd forgotten about her tox screen.

"Anyhow, Officer Perry recommended mental health court when he brought you in; given your pressured speech and aggressive behavior, he was convinced you were high on meth. You're lucky he didn't add battery on a police officer to your charges. Probably would have, if . . ."

Hannah finished his sentence in her head—if she wasn't white and blonde and pretty, with adorable daughters and an address in a decent neighborhood. She'd spent enough time at Cook County to know luck had nothing to do with it.

The doctor cocked his head and studied her, as if she were one of those 3D stacking puzzles you could solve by approaching from a different angle. "I'd have bet money on meth. But if you say you're on antidepressants . . ." He eyed her again. "Any other symptoms? Racing thoughts, sleeplessness, hearing or seeing things that aren't there?"

Hannah vehemently shook her head. Her insomnia was not the issue here. Besides, she'd rather fight a misdemeanor charge than have social workers and psychiatrists breathing down her neck. "Thanks for your concern, but I'm fine. Perfectly fine. Or I will be, once I get my kids back."

The doctor frowned. "Well, you said you're on antidepressants, and major depression would qualify you for the program. The charges could be wiped from your record if you agree to enter a—"

"No." Hannah had spent her whole life fighting against her mother's voice in her head, telling her she wasn't focused enough, competent enough, strong enough to stand on her own two feet. When Hannah's dark moods first began disrupting her adolescence, Elaine was quick to dismiss them. "She doesn't need a therapist," Elaine had snapped when a school counselor suggested Hannah's plummeting grades might be a sign of a deeper issue. "She just needs to stop feeling sorry for herself, to buckle down and focus on something besides all that moody artwork."

Now this doctor was triggering every shame button in Hannah's extensive repertoire. "Sure, I've been struggling since my husband died," she said, "but I don't need a treatment program. You try raising two kids alone, with a crappy life insurance policy and no savings in the bank, and let's see how peppy you're feeling."

The doctor sighed and set down his pen. "Suit yourself. But if you're not going through mental health court, the judge will need documentation to explain that tox screen. Driving to the grocery store under the influence, with kids in the car? That would bring your misdemeanor right up to a felony."

Hannah fought to stay calm, and once again, her thoughts jumped to her mother. As heartless as Elaine could be, she was a legal wrecking ball—with a few words of legalese, she'd somehow make all this go away. Hannah tried to channel her mother's cool, commanding voice. "Once I've posted bail and picked up my girls, I'll send over those records just as soon as I can." She gave the doctor the biggest smile she could muster, suddenly conscious of her tangled hair and bruised cheek.

He made a strange sound, a cross between a snort and a sigh. "This isn't a neighborhood clinic. You can't just *send over your records*; your lawyer will have to present them to the judge." He picked up Hannah's file and strode toward the door. "If you're not interested in mental health court, there's not much I can do for you. I'll tell George to set you up with an overnight kit."

"Overnight?" Hannah's voice cracked.

"It's past four, so no way your arraignment's going to happen tonight. Might as well get comfortable." He tossed her a pair of orange scrubs and some ugly rubber sandals, then left the room, locking the door behind him.

Four

After Hannah quit speaking to her last year, Elaine had cleared every trace of her granddaughters from her office. She'd had no choice—each time she glanced at the framed photo on her desk and saw Wren and Ivy's delighted faces, sticky with ice cream as they licked chocolate cones on the front stoop, she felt a pang and momentarily forgot her work. With the other senior partners dropping not-so-subtle hints about retirement, she couldn't afford to lose time.

Elaine had buried the picture under rubber bands and rolls of tape in her top desk drawer, although now and then she pulled it out, unable to help herself. Today, she'd just slid the drawer open when she noticed young Tobias Greenbaum striding toward her glass-walled office, a wide grin plastered on his face. Elaine cringed.

Her boss should not have been smiling. He should have been furious, because yesterday she'd committed the cardinal sin of corporate law—violated attorney-client privilege—and possibly lost the company a multimillion-dollar case, all because she'd sent an email to the wrong address. In her defense, the client and the opposing counsel had eerily similar email addresses. One careless autofill and their litigation strategy had gone sailing through the ether and landed in the greedy paws of the attorneys for BioNu AgroChemical Incorporated.

"Got a minute?" Toby asked, poking his square-shaped head and overly broad shoulders into Elaine's office. Without waiting for an answer, he waltzed inside and balanced himself on the arm of the white leather couch beside Elaine's desk. She'd never gotten used to Toby taking over for his father. Mr. Greenbaum Senior would have taken a proper chair. For a moment, her youthful boss gazed out the window, silently admiring the Chicago River as it wound its muddy way through the neighboring skyscrapers.

"Lots of boats out there today," he said, still looking at the view. Being on the thirtieth floor was not without its advantages. "Ever been on a sailing trip yourself?"

"Get to the point, Greenbaum." Elaine tapped her pen against the stack of paperwork on her desk, and Toby blinked. For a second his brown eyes looked cloudy, almost wistful.

"Hate to be the bearer of bad news. But you remember our conversation last year, I'm sure. About our policy regarding retirement?"

Not this again. "Of course I remember. The conversation involved *me* reminding *you* that the policy doesn't apply to me. I signed a contract making me an equity partner in 1985, and there was nothing in that contract about a recommended retirement age."

Toby flexed his knuckles, unleashing a ripple of cracks that sounded like popping corn. Elaine fought the urge to lecture him about early-onset arthritis. "Elaine," he said, "you know how much we value your experience here at Greenbaum & Sons."

She nodded, eager to remind him of her worth. "Last year my portfolio raked in over twenty percent of our total revenue. Pretty valuable, I'd say."

Her boss sighed, studying the diagonal navy stripes that crisscrossed the rug beneath his feet. "But this year, it's a different story. You've lost two of your major clients due to a series of careless errors. Now, thanks to this email snafu, we're about to lose a third."

"I promise you, it won't happen again. I've worked out a strategy where I'll route all my emails through Marie before they go—"

"It's not just the emails." Toby picked up a glass paperweight from the coffee table and turned it over in his hands. "It's also how last month you lost your cool with a judge, who almost found you in contempt.

It's how you mixed up court dates and ended up in Bridgeview when you should have been in Skokie, how you insulted Louise Skinner and made her cry."

"Louise has thin skin. That one's not my fault." Sure, Elaine had messed up a few times since Steve died, but she'd admitted her mistakes and done her best to fix them. Didn't a grieving widow deserve a little slack?

Toby sighed and stood up from the couch. "Elaine, you're seventy-six years old. I'm telling you this as a friend and as someone who deeply admires you: it's time to retire."

Please. She'd wiped drool off Toby's chin when he was a baby; he wasn't exactly what she'd consider a "friend." All this talk of retirement was getting tiresome. "You know as well as I do: the firm can't afford to lose my accounts. Now, if you'll excuse me, I have work to do." She closed the top drawer with a bang, rattling her granddaughters inside their frame. Instead of leaving, Toby stepped closer and leaned against the desk. Elaine hunched over her keyboard, opened a random email, and began to type.

"I've already talked to your clients," he said. "They're all on board with the transition." He stood so close Elaine could smell the chicken sandwich on his breath, and the scent made her stomach turn. At one time, she'd planned for this year to be her last at the firm, but that was before Steve had died and Hannah had disowned her. Now, with no husband and no daughter or granddaughters, Elaine aimed to work herself into the grave.

She glared at her boss, who'd taken the liberty of perching his bottom on her desk. "Still, you can't remove an equity partner without a unanimous vote." She lifted her fingers from the computer keys and hid them under the desk so he couldn't see the way her veined hands had begun to tremble. "Even if you get everyone else to agree, Smith and Parker-Jones would never vote against me. Now, get your derriere off my desk, young man."

Toby hopped down, shaking his head. "Don't force a vote. No reason to make this harder on yourself than it needs to be. I'll give you a three-month leave of absence—starting now, and paid, of course—to think it over, and during that time we can work out the details. I assure you, the package will be generous."

He fled the office without waiting for a response, and Elaine pressed her lips together to keep from shouting after him. She'd given Greenbaum & Sons the best thirty-two years of her life, including countless late nights and weekends away from her family, away from the daughter who now refused to speak to her and the husband who'd just died.

She pushed away a familiar stab of guilt. But Steve's death wasn't the one on her conscience. Hannah's accusations were plain wrong. After all, she and Steve had made every decision together. He'd wanted to stay in the hospital for his treatments, preferring to be taken care of by strangers than to become a burden on his wife. "Full steam ahead," he'd told her, encouraging her not to beg off the Harper-Jackson case. "Don't slow down on my account."

Now, in exchange for all her sacrifice, the firm was offering a "generous" package. What was she supposed to say—*Thank you*? Packing up her desk, Elaine didn't bother to keep the files tidy; flinging random papers into boxes felt satisfying, and if her replacement floundered, Toby might come crawling back and beg her to return. Elaine left most of her things behind, out of spite and also because she didn't want silver pens and brass plaques with the G&S logo. Just before leaving, she rescued Wren and Ivy from beneath the rubber bands, slid them into a manila envelope, and tucked them into her briefcase.

As she walked out the revolving door into the stiff November wind, Elaine felt a strange sense of elation and purpose: she had three months to make a plan and get her job back.

—⁓—

Two days later, Elaine sat at her kitchen table and sipped ice water, trying to stave off a headache. As the hands of the wall clock ticked down one useless hour after another, she feared all her buoyancy had been denial. When she'd called her friends at the firm, they'd offered sympathy but no support.

"I'm only a few years younger than you," Zachary Smith told her. "I can hardly afford to lead a coup." He spoke in a muffled whisper—still in the office, even at 9:00 p.m.

"All the more reason you should stand up to them," she said. "You'll be next."

"No way. If I tried to block the vote, they'd boot me out along with you. I just need to make it two more years, then the wife and I are moving to Florence."

After Beatrice Parker-Jones said the same thing in different words, Elaine cursed herself for choosing such lily-livered friends. If she couldn't spend the rest of her life working, what on earth was she supposed to do? In the two days since being forced into retirement, she'd already alphabetized her bookshelves and reorganized her ample walk-in closet, arranging the pantsuits by color from light to dark and lining up her pumps by heel height.

Now, feeling out of sorts, Elaine reached automatically for her briefcase, which she'd placed in its usual spot at the center of her kitchen island. But when she popped open the brass clasps, instead of finding a satisfying stack of legal briefs, she found the manila envelope with her granddaughters' photo.

Wren and Ivy grinned at her with chocolate-covered faces. She'd taken this photograph thirteen months ago, two days after Steve's funeral and mere hours before Hannah discovered the document that severed their troubled relationship for good. In the photo, Ivy's coconut-milk ice cream was melting, splattering gooey drops of chocolate on her dress, and a strand of Wren's hair had fallen into her cone. Hannah sat off to the side with a vacant expression, oblivious to the dripping mess in her hands. She'd scared Elaine that day, seeming even more unhinged after her father's death than when her own husband had died less than a year before. But who could blame her? Hannah and Steve had shared a special bond.

Elaine herself had woken up that morning confused and adrift, unable to find her glasses or put on makeup or even remember what day of the week it was. Without Steve, the world looked blurry and tilted, as if its axis had shifted toward the gaping hole he left behind. But after a few minutes of fumbling through the grief-dark, she did what she always did: marshaled her emotions into action, focusing on a concrete set of tasks—one, two, three—that would keep her sane. The girls missed their grandpa, so Elaine bathed them and dressed them and marched them down the street to the neighborhood ice cream shop.

As she looked at the photo, a familiar anger flared in Elaine's chest—she'd held such high hopes for her relationship with her granddaughters, before Hannah's stubbornness ruined everything. Elaine had tried calling a dozen times after their big fight, but not once had her daughter picked up the phone. Then Hannah had the gall to email asking for the deed to Steve's cabin on Whidbey Island, planning to sell the very project he'd been working on before he died—and Elaine had snapped. If Hannah didn't want Elaine's presence in their lives, she sure as heck wasn't getting her money.

But now, Wren's thoughtful blue eyes seemed accusing: *Where have you been, Nana?* Elaine was seized by a desperate urge to see her granddaughters, if only to make sure they still had a roof over their heads and a mother who remembered to feed them. Sure, Hannah had threatened a restraining order, but what cause did she have? You couldn't file a restraining order simply on a whim. Besides, Hannah was hardly the type to involve lawyers or police. With a surge of determination, Elaine yanked her laptop from its case and opened Flights.com.

This ridiculous estrangement had dragged on long enough. Hannah could refuse her calls, but she'd have to answer the doorbell.

Five

Peeking into the hallway, Julie checked to make sure the door to the guest bedroom was still closed. Perfect; she'd shower, whip up a nutritious breakfast, then wake the girls and explain her plan for the day. She'd learned about the "honeymoon period" from her training instructor—the early days of a placement when most foster kids behaved like angels, too shocked and scared to cause any trouble. Wren and Ivy had arrived on a Friday night, so Julie figured they'd spend their "honeymoon" touring all the best kid spots in Seattle— Woodland Park Zoo, the Pacific Science Center, Alki Beach—all the fun places she took her nephews when they stayed for the weekend. Keeping busy would hopefully distract the girls from the worries swirling in their heads, and Julie wasn't above resorting to a little retail therapy.

But the moment her bare feet touched the hardwood floor downstairs, she knew her strategy was flawed. Something gritty rolled beneath her toes, and she heard giggling and thumps. Rushing into the kitchen, she found her countertops and floor liberally dusted with a substance resembling kitty litter. Ivy sat in the middle of the largest pile, pouring the stuff from one hand to the other and watching it trickle through her fingers. Wren, teetering on a folding chair, leaned over the stove and stirred a pot.

"What in the—" Julie clapped a hand over her mouth. She took a deep breath and started over in the calmest voice she could manage.

"Wren, love, what are you doing?"

Wren kept stirring, not looking up. "Cooking."

"Cooking what?"

"Breakfast." Wren kept her eyes determinedly fixed on her concoction. "You didn't have any regular cereal."

"Do you have the stove on?"

"Of course." This time Wren glanced up and shot Julie a shriveling look, as if she'd somehow been saddled with the densest grown-up on the planet. "You can't cook without turning on the stove."

"It's just, well—you're seven."

"Seven and a half," Wren corrected.

"Sure, but still. I don't want you to burn yourself."

"I won't. I cook all the time. How else is Ivy gonna eat?"

Julie felt something inside her crack. If this precocious seven-year-old regularly cooked for her sister—Julie didn't want to think what other burdens she might have had to shoulder. "It's okay, sweetie." She walked over to Wren and gently lifted the wooden spoon from her hand. "I'm taking care of you now. I'll cook breakfast."

Wren made a grumpy face but hopped down from the chair and went to sit by her sister on the floor. "Ivy, you shouldn't waste this stuff. It costs money."

"Is that . . . cat litter?" Julie wasn't sure she wanted to hear the answer.

"Malt-O-Meal," Wren said matter-of-factly.

Of course. Julie connected the dots between the gray slop bubbling in the pot and the grits scattered across her otherwise spotless floors. "I didn't even know I had Malt-O-Meal. Where the heck did you find it?" Julie picked up the faded box on the counter, and a trail of grains spilled out from a ragged hole in the bottom. Some creature—Popsicle, hopefully, and not a rat—had chewed off the corner.

With a start, she realized she hadn't seen her cat all morning. The orange fluff ball had been missing from his usual spot on the bed when she woke up, and by now he should've been weaving himself through her legs, meowing for breakfast. "Girls," she said. "Where's Popsicle?"

Wren waved her hand toward the window seat, and sure enough, the great orange beast lay sprawled on his back, paws in the air, soaking up the morning sunshine. "I fed him too."

So much for the honeymoon period, Julie thought. This child was already one step ahead of her. She looked ruefully at the kibble overflowing Popsicle's dish. At this rate, her already fat cat would balloon into a zeppelin. But she had to admire Wren's industriousness: not yet seven o'clock and look what she'd accomplished.

Wren stood up and put her hands on her hips. "We're ready to go back to Mom now."

Julie gulped, remembering Rhonda's instructions. "Yeah, so your mom . . ." She stalled, trying to find the right words. "Your mom's not feeling well." Ivy's heart-shaped face snapped up, and Wren's eyebrows knitted together. "No, not like that. She'll be fine. She just needs a little rest."

Wren gave a small snort. "She can rest with us around. She always does."

As Julie digested this bit of information, she glanced at the Malt-O-Meal, trying to decide if it was safe. Making a batch of fresh oatmeal might offend the seven-year-old chef, so she dipped a spoon into the mush and took a tentative bite: bland and flavorless, like always.

"Can we call her at least?" Wren asked, tapping her foot against the floor.

Julie frowned, wishing she could reassure them with concrete details about their mom's whereabouts. "I'm not sure, actually. I can ask Rhonda, but let's have breakfast first. She might even call while we're eating."

After sneaking a glance at the bottom of the Malt-O-Meal box—expiration date still six months out—Julie sliced strawberries and dusted brown sugar on the steaming cereal. But when she started to pour milk into the bowls, Wren grabbed for the carton, looking horrified.

"No cow milk for Ivy. She's allergic."

Julie jerked back the milk, imagining swelling hives and closing throats. Unbelievable that DSHS had entrusted her with a child without telling her this crucial fact. "Allergic how?"

"She barfs. A lot. It's gross." Wren looked affectionately at her sister, who'd abandoned the spilled grains and was climbing into one of the metal chairs by the breakfast table.

Well, throwing up was better than anaphylactic shock, but what other details had Rhonda failed to mention? Julie really wished she'd gotten that medical form. As she watched the girls scramble into their seats, she realized Wren was the only one who'd been talking. Shouldn't a three-year-old be able to speak, or babble at least? At that age, her nephew Henry had been a fountain of meaningless chatter. Ivy seemed awfully small for her age, and awfully young. Julie set a bowl in front of her, sans spoon, hoping she might speak up and ask for one. Seconds later, Wren swooped in with the necessary utensil.

"Here, Ivy." Wren blew on a spoonful of cereal before guiding it into her sister's mouth. After the third baby-bird bite, she handed Ivy the spoon and tucked into her own breakfast.

Julie leaned on the table. "Ivy, what do you want to do today?" Maybe a direct question would coax out some words.

Ivy focused on her bowl and didn't make a sound. "She wants to go home," Wren said. "We both do."

"Right." Julie sighed and headed back to the stove to ladle out her own bowl of Malt-O-Meal. Clearly she'd have to up her game if she was going to distract them from missing Mom.

—◊—

At the zoo, the girls loved imitating the penguin's funny waddle, and Julie paid extra for each of them to drop a slippery herring into a bird's waiting beak. Ivy was mesmerized by the snow leopard pacing back and forth behind the glass, and they all oohed and aahed at the mama gorilla nursing her baby. Julie was about to congratulate herself on an excellent choice of first-day adventure, when they arrived at the otter exhibit.

Julie had talked up the Asian small-clawed otters a bunch: Cutest animals at the zoo, she'd said, just wait until you see those sleek brown tails and puppy dog faces, sliding on their bellies into the waterfall. A litter of pups had been born the previous spring, and usually the play-ful antics of seven adolescent otters made for quite a show. But today, when Julie parked the stroller in front of the cloudy glass enclosure and hoisted Ivy to her shoulders, she found the whole otter family asleep in their den. No matter how effusively Wren and Julie pointed—"See, a bit to the left of the opening, that patch of brown fur peeking out from the straw?"—Ivy couldn't make out their dark shapes inside the rocky cavern.

This cruel slight of a clearly malevolent universe made Ivy furious. Words were unnecessary—with shrieks and kicks and tears, she com-municated her frustration to every patron in a half-mile radius. Her cries went on and on, attracting a small crowd of other parents who began offering advice. How about trying some water? A snack? Maybe a diaper change? But Ivy refused to touch the whole-grain crackers Julie had packed, and they'd just gotten back from the bathroom. Ivy man-aged to kick off both shoes and was starting to claw at her hair, when Julie finally found an ancient, crusted lollipop at the bottom of her purse. She popped the orange globe into Ivy's mouth, and the tantrum ceased mid-scream.

The onlookers turned back to their own children, but Julie could tell from their sideways glances that she'd broken some fundamental code of proper parenting by rewarding a screaming fit with candy. Blushing, she told herself she'd do better next time.

"Why don't we take a little detour to the downtown Target on the way home?" Julie asked, after they'd had their fill of animals. "We can buy you some clothes to tide you over for the weekend."

Julie had called Rhonda twice but gotten her voicemail. She wanted an update on the girls' mom and to ask if there was any chance of retrieving some of their belongings. Wren had again turned up her nose at the offer of a fresh outfit, and Julie refused to let another day pass in those filthy footies. She figured if Wren picked out her own clothes, she'd have no excuse not to wear them.

But as they passed two obviously intoxicated men arguing in the CityTarget parking garage, Julie regretted her choice. Downtown Seattle seemed to get grittier with each passing year, and having the girls with her made her feel doubly vulnerable. Clutching their hands, she triple-pressed the elevator button with her elbow, willing the doors to open.

Inside, under the bright fluorescent lights, Julie relaxed her grip, and once they made it to the children's section, she let go altogether. As the girls chased each other through racks of skirts and sweaters, Julie reveled in polka dots and sequins. She'd always dreamed of shopping for little girl clothes—so far every baby born to her brother and cousins had come out boy—and now she finally had her chance. Pulling a cozy purple sweater in size seven from the rack, she turned to get Wren's opinion.

"Feel this bouclé, it's so soft. What do you—?"

Julie stared at the empty space where moments ago her foster daughters had been giggling and jostling each other. The store had gone eerily silent. She listened hard, expecting to hear their muffled snickers from behind a nearby display.

"Wren? Ivy?" Julie's voice wavered. "Come out from wherever you're hiding." She switched into teacher voice, on purpose this time: "This isn't funny."

Nothing. Julie blazed through the girls' department, hollering their names. She flung hangers aside to peer between the racks and even crouched on the dirty floor, desperate to spot little feet beneath the shelves. Finally, she bumped into another shopper. "Have you seen two little girls go by? A tall skinny one with short brown hair, and a little one, blonde curls?"

The woman gave Julie a sympathetic glance but shook her head and went back to pawing through velvet holiday dresses.

Julie told herself not to panic, trying to think where the girls might go. Pet department? Toy aisle? But she didn't want to leave the clothing section in case they were simply experts at hide-and-seek.

Seconds ticked by, and Julie imagined calling Rhonda and admitting she'd lost her foster children on her very first day, at the downtown Target, no less. Maybe they'd left the store entirely and were trying to make their way home to Mom, through the horde of drug dealers milling about on Second Avenue. Or worse yet, maybe some child predator had snatched them up, forced them into his car, and was now speeding across state lines. Julie gave up on finding them herself and raced toward the front desk to ask them to call over the PA system.

Halfway through home furnishings, she nearly tripped over a quiet pair of girls, holding hands and walking serenely back to the children's department.

"Where did you go?" Julie seized Wren's shoulders, her muscles trembling with adrenaline and the effort of not shaking her wayward charge. "You can't run off like that. I panicked."

Wren's eyes flashed, despite the smile pasted on her lips. "I took Ivy to the bathroom. She had to pee."

Julie clamped her mouth shut, too mad to respond. Taking the girls by the hand, she dragged them back to the clothing department. What kind of seven-year-old didn't know to tell an adult before disappearing to the bathroom? The concept of supervision seemed completely foreign to these girls, as if they'd never had an adult take care of them before. *As if they'd never . . .* Julie slowed her stride, feeling guilty for her harsh demeanor.

"Okay," she said, trying to make her voice cheerful again. "Time to try on a few outfits." She plucked a red shirt off the nearest stack. "Ooh, Wren, you'll like this one—it's the Incredibles." Wren gave her a blank look. "They're superheroes, like Batgirl."

Wren snatched up the shirt, along with two more from the pile, and stalked off to the dressing room. Still hanging on to Ivy, Julie grabbed several pairs of black leggings and followed as fast as she could.

"Wren?" She tapped on the changing stall. "You forgot pants." No answer, so Julie knocked harder. The door swung open, and Wren stood with her bare back to the door, pulling a mustard yellow T-shirt over her head. Julie gasped.

An enormous purple-and-green bruise stretched across the left side of Wren's torso, and the edge of a second mark peeked out from the elastic of her underwear. The blood drained from Julie's face. Was *this* why she'd refused to change out of her pajamas?

"Wren, your back. What happened?" Julie took a step forward and tried to pull the shirt back up. Wren yanked it down, glaring.

"It's nothing. I fell off a . . ." She bit her lip. "It's nothing. I bruise easily."

Julie felt like she might cry, or vomit. Wren cooking breakfast. Ivy's tantrums and refusal to talk. Both girls disappearing in downtown Target—it was all too much. And now the bruises: these girls weren't the victims of an innocent, one-time mistake. They'd been severely neglected, if not outright abused.

Wren refused to say anything more, and Julie tried to act normal as they finished picking out leggings and T-shirts. At the front counter, as a bored-looking cashier stacked their purchases in a pile, Julie's phone buzzed in her purse.

Finally, a text from Rhonda.

Mom getting out of jail. Girls probably going home Monday.

No. No, no, no. Julie fumbled with her phone, pressing three wrong keys before she punched the call button for Rhonda. No way these girls were going home. Not until CPS investigated those bruises.

Six

Hannah had spent a miserable night in her cell, tossing and turning on the thin foam mattress of the bottom bunk. No one occupied the top bed, thank goodness, but at any moment Hannah expected the door to swing open and the corrections officer to deposit a second unfortunate soul into her purgatory. Minutes had turned into hours, spinning the world from day to night. Which meant that somewhere out there, Wren and Ivy also slept in an unfamiliar bed. As hard as Hannah tried not to think about it, she couldn't stop imagining the scene: a stranger helping her daughters into pajamas, tucking them under covers, flipping off the light.

Her nightmare scenario.

All throughout her own childhood, Hannah just wanted her mom to *be there*, but Elaine never was. Even when physically present in the house—which wasn't all that often, given her late nights in the office and frequent business trips—she was always at her desk, nose buried in a file and barking orders to her assistant over the phone. Or else holed up in her bedroom with another headache, the migraines that always seemed to strike when Hannah needed her, but never in the court-room. All the caregiving had fallen to Hannah's dad or, on evenings when Elaine insisted he escort her to one company gala or another, to one of the babysitters in Elaine's fat Rolodex. Hannah had hated those syrupy mother substitutes, pretending to care as they cheerfully pulled the comforter up to her chin, secretly counting the minutes until they could escape downstairs to watch TV.

Which was why, as a mother herself, Hannah refused to consider hiring outside help. Even after Alex died, Wren and Ivy had never had a babysitter or a nanny, never been tucked into bed by a stranger. Until now.

Hannah shook her head, trying to block the image of a foster parent from her mind. Instead she returned to the doctor's ominous words: *Documentation to explain that tox screen . . . driving under the influence . . . misdemeanor right up to a felony.* Hannah moaned, turning over to face the wall. She pressed her forehead against the cinder block, wishing it was cold enough to chill her overheated brain. Somehow, in addition to posting bail and finding a lawyer and getting her car out of the impound lot—not to mention fixing the new hole in her passenger-side window—she also needed to befriend a doctor. Someone willing to ID the pills she'd been taking and testify they'd caused a cross-reaction.

"What a mess, Alex," she said out loud. "How am I going to get us out of this one?" As if in reply, a door banged shut somewhere in the compound, and the heavy thud made Hannah jump. She shuddered. Ever since that night two years ago, she couldn't stand the sound of slamming doors. Now a second door crashed closed inside her mind. Through hot tears, she saw her husband's face, cheeks flushed and eyes wild, before he turned away and stormed out of her life. "I'm sorry, love," she whispered. "I've tried so hard."

—⁂—

On that rainy night in late October, Hannah had tucked Wren into her big-girl bed and nursed baby Ivy to sleep. She'd washed and dried the dishes, returned each Duplo to its proper bin. Now she had nothing to do but watch the minutes tick toward midnight on the clock. From the dining room table, she had a direct view of the front door—for this vigil, a hard-backed wooden chair felt more appropriate than the living room sectional. If Alex walked in and saw her lounging, he'd assume she'd spent a relaxing evening reading art magazines or watching a documentary. Hannah wanted him to see her sitting bolt upright at the table, doing nothing but glaring at the door.

On the phone earlier that day, Elaine had given voice to the nagging frustrations Hannah had been brushing aside for months. "I told you this was going to happen when you closed your photography business. Alex works a nine-to-five, sure, but he shouldn't expect to come home and put his feet up." Elaine paused, and Hannah imagined her mother shaking her head, the cordless phone pressed against her sleek silver-white bob, her lipsticked mouth pursed into a familiar frown. "This isn't the fifties anymore, thank God."

At the time, Hannah had defended Alex. Sure, he missed dinner several nights a week, but most of those evenings away were unavoidable, client dinners or overnight trips to the Bay Area for board meetings. Hannah fudged to her mom, claiming that when Alex was home, he cooked for the family and took charge of the girls.

"Pajamas, books, diapers, he does it all," she fibbed. "You should taste his linguine alla carbonara." In truth, Alex had made dinner exactly once: spaghetti alla Ragú. And yes, he would brush Wren's teeth, but only after Hannah applied strawberry toothpaste and handed him the brush. But she'd never tell this to her mother, who'd warned Hannah not to stop working after Ivy was born. "You'll regret it," Elaine had said. "You'll be crawling out of your skin with boredom."

Of course Elaine would assume that—she'd clearly found motherhood terribly tedious herself. But Hannah was nothing like her mother. No matter how bored she got, her daughters would always come first. Besides, her freelance work never took off in Seattle the way it had in Chicago, and her family photo shoots hardly earned enough to justify a nanny. Staying home made sense.

Except now, after months of endless baby care, Hannah's world had shrunk so tight she scarcely recognized herself, this woman who locked the bathroom door for two minutes of solitude, who stuffed down dark fantasies of climbing into the car and driving away from her life.

But each time Hannah opened her mouth to tell Alex how overwhelmed she felt, the words stuck in her throat. She started dropping not-so-subtle hints—like the cheesy bedtime routine pinned on the girls' wall, with "Daddy changes diapers" right there on step two. He should've been shocked, given how much she abhorred confining schedules and tacky star charts. Before kids, they'd promised each other never to stoop so low. But apparently Alex was too absorbed in the sparkly, fast-paced world of his tech start-up to notice his wife being gobbled up by full-time motherhood, one chunk of identity at a time.

All that day, desperate for adult conversation, Hannah had counted down the hours until Alex would be home for dinner. She'd made his favorite pizza, a peculiar pairing of onions and pineapple, and swapped their usual place mats for an actual tablecloth. The girls even helped her arrange a centerpiece of colorful fall gourds. But when Alex breezed in the door just before seven, he didn't even glance at the table.

"Off to game night, Hannah-banana." He grabbed his poker chips and headed back to the door. "We're at the Raconteur tonight, so I'll bring home one of those double-chocolate brownies you love."

She'd forgotten his monthly game night. "Have a great time," she said, forcing her voice to sound cheerful. "Don't let a wife and kids hold you back from those precious card games."

Dropping his hand from the doorknob, Alex turned around. "You know it's not about the poker. One of our biggest potential investors is coming tonight."

Right. The all-important investors, Alex's excuse for everything.

"Anyway," he continued. "It was on the calendar." Which Hannah never checked, because her life ran on baby time, a demanding and mercurial chronology that existed outside the realm of planners.

Finally noticing the beautifully set table, Alex gave her a sympathetic smile. "But I'm sorry to miss all this." He picked up a gourd and tossed it from one hand to the other. "Why don't you plan a girls' night one of these evenings?"

Hannah rolled her eyes. "A girls' night with who?" Marching into the kitchen, she began to saw at the steaming pizza with fast, uneven strokes. "You're the only one with time to make friends."

"The only one who makes an effort, you mean. What about that artist I introduced you to—Rob's wife, who does the oil painting? I gave you her number, but Rob says you never called."

Celeste was indeed an artist, a popular one whose portraits were featured in a gallery down the street. The kind of artist Hannah would've befriended in a hot minute back in Chicago but who now seemed intimidating. What would glamorous Celeste want with a boring stay-at-home mom like herself?

Hannah was saved from explaining this to Alex because Ivy started to wail. She plucked their chubby eleven-month-old from the playroom floor and bounced her up and down. "Wren," Hannah called. "Dinner!"

A stampede of footsteps came down the stairs, and five-year-old Wren clambered into her chair. Hannah handed her a plate of pizza and carrot sticks and tucked a cloth napkin into the front of her shirt. Making a face, Wren yanked the napkin back out and threw it on the floor.

Hannah stooped to pick up the napkin. "Just go," she told Alex. "We're fine." She walked to the stove, feeling his eyes boring into her back.

"If you're mad at me," he finally said, "just say so. I'm tired of guessing all the time, while you silently seethe, expecting me to read your mind."

Still bouncing Ivy on her hip, Hannah placed two slices of pizza on a chipped plate and grabbed a sparkling water from the fridge. She stepped around Alex without looking at him, then sank into a chair and lifted her shirt. Ivy had begun to fuss again, but her cries stopped when she found Hannah's nipple.

"Do you really need me to spell it out for you?" Hannah scratched her thumbnail against a spot of crusted food on the table. "I'm here twenty-four seven, alone with the girls. Go Fish is basically the highlight of my day, because at least it has actual rules, written down on paper, that don't change based on the whims of a five-year-old. Meanwhile, there's you, out in the world, being a real person—"

"Hannah, stop." Alex cocked his head toward Wren, who hadn't touched her pizza and was staring at them with wide, glittering eyes. "Let's save this conversation for when we're alone."

"Fine, sure." Hannah tried to soften her voice, but the words came out brittle. "Except when's that going to be? At night, after you've been out all day, God forbid you come home and spend a little time with your family."

"I'm not *out* all day. I'm at work." A blotchy red stain crept up Alex's neck. "Do you think I enjoy dealing with all these power-grubbing hacks, the prissy founders, the a-hole clients? I leave the office with every nerve fried, only to come home to your endless badgering." He brushed both hands through his thick sand-colored hair, making it stick up in tufted clumps. "Sure, I'll change Ivy's diaper, but give me a minute to relax. Jesus."

So many times, Hannah had looked back on that moment and wished she'd stopped there, taken him into her arms, and murmured something sweet and conciliatory to prove they were still on the same team. But the stress of caring for babies, day in and day out, had sapped her empathy reserves. "You're not taking a minute," she spat back. "You're taking the whole evening, three or four or five nights a week. You're starting to remind me of my mother."

Alex gave an exasperated sigh. "And tell me again, what's so terrible about Elaine? A successful, groundbreaking lawyer working hard to support her—"

"Your daughters hardly know you."

The color drained from Alex's face. "Who do you think I'm doing all this for?" His voice was only a whisper, but sibilant like an angry snake. "I work the hours I do so someday the girls can go to private school, to summer camp, so they can have a childhood like I never did. I *had* to take this job, because your art sure as heck wouldn't pay the bills."

Yet again, Alex had twisted the conversation so she became the villain. "Go," she said. "Just get out. We don't need you here."

Rage contorted Alex's handsome features into a grimace. He stalked out of the house, slamming the door behind him with enough force to make the walls shudder. Wren dissolved into tears.

"Oh, baby." Hannah buried her face in Wren's chestnut hair. "Daddy will be back soon. Don't worry."

But hours had passed, and now Hannah was the one who needed reassurance. She listened to the rain pelting the windows and pictured Alex walking through the door, apology flowers in one hand and her double-chocolate brownie in the other. "So sorry, Hannah-banana," he'd say. "I know how hard you're working, and how lonely you get." Maybe he'd offer to fly her parents out for a few days to give the two of them a chance to get away. She imagined holding hands with her husband on a barefoot stroll along the beach, or maybe they'd rent a cottage in the mountains—

Three raps on the door startled Hannah awake. She'd fallen asleep at the table, and the imprint of her watch band throbbed on her cheek. Wiping a thin dribble of spit from her chin, she glanced at the clock. Past 1:00 a.m. "Alex?" she called, expecting to hear his familiar voice telling her he'd forgotten his key.

Three more knocks, louder this time, and Hannah leaped from her seat. Alex wouldn't bang like that. She crept toward the door, trying to get a glimpse out the window without being seen.

"Police!" called a gruff female voice. "Please open the door."

Hannah fussed with the dead bolt, her fingers thick and useless. Two police officers stood on the porch, faces arranged in careful, solemn expressions. "Hannah Sawyer?" The woman locked her deep brown eyes on Hannah's. "There's been an accident."

For a second, Hannah's anger flared again. Just like Alex, to get injured and earn a hospital vacation. Now she'd have three bodies to tend instead of two. But the police officer's mouth kept moving, her lips like two bloated worms writhing on the sidewalk. Hannah was too distracted by those lips to understand the words: *head-on collision, drunk driver, dead on impact*. None of it made any sense, and now an eerie wail drowned out the officer's voice. Hannah squinted into the darkness, desperate to find the source of this terrible howl.

But no siren-blaring truck came screeching down the street, and in the next moment, the truth shattered over her like a rainstorm of glass. She collapsed against the doorframe. One moment of neediness; one silly, stupid fight—and Alex was dead.

—⁂—

By the time an officer came later that morning to collect Hannah from her cell, blood pounded in her head like the Lake Michigan surf. On Saturdays, arraignments took place in the single courtroom at the correctional facility, so Hannah was spared a long walk in handcuffs across the sky bridge to the courthouse. She'd dreaded meeting the judge and hearing her charges read out loud, but when her name was called, she felt numb: one more body in a parade of offenders pleading not guilty. As expected, the judge raised his eyebrows at her positive tox screen and mandated a full psych evaluation as a condition of her release.

"You'll want to get that done as soon as possible," the public defender told Hannah after they left the bench. She'd also dreaded meeting with a lawyer, but Mr. Gorman seemed sympathetic and approachable, if a bit distracted. "Once you get the bit about the amphetamines cleared up," he said, "we're in good shape to negotiate a plea bargain and avoid a criminal trial altogether."

Fine, Hannah told herself. She'd see a doctor. But not until she'd sprung Wren and Ivy from their own version of prison, whatever foster home they'd been sent to by CPS.

Seven

Julie whipped open the front door and practically fell into her best friend's arms. "I can't believe—this is so stressful—their social worker won't even return my calls."

Anitha patted her on the back. "Deep breaths, new mama. We'll figure it out."

Julie complied, and after a few moments of drinking in Anitha's calm, she felt the tension in her shoulders begin to melt away. Standing on the stoop, her best friend looked the way she always did: effortlessly gorgeous, even in a sweaty tee, with her wavy black hair swept up in a ponytail and her amber skin still glistening from a workout.

"So what happened?"

Two hours earlier, Julie had started to call Rhonda from the Target checkout line. But as she listened to the rings, composing impossible sentences in her head, she'd hung up. There was no delicate way to explain a child had been abused, and she could hardly discuss Wren's bruises in front of her. Especially not in line at Target.

Need to talk, Julie had texted Rhonda. Will call in thirty.

But over an hour passed before she managed to get the girls home and distracted with some of her old toys, and by then Rhonda didn't answer her phone. After the fourth try, Julie couldn't take it anymore. She speed-dialed Anitha and caught her best friend panting on the cross-trainer. Julie didn't know how a mom with three boys under ten found time for exercise, let alone time to drop everything and fly across town to her friend's rescue. But here was Anitha, holding up two brown paper bags. "I left the minute Nick got home, and I brought groceries." Her dark eyebrows scrunched into a frown. "You look terrible. Can I come in?"

Julie nodded and led Anitha into the kitchen. "Sorry, I didn't want to explain over the phone. I took the girls to the zoo, but Ivy had this giant tantrum, and then Wren wouldn't change her clothes, so we had to go shopping, and then they ran away in CityTarget—"

"Wait, what? Slow down."

"Basically, I'm bungling everything, and they've been here less than twenty-four hours."

"Oh, honey." Anitha set her grocery bags on the counter. "I'm sure it's not that bad."

"That's not the worst of it. Hang on a sec." Julie walked to the landing of the stairs and listened for a moment. Good. The girls were still up in their bedroom, giggling as they dug through a box of ancient stuffed animals. Back in the kitchen, she lowered her voice to a whisper. "I found bruises—huge horrible welts—all over Wren's back, and no matter how many voicemails I leave, their social worker won't call me back. I'd take Wren straight to the emergency room, but I still don't have the medical consent form I was supposed to get."

Anitha's dark eyes widened.

"Awful, right?" Julie pressed her palms against her cheeks, trying to calm down. "But now that you're here, I feel silly for making you come over. This is what I signed up for—I knew it was going to be hard." She studied her feet, all the excitement and fear and confusion of the past day churning in her gut.

"You're never silly for asking for help." Anitha stepped closer and squeezed her hand, making Julie dissolve into tears.

"The girls don't even like me. I don't know why I'm doing this."

"Of course they don't like you," Anitha said, her voice low and soothing. "They don't know you yet. But it's not true you don't know why you're doing this."

Only a few weeks ago, Julie had explained it to Anitha, like she'd explained it to her parents and her brother and all her other friends. She wasn't fostering because Seth had broken off their engagement, or because she couldn't find a decent guy, or even because she couldn't face another pregnancy loss. She was fostering because she'd always wanted to be a mother, and all her struggles up until this point seemed like a sign: maybe *this* was how she was meant to contribute to the world.

But now, massaging the bumpy acne scars along the crest of her cheekbones, Julie was consumed by doubts. What if she didn't have the guts to handle children who'd been neglected and abused? The training program was supposed to have prepared her, but after only twenty-four hours, she already felt in over her head.

"Have you changed your mind about fostering?" Concern flickered in Anitha's eyes. "That would be totally understandable, especially since you were planning to get a baby. Besides, this is only a temporary placement. You could always tell your social worker it's not working out."

Julie thought of last night, the way she'd rocked Ivy in her arms and watched her sleep. No. Fostering would not be another thing she quit, not like she'd quit teaching and law school and even dating. Motherhood was her calling, the one thing she wanted more than anything else. "Of course not. The bruises just freaked me out. And the caseworker texted me that they're going home Monday, but obviously that can't happen now, not if their mom's beating them."

Anitha nodded. "Sounds like they've been through a lot." She dug through the grocery bags and pulled out a carton of vanilla ice cream. "Dessert's not going to fix all your problems, but I thought it couldn't hurt. Better stick it in the freezer, though." As they unloaded taco supplies onto the counter, Anitha kept talking. "You may not want to hear this, but parenting is tough no matter where your kids come from."

Julie swallowed. Anitha's oldest son suffered from asthma and severe food allergies, and her youngest had mild autism. Her best friend had weathered endless ER visits and therapy appointments, not to mention the typical kid-troubles with school and friends and sibling rivalry. Yet whenever Julie praised her friend's commitment, Anitha brushed her off. "Moms do what they have to," she always said. "Besides, we have lots of help from my parents and our nanny."

Now, Anitha grabbed an onion and a cutting board from the drying rack and started chopping. "If you're really sure you're up for this," she told Julie, "you've got to keep calling that social worker. Or texting, or emailing, or whatever. Make sure she understands how badly they've been treated—and get ready to fight like heck for those little girls."

Julie sniffed, wiping her eyes on her sleeve. Anitha was right. Of course she was right; she was the best mother Julie knew.

"It's just—well, I never thought I'd be doing this single, you know?"

Anitha made a face. "Don't tell me you're missing Seth. All this would be a thousand times harder with a verbally abusive boyfriend added to the mix."

Julie wanted to protest—Seth hadn't been abusive, not really. Just type A and too much of a perfectionist for his own good.

When they'd met at a mutual friend's thirtieth birthday, Julie had been shocked by their instant chemistry. After less than six months of dating, they'd moved in together, to a swanky Ballard apartment financed primarily by Seth's Amazon salary. But as time went on, he became more and more demanding of Julie's time and increasingly critical of her choices and friends. If she had to work late, he'd ask, "Why are you wasting your life at that dead-end job?" Or if she bowed out of a social obligation to curl up on the couch with a book, he'd make some snarky comment about how he didn't know Wazzu grads could even read—ironic, because despite his fancy Stanford pedigree, Julie was pretty sure Seth had never finished more than the CliffsNotes of a novel. Sometimes he'd lose his temper—especially if he'd been drinking—and rage against all the things Julie did wrong, from leaving half-empty water glasses around the apartment to cutting her hair too short.

By the time they'd been together for three years, Julie's family and friends were all begging her to dump him. But she had a hard time seeing what they did—after all, Seth's negative judgments echoed her own self-doubts. When he got down on bended knee and offered her the most gorgeous diamond she'd ever seen, Julie couldn't resist saying yes. Every relationship had its bumps, she told herself, and Seth's critical nature stemmed from his tough childhood—he'd calm down once they got married.

But six weeks before the wedding, Seth called from a ski trip in the mountains. "I'm not ready for something this serious," he'd said, his words sloshing against the sound of party music in the background. "Or not with you, anyway. We've got to call it off."

In the weeks that followed, Julie was forced to return her dress, cancel the caterers, and explain to every person in her life how she'd been rejected. But worst of all, Seth's cruel words had wormed their way into her psyche. Long after he was gone, his criticisms played on repeat in her head, a twenty-four seven tirade that sapped her energy and turned her personality from bubbly to flat.

Julie came back to the present, aware of Anitha's hand waving in front of her eyes. "Earth to Julie. Stop thinking about Mr. Shit-Face."

She shook her head, shoving away thoughts of her ex. If that was what love did—well then, she was doing the right thing, skipping the love part and going straight to babies. "Right. Sorry." Julie grabbed a knife and cutting board to start slicing tomatoes.

"Did you even hear what I just said?" Anitha asked. "I told you, I've got juicy news."

Julie braced to hear about another pregnancy in their friend group, or maybe an engagement. These days she felt like they were all playing the Game of Life, and she'd landed on three "Lose a Turn" spaces in a row.

"Guess who moved back to Seattle?"

Julie shrugged.

"Guess," Anitha insisted.

"No idea. Just tell me."

"You're no fun. Fine, I'll tell you, but only if you set down your knife first."

All They Ask Is Everything

"What, because I might faint from the shock?" Julie gave an exaggerated eye roll but stopped chopping.

"None other than . . ." Anitha drummed her fingers on the cutting board. "Jake Lankowski, your seventh-grade sweetheart."

Julie's stomach gave a lurch, but she picked up her knife and resumed dicing. "It was never like that. We were just friends."

"Friends who were in love with each other."

Julie scoffed. "Friends who were so nerdy no one else could possibly love them." Jake had been Julie's best friend in middle school—her only friend, really, since Anitha's dad had gone on sabbatical and temporarily moved their family overseas. But she and Jake had lost touch over the years, and random 3:00 a.m. fits of Facebook stalking had never turned up any leads. "How do you know he moved back?"

"Nick was telling me about some new lab equipment he installed at Harborview and mentioned his name. I did a little digging, and sure enough, he's your very own Jakey-boy, in the flesh. A doctor now, and apparently a professor too."

Julie sighed. Of course he was. Also probably had a gorgeous wife to go with his successful career. But before her thoughts could take their usual self-deprecating spiral, Ivy raced into the kitchen, waving a stick with a long string tied to it, both Wren and Popsicle in hot pursuit.

"Wait, first you're supposed to let me tie on the fish we—" Wren spotted Anitha and froze.

Julie tried to recall the advice for introducing foster kids to friends and family. Slowly—that was the main thing, giving them plenty of time to observe new people before having to interact. But as always, Anitha knew the right thing to say. "I've got kids just about your age, and I brought you something of theirs to play with." She pulled out two plastic retractable lightsabers from her purse on the counter, and Wren's eyes grew round. "Familiar with Star Wars?"

Wren shook her head.

"Then allow Julie and me to demonstrate." Bowing, Anitha held out a saber. "Princess Julie, I challenge you to a duel for the honor of

59

chopping this avocado." Before taking the toy, Julie checked the girls' faces—both were wide-eyed with interest, and Ivy was grinning.

"Huzzah!" With a flick of her wrist, Julie extended the blue plastic "laser" and advanced on Anitha, who brandished her own weapon and pretended to fight back. Sabers clacking, they chased each other around the kitchen island until Anitha moaned and fake-melted into the floor. "I am defeated. I shall surrender the avocado!" Ivy dissolved into giggles.

Wren didn't quite crack a smile, but Julie saw the corners of her lips twitch before she forced her face back into a scowl.

—⁓—

Late that night, after Anitha went home and the girls were in bed, Rhonda finally called back. Dinner had gone so well that Julie had almost forgotten the horrible events of earlier in the day, but Rhonda's all-business voice brought her worries flooding back. "Document everything. And I sent over your consent form—first thing in the morning, take them to the hospital. It's for your protection, too, since the bruises weren't discovered until after the girls were in your care."

Julie tried not to think about the whispered stories she'd heard in her training class, about bio parents who flipped investigations upside down by pressing charges against their foster families. "Shouldn't the girls have seen a doctor first thing, before you even brought them to me?"

Rhonda didn't have a good answer, except to say not all kids got a physical exam when they went into emergency custody. "We only took the girls because their mom got arrested and there were no relatives to take them. Nobody filed an abuse allegation."

But now that bruises had been found—along with the other evidence of neglect Julie reported—Rhonda didn't think the girls would be going home anytime soon. "In fact," she said, "now that I'm digging into the records . . ." The caseworker paused, and Julie could hear her fingers clacking across a keyboard in the background. "I see another complaint, made just last week. Looks like a neighbor called after she'd seen the girls wandering outside by themselves."

Julie wasn't surprised. Seemed like these girls did everything by themselves.

An hour later, she still couldn't get the image of Wren's bruises out of her mind. Without sleep, she'd never be able to make it through the next day. But just as she flipped onto her stomach and pulled a pillow over her head, a loud whimper came from the guest room. Hurrying down the hall, Julie expected to find Ivy crying for her mama again. But the toddler slept soundly, thumb in her mouth and tangled curls spilling over the pillow. These sobs came from a bigger lump, quivering under the blankets.

"Wren?" Julie said softly. "Honey?" She placed her hand on the covers, and the cries stopped abruptly. Peeling back a corner of the comforter, Julie found Wren curled in a tight ball, like a pill bug fending off attack.

"Go away." Her voice sounded muffled and shaky.

"Trouble sleeping? I'm sorry about the doctor visit tomorrow. They just want to check your bruises, make sure everything's okay."

Wren yanked the covers back over her head.

Julie paused for a moment, choosing her words carefully. "Bet you miss your mom."

A loud sob told Julie she'd guessed right.

"I'm sure she misses you too. Rhonda says it'll be only a few more days until you can see her."

Wren lifted her head from the blankets, face puffy and blotched from crying. "Go away," she hissed. "I hate you."

"It's okay to be mad." Julie replaced the covers but sat down gingerly on the edge of the bed. "But you're safe here. I promise to take care of you and Ivy."

The lump under the blankets shook as whimpers gave way to wails. Julie worried Wren's crying would wake her sister, but Ivy slept on. Julie sat in silence, not wanting to leave Wren alone but not daring to touch her again. Finally, the cries turned into hiccups, and Wren's nose peeked out of the blankets.

"You're still here."

"Still here," Julie said.

"I still hate you."

"Okay." Julie nodded. "I'll still take care of you. And tomorrow— let's read that *Batgirl*."

Too tired to argue, Wren lay her head back on the pillow and closed her eyes. Julie waited until her breathing slowed to a steady rhythm, then pulled the comforter up to her chin, smoothing it around her shoulders. "Sweet dreams," she whispered, and tiptoed down the hall.

Eight

"You must be Hannah. Wren and Ivy's mother?"

Hannah shook the social worker's hand with more confidence than she felt. During her night in jail, she'd played out the scene over and over in her mind. Forceful but composed, she would give the caseworker exactly what she deserved: a tongue-lashing laced with hints of a lawsuit if her daughters weren't returned that very afternoon.

But as Rhonda unlocked the door to her office and ushered her inside, Hannah's certainty melted away. After getting out of police custody, she'd spent the past twenty-four hours sweeping up scattered fragments of her life, first charging bail to their last remaining credit card (Alex may have skimped on life insurance, but thankfully he'd always been good about credit), and then paying another $300 to get the Volvo out of an impound lot. Who knew how much the mandated psych evaluation would cost, but Hannah refused to think about any of that until Wren and Ivy were safe in her arms.

"Sit down," Rhonda said, pointing to a folding metal chair in front of her desk. "We've got a lot to talk about." Her dark eyes traveled up and down Hannah's thin frame, taking in the faded jeans and cotton sweater. Next to Rhonda's coiffed hair and tailored black pantsuit, Hannah felt naked. At least she'd convinced the caseworker to conduct their first appointment at the CPS office—she wasn't about to let Rhonda see the state of her house.

"So." Rhonda leaned forward, drumming manicured fingernails against the inch-thick stack of papers on her desk. "I'm here to help you get your girls back."

Hannah's mind flashed to her sour-faced sixth-grade teacher, who'd always said *help* like a dirty word: "Any student who needs *help* with their equations can come to the front of the room." Clearly Rhonda wasn't Hannah's ally; she was the one who'd stolen Wren and Ivy in the first place.

"But to help," Rhonda continued, "I'll need your full cooperation."

Hannah nodded, trying to keep her emotions in check. "Of course. Whatever I need to do. But first—can I give you these?" She reached into her purse and pulled out two plush dolls: Wren's beloved Batgirl and Ivy's Belle. "I've got a whole bag of clothes and toys for them in the car, if that's okay. But these—" Hannah choked on her words, wanting to cling to the lovies herself. "These are their favorites. They can't fall asleep without them."

"I'll make sure Wren and Ivy get them straightaway." Rhonda traded the dolls for a tissue box, and Hannah blew her nose. Even after the social worker tucked the stuffies into an oversize satchel by her feet, Hannah could still see the purple tips of Batgirl's ears. Listening, keeping her honest.

Rhonda opened the manila file and began asking all sorts of questions: at what ages Wren and Ivy walked and talked and potty trained, what they liked to eat and play, who cared for them during the day while Hannah worked.

"I don't work, not at the moment. I used to be a photographer, but I shut down my business after Ivy was born."

"No one else cares for them, then? Not Grandma, or a neighbor, or a friend?"

Hannah wondered where this was going. "Well, sure. Wren plays with a neighbor girl down the street sometimes." Or at least she used to; after Rhonda asked her to write down the friend's name and address, Hannah realized Wren probably hadn't seen Ellie in years.

"Anyone else?"

Hannah thought briefly of old Mr. and Mrs. Ashford, their closest neighbors on Whidbey Island. When the girls tired of watching Hannah sand floors or spackle walls, they wandered over to the Ashfords' two-story bungalow, where they'd learned the joy of dunking graham crackers in milk and Mrs. Ashford had taught Wren to play checkers. But mentioning Whidbey would lead to questions about why Hannah was on the island in the first place, and explaining that she'd been illegally remodeling a house she didn't own seemed like the wrong way to win Rhonda over. "No. No one else."

"Then we've got a problem." A note of steel crept into Rhonda's voice. "Right now your daughter is at the emergency room, undergoing an abuse assessment." She described bruises the size of softballs on Wren's back, and something about x-rays for cracked ribs. Hannah couldn't follow. She kept opening and closing her mouth, trying to find the words to express her disbelief.

"How—what—how could this have happened?" Hannah leaped up, almost toppling her chair. "You stole my kids to keep them safe, then stuck them in an abusive foster home?"

"Not at all." Rhonda shook her head, infuriatingly calm. "Some bruises appear nearly a week old, so Wren must have gotten them while still in your care. Based on the pattern of bruising, the doctors suspect nonaccidental injury."

"No." Hannah turned away and began to pace, fists balled at her sides. "That's impossible. Maybe I haven't been a perfect mother—I won't pretend it's been easy since their dad died. And sure, I lose my temper sometimes, but I would never—" She couldn't even say it. This Rhonda woman knew nothing about her family, nothing about the sacrifices she'd made for her children. How she'd breastfed baby Wren for two whole years and carried her day and night in a sling, long after other mothers switched to strollers. How she'd given up her photography career—the one thing that made her feel alive—to always be there for her girls.

"Then how did she get those bruises?" Rhonda asked. "You must have noticed them."

Hannah scrolled through her memory, trying to recall the week before her arrest. She remembered sleepless nights and frantic days, a feeling of inexhaustible energy and boundless possibilities. But as hard as she tried, the details stayed fuzzy. She thought they'd spent a few days at the Whidbey cabin, but she couldn't be sure. Had Wren had an accident she forgot about? "Wait." Hannah's mind began to spin. "What kind of bruises are we talking about? Like actual, serious bruises, or just regular ones?"

Rhonda's eyes narrowed. "Ms. Sawyer, there is nothing *regular* about bruising on a child. Your daughter has black-and-blue marks across her back, side, and buttocks, and she keeps changing her story about how she got them. Are you saying this happens all the time?"

"Of course not." Hannah's mind flashed to the day she'd yanked her daughter back from the street, leaving a purple handprint that lasted a week. Or the time she'd bruised Wren's ribs, squeezing too hard while lifting her out of the bath. "She bruises easily, is all I'm saying."

"You mean you've left marks on her before?"

"No. I mean, definitely not on purpose." Hannah's heart began to pound, and her voice rose an octave. "I would never hit my daughters; I don't even believe in spanking. But one time Wren ran into the street, and I—"

She clamped her mouth shut, realizing Rhonda was scribbling down every word she said. "I want to talk to a lawyer."

"Of course." The caseworker instantly ceased her questions and became all-business. "As soon as the state files an official dependency petition, you're entitled to a public defender."

Feeling lightheaded, Hannah sank into her folding chair. "A dependency petition?" She wasn't sure she wanted to find out what that meant.

"Basically, it asks the state to assume responsibility for your daughters while we evaluate their safety. An emergency hearing has been scheduled for tomorrow morning at eight o'clock. While CPS investigates, I expect the judge to award temporary custody to their foster mother."

Hannah's mind whirled, but she sat perfectly still, as if by refusing to move her muscles, she might avoid inhabiting this terrible new reality.

"I know it's a lot to take in," Rhonda said, and the sympathetic lilt in her voice made Hannah's skin crawl. "Here's your *Parents' Guide to Child Protective Services*." She thrust a thick purple packet into Hannah's lap. "It'll answer all your questions and explain the terms, and there's a Dependency 101 class you can sign up for."

Hannah eyed the sad-faced children on the booklet cover—her cheerful, confident girls had nothing in common with these tragic waifs. She had a flashback to her first moments as a mother, cradling a tiny pink Wren still covered in cheesy vernix. Gazing into those gray-blue newborn eyes, the exact color of a rainstorm, Hannah had promised: no matter what else happened, she would keep her daughter safe. The universe had thumbed its nose at her plans for a carefree childhood, yet she'd always made mothering the center of her life. How had her good intentions gone so awry?

—⁓—

For two months after Alex died, Hannah didn't wash the sheets. At first, his familiar scent radiated from the left side of their queen mattress, and if she inhaled deeply enough, she could imagine he was still beside her. But by the third week, even the spicy note of his cinnamon aftershave had faded. Instead, the sheets smelled like the sea after the tide goes out: salt mixed with a faint whiff of something rotten. She'd been lying in that bed for weeks and had cried an ocean of tears.

On the night of the accident, after the police had helped Hannah to the sofa, they tracked down her cell phone and punched the number labeled "Mom." Elaine answered on the first ring, sounding breathless and shocked even before getting the news. Hannah's parents took the first flight out of O'Hare the next morning, but Elaine barely made it through the funeral before racing back to Chicago. Ostensibly for an important case, but really, Hannah suspected, because she couldn't stomach watching her daughter grieve.

Her dad stayed behind and became her life ring during those early days of stupor, when each wave of grief hit like a fresh concussion. She couldn't drag herself into the shower, let alone care for two young kids, so Grandpa Steve held Wren as she cried and answered her endless loop of questions: *Where is Daddy? When is Daddy coming back? Why would Daddy go somewhere and not come back? Where is Daddy?*

He even got up in the middle of the night with Ivy, who'd always been a fussy sleeper but now reverted to the habits of a newborn, waking up screaming two, three, four times per night. For Hannah, it was bad enough to wake each morning and discover Alex's absence anew; she couldn't repeat the painful cycle all night long. Even during the day, she avoided her one-year-old daughter, whose blonde curls and wide grin made her a perfect mini Alex. Hannah couldn't bear to look into those clear blue eyes as Ivy nursed, so she let her breasts grow taut and heavy while her dad fed Ivy toddler formula from a sippy cup.

At first she'd been too overwhelmed by grief to care that she'd relinquished the role of primary caregiver. But in December, when Elaine showed up for a ten-day visit, everything felt wrong. Unlike Steve, who'd faded into the background as he quietly kept them all afloat, Elaine strutted about the house as if she owned it. A paragon of efficiency, she'd delighted in reorganizing Hannah's kitchen cupboards and taking the girls to get their first "proper" haircuts in a salon. The day Wren burst into Hannah's bedroom, dragging a magnetic chore chart and multiplication flash cards—presents from Nana, of course—Hannah knew it was time to reclaim her life.

Her limbs remained heavy, coated with sadness like a layer of wet sand, but her brain felt less sluggish and she considered getting dressed. She imagined walking down the stairs and saying a bright hello to Wren, who'd leap into her arms, thrilled to have Mommy back after so much separation. Ivy might start to cry at the sound of her voice, but she'd stop as soon as Elaine handed her over. Hannah would gaze into the round, babified version of her husband's face, and smile instead of sob.

She dug through the pile of clothes on her floor, searching for a pair of jeans to swap for her tired sweats. But when she pulled them on, she cringed at the way they hung off her hips. Maybe she'd take Wren for an ice cream later too. The floorboards creaked as she walked down the hall, and in the quiet she wondered if Elaine had gone with the girls to the park. Then Wren's voice, hardly louder than a whisper, floated out from the girls' bedroom. Elaine had apparently taught their wild child the meaning of *inside voice*.

Hannah peeked into the room and saw Wren leaning over her dolls, fierce concentration on her face. She'd carefully lined six of them in a row on the pink braided rug, as if she were about to serve tea. But instead of passing out cups, Wren picked up her Princess Moana doll and flung it aside. She fussed with the five remaining dolls for a moment, whispering to them as she arranged and rearranged the order, then abruptly pitched another one behind her. Each time a doll went flying, Wren muttered a phrase she couldn't decipher.

"Hey, Wren-baby," Hannah said in a soft voice. Wren didn't look up but threw another doll toward the door. Hannah stepped into the room. "Wren, honey, what are you doing?" She continued the game without acknowledging her mother, but now Hannah stood close enough to hear the words.

"Now, baby goes to heaven," Wren said, hurling the last doll against the wall. The bald, naked infant landed with a thud, and one of its brown eyes flew open and stuck there. Hannah gaped at the winking doll, unsure how to reconcile this angry, whispering version of Wren with the exuberant daughter she remembered.

"Want to play girl-power superhero squad?" Hannah asked, her voice scratchy, as if she hadn't spoken in months.

"No."

"How about making your Calico Critters go camping?" Hannah picked up the baby doll and fixed its staring eye.

"No."

"A walk to the ice cream shop?"

Wren looked up, her eyes puffy around the edges. "No," she said fiercely, and snatched the doll out of her mother's arms. She threw it against the wall a second time and ran from the room.

Hannah sighed. Her mama instincts screamed that she should run after her daughter and wrap her arms tightly around that small suffering body. But the damage from Alex's death would take years to heal, and even baby steps toward recovery felt too daunting. Hannah wasn't ready, not yet. Instead, she wandered down the hall in search of her younger daughter. A cheerful baby seemed more manageable than a grieving five-year-old.

Hannah found her mother rocking Ivy in the glider downstairs. She watched them for a moment, Elaine's silver head bent forward, crooning "Hush Little Baby" as Ivy's eyes drifted closed. Hannah wanted to take a photo—the most maternal her mother had ever looked.

"Here," Hannah offered, "I'll put her down for a nap." But as she reached for Ivy, her daughter shrank back and buried her face in Elaine's armpit. Hannah's cheeks stung as if she'd been slapped. It might have been a day or two since she'd last held her, but Ivy had never turned away from her before. She told herself not to be silly. A baby couldn't forget its mother.

Prying a squirming Ivy from Elaine's arms, Hannah pulled her close and kissed the top of her head, only to wrinkle her nose: Ivy's vanilla-sugar scent now mingled with the unfamiliar tang of soy formula. Hannah bounced and shushed Ivy, but she only cried harder.

"Na-na! Na-na!" she wailed, reaching for her grandmother.

Shocked, Hannah almost dropped her. At thirteen months, Ivy had been babbling for a while, but so far she hadn't said *mama* or *dada* or even *dat*, which had been Wren's first all-purpose expression.

"Nana? *Nana?* You didn't tell me she'd said her first word."

Hannah glared at her mother, who kept cooing as if she hadn't heard. "Shh, Ivy, don't cry. Nana's right here."

Hannah seethed. "When did she start talking?"

Elaine's lips tightened to suppress a smile. "It's no big deal. She's been saying *Nana* for a few days now, when she's hungry or wants to be picked up."

Ivy still thrashed in Hannah's arms, arching her back and crying for her grandmother. "Here." Hannah dumped the baby into Elaine's lap. "She clearly wants you." Stalking out of the playroom, Hannah rushed back to her safe haven and dove into bed, where she pulled the covers over her head. If only the comforter could block out thoughts as well as light.

Her breath came in ragged gulps. She knew she shouldn't be angry with her daughters, who were too young to understand, but it felt like they'd abandoned her too. First she'd asked her husband for help and lost him forever, and now leaning too much on her parents was costing her the girls. Alex was never coming back. Time to pull herself together and be a mother again.

Hannah stood up and ripped the sheets off their bed. *My bed,* she corrected herself, stuffing the ball of linens into the washer and setting the machine on extra hot.

Two days later she drove her parents to the airport for a red-eye back home. As she kissed her mother goodbye, Elaine's floral perfume made Hannah's nose sting. "Are you sure you're up for solo parenting?" Elaine asked. "You could bring the girls to Chicago, you know. We've got room."

"Thanks, Mom." Hannah nudged her toward security. "I've got this."

—※—

For a while, she did. Burying her grief under layers of intensive mothering, Hannah packed her days with Gymboree classes and library story hours. She dusted off the baby-size blender to make Ivy elaborate fruit-and-veggie smoothies and taught Wren to spell with shaving cream and magnetic letters. At night, after the girls fell asleep and the noxious gas of silence filled her empty bedroom, Hannah called her dad, always dialing his cell so there'd be no chance she'd have to talk to Elaine, who asked dozens of questions but never bothered to listen to the answers. Steve didn't say much, but he let her stay on the phone as long as she needed. His breath on the other end of the line kept Hannah from contemplating ways to join Alex in the hereafter.

Then, in March, her dad phoned with a wild idea. Newly retired after forty years as a general contractor, he was bored with his part-time desk job. What if he used a chunk of their ample retirement funds to buy a fixer-upper near Seattle? He'd already picked out the perfect property, a crumbling cottage on five acres of forest in the center of Whidbey Island. As soon as the sale went through, he'd fly out to Seattle and they could start the remodel together, ripping the building down to its studs and turning it into a summer house for Hannah and the girls, or a rental property if she needed the money. All Hannah had to do was drive up to the island and make sure she liked the location.

"Really, Dad?" Hannah asked, charmed by the idea but amused by his naivete. "That's all I need to do? And I suppose Mom has approved this plan?"

"She has . . . acquiesced." From the smile in his voice, Hannah could tell her frugal mother had been dragged kicking and screaming into agreement.

Hannah knew she should say no. Alex's start-up had been stingy with benefits, and with only a $100,000 life insurance policy, she should've been spending every minute job hunting, or else getting her photography business up and running again. But her dad insisted she wouldn't have to pay a cent, and he promised rebuilding the cottage would also rebuild her spirit.

"Why do you think I left law school to become a contractor? Restoring old houses feeds the soul." Hannah heard the unspoken truth in her father's words: construction work had helped him manage his own difficult moods. She knew he'd been in a dark place when he dropped out of law school, but if she ever pressed for details, he changed the subject. Mental health wasn't something they talked about in the Montgomery family. "Besides," her dad continued, "maybe I can teach you girls a thing or two about construction." Hannah knew he'd always dreamed of a father-daughter building project, and in the end, he convinced her by describing all the photos she could take: shot after shot of the girls wielding hammers and paintbrushes, dappled forest light dancing across their faces and a cottage taking shape in the background.

Indeed, the moment she saw the property he'd chosen, she'd fallen in love. This was the sort of unspoiled forest where you could imagine fairies flitting between the trees or dancing among the trillium blooms. A carpet of jade moss covered the ground, sage-colored lichen clung to the trunks and branches, and lush clumps of apple green ferns sprouted everywhere, casting the whole place in a soft emerald glow.

The week in April they'd spent on demo was the first time Hannah felt hopeful since Alex's death. For the initial heavy lifting, they left the girls in Seattle with Elaine and camped in a tent on the property while they worked. Her dad insisted on deconstructing the old cottage by hand so they could salvage as much of the wood and raw materials as possible. That first afternoon, when he handed Hannah a well-worn sledgehammer, she nearly dropped the fifteen pounds of metal on her toe. But after he'd taught her to plant her feet off to the side, with her weaker left arm closer to the target and her stronger right one controlling the hammer's arc, she found the rhythm of demolition as soothing as a yoga class: inhale, lift; exhale, smash.

Hannah hadn't told anyone about her fight with Alex on the night he died, and the secret continued to fester. But with each crash of her hammer against concrete, her shame loosened a tiny fraction. The island air soothed her lungs, and as she piled reclaimed boards—weathered gray from decades of sun and rain—beneath a centuries-old Douglas fir, she thought perhaps she might survive after all.

"You're a proper wrecking ball," her dad said, surveying the crumbled concrete steps after her first day of work.

"Learned from the best of them, sir." Hannah gave him a mock salute, and they both laughed. He slung an arm around her shoulder, and the familiar scent of sweat mixed with sawdust transported Hannah back to childhood. His breath tickled her ear.

"I'm still here for you. Always."

Three weeks later, after her father had returned to Chicago for a short break from their construction project, Elaine called to tell Hannah he wasn't feeling well. Two weeks after that, his minor flu bug turned out to be metastatic pancreatic cancer. In six more months, Hannah's father was dead.

—⁓—

That's what made the dominoes fall, Hannah decided. Not crepes or Mrs. Li's pills or even Alex's accident, but her father's unexpected death. His cancer had been the final blow to her fragile trust in others, and at his funeral, she promised herself she'd never again make the mistake of depending on another person for support.

"Now, if you need a ride to the courthouse tomorrow—" Rhonda slapped Hannah's file shut and rose from the desk. "I'd be happy to call one of our parent liaisons. These are moms who've stood in exactly your shoes—been through the system and gotten their kids back—and now volunteer to walk others through the process."

"No need." Hannah scraped back her metal chair. "I can find the courthouse."

Annoyance flickered across Rhonda's face, and her grip tightened on Hannah's file. "Suit yourself. But don't be late."

Nine

Elaine's laptop rattled against her tray as the captain announced yet another bout of turbulence. Frowning at the illuminated fasten seat belt sign, she wondered if she could sneak past the stewardess to the lavatory. All four hours of this flight had been bumpy, rattling her bones and making her wonder yet again whether this trip was a good idea.

As the plane sped through the clouds toward Seattle, Elaine read case reports of wrongful termination lawsuits, gearing up for a fight against her own firm. But with each verdict, her spirits sagged—forced retirement based on age alone was illegal, but she found plenty of precedent for forced retirement after a series of screwups.

It didn't help that she'd been seated next to a whiny toddler, who kept squirming in his chair and kicking the seat backs. His young mother plied him with every video game and TV show known to man, not to mention gummy bears and Skittles, but the screen time and sugar only exacerbated his wiggling.

Giving up on the dismal retirement lawsuits, Elaine pulled out her Kindle and clicked on her latest guilty purchase. But she'd hardly settled into the seventeenth-century Scottish Highlands when another swift kick to the seat back sent her coffee sloshing over the edges of its Styrofoam cup. She turned to glare at the boy's mother. "You might consider switching places with him. Then at least he could see out the window." And then, more importantly, the boy would be farther away.

But his mother gave Elaine a withering look and gestured to the window: they were in the middle of clouds, socked in by white in all directions. "He's only three, and this is our third flight in a row." She glowered at Elaine with bloodshot eyes. "Cut us a little slack, will you?" Indeed, the woman looked like hell, with most of her dark hair escaping from her ponytail and a smear of what looked like ketchup across the front of her shirt. She yanked a baggie of orange crackers out of her bulging purse and dangled them in front of her son. "More Goldfish?"

"Not crackers. Candy." He stuck out his lower lip.

The mother sighed. "You've had enough candy for this flight. How about PB and J?" She pulled another Ziploc from the enormous handbag, this one containing a smushed brown blob that at some point must have been a sandwich.

"I . . . want . . . *candy*." The boy's lip began to quiver, and on the last word, his voice rose to a screech. Other passengers turned in their seats, and the mother's shoulders sagged as she once again passed him the family-size bag of gummy bears.

Elaine shook her head. Seated next to this little devil, she couldn't even focus on escapist fluff. What was the world coming to, if parents couldn't stand up to their children? She thought of Wren and Ivy, wishing for the hundredth time that she could be part of their lives, to make sure Hannah raised them right. Elaine couldn't claim she'd been a perfect mother herself—at the time, she'd been distracted by the demands of her career, desperate to prove everyone wrong by making partner twice as fast once she'd had a baby. But now, thanks to ungrateful Greenbaum Junior, Elaine had nothing but time.

After tucking her Kindle into the seat-back pocket, she opened the photo app on her phone. In the past year she'd discovered whole hours could slip by this way, as she dipped into happier times. She had only a few recent snapshots of Wren and Ivy, mostly ones she'd taken herself on visits to Seattle. But she had hundreds from the years before Alex died, when Hannah never went anywhere without a camera around her neck. Not surprisingly, she'd documented every moment of Wren's babyhood, and now Elaine clicked through the images, admiring newborn Wren as she waved splotchy arms in the bathtub, toddler Wren taking wobbly steps across the playroom rug, big-kid Wren showing off her purple superhero costume at Halloween.

It seemed a bit silly, all this endless snapping of pictures, as if you could slow down time by freezing it into pixels on a screen. Didn't parents realize their children would grow up anyway, no matter how many photos and videos they took? They missed the best moments, eyes glued to their phones as they checked to make sure no one blinked. *YOU missed the best moments,* Elaine's brain argued, *even without a smartphone to distract you.* Shoving that irksome thought to the back of her mind, she refocused on the images of her granddaughters.

As much as she pooh-poohed her daughter's profession, she had to admit Hannah had talent. With her background in photojournalism, she'd never stooped to dangling a cheap toy in her subjects' faces and begging them to smile. Instead, she let herself blend into the surroundings. "My favorite shoots are what I call 'A Day in the Life,'" she'd once written on her website. "I spend hours with a family, chronicling not just the sweet moments but also the rotten ones, when the baby is shrieking and the toddler drops a whole carton of orange juice on the floor; when Mom's milk is leaking all over her silk blouse, and Dad's about to lose his cool." Hannah used to glow when she described her art, excitement all but erasing the worry lines between her brows.

But that website no longer existed, and the Hannah that Elaine had seen most recently—the one who'd smashed a coffee mug and threatened a restraining order—hardly seemed like the same person who'd taken those luminous photographs. Elaine sipped her decaf, bitter and cold in its throwaway cup.

Swiping through more photos, she spotted a rare one of Alex and Hannah together, bending over an inflatable kiddie pool in the backyard. The camera had caught Alex midblow, cheeks puffed out with exertion, while Hannah pumped her fist and cheered him on. They looked happy and content, like any pair of exhausted new parents hosting a neighborhood barbecue. Parents who expected to watch side by side as their babies grew up, through diapers and lunch boxes and driving tests. Elaine's throat turned dry and she took another gulp of coffee, wishing it was brandy instead.

"You have nothing to feel guilty about," Steve had told her a thousand times. "It was still an *accident*." But he'd made her swear never to tell Hannah, worried the truth might be the final wedge to drive them apart. Elaine shared his fear; after all, Hannah had spent a lifetime blaming her for everything.

On his last lucid afternoon, Steve squeezed Elaine's hand with fingers that already felt cold. "I've got to know my girls will stick together. You and Hannah need each other." So Elaine had kept her mouth shut, but it didn't matter: apparently Steve had been the tether holding their family together. Now that he was gone, she and Hannah were adrift on separate oceans.

She closed her eyes and tried to imagine what she'd say, once she stood in front of her daughter. *Sorry* might be a good start, because she had said some awful things that night. But Hannah's accusations cut deep, and part of Elaine was still furious. True, she'd kept working despite Steve's diagnosis, and true, she'd thought he needed more care than she could provide herself—but how could she have guessed he'd catch pneumonia at the nursing home? The doctors had been so confident in their cocktail of poisons. If she'd known how fast Steve's cancer would take him, she would've made different choices. Of course she would have.

A quick elbow jab to the ribs knocked her out of her reverie. "We're landing! We're landing!" the little boy squawked. As the stewardess walked by to collect their garbage, his mom handed Elaine a dozen candy wrappers.

"I'm on the way to visit my granddaughters," she blurted. "The little one is just about your boy's age."

The mom looked at Elaine as if she'd sprouted a second head.

"I know. Don't seem like the grandmotherly type, do I?" Elaine flashed a smile that surprised them both. "But I haven't seen my girls in almost a year, and to tell you the truth, I'm a bit worried about them . . ."

Once Elaine got talking, she found it hard to stop. She'd been home, alone, for the entire week since Greenbaum & Sons booted her out, and thinking about Hannah reminded her just how complicated parenting could be. By the time their plane landed with a jarring thud—making the little boy squeal with glee—Elaine had told this stranger all about Hannah's childhood and her own struggles as a working mom. As she helped the woman maneuver her stroller, rollaboard, and three backpacks down the jet bridge, Elaine felt lighter than she had in days. So what if there'd been fireworks the last time she'd seen her daughter? She was a different person than she'd been a year ago—clearly, because the old Elaine would never have befriended an unkempt mother and her obstreperous son.

Perhaps she and Hannah were finally ready to start over, let past transgressions be water under the bridge. Maybe she'd get to be a real grandmother yet.

Ten

Hannah had planned to wake up early Monday morning, with enough time to wash her hair and drag the ironing board out of the closet so she could battle Rhonda's pantsuit with slacks and a dress shirt of her own. But then she'd lain awake until 4:00 a.m. and finally downed a Benadryl out of desperation. She must have hit snooze on the alarm at least twice before the angry buzz pulled her from her dreamless sleep, and when she finally dragged herself out of bed, she had no time to shower or deal with the wrinkles in her clothes. As she dabbed concealer on the purple shadows beneath her eyes, Hannah tried to convince herself it wouldn't matter.

More precious minutes went by as she waited for the bus—late, of course—but trying to find parking near the courthouse would take even longer. She raced through the doors of the King County Youth Services Center with only minutes to spare. Dozens of people already crammed into the too-small waiting area, and Hannah tried not to breathe the stale air as she tore off a number from the ticket dispenser. "Take a seat," the sign said, except there were no seats left. Hannah's head pounded and she felt almost feverish as she paced the crowded room.

Finally, an attendant called number three seven zero, at six minutes after eight, but when Hannah handed over her paperwork, the woman shook her head. "You're in the wrong court, ma'am. See right here?" She thrust the court order back into Hannah's hands, jabbing at the bold print across the bottom. "Your hearing's over at the main courthouse, about a mile down the street."

Hannah wanted to scream, or throw something, but instead she sprinted down Twelfth Avenue through the misty drizzle, cursing the flimsy heels she'd worn to look professional. She arrived at the imposing brick building downtown soaked in equal parts rain and sweat. A far cry from the shabby Youth Services building, the ornate foyer of the municipal courthouse—complete with mosaic marble floors and framed portraits of Seattle's stodgiest dead white men—only served to highlight her disheveled appearance. As she stepped into one of the brass elevators, Hannah would've given anything for a hairbrush and a dry shirt.

Hearings were already underway when she slipped into the courtroom.

"Ms. Sawyer," the judge said, his voice frowning so his mouth wouldn't have to make the effort, "we started your case ten minutes ago." He called her to the bench and asked her to swear under oath.

Hannah's arm trembled as she raised her right hand, and adrenaline battled the foggy vestiges of Benadryl as she struggled to form coherent answers to the judge's questions. She tried to explain what had happened in the grocery store, how a momentary obsession with crepes had led to helping a sick old lady—but the judge shook his head. Apparently, the cops had gone inside the store to investigate and found no evidence of a woman in distress. Instead, the judge seemed to think her positive tox screen explained everything, and that her outburst at the cop represented not one-time panic but a tendency toward aggression. When Hannah finally stumbled to the end of her narrative, the judge scribbled a few notes and called Ms. Rhonda Thompson to the bench. The woman's orthopedic heels clacked with reproach as she sauntered to the front of the room.

"Your Honor, it is the opinion of the department that Ms. Hannah Sawyer has exhibited a pattern of conduct evidencing serious disregard of consequences and constituting a clear and present danger to her children's safety." As Rhonda switched from legal jargon to storytelling, her voice became more animated. "Namely, she left her daughters strapped into their car seats, alone, while she went about her shopping. The vehicle was in direct sunlight with no ventilation, and her youngest child, three years old, began crying for help . . ." Hannah cringed as she listened to Rhonda's version of events. Had she really been in the grocery store for forty minutes? The police report described her actions as *erratic*, her speech *unintelligible*. By the time Rhonda described the bruises covering Wren's back, Hannah knew she didn't stand a chance.

The judge made his ruling immediately: Wren and Ivy were to remain in out-of-home care until CPS could complete a full investigation. The sordid details of said investigation would be revealed at a second hearing, within seventy-five days or less, at which time Hannah would get another chance to convince the judge she deserved to raise her daughters. Her babies, for whom she'd given up eighteen months of wine and soft cheeses, three years of sole proprietorship of her breasts, and thousands of hours of sleep. For whom she'd gladly give another decade of her life, if only she could take them home immediately.

Hannah listened numbly as the judge recited her parental rights: weekly supervised visits; the right to give input on any medical or educational decisions; the right to either a private or court-appointed lawyer. When the judge banged his gavel three times to adjourn the hearing, Hannah couldn't hear the blows: a swarm of buzzing hornets had filled the space between her ears. She staggered out of the courtroom and darted into the nearest bathroom just before her stomach seized. It didn't matter that she'd skipped breakfast—even the acid in her belly was too much.

She was still in the stall, crouched over the toilet, when the bathroom door creaked open. "Yes, that's right. New to care."

Hannah recognized the voice and froze, a wad of toilet paper pressed against her lips. Rhonda was the last person she felt ready to face, but maybe if she hid out long enough, the caseworker would go into a stall and she could escape unnoticed.

"Ages seven and three," Rhonda continued. "The caregiver works full time, so she needs them to start as soon as possible."

Seven and three. Wren and Ivy.

"If you're getting an error, you must've entered it wrong." Now the caseworker sounded mildly annoyed. "Julie Abbott, with two *b*'s and two *t*'s. Here, I can spell it out for you. *J-u-l* . . ."

Julie Abbott. Either Rhonda had more than one new case involving kids ages seven and three or that was the name of their dreaded foster mother. A fresh wave of outrage flooded Hannah's mind at the thought of her girls with a stranger. She jammed on the flush button, no longer caring if Rhonda saw her. The state had had no right to take her kids, and this caseworker had no right to make her cower in a bathroom stall.

Hannah flung open the door and met Rhonda's startled brown eyes in the bathroom mirror. The social worker clutched a lipstick, one half of her mouth redder than the other.

"Oh, I'm glad you're here," Rhonda said, recovering her poise in an instant. "I tried to find you after the ruling, but you'd already disappeared."

Hannah nodded, busying herself with water and soap at the second sink.

"Wanted to make sure you've got my number, in case you need anything. I'll be in touch to set up the visiting plan. Let me know if you need help finding a lawyer."

"Thanks, but I'm all set," Hannah said, loath to accept anything from Rhonda. Besides, she already had a court-appointed lawyer from her misdemeanor charge.

Hannah hoped Rhonda would leave then, but instead she took a step closer to Hannah's sink. "Please consider coming to our support group. It's run by one of the parent liaisons I told you about, and it meets once a month on Tuesday nights." She reached out as if to pat Hannah on the arm, then stopped, her hand hanging awkwardly in the air. "I know how hard these situations can be, on everyone involved."

It took all of Hannah's self-control not to roll her eyes. Rhonda had no idea what it was like to have your daughters kidnapped by the state; to have your words and actions twisted into something foul; to be accused of failing at the one thing you'd built your life around. Forcing her lips into a tight smile, Hannah stepped carefully around Rhonda, yanked a paper towel from the dispenser, and escaped into the hallway.

—⁂—

Back home, she collapsed onto the sofa next to a pile of greasy week-old potato chips. Lifting a crumb to her lips, she tasted this salty remnant of her daughters, who never could remember the rule against eating on the couch. Hannah had left for the shelter care hearing nervous but in high spirits, convinced that if she played her cards right, she'd return with Wren and Ivy. Now it felt surreal to be back home, alone. So many times she'd begged the girls to quit bickering, quit singing, quit jabbering nonstop—to give her just one moment of peace so she could focus. Now the silence throbbed like a headache.

Hannah gulped down the last sip of her lukewarm beer. She'd never been much of a drinker, but in the past few months a flock of wine bottles had taken up residence on the kitchen counter. After the total disaster of the hearing, she'd headed straight to her stash, only to find it empty. Ransacking the house in search of something to numb her panic, she'd unearthed this single can of Miller Genuine Draft, likely leftover from one of Alex's backyard barbecues, and nearly choked on its sour taste—a mix of corn, metal, and armpit.

Now, as she wandered into the kitchen with her empty beer can, Hannah fantasized about stealing back her daughters and escaping to her dad's cottage on the island, where a barricade of conifers could hide them from the court's judgmental eyes. Instead, she picked the least filthy glass from a graveyard of dishes and turned on the tap. Water gushed into her cup as she considered all they'd asked of her: everything from parenting courses and home visits to a class on how to manage her "anger." Even a twelve-step program and drug counseling, despite her insistence she wasn't an addict. Which reminded her: she still needed to find a psychiatrist to ID those pills. Even when she'd gone back and scrutinized the label, Mrs. Li's helpful reminder—**MOOD PILLS** in thick black Sharpie—made it impossible to read the medication name underneath.

Hannah glanced around the kitchen and groaned, imagining how her home would look to a visiting caseworker. She hardly recognized the junk strewn about the room. Two pink LEGO kits had been dumped out on the kitchen table, and a mess of shopping bags lay underneath, contents spilling onto the floor: a set of oil paints, three boxes of girls' shoes, a wedge of cheese that should have gone into the fridge days ago. She couldn't remember buying any of it.

An icy feeling in her hands jolted her attention back to the sink. Water spilled over the brim of her glass and cascaded down the food-encrusted drain. She lost her grip, and the glass clattered into the sink, cracking against the porcelain. A stream of obscenities poured from her lips as she collected the jagged pieces. If she couldn't fill a simple glass of water, could she really blame the state for taking custody of her daughters?

Hannah imagined Wren and Ivy running into the kitchen, laughing and jostling each other for the single stool at the table, the best seat for building LEGOs. She dumped the glass shards into the garbage but couldn't stomach the idea of cleaning. Every item she tossed away would be one fewer link to her missing family—even Alex's beer can felt too precious to recycle. Instead, she wandered over to her desk, where a fine layer of dust coated the computer screen. She pressed the power switch and tapped her fingers against the wood as she waited for the machine to boot up. If she didn't hurry, she'd lose her nerve. When the screen finally loaded, Hannah's fingers flew across the keys.

Within seconds, Whitepages.com had found twenty-six entries for "Julie Abbott" in Washington State.

Eleven

Julie chewed on a flap of skin hanging off her cuticles and held the cell phone tight against her ear, hoping the dresses and coats in the closet would muffle her voice. The girls were watching a movie in the next room, and Wren's keen ears were always listening. "They must have decided by now. What if the court doesn't understand how bad those bruises were? What if they get sent home anyway?"

On the other end of the line, her brother, Drew, made a tsking sound. "Jules, you're getting too emotionally involved. Already." Four years older, Drew had been protecting Julie from imaginary dragons since she'd learned to crawl. "Your job is to give these kids a loving home until they can go back to their mom, right? It's not up to you to decide when."

Julie sighed, shifting around to find a comfortable seat in the cramped space. She'd called to decompress after yesterday's stressful stint in the emergency room. At the hospital, a dozen white coats had examined and photographed Wren's back, and a team of social workers insisted on questioning her privately. When the doctors looked at the x-rays, they were surprised to find nothing broken. With the extent of the bruising, one pediatrician said, they would have expected a fracture underneath, especially if the cause had been a fall, like Wren said. But first she claimed she'd fallen from a stepladder, then later changed it to a tree.

Julie tried to comfort her during all the poking and prodding, but Wren became ever more sullen as the ordeal dragged on. After five long hours, when it was clear she would offer no more details—and after Ivy had been examined, too, and pronounced bruise-free—the doctors finally let them go. Julie stopped to get the girls doughnuts on the way home.

"She refused to pick a flavor, Drew. Finally I went ahead and ordered glazed chocolate, because who doesn't like glazed chocolate?" Julie paused to attack her thumbnail again, but her brother offered no comment. "She took three halfhearted nibbles before tossing it into the trash. I wanted to cry."

Drew cleared his throat. "Jules, I admire your big heart. You know I do." She could already hear the *but* in his voice. "I just don't understand why you're putting yourself in the middle of all this tragedy, trying to play the superhero. These aren't your problems; these aren't your children. I know you want to be a mother, but you're only thirty-five and . . ." Drew didn't have to finish his sentence, because they'd had this same conversation several times already. Why didn't she just meet a great guy, get married, and have babies of her own?

Julie fiddled with her silver necklace, wrapping the chain tight around her pinky finger. Her brother knew her first attempt at single motherhood had ended in a loss, but he had no idea she'd tried—and failed—two more times.

Eighteen months ago, after she'd finally scraped off the greasy residue of Seth's rejection, Julie had marched straight into her gynecologist's office and inquired about fertility options. After all, except for the whole sperm-meets-egg part, who needed a guy? She'd just been promoted to medical records coding manager and moved into a bigger town house in family-friendly Fremont.

With the first baby, Julie hadn't found out until twelve weeks, after they'd squeezed cold jelly on a plastic-sheathed probe and asked her to spread her legs. She held her breath as the doctor assessed her uterus, pressing lightly at first, then hard enough to make her gasp. No flicker.

The second time, she'd lost the baby at nine weeks, and the third time, she'd known before even scheduling an ultrasound—every morning she peed on a new stick, and every morning the pink line grew fainter. When the cramping and spotting started, Julie couldn't bring herself to call Anitha or her mom. Just sat on the toilet, dry cheeks burning with shame, waiting for another bloody tide.

After running a host of tests, the doctors declared her triple misfortune an incredibly unlucky fluke, likely caused by separate, random blips in her babies' DNA. "Don't lose hope," they said. "There's no reason you can't get pregnant again." But to Julie, three losses felt like a sign from the universe, telling her she'd taken a wrong turn in her path toward motherhood. Someday she might be brave enough to try again—but not now, and certainly not without a partner.

"If you're bored in medical records," Drew said, "why not go back to school, get another degree?" Julie swallowed the lump in her throat. "It doesn't have to be law. Heck, like Dad's always saying—you could go to med school."

She unwound the chain from her throbbing finger, now crisscrossed with angry purple streaks. Her overachieving family didn't get it. Everything for them was about climbing the corporate ladder or accumulating rolls of parchment, and these days even her mom was busy with her new real estate license.

"It's not about being bored. These girls need me."

"Okay, but don't you still want to meet someone? With kids at home, how can you—"

Call-waiting buzzed in Julie's ear, and she gulped, clicking away from Drew without an explanation. It had to be Rhonda.

Sure enough, the caseworker's clipped voice barked in her ear: "You've got them until the fact-finding hearing on January twenty-fifth. Two months for sure, and likely more after that."

Julie sucked in her breath. "Oh, wow. Fantastic! I mean—" Realizing how callous that sounded, cheering for a mother to lose her children, she started over. "I'm glad the court will have time to make sure the girls go home to a safe environment. But I'm sorry about their mom."

"The important thing is protecting the girls," Rhonda said, "and this mom is really struggling. She showed up half an hour late to the hearing, all sweaty. Said she got the buildings mixed up and had to run all the way from Cherry Hill. Besides, her tox screen came back positive for amphetamines. No wonder she became violent toward the cop."

Julie pictured the purple blooms on Wren's back and shuddered. Apparently, a policeman wasn't the only person she'd attacked.

"Anyhow," Rhonda continued, "once the judge heard the words *abandoned in a motor vehicle* and *extensive bruising,* it was all over." For the next two and a half months, the girls would stay with Julie while CPS conducted their investigation. At the fact-finding hearing in January, a judge would weigh the evidence and decide what conditions must be met for the girls to go home. "We can't force parents to do anything," Rhonda said, "but if they're not compliant with their case plan, they're not likely to get back custody."

Julie heard two thumps and a squeal in the background, and realized Rhonda must be at home with her own kids. The caseworker lowered her voice, almost to a whisper. "Between you and me, given the extent of the bruising you found, I'm afraid Wren and Ivy are unlikely to be returned home. Even if their mother follows every recommendation to a T, it's hard for a judge to see those black-and-blue marks and think anger-management classes will fix everything."

Julie's heart beat faster. Rhonda was talking like adoption might become a real possibility. She felt excited, until she remembered Wren still asked for her mom about a hundred times a day. "But they'll have visits, right?"

"Of course. Supervised ones. And their approval at Green Harbor Childcare should be coming through any day now." Julie nodded. She'd been given ten days of family leave, but once the girls got into this nonprofit daycare center for high-risk kids, she could get back to the office. "Ivy can attend all day," Rhonda said, "and they'll coordinate with the nearby elementary so Wren can enroll and finally start learning something. Apparently she's never set foot in school, even though she ought to be in second grade."

"Actually—" Julie wasn't sure how to explain what she'd discovered while baking with the girls: Wren could not only read, but she knew how to convert teaspoons to tablespoons and add half cups and quarter cups in her head. Perhaps Wren's mom had neglected to send her to school, but the seven-year-old was well on her way to an education.

Julie heard another crash on Rhonda's end. "Talk soon," the caseworker trilled, and the line went dead. Julie didn't bother switching back over to Drew; he'd probably hung up ages ago, and she didn't want to explain the uncomfortable mix of hope and fear fluttering in her belly. Unfolding herself from the closet, she went to check on the girls: still parked in front of the TV, mesmerized by the Hundred Acre Wood despite Wren's initial protests.

"Wait," she'd said, grabbing the remote from Julie's hand. "We're not allowed to watch TV. Mom says it rots your brain."

"Not allowed—?" Julie shook her head, trying to reconcile a mother who would abandon her girls in the car with one who worried about the cognitive effects of television. "Well, one movie won't hurt. And Winnie-the-Pooh is a classic. Soon we'll go to the library and get audiobooks."

Now that she'd hung up with Rhonda, Julie wanted to get the girls off screens and onto something more interactive. Earlier that day her mom had dropped off another box of Julie's childhood treasures, this one filled with jigsaw puzzles. At least half of them featured superheroes, and she couldn't wait to share them with Wren. Peeking into the next room, Julie was overwhelmed by the cuteness of seeing them side by side on the carpet—one brown head and one blonde one, both perched on straight little backs with perfect posture.

"Okay, who wants to try a puzzle marathon?"

Four school-free days later, Julie collapsed on the couch, exhausted. She never would've admitted it out loud, but before fostering she'd been the teeniest bit judgmental of her friends with kids, who often seemed desperate to escape their offspring. If you didn't like spending time with children, why procreate in the first place?

Julie assumed that when she finally had her own kids, she'd be one of the "fun moms," up for anything, like her own mother had been, with boundless reserves of patience. But after a mere week with Wren and Ivy, she'd developed some compassion for her beleaguered mama friends—as an adult, playing nonstop with children was *work*. So far that day, she and the girls had built cardboard box castles (and suffered through Ivy's tantrum when Julie wouldn't let her use the big scissors), baked gingerbread cookies (while covering the entire kitchen in flour), and played at least a dozen games of Candy Land (which ended with Wren flinging the board across the room, unable to endure the indignity of being beaten three times in a row by her little sister). When the girls asked to make a leash to walk Popsicle around the courtyard, Julie suggested another movie, unable to stomach yet one more project.

Now she glanced at the clock and groaned. Past four already. She hardly felt like eating, let alone cooking, but the girls would be hungry for dinner. No skipping meals, she chided herself, and walked into the kitchen to survey the contents of the cabinets. Rice crackers, reduced-fat peanut butter, and dried beans—hardly the stuff of a balanced diet. She added "meal planning" to the list of real-mom chores she needed to get better at. Sorting socks and braiding hair had already made the list.

"Ivy! Wren!" she called. "We need to make a grocery run." The affable voice of Jim Cummings floated out of the guest bedroom. Another thing a real mom wouldn't do: let the girls watch the same Winnie-the-Pooh movie three times in less than twenty-four hours.

Julie's head ached as they drove to the store, the girls squabbling in the back seat. Once inside, they argued over whether to buy pasta in bow ties or spirals, and then over whether to buy mushroom sauce or plain. For a nonverbal child, Ivy managed to make her wishes surprisingly clear. In fact, as the three-year-old grunted and shrieked, Wren responded as if her sister had been speaking perfect English.

"Wait a second." Julie rescued the jar of marinara before the tug-of-war ended in broken glass. "Is Ivy *talking* to you?" Seven days had passed without a single word from the three-year-old, except for crying "Mama" in the night. Julie was pretty sure that wasn't normal.

But Wren ignored the question and lunged again for the mushroom sauce. "Stop fighting," Julie said. "We can get both." Kneeling down to Wren's level, she looked into her gray-blue eyes. "But first, I really want to know—can you understand what your sister says? Because it all sounds like gibberish to me."

The color drained from Wren's face, and she drew back.

"Oh no, sweetie," Julie said. "I'm not mad, I just—" But Wren's wide eyes were fixed on something above Julie's left shoulder. Julie whirled around, expecting an oversize spider or a kid in a Halloween mask. Instead, she found herself inches away from a stern-faced woman in her seventies, with a bright white bob and unnaturally straight posture.

"Who," the woman demanded in a frosty voice, "are you?"

Twelve

There were plenty of things Hannah should've worked on during that first week without her daughters: scrubbing the toilets in preparation for Rhonda's home visit, attending the dreaded twelve-step meetings, or working through the recommended online anger-management classes. But each interaction with the "system" left her more discouraged. She'd left three messages with the public defender; when he finally called her back, he seemed preoccupied—and far too interested in the option of avoiding a trial by signing the dependency agreement.

"It doesn't mean giving up your kids," he said. "You'd just be letting the state take temporary custody while you get back on your feet."

Hannah clenched her teeth, glad they were having this conversation by phone so he couldn't see her beet red face. "Mr. Gorman, they're saying I abused my daughter, and I'll never sign anything that states that."

He paused. "You have no idea how she got those bruises?"

Hannah squeezed her eyes shut. She'd been trying all week to piece together what might have happened, but it was as if someone had taken a blending brush to her memory of the days before her arrest, swirling the details together like wet paint. No matter how hard she tried, the images wouldn't crystallize. "I told you, Wren bruises easily. She's seven, and she's a klutz. If she said she fell off a ladder, that's probably what happened."

"Except then she changed her story, and said it was a tree."

This part made Hannah's skin prickle: she'd never known her daughter to lie, and it scared her to think what Wren might be covering up. But to her lawyer, she only said, "Look, I'm as concerned about the bruises as anyone. Did you call that doctor in Chicago I emailed you about? She can tell you how many times I brought Wren in as a toddler, worried about her purple shins."

Mr. Gorman sighed. "Apparently Wren's former pediatrician retired three years ago. Her clinic faxed us Wren's medical records, but it's all a bunch of growth charts and vaccination dates. Nothing to explain the abuse."

Hannah wanted to fling the phone across the room. *The abuse.* No matter what she said, even her own lawyer didn't believe her. So instead of following the judge's orders, Hannah focused on things she could control. Like escaping to Whidbey Island to finish painting her dad's cabin and staking out the various addresses occupied by the many Julie Abbotts of Seattle, desperate for a glimpse of the girls. So far she'd crossed off three addresses in the Central District, one in Laurelhurst, and two in Ballard, but had found no trace of Wren and Ivy.

Today, though, she'd had a stroke of luck: a last-minute cancellation at the Presley Center for Positive Mental Health meant she no longer had to wait three months for an appointment. Now all she had to do was convince a sympathetic doctor to explain away her tox screen.

On her way out the door, Hannah grabbed the offending pills from her medicine cabinet, giving the bottle a wistful shake. She'd stopped taking them since that disastrous day in the grocery store, and the buoyant effects of the medicine had worn off, leaving her sluggish and weak. Until her thoughts slowed down, she hadn't realized how much pressure she'd been under—pressure to talk, pressure to move, pressure to make art and bake crepes and reorganize her life. Without the pills, she could take a deep breath, but she missed vibrating through life like a resonant string. And deprived of her endless supply of energy, the plan she'd hatched to dig the family out of financial ruin seemed dubious at best. Even if she somehow managed to forge the deed and sell the cabin, Elaine would never let her scheme go unpunished.

Hannah missed the reckless optimism she'd felt on the pills, but after all the trouble they'd caused, she didn't dare swallow another bright-green capsule. At least not until she confirmed what they were.

—⁓—

"Fluoxetine. Thirty milligrams." The psychiatrist raised his eyebrows. "You got these from your neighbor? You know that's a terrible idea, right? Not to mention illegal."

Hannah suppressed a laugh. "Believe me, I've been sufficiently punished for my sins. I'd gladly have gone to a doctor, if I'd had health insurance or money to pay for it. As it was, borrowed pills were my only option."

"But now you've got insurance?"

"Medicaid, thanks to a very helpful social worker I met in jail."

"Right." The doctor rubbed his chin. "Why don't you tell me how all this started?" His hand hovered above the clipboard on his lap, pen poised to write notes.

Hannah sat in silence for a moment, tracing her finger up and down the fossil-gray couch and stealing glances at the psychiatrist, whose ID badge read **DR. ERIC BANNING**. With smooth brown skin and a soft jaw, he looked too young to be a doctor, and his expression too kind and concerned to be genuine. She thought about telling him it had all begun with Alex's accident, or with her father's death, but she didn't want to talk about the days and weeks she'd spent in bed, leaving the girls to fend for themselves. This doctor needed to understand she was a perfectly competent mother who'd made a simple, innocent mistake.

"With crepes," Hannah finally said. "I'm here because I planned to make pancakes, but got distracted by strawberry jam, and then arrested for trying to cook a picnic breakfast."

Dr. Banning grinned, the smile of an overeager puppy ready to play fetch. "Heard a lot of stories in my life, but never heard anyone blame their arrest on pancakes. You'll have to tell me more."

Hannah tried to explain from the beginning, the girls falling asleep and the pregnant lady calling 911, and the belligerent cop whose now-faded handprint still lingered on her forearm. The psychiatrist didn't say anything, just kept nodding and smiling, a disarming grin not so much on his lips but in his hazel-brown eyes, crinkled at the edges. Like Alex's eyes, Hannah realized. Her husband had always been laughing, and once he'd turned forty, the evidence showed on his cheeks. Hannah, on the other hand, sported an entirely different set of wrinkles—twin parallel divots between her brows that announced to the world she worried too much. "Or just that you don't wear enough sunscreen," Alex would say. Then he'd kiss that spot on Hannah's forehead, as if all her worries could be erased with a kiss.

She paused, realizing that while she'd been imagining Alex's lips on her forehead, she'd continued yammering to the doctor about picnics and groceries and sick old ladies, and now she had no idea what she was saying. Dr. Banning kept looking at her expectantly, and somehow those laugh lines wore her down.

"Fine. I was depressed. The walls of my life had closed in so tight, it was like I was living in a tunnel." She picked at her thumbnail. "My neighbor realized I was struggling and offered me those." Hannah gestured to the pill bottle and looked up. Dr. Banning was scribbling furiously.

"How much did you take?"

"One pill, two times a day." Hannah paused, struggling to remember. "Or sometimes maybe three?"

Dr. Banning whistled. "That's a hefty dose, especially for someone your size. But we've got your diagnosis at least. Drug-induced mania. On top of major depression, sounds like." He squinted at her. "There's also a condition we call 'complicated grief.' You said your husband died a few years back?"

Hannah stiffened. Her grief was complicated all right, but she had no desire to discuss Alex with this prying psychiatrist. "Several years ago now. Not related."

"Sure, right." Dr. Banning jotted down another note. "How did he die?"

Hannah's eyes darted to the door, and she fanned her face, desperate to finish the interview and get out of this overheated exam room. "A heart attack. While running a marathon." She hadn't meant to lie, but after the words popped out, she felt safer—glad to have an insulating layer of fiction between them.

"That must have been a shock." Dr. Banning paused, studying her face. When Hannah stayed silent, he moved on. "The racing thoughts, sleeplessness, and elevated mood—you're sure this has never happened before?"

Hannah bit her lip. She'd been mulling over that question ever since her interview with the jail doctor. Something about the electrified feeling she'd gotten from the pills felt familiar. She remembered late nights during her MFA, ecstatically developing print after print in the darkroom, or standing in front of her easel, madly splashing color onto canvas as energy pulsed through her veins. And years later, setting up her portrait photography business, she would put baby Wren to sleep and stay up for hours, spinning out dreams as she designed the perfect website. More than once, Alex had told her to ease up, calm down, go to bed. Cut down on the crazy, he'd said. But that wasn't mania—that was just being an artist.

"Nope," she said. "Must have been the pills. Honestly, they made me feel better than I had in a long time. Except for getting arrested and losing my girls, I was practically flipping cartwheels." Cartwheels she now couldn't remember. Hannah wanted to ask whether it was normal for antidepressants to leave your memory blurry and riddled with holes, stretches of time so empty and blank you couldn't be sure what you had done. But she shook the dark thoughts from her mind. She never would've hurt her daughters, and she couldn't trust this doctor not to misinterpret her questions.

"What happened when you quit taking them?" he asked. "Any nausea, dizziness, flu-like symptoms?"

Hannah shrugged. She'd vomited in the courthouse bathroom and suffered a nonstop headache since her girls had been taken, but she'd assumed all her symptoms were from stress.

"Whatever you do, don't take any more borrowed pills—fluoxetine can cause mood-switching in susceptible individuals." Dr. Banning frowned. "That's why it's a *prescription* medication, meant to be taken under the advice of a physician. But don't worry, we'll get you into an outpatient treatment program and find you the right medication—probably a mood stabilizer to start."

Hannah clutched the arm of the couch. She hadn't considered this might be more than a one-time visit. "That won't be necessary. I feel fine now. Really, I just came to see you because of the court order. And because—" It was now or never. "I need a doctor to verify I was taking those pills."

Dr. Banning narrowed his eyes. "To verify—? What for?"

Hannah took a deep breath. "Amphetamines popped up on my drug test. But I swear, I never took anything but those green capsules. My lawyer says I need a written statement from a doctor, explaining how my antidepressants could have caused a positive result."

"Well, sure, fluoxetine can cross-react. But I wasn't the one who prescribed the pills, and your name's not even on the bottle. I can hardly testify you were taking them, especially if you're not my patient."

Crap. Hannah leaned her elbows on her knees and pressed the heels of her hands into her brow. Dr. Banning was just about the most sympathetic doctor she could hope for. If he wouldn't help her, no one would. She looked up with red-rimmed eyes. "The public defender said if I can just get the tox screen cleared up, he'll negotiate a plea bargain. I can't afford a criminal conviction, not while I'm fighting CPS for my kids."

Dr. Banning sighed. "I'm not going to lie for you. But maybe there's a way I could speak truthfully on your behalf—I'd be happy to write up a statement explaining how fluoxetine can mimic amphetamines on a drug screen. However—" He gave Hannah a stern look. "The dependency judge will expect you to take your mental health seriously. Best thing you can do is comply with treatment; start getting healthy so you have the best chance of getting your girls back."

Hannah recoiled at the phrase *best chance*, as if returning her daughters was a question rather than a certainty. As if she'd leave the two people who mattered most—the only people who mattered—up to chance. "I'll do whatever's necessary," she snapped, "so my girls can come home."

The doctor smiled again, but his crinkled eyes had lost all appeal. "In that case, you may want to consider our partial-hospitalization program . . ."

In the end, they compromised. For Dr. Banning's help with the tox screen, Hannah traded 180 hours of her life. Every Monday, Wednesday, and Friday for the next twelve weeks, she'd attend structured outpatient therapy from 10:00 a.m. to 3:00 p.m. During that time, the program brochure promised, she'd learn the "cognitive, behavioral, and interpersonal skills needed to create a life worth living."

Hannah shuddered at the thought of sharing her feelings with a group of strangers. But the only life worth living was one in which she had her daughters back: if therapy was what it took to regain custody, then therapy was what she'd do.

Thirteen

At first Elaine didn't think those girls could be her granddaughters—too tall. But even from across the grocery store parking lot, the brunette reminded her of Wren, the way she led with her chin through the sliding glass doors, so confident and purposeful. Wren had always taken after her grandmother that way.

Once inside the store, Elaine didn't mean to follow the trio, but there were only so many ways to proceed through an unfamiliar supermarket. She kept a good distance from the girls, only stealing a sideways glance now and then. As lonely as she was, she refused to become one of those desperate grandmas, fawning over other people's children in a store.

That is, until the little blonde turned around and looked Elaine straight in the face. She'd grown up from the chubby infant Elaine remembered, but those puckered brows—all scrunched up with the kind of concern you didn't usually see on a toddler—left no question. That child was her granddaughter Ivy.

Elaine's heart thudded in her chest, and she gripped the cart for support. She'd spent her first twenty-four hours in Seattle trying to decide how best to approach Hannah without getting a door slammed in her face. Three times she'd circled their neighborhood in Beacon Hill, hoping to catch a glimpse of the girls, but she never imagined finding them wandering the aisles of the Fremont Marketime Foods with a babysitter. Part of her wanted to rush across the store and hug them, but she held back, feeling inexplicably nervous. Hugging had never come naturally to Elaine.

Instead, she studied the sitter picking out greens. Her petite frame had been swallowed up by a gigantic puffy coat, and she kept placing items in her cart only to take them out again, apparently flummoxed by the mundane choice of romaine versus baby spinach. But despite the dithering of this squat, round-faced caregiver, Elaine felt relieved: if the girls were with a sitter, Hannah must have finally hired some help. And if she'd hired help, that meant she hadn't fallen into complete destitution, one of the many fears that had haunted Elaine all year. Sloppy ponytails notwithstanding, the girls bore fresh faces and clean clothes—more than she could've said the last time she saw them.

Ivy gave Elaine a long, questioning stare, but if she recognized her grandmother, she didn't breathe a word of it to Wren or the babysitter. Just squeezed the woman's hand a bit more tightly, maybe, and followed her around a tower of baked beans into the next aisle. By now Elaine had forgotten all about buying groceries to stock the kitchenette in her hotel suite, and she crept after them, as stealthily as she could with a cart clattering along in front. In aisle four, she watched her granddaughters bicker over pasta shapes.

"Not spirals," Wren said. "They're too squiggly, and wiggly, and they make me choke." She snatched the bag of pasta from Ivy and shoved it back on the shelf—knocking off several other boxes in the process. Ivy grabbed two off the floor and tried to dump them in the cart, but Wren, a head taller, blocked her efforts. Meanwhile, the poor sitter looked on, her head flipping from one child to the other as if watching a tennis match on TV. Elaine longed to step in and demonstrate how to handle unruly little girls, but Hannah had called her meddlesome one too many times.

She managed to keep her distance and hold her tongue—until they started up again over jars of sauce. Her granddaughters were yanking back and forth on a bottle of Prego and about to drop it on the floor.

Any grandmother worth her salt would have intervened at that point, and Elaine strode forward before considering what to say.

The moment Wren spotted her grandmother, all arguments died on her lips, and she let go of the jar, mouth agape. Elaine gave a wave and a smile, proud she'd halted the sauce argument so promptly. Then the sitter turned around, a confused expression on her face. Up close, tiny crow's feet and shadows under her eyes made the woman appear older than Elaine had guessed, but no less empty headed.

"Who are you?" Elaine asked, and the babysitter jumped back as if she'd spotted a venomous snake.

"Um. Julie Abbott, ma'am. And you?"

"Wren and Ivy's grandmother."

At that point, Elaine could have knocked over young miss Julie with a feather. Her face turned the unappealing gray-white of leftover oatmeal, and she gripped her cart for support. "Their *grandmother?*"

"Their mother's mother, to be precise." The nanny's mouth continued to flap open and closed, and Elaine wondered if she suffered from a speech impediment. She crouched down to address the girls. "My, look how you've grown. A kiss for Nana?"

Wren gave Elaine a chaste peck on the cheek, but Ivy hid behind the sitter's legs. Elaine frowned. All those nights rocking her to sleep, yet Ivy seemed to have forgotten her grandmother. The nanny whisked the toddler away, plopping her into the child seat on the cart.

"Never mind," Elaine said, her bad knee popping as she stood. "We'll get reacquainted soon enough. I haven't told your mother, but I'm here in Seattle for a month . . . on a special case." True enough; reconnecting with Hannah would require all of Elaine's lawyerly finesse. She turned back to the sitter, who still looked like she'd seen a ghost. "Is Hannah home?"

"I don't . . . I don't know."

"Well, when will she be back, then?"

The woman's mouth twitched, but she didn't speak. Meddlesome or not, Elaine's first order of business when she confronted Hannah would be convincing her to hire a more competent sitter. Elaine turned to Wren. "Dear, when is your mother due back?" Wren could be counted on to know such things; ever since Elaine had taught her to tell time at age four, she'd been fixated on schedules and organization. A sensible child, so like her grandmother.

"Nana, Mommy's not . . ." Wren trailed off, and her uncharacteristic hesitation gave Elaine goose pimples. Something was not right.

She squinted at Julie, who'd taken the jar of mushroom sauce from Ivy and was turning it over and over in her hands. "You're the nanny. You must know when their mother will be back." Julie shook her head, as if clearing whatever vexing spirit had possessed her, and finally looked Elaine in the eye.

"I'm not their nanny. I'm their foster mom. And I'm prohibited by the state from giving you any more details, so if you'll please step out of the way, we'll continue with our shopping."

Now it was Elaine's turn to gape. Good Lord, their *foster* mom? Something like rage bubbled in her belly. Not even in her worst nightmares had Elaine imagined her daughter bungling up her life this thoroughly. And apparently Hannah's stubbornness knew no bounds: instead of swallowing her pride and calling Elaine for help, she'd preferred to give Wren and Ivy over to foster care. Elaine wanted to storm out of the grocery store and straight to Hannah's doorstep. Unless . . . the color drained from Elaine's face.

"Wren, your mother's not—injured, is she?"

"Their mother is fine." Julie put an arm around Wren's shoulders. "But like I said, I'm not allowed to give you any more information. You'll have to call social services."

Before Julie could push by with her cart, Elaine grabbed the metal lattice, steadying her shaking hands. "Miss Abbott, allow me to formally introduce myself." Her voice got stronger as she spoke. "Ms. Elaine Montgomery, attorney-at-law. This is the first I've heard of my granddaughters somehow ending up in the foster care system, but I assure you, I will rectify the situation quickly. You may of course proceed to select your groceries, but you will be hearing from me in short order."

Elaine released the cart, and an ashen-faced Julie hurried the girls away without reply. "Goodbye, my loves," Elaine called, as the trio rounded the corner and disappeared. As she blinked at the space her granddaughters so recently occupied, Elaine's whole body trembled.

Abandoning her groceries, she marched out of the store and climbed into her car, determined to drive straight to Hannah's.

—⁂—

When Elaine arrived, the house looked abandoned—no Volvo in the driveway, every window black. Though it wasn't yet 6:00 p.m., darkness hung like a thick wool blanket over the street. Elaine parked in front of the house, under the maple she'd watched Wren climb so many times, and sat idling the engine of her rental car, wondering whether Hannah was hiding somewhere inside. Then again, a year had passed—maybe she didn't even live here anymore. Elaine clenched her teeth, furious again at how thoroughly her daughter had shut her out.

Storming up the walkway, she cringed at the shotweed choking the garden bed and the broken sconce hanging crooked next to the front door. She pressed the doorbell but heard neither chime nor footsteps. Banging on the door produced the same null effect, so Elaine jiggled the doorknob: locked. She wandered around the side of the house to peek into the windows, but every blind was shut tight. No garden hoses attached to the spigots, no shoes by the door, no abandoned toys in the yard—nothing to prove Hannah still lived here.

Elaine pulled out her cell and dialed the number for Hannah's house phone. Three beeps and an infuriatingly chipper voice informed her the number was no longer in service. A call to Hannah's cell phone also went straight to voicemail, the box too full to leave a message.

Defeated, Elaine retreated to her car and sat in the driver's seat, shivering from frustration as much as cold. Even in the dark, she could tell how much the neighborhood had changed. Light streamed from every window of the house next door, casting its fresh yellow-green paint in a cheerful glow. Three years ago, the craftsman had been all but abandoned, with broken windows and a sagging roof. Alex had railed against that house and its ever-expanding tower of tires, moldy mattresses, and paint cans in the backyard, but he never got to appreciate its transformation—he'd died only days before renovations began. Elaine would forever associate the pulse of jackhammers with shock and guilt.

Her eyes watered as she surveyed the next-door property, sparkling with its new in-ground lighting and manicured grass. Maybe Alex would still be here if she could go back to that wretched night and simply not pick up her phone. But like Steve had told her a hundred times, it was an *accident*, and no amount of self-recrimination would bring her son-in-law back. Nor could she sit here in a freezing car all night, waiting for a daughter who might never come home.

Wren and Ivy were her priority now: first thing tomorrow she'd call social services and demand to know what the hell was going on.

Fourteen

The minute Julie escaped from the snow-haired ice queen of a grandmother in aisle four, she wanted to whip out her phone and call Rhonda. But she worried the woman might be lurking around the corner, eavesdropping. Her ramrod-straight posture and piercing blue eyes sent prickles down the back of Julie's neck, and Wren and Ivy seemed oddly terrified of her. Julie stole a sideways glance at Wren, longing to pepper her with questions. But Wren's lower lip still quivered, so she trod lightly.

"Was that your grandma?"

Wren nodded and climbed onto the side of the cart, a trick Julie had forbidden three times already. This time, she let the cart-surfing slide. "I didn't know you had a grandma." More silence. "You don't have to tell me if you don't want to, but I'm wondering why you seemed so scared."

Wren's head jerked up. "Not scared. But we haven't seen her for a long time, since after Grandpa died. She used to take care of us sometimes, and she's . . . strict." Julie waited, hoping for more, but they'd rounded the corner into the cereal aisle, and Wren moved on to more pressing topics. "Can we get peanut butter Panda Puffs? Please, Mama Julie, please?"

She froze. *Mama Julie.* She'd told the girls they could call her whatever made them comfortable—Mama Julie, Miss Julie, or just plain old Julie—but she'd secretly doubted Wren would ever call her mama, let alone so soon. Julie beamed, and Wren looked back at her with round puppy dog eyes.

"Puh-lease?"

Julie laughed and tossed the Panda Puffs into the cart. This seven-year-old knew her audience. She leaned down and gave Ivy a spontaneous kiss on the forehead. "You know what, girls? Let's buy these groceries and get out of here. We'll save cooking for another night and go to Zeeks for pizza. It's been a wild day."

—m—

Julie called Rhonda's cell twice from the restaurant bathroom and another couple of times from home, but only reached her voicemail. Finally, twenty minutes after the girls were tucked in bed, the case-worker answered.

"You're not going to believe this," Julie said. "The girls have a grandmother."

"Wait, that's why you called me six times?" Rhonda sounded annoyed.

"I just thought—"

"Every foster parent imagines they're the only family on my case list. But guess what? I've got twenty-seven—no, twenty-eight if you count the emergency removal I just did. Can you even conceive of that much paperwork? How many court cases and permanency plans and home visits?"

Julie sat in silence, shocked by this crack in Rhonda's normally professional demeanor. Before she could decide how to respond, Rhonda resumed her tirade. "Know what the state-recommended case limit is? Of course you don't. It's *twelve*." She spat out the last word like it tasted bad.

Clearly, Julie should have sent an email. But as she started to apologize, Rhonda gave a huge sigh. "Sorry for the rant. It's been a tough week, and I just missed my own kids' bedtime for the fourth night in a row."

"Gosh, I'm sorry. If you'd rather call me tomorrow—"

"No, no, it's fine. The last thing I want to do is unload on my foster families. If I scare you all off, the next option is booking kids into a hotel."

Julie gave a nervous laugh.

"You think I'm joking, but we really do stick kids in hotels. Not ones as young as Wren and Ivy, of course, but sometimes it's our only option." Rhonda sighed again. "Anyhow, what was this about a grandma?"

"We bumped into her at the grocery store. Said she didn't know the girls were in foster care, but now that she knows, she seems pretty upset."

"Did you get her name?" Julie heard Rhonda rustling through papers. "But don't worry. This is normal. Relatives always come out of the woodwork after kids are placed."

"They do?" Julie imagined uncles and cousins popping out like Nightcrawler, magically appearing from thin air. "Could she . . . I mean, could this grandmother try to get custody?" Julie bit her lip, remembering how she'd laughed with the girls earlier that night, the three of them squished into a booth meant for two. Ivy had opened her mouth wide to attack a slice of pizza the size of her head, and Wren squealed, "Watch out, pizza, it's Tyrannosaurus Ivy!" They'd laughed so hard Wren knocked over her milk. Julie couldn't help it; already she couldn't bear the thought of going back to her old life.

"Maybe. Kinship care is the preferred option, but not against the wishes of the parents. Their mother went so far as to deny this grandmother's existence, so that speaks volumes."

Julie nodded. *Something* must have been off about the grandmother, for Wren to act so nervous.

"Besides," Rhonda continued, "the judge awarded you custody until the fact-finding hearing, so not much this woman can do until then."

Julie fiddled with her necklace, sliding the pendants up and down the chain. "I don't know if this means anything, but the girls seemed a bit . . . scared, I guess, of their grandmother."

"Hmm." Rhonda's flat tone indicated she found this information highly irrelevant, and she moved the conversation along to the girls' placement at Green Harbor Childcare. She'd secured them an opening, but they couldn't start for a few more days. Inwardly, Julie both cheered and groaned—more bonding time, but also more long uninterrupted days to fill.

At least this would give Wren's bruises more time to heal. They'd already begun to fade, so by the time Wren started school, Julie hoped they'd be nothing more than a bad memory.

Fifteen

A sour taste crept up Hannah's throat as she slowed to a stop in front of the town house complex: 4510 Fremont Avenue North, the final address on her list of Julie Abbotts. She'd gotten bolder on her most recent excursions, knocking on doors and chatting with neighbors instead of simply spying from the Volvo. But today she planned to stay in the car: she didn't have much time, and besides, unit 3B was her last hope. After meeting with the public defender again this morning, she felt too fragile to face an abrupt dead end.

According to her lawyer, everything was going according to plan. He'd brought all the necessary paperwork to file for a plea bargain, which would hopefully get her criminal charges dismissed. But while he waited for her to read and sign the documents, he'd tapped his pen impatiently and kept glancing at his watch. She couldn't help feeling like one more checkbox on this busy man's to-do list. Now, as she leaned her forehead against the passenger window and scrutinized the eight identical redbrick units, she burned with an unexpected longing for her mother. How different it would be to face the judge with all the force of Elaine's acidic tongue and glass-sharp intellect behind her. Except that was impossible. The threads of their relationship had been fraying for years—their problems traced back decades, perhaps all the way back to Hannah's unplanned birth—and her dad's death had been the final cut.

They'd argued about it for weeks. Hannah thought her dad should spend his final months at home, while Elaine insisted he needed more help than she could provide: "The care center has doctors on call twenty-four seven. They can manage his pain better than I can."

Hannah wondered whether her mom was simply too busy to bother playing nurse. Despite her dad's terminal diagnosis, Elaine hadn't cut back her hours. If anything, she was working more than usual, immersed in some high-profile case involving antitrust violations. How defending a bunch of corporate schmucks could possibly be more important than spending time with her own dying husband, Hannah would never understand.

Each time she called to ask whether she should fly home, Elaine told her no. "The doctors say he's got months," she kept saying, "maybe even a whole year."

But then Steve's condition deteriorated faster than either of them expected, and Hannah and the girls were still on an airplane when he took his last breath. She begrudgingly acknowledged her mom had been right about one thing: perhaps her dad had needed more care than she'd realized. Until two days after the funeral, when Hannah sat at her mother's breakfast table peering at a document that didn't make sense. She'd picked up the autopsy report without realizing what it was, and she blinked at the words "proximal cause of death: nosocomial pneumonia." That couldn't be right. "Mom," she called into the kitchen. "Why does it say *pneumonia* on Dad's autopsy report? You never told me he had pneumonia."

Wiping her hands on a dish towel, Elaine came to hover over Hannah's shoulder. "No, it says cancer." She pointed at a different line on the report. "See: 'due to, or as a consequence of: stage IV pancreatic cancer.' Pneumonia is common when somebody's that sick."

"But what's *nosocomial*?"

Elaine looked uncomfortable. "It means he caught it from the nursing home."

From the nursing home. If her mother hadn't been so selfish, or if Hannah had been more insistent, would her dad still be alive? She narrowed her eyes. "Where *you* demanded he stay. Why didn't you tell me he caught pneumonia there?"

Elaine snatched the paper from Hannah's hands. "It doesn't matter where he got it. His cancer wasn't getting better, and they did everything they could."

Hannah couldn't stand the way her mother brushed aside her own culpability. Elaine had said it herself: Steve should've had months to live. But because of her mother's stubborn negligence, Hannah didn't even get to say a final goodbye. Tears burned at the corners of her eyes, but before she could figure out what to say next, Ivy came toddling over, holding out her arms to be picked up. Hannah pressed her lips into a line—some words weren't fit for a child's ears.

All day she held back her anger, and by the time the girls were in bed that night, she was too exhausted to start a fight. Instead, she stood next to her mother at the sink, silently drying each dripping plate Elaine handed over.

Hannah stared at the gray dishwater, tracing her finger over the flowers and vines embossed into the sink's copper surface. She and her dad had both despised this sink—gaudy and impractical—but for some unfathomable reason, Elaine adored it. And when Steve made remodeling their kitchen his first postretirement project, he'd been determined to give Elaine everything she wanted. "You don't realize, Hannah-banana," he'd said. "Your mom's had a rough go of it. These days women are encouraged to become lawyers or doctors or scientists, but back when we went through school, Elaine had to fight for every single rung up the ladder. An ugly copper sink is the least I can give her for the life of luxury she's provided us."

Hannah had rolled her eyes. She'd never understood her dad's uncritical praise of her mother's "success." Sure, Elaine had managed a booming law practice, but she'd never made it to a single soccer game or art exhibition, and Hannah considered her mother's complete lack of involvement nothing short of cruel. Elaine couldn't care less about her only daughter, yet she dug in her heels about a copper sink. Just another slight in a lifetime of misplaced priorities.

Now Elaine handed Hannah an I-heart-NYC coffee mug. "Guess I'll be moving up to Seattle once this Harper-Jackson case finishes up." Hannah almost lost her grip on the mug. Elaine had dropped her bombshell as casually as if she were commenting on the weather. "The case will drag out for another three months or so, but after that, I'll give my notice."

"But *why?*" Hannah asked, her mind whirling. Elaine complained bitterly every time she visited Seattle, whining about the damp gray air, the cold summers, the endless traffic across the bridges. Even the salty air of the Puget Sound annoyed her. "You love Chicago. Your work is here, your friends. The house Dad built you. Why would you leave?"

Elaine frowned, deepening the lines around her mouth. A faint yellow sheen glistened over her pink-rimmed eyes, and her hand shook as she gripped the sponge. Hannah's always fresh, always competent mother looked suddenly old, and for a second her resentment softened. Maybe Elaine needed help.

"Why, to give you a hand with the girls, of course." Elaine's voice was cheerful and assertive. "Now that your dad has passed, I can finally give you the support you need."

The mug in Hannah's hands was long past dry, but she rubbed it harder with the dishcloth, wishing she could buff that pale pink heart right off. "Mother," she said, trying to keep her voice civil, "exactly what sort of *help* do you think I need?"

"You know, sweetie." With a crash, Elaine dumped another pot into the sink, splashing soapy water on Hannah's forearm. "Not to criticize, but you've let things slip a bit since Alex died, don't you think? That morning glory has invaded every inch of your garden, and it's threatening to take over the porch. Your roof's got an inch-thick carpet of moss. The girls never have clean clothes in their drawers, and the last time I bathed Ivy, when I peeked behind her ears, there was this green gunk—"

"Enough." Hannah glowered at her mother. "This is preposterous, coming from you."

Elaine blinked, her wide eyes the picture of innocence. "Coming from me?"

"The one who never did a load of laundry in her life, or kept a garden, or bothered to give her own kid a bath. Dad basically raised me as a single parent, so what's with all this new grandmotherly concern?"

"You know I had to provide for the family."

"Provide?" Hannah spat back the word. "You mean you had to buy yourself a bunch of fancy suits and a luxury Mercedes. We could've lived off half as much if you hadn't been addicted to Barneys and your business trips to New York City. Besides, Dad made good money with his historic reconstructions."

Elaine snorted. "Apparently you have no idea how much it costs to raise a family. Alex always took care of those little details, didn't he? So you wouldn't have to worry your pretty little artistic head about something as menial as finances. But now, pray tell, what will you do when the life insurance runs out?"

"That," Hannah hissed, "is none of your business." She glared at the side of her mother's round white head. Elaine made a show of scrubbing a spot of crusted tomato off the casserole dish before looking up.

"My granddaughters surely are my business, and you hardly own the city of Seattle. If I choose to move up there, that's my prerogative. Someone's got to make sure the girls are cared for properly."

Rage exploded in Hannah's chest. "What do you know about caring for someone *properly*? You're the one who let Dad die because you were too busy with your beloved court cases to care for him at home. Don't you realize? He might've lived another six months if he hadn't caught pneumonia from that germ-infested place."

Elaine stepped back as if she'd been hit, but Hannah didn't stop. "You refused to care for me, you refused to care for Dad. But now you're desperate to care for Wren and Ivy, to save them from my inadequate mothering?" Hannah's hand slipped, and the mug she was still holding crashed to the floor.

Elaine gave a surprised yelp, but her voice came out cold and even. "You always were the drama queen."

"And you always played the evil stepmother. You don't care two hoots about the girls. Maybe you're just afraid to be alone."

Elaine's eyes narrowed. "I should think you could give me quite a lesson on the fear of being alone. Wasn't that what you argued with Alex about on the night he died? You were lonely, a poor little housewife stuck at home all day, so you badgered him until—" Elaine stopped abruptly, but Hannah filled in the missing words. Until he charged out of the house and sped down the street, straight into the path of a drunk driver.

Hot tears blurred her vision. How did Elaine even know about that fight? Had Wren told her? Hannah hurled the towel across the marble countertop, stalked out of the kitchen, and threw open the door of the guest bedroom, before wheeling around once more. "Move to Seattle if you want, but don't you dare come near me or the girls. I'll file a restraining order if I have to." She slammed the door and locked it behind her.

All night Hannah waited, half expecting her mother to knock at the door and apologize, but the next morning Elaine left the house before Hannah and the girls got out of bed. For their last two nights in Chicago, Hannah packed their bags and moved them into a Motel 6. A month later, when Elaine finally left a string of voicemails, Hannah deleted them all unopened. Life would be easier without her mother.

—∞—

A garbage truck honked, and Hannah startled awake, bumping her knee on the steering wheel. Her neck felt sore from slouching against the window, and she checked her watch: only a few hours left to clean the house before Rhonda's first home visit. But as she glanced one more time at the plain brown door of 3B, hope bloomed in her chest. There, parked on the porch, was something she hadn't seen before.

A stroller. Bright pink with tags still dangling from its shiny chrome handles, it was brand new but cheap: exactly the kind of umbrella stroller a foster mom would buy when she found out she was getting a three-year-old.

Seconds later, the door swung open. First Wren, then Ivy appeared on the stoop, and for a moment Hannah couldn't breathe. Holding hands and wearing matching yellow raincoats, her daughters looked smaller and more vulnerable than she remembered. Two lonely ducklings, bobbing next to each other in an otherwise empty sea. Hannah fumbled with the door handle, ready to burst from the car and rush up to kiss them, until a woman stepped onto the porch.

Julie Abbott, in the flesh: the subject of all Hannah's nightmares from the past few weeks. She squinted, unable to believe they'd given her daughters to a teenager. No more than five foot two and dressed in polka dot leggings and a Wonder Woman sweatshirt, the girl hardly looked old enough to drive, let alone steal someone's children. Her drab brown locks were pulled back with a pink elastic, but her hair was so short the style resembled a rottweiler's tail more than a pony's. On the side she'd added sparkly plastic clips, the kind Hannah put in Ivy's hair to smooth down flyaway curls, and she'd topped off the look with a heavy layer of foundation and shimmery lip gloss. As this foster "mom" herded Wren and Ivy down the street, Hannah wanted to scream.

She shouldn't—couldn't—follow them. Her house was still a wreck, with only a few hours left until Rhonda's home visit, and she didn't want to think what might happen if she got caught trailing Julie. But as her daughters disappeared around the corner, Hannah gripped the steering wheel and shifted into drive. Just one more glimpse, and then she'd tear herself away.

Sixteen

"You'll love this library," Julie gushed to the girls as they bumped along on the bus.

Over the past seven days, she'd taken them on a tour of Seattle museums: IMAX and the butterflies at the Pacific Science Center, sharks and seals at the aquarium, space shuttles at the flight museum. Now they were en route to the central branch of the Seattle Public Library, an architectural gem of steel and glass in the center of downtown. Composed of nearly ten thousand diamond-shaped windows, it looked like a geodesic dome, except with lots of corners. From trips with her nephews, Julie knew they had an unparalleled selection of children's books on tape.

The bus jerked to a stop, and Julie gripped Ivy's stroller to keep it from sliding forward. "There's this open area with books and puzzles and games, and even a little wooden dollhouse. Do you like dollhouses, Ivy?"

Ivy just blinked and chewed on her fingernail, and Julie frowned. She *knew* a great deal was going on inside that little cherub's head: her earnest blue eyes followed Julie's every move, and comprehension simmered under the surface of her gently wrinkled brows. Yet she refused to talk. Wren's personality was complicated—spunky, smart, and too sophisticated for her age—but at least Julie could get a sense of it. She still hadn't cracked Ivy's silent wall, and the not-knowing bothered her.

As skyscrapers flashed by outside the window, Julie kept up a steady chatter, describing how her own mom had taken her downtown on the bus as a kid, and how much had changed. "The library we're going to wasn't even here back when I was your age. It wasn't built until 2004, after I'd left for college. I was so excited to come home at Christmas and see the—"

"We've been there before," said Wren, who'd been staring out the window. "Lots of times."

Of course. Julie bit her lip, feeling silly. Somehow she'd assumed their mom was too—what? Neglectful? Depressed?—to take them to the library.

The loudspeaker announced their stop, and Julie was thankful for the distraction. "Yup, that's us. Third and Marion. Wren, want to pull the cord?"

The bus slowed to a stop, and they tumbled onto the street. Holding tight to the stroller and gripping Wren's hand, Julie looked around, both exhilarated and anxious. She loved the way strangers treated her now, beaming at the girls and saying things like, "Got your hands full, huh, Mama?" Such a welcome change from the typical Seattleite stranger treatment: *Don't look at me, and I won't look at you. Try to talk to me, and I'll stuff in my earbuds.*

But Wren kept letting go of her hand and skipping three paces ahead, and Julie still felt scarred by their misadventure at Target. "Stay close. The library's just up this hill."

Once ensconced in the cheerful expanse of the children's section, Julie breathed a sigh of relief. With a security guard stationed at the entrance, she felt comfortable letting go of Wren's hand and letting her roam among the thousands of picture books. Ivy beelined straight for the play area, a set of three tables covered with puzzles and surrounded by blocks, benches, and the promised dollhouse. She flipped over a wooden puzzle, and five blue circles in ascending size clattered onto the table. As she placed each circle in its hole, her lips formed what looked like silent words: "One, two, three . . ."

Excited, Julie turned to Wren. "I knew it. Your sister used to talk just fine, didn't she?" But Wren had disappeared again. Julie had to smile at her magical prowess—even at Hogwarts, you had to be seventeen to disapparate.

Two rows over, she spotted Wren's brown head bobbing above the bookshelves. "Stay where I can see you," she called, telling herself not to worry—as long as Wren stayed in sight, she was old enough to pick out books by herself. Julie returned her attention to Ivy, who'd finished circles and moved on to placing pigs, ducks, and chickens into a wooden barn.

Moments later, Wren's voice exploded from the stacks, loud and indignant. "Hey, that's mine!" Julie rushed around the corner of the bookshelves and found Wren locked in a tug-of-war match with an oversize toddler in red denim overalls. They clutched opposite covers of *The Perfect Puppy Princess*, and the paperback was about to rip in half.

"Whoa, whoa, whoa." Julie rushed up and placed her hands on Wren's shoulders. "Honey, just give him the book. He's too little to understand."

"And he's too little to read it." Wren didn't let go.

"True, but there's probably another copy, or a different book you could read." Julie pried Wren's fingers off *Puppy Princess*, and the round-faced boy examined his prize, beaming. He crammed a corner of the pink paperback into his mouth.

"He's going to ruin it." Wren sprang forward and snatched away the book, surprising the toddler and knocking him off balance. He plopped to his diapered bottom and stared at them for a long moment, wide-eyed and silent. Then he opened his mouth and let out a wail that brought his dad running from the stacks.

"Gosh, I'm so sorry," Julie said as the man crouched down to comfort his squalling son. "She just wanted her book back. Of course I said she should get a different one, but—"

"It's fine." The dad chuckled as he turned to Wren. "You're quite right; he's far too young for *Puppy Princess*." He pulled a board book from the nearest shelf and handed it to his son, who promptly stopped crying to sample a cardboard corner. "Happens all the time. Sam's quite a bruiser, and he's got a thing for older women."

As the dad unfolded his gangly limbs to stand, Julie looked at his face for the first time and gasped. He'd gained several inches of forehead and a scruffy new beard, but she would recognize those pale, almost translucent blue eyes anywhere.

A huge smile spread across her face. "Jake Lankowski, I don't believe it. I heard you were back in town."

The man looked confused for a second, and then his eyes lit up. "Jules? No way. Jules!" Laughing, he crushed her with a spontaneous bear hug. Julie remembered these exuberant hugs; like always, her nose came up only to his sternum. After a moment, Jake stepped back and looked her over. "You're like a time machine. Haven't changed a bit."

Julie blushed, regretting that she'd let the girls pick out her clothes and "style" her hair that morning. Of course Jake thought she looked the same: her short brown hair was clipped back with plastic barrettes, and the girls had dressed her like a twelve-year-old.

When they'd first met in sixth grade, she and Jake had bonded over a mutual dislike of Mrs. Murphy, the math teacher who insisted on pairing them together for every project and made a big production of giving them separate work from the rest of the class. "Something special for my star pupils," she'd trill, waving a thick packet of extra worksheets. At first, young Jake and Julie were mortified, shrinking into their seats and dreading the inevitable schoolyard taunts that followed. But once they discovered their shared passion for Marvel comics and Miyazaki films, they stopped caring whether other kids sang about k-i-s-s-i-n-g.

That was the year before Julie's face erupted into a volcanic wasteland. "Don't listen to them," Jake would say when kids teased her. "They're bullies, and they tease everyone. You've heard them call me Yeti-Boy." Jake was a head taller than the other boys in class and twice as skinny, with pasty skin, almost nonexistent eyelashes, and white-blond hair that hung below his chin. It didn't help that his jeans stopped above the ankles or that his sneakers came from the women's department at Payless. Even so, the crime of being pale, scrawny, and poor was nothing compared to the social suicide of Julie's pustular skin.

But Jake didn't seem to care what the other kids thought, and he vastly preferred Julie's mom's all-you-can-eat taco dinners to the meager rations at his own house, where his mother had to stretch a nurse's salary to feed and clothe five kids. As Jake spent more and more of his after-school hours at Julie's house, their friendship became her lifeboat in a sea of seventh-grade sharks.

The following year, when Jake's mom moved their family back to Ohio, Julie was devastated. She flew out to see him once in high school, but by then he'd joined a band and become one of the cool kids. Intimidated by his new, more popular self—and also by his clear-skinned, guitar-playing girlfriend—Julie quit calling and writing letters. By senior year, they'd lost touch completely; she'd never even learned where he'd gone to college.

Now that her old friend had appeared in the flesh, Julie couldn't stop staring. His skin was still startlingly pale, but his lanky frame had filled out, and he no longer stooped his shoulders like an anxious adolescent. Those clear blue eyes radiated confidence.

"What brings you back to Seattle?" Julie asked, feeling suddenly awkward. "Oops, there goes your son." Apparently bored of pulling picture books off the shelf, the little boy had slipped around a corner into the stacks.

"Wait, Sammy, come back here." Jake chased after the toddler, caught him by the overall straps, and flipped him expertly over one shoulder. The boy dissolved into a fit of giggles. "This is Sam. Remember my youngest sister, Eva? Sam is her kid, and they live right down the street, so I borrow him all the time." Julie felt a flutter of excitement as she realized the boy wasn't Jake's son after all. She snuck a peek at his left hand. No ring.

"To answer your question," Jake said, "I moved to Seattle for work. And to live closer to this little guy, of course." He smiled down at Sam, who'd wriggled out of his arms and gone back to dumping books on the floor. "I just finished my pathology fellowship, and now I'm starting my own lab at UW."

Julie raised her eyebrows. "A doctor, wow. Lab path or anatomic?"

"Anatomic." Jake laughed as she wrinkled her nose. "You must be in medicine, too, if you're familiar with the branches of pathology."

"Billing, yeah. I'm a supervisor, but it's not very glamorous. I spend my day correcting coding errors, and then I'm the one who saddles Grandma with the astronomical bills she can't pay."

"Well, I spend my days with cadavers and resected livers, so try that on for glamour." As they both laughed, Julie felt transported back to junior high, when they used to crack each other up so hard their sides ached. Jake cleared his throat. "And who are these beautiful young ladies?"

Bored with grown-up talk, the girls had plopped onto the floor and were paging through a picture book together. Julie hesitated for a second, trying to decide how to introduce them to Jake. A whispered explanation would activate Wren's Spidey-sense hearing and arouse suspicion, but she wanted Jake to know they weren't her biological daughters.

"Oops, forgot to introduce you," she said in a bright voice. "Meet Wren and Ivy, who are staying with me for a while. Girls, this is my old friend Jake."

A flicker of surprise crossed Jake's face, but he didn't ask questions. "Nice to meet you, Wren and Ivy." He bent down and offered his hand to the girls, but they ignored him. "I don't blame them. *Berenstain Bears Go to Camp* is pretty riveting."

Wren glanced up. "It's a bit babyish, but Ivy loves the sleep-out part. I prefer chapter books with a real plot. And suspense."

"Right." Jake smiled. "*The Perfect Puppy Princess* sounds very suspenseful."

Wren giggled. "It is, really. She's tired of being a princess, so she runs away from the castle, but then everyone is looking for her, and—well, you should just read it."

"Maybe I'll read it to this little guy, when he's old enough." Jake ruffled Sam's hair and turned to Julie. "I promised my sister I'd have him back by five, and now that he's pulled the whole library collection down on the floor, I think that's our cue to leave." He knelt to start reshelving books, and Julie stooped to help. "But hey—" Their eyes locked. "Can I buy you a beer sometime? I'm dying to hear what the brilliant Julie Abbott has been up to for the past two decades."

Julie looked down at her feet. Sure, she'd been a math whiz in junior high, but what had she really done with her so-called brilliance? She'd started law school but then quit to become a teacher, only to burn out after a year of substitute teaching. Hopping from one underfunded elementary to the next was exhausting, and when a friend mentioned that Virginia Mason was training new recruits for its medical records department, Julie jumped at the chance. Her job was easy and predictable—but nothing to brag about. Fostering was the only interesting thing in her life right now; at least she could talk about the girls.

"Of course. I'd love to get a drink, anytime. Except—" She frowned, trying to recall the rules. Could she just hire a regular sitter, or did they have to be specially approved? "I'll need to schedule a babysitter."

"No worries." Jake pulled out his cell phone. "I've got a week of night shifts coming up, but let's try for next weekend. What's your number?" Julie rattled off her digits, and Jake punched them into his phone. Her purse vibrated, and she felt a warm thrill, knowing Jake Lankowski's contact information was secure in her call history. He gave her another quick hug, and for a second, with her ear pressed against his flannel coat, she could feel the thump of his heartbeat. He smelled like peppermint Life Savers.

"Julie Abbott," he said, pulling away and holding her at arm's length. "Who would have thought? I'll be in touch." He let go of her shoulders and grabbed Sam's hand. "Lead the way, little buddy."

Julie's stomach did a flip-flop as she watched them walk hand in hand out of the children's section. Jake loomed like a giant next to his toddling nephew, whose chubby legs pumped furiously to keep up. With a sigh, she turned to the girls.

"Okay, time to find that audiobook."

Seventeen

Following the bus proved tricky—every time it stopped, Hannah had to pull over to wait, and once she almost rear-ended a taxi. Finally, at Third and Marion, Wren's fuzzy purple sweater emerged from the open doors, followed by Julie holding a squirming Ivy on her hip and dragging the stroller behind. Hannah pulled into a five-minute loading zone and watched the trio trek up the steep hill toward the Central Library. Julie gripped Wren's hand as they wove through the crowd, until they turned a corner and Hannah lost sight of them. Desperate for another glimpse of her daughters, Hannah maneuvered her car into the underground library parking garage. The twelve-dollar fee would just have to go on her credit card.

The bigger problem was how to enter the library without being seen. The last thing Hannah needed was to be accused of unauthorized visitation. Rummaging around in her cluttered trunk, Hannah found a black pashmina scarf with a rip down the middle. Wrapping one end over her mouth and nose and looping the remaining fabric over her head, she tucked the loose tail behind her neck. Hannah glanced in the rearview mirror: she looked like a bank robber, but hopefully the disguise would keep Wren and Ivy from recognizing her if she happened to bump into them.

She snuck into the children's section. The shelves of picture books were only three feet high—designed for toddlers—but if she squatted down, she could inch along the stacks while staying out of sight of the play area. Hannah had just made it to the end of the first row and spotted Julie on the couch with the girls, when a tap on the shoulder made her jump.

"Ma'am, are you all right?" Still hunching over, Hannah whirled around and lost her balance. Tumbling backward, she bumped several books off the shelf. The pashmina slid off her head and puddled on the floor next to a pair of shiny black boots. Hannah looked up, into the bemused face of a library security guard. "This area is only for children and their caregivers."

"Right, of course." Hannah scrambled to collect the fallen books. "I'm just . . . ah . . . looking for a book for my toddler." She picked one at random and held it up to him. *CogAT Prep for Kindergarteners.* "She's advanced. Private schools these days, you know, just getting her ready." The security guard narrowed his eyes, clearly debating whether her vibe seemed more tiger mom or kidnapper. Hannah batted her eyelashes.

The guard shrugged. "Just ask the librarians if you need anything. And here's your scarf." He lifted the torn pashmina by one corner, pinching it between his thumb and forefinger as if it might be contaminated.

"Thanks." Taking her scarf, Hannah turned back to the books and waited until she could no longer hear his heavy boots clomping along the laminate floor. Then she wound the slippery fabric back across her face, tighter this time. She could feel the guard's eyes, still watching her from his desk just outside the glass walls of the children's section. Beneath the folds of wool, she stuck out her tongue.

When she peered around the stacks a second time, Ivy sat alone at a table in the play area, head bent low over a puzzle. Where had Julie disappeared to? Until recently, Hannah would have thought nothing of leaving Ivy alone for a minute while she and Wren picked out books, but now that Washington State had gone to such lengths to point out her negligence, she burned with indignation at this foster mom's lax supervision. Ivy stood up from the table and wandered into the stacks on the other side of the play area, and Hannah darted after, unable to help herself. But as she rounded the first corner, she stopped short.

There stood Julie, completely ignoring the girls, flirting with a man she'd clearly just met. The puppy love grin on her face made Hannah sick, and when Julie stepped forward and *embraced* him, Hannah had to clap her hand over her mouth to keep from calling out.

Just then Wren glanced in Hannah's direction, forcing her to duck behind the stacks again. Determined to hear the conversation, Hannah snuck closer, leaving a single bookshelf between her and the girls.

"And who are these beautiful young ladies?" the man asked, fixing his startlingly pale eyes on the girls. Julie's replies sounded loud and self-conscious, reminiscent of an adolescent's text: every phrase followed by an exclamation point or happy face emoji. Then Wren spoke up, and Hannah grinned despite herself. She wished Rhonda could hear Wren's lilting little-girl voice now, describing her preference for chapters and suspense—the social worker had been horrified to learn Wren had never been to school, but clearly she hadn't spent much time with Hannah's "uneducated" daughter.

Rhonda! Hannah checked her watch. Nearly 3:00 p.m., less than two hours until she needed to meet the social worker across town. At the house. She'd meant to spend the whole afternoon cleaning, but once she'd spotted that pink umbrella stroller, all thoughts of Rhonda had flown from her head. Even now, she couldn't bear to think of walking out the library doors without her daughters. Her knees ached from squatting behind the bookshelf, and her nose itched under the scarf, but being so close to Wren and Ivy loosened the knot of emptiness in her stomach.

Just as she was about to turn away, Ivy crept around the other side of Wren, bringing her close enough that Hannah could've reached between the books and wrapped one of Ivy's silky curls around her finger. Instead, she leaned in and inhaled, expecting the soft honey scent of her daughter's baby shampoo. Hannah nearly choked. Ivy smelled like she'd been assaulted with grape-scented air freshener.

Thus far, Hannah had kept it together on her reconnaissance mission. She'd watched this strange, bubbly foster mom perform all the tiny movements a parent made without thinking—snatching up Wren's hand as she stepped into the street, hoisting Ivy onto her hip—and hadn't cried. But the sickly stench on Ivy's hair was more than she could bear. Tears pricked her eyes, and Hannah leaped up, no longer caring who spotted her. As she raced past the librarian's station, the scarf slipped from her head and fell to the floor, but she didn't stop.

What had she been thinking, letting herself forget the appointment? No matter how much she wanted to pretend the last two weeks had been nothing but an incredibly realistic nightmare, she wasn't going to randomly wake up one morning and discover the girls back in their beds. She needed to stop feeling sorry for herself—stop wasting her time on foolish errands like stalking Julie—and fight, harder and smarter than she'd ever fought in her life. She loathed the idea of primly sitting next to Rhonda at her own kitchen table while the social worker drew up a "visiting plan" to give her a fraction of the hours she deserved with her children. But cooperating with the enemy was the only way to win this war. Hannah vowed to paste on her best fake smile and prepare for battle.

—⁓—

She'd never cleaned faster in her life. After snatching three garbage bags from under the kitchen sink, Hannah crammed in armloads of junk from the floors, counters, and table. Vacuuming with one hand while waving a feather duster in the other, she reveled in the quickly dissipating filth. Even the mantelpiece above the fireplace got a quick pass. Hannah paused at her wedding portrait, Alex's face now a gray smudge. With a rag and cleaning spray, she carefully wiped the dust from his adoring grin. For a moment she pressed her lips against the glass, remembering the giddy indulgence of that day. Then she wiped the frame a second time and placed the photo back where it belonged, between chubby baby Wren and a squalling newborn Ivy.

When the doorbell rang, Hannah's face was flushed and sweaty, but the house looked better than it had in months. She stuffed the last of the garbage bags into a closet and hoped the smell of bleach wouldn't give her away. Opening the door, she ushered Rhonda into the now sparkling kitchen.

"May I offer you a drink?" she asked, smiling sweetly at her pantsuit-clad nemesis.

Rhonda shook her head. "Better get down to business. We've got a lot to talk about." The caseworker parked herself at the kitchen table and pulled out a giant manila file. Somehow, less than two weeks of foster care had generated an inch-thick paper trail, and Hannah longed to stuff the entire folder into Alex's paper shredder, or better yet, toss it in the fireplace.

"The visiting schedule, then," Hannah said. Maybe if she spoke first, she could control the conversation.

"Visitation is no longer the most pressing issue. First, let's talk about your mother."

Hannah went rigid. "My *mother*? She has nothing to do with this."

Since their final fight, her only contact with Elaine had been a heated battle for the Whidbey cabin, conducted over email. The moment they'd arrived home in Seattle, Hannah had wanted to get back to the island, to honor her dad by finishing the project they'd started. But when she emailed Elaine to ask for the deed transfer—naturally, since he'd bought the place for her in the first place—her mother balked. Her message was curt: "If your father meant to leave you the cabin, he didn't bother to mention it in his will. You will not be selling that property, and unless you want a lawsuit, I'd advise you not to set foot on the premises." Typical of Elaine—dramatic and selfish. With her mother's ample bank account and deep loathing for the Pacific Northwest, Hannah couldn't imagine why she'd want to keep the cabin.

But none of this explained why Rhonda was asking about Elaine. Hannah remembered *considering* forging the deed transfer, back when she was manic on those pills, but she'd never done it, had she? All she didn't need was more legal trouble. "What do you know about my mother?"

"Her name's Elaine Montgomery, she's a lawyer, and she won't stop calling me about getting access to your case file."

Hannah sucked in her breath. "I haven't spoken to my mother in over a year. How does she even know the girls are in foster care?" She imagined a private detective stalking Wren and Ivy down the street, or a secret tracking device pinned inside their T-shirts.

"Apparently she bumped into them at a grocery store," Rhonda said.

"Here? In Seattle?" After their fight over the Whidbey cabin, Hannah had blocked her mother's phone calls and set up a filter to delete her emails, but what Elaine had said was true: *You hardly own the city of Seattle.*

Rhonda nodded. "As you may know, relatives are always our first choice for out-of-home care. We only sent the girls to a foster home because you claimed they had no relatives at all. Now that Ms. Montgomery has stepped forward, we need to discuss—"

"She can't take the girls." Hannah's thoughts were muddled and her head had begun to pound, but one thing was clear: she would never win a custody battle against her mother. Julie was annoyingly cute and bubbly, but she was an opponent Hannah could handle. "The law says I have the right to provide input into the plan for my daughters' care. My input is that absolutely, under no circumstances, can they go live with their grandmother."

Rhonda frowned. "What's so wrong with their grandma? Her voicemails have been a bit excessive, but she sounds competent and professional."

That, precisely, was the problem. All throughout Hannah's child-hood, her mother had been the essence of competent and professional, oozing cool and calm with every demure nod and casual wave of her hand. Not once had Hannah seen her mother break down and cry, not when Elaine's own mother died when Hannah was nine, not after

Alex's accident, and not even when they got the news that Steve's pancreatic cancer had spread beyond hope. But if Elaine numbed herself to life's emotional lows, her highs were even more blunted: she rarely laughed and was always stingy with hugs and kisses. Even her mother's smiles seemed more calculated than spontaneous. No, Hannah refused to doom her daughters to the emotional flatland of her own girlhood, especially since they wouldn't have her dad's booming laugh and warm embrace to melt Elaine's frost.

"My mother has never been what you'd call maternal," Hannah said, twisting a strand of blonde hair around her finger. "She's a brilliant and accomplished lawyer, but she never wanted children. Wouldn't have had me in the first place, except she accidentally got pregnant. I can't imagine why she wants to care for her granddaughters now, and frankly, I don't think she's up to the task."

Hannah could see the wheels turning in Rhonda's mind, weighing Hannah's qualifications as a mother—grossly negligent, nearly destitute, possibly abusive—against Elaine's impeccable manners, smooth lawyer-speak, and ample pocketbook. On the social worker's scale, the balance clearly tipped in Elaine's direction. "The data shows children suffer less emotional damage when placed with relatives," Rhonda said. "And moving the girls to their grandmother would open another foster bed."

Hannah scrambled to think of an argument Rhonda would find compelling. "Wait, do you realize my mother lives in Chicago?"

Rhonda sat up straighter. "Chicago? The case falls under the jurisdiction of Washington State, and for the girls to move—" She shook her head. "That's quite impossible. But Ms. Montgomery never mentioned living in Illinois. Perhaps she plans to relocate? Or has already?"

Hannah vehemently shook her head. "My mother hates the West Coast. Says we're all a bunch of whining liberal softies. Besides, she's married to her law firm."

Rhonda pursed her lips. "I see. Well, yes. That presents a problem." She scribbled a note on the stack of papers in front of her. "As their mother, you've got considerable sway with the judge regarding the girls' placement. If you'd prefer they stay in foster care, I'll communicate that to the team and recommend we leave the custody arrangement in place. For now, at least."

Hannah breathed a small sigh of relief but harbored no illusion that she'd conquered the two-headed dragon that was her mother. She added a new item to the top of her to-do list: gather concrete evidence of Elaine's incompetence as a parent. Hannah knew all about this chink in her mother's armor; she just needed to prove it.

Eighteen

It had taken Elaine four days of calling child protective services, with eight instances of "Let me transfer you to the right department" and sixteen recorded voicemails, to finally get Ms. Rhonda Thompson on the phone. When they spoke at long last, the conversation was less satisfying than she'd hoped. Like a scratched record, the woman kept repeating herself. "All details about the case are confidential, ma'am," and then, "No information can be provided without written consent from the parties under investigation." Elaine politely explained that she couldn't get consent because her daughter wasn't replying to phone calls or emails, but Rhonda refused to give out Hannah's current address. When Elaine asked whether she could at least find out why the girls had been taken into custody, the conversation went full circle: "All details about the case are confidential, ma'am."

Only when Elaine threatened to file an official grievance regarding the department's failure to make a good-faith search for relatives did Rhonda take her seriously. Even then, she insisted there was no higher authority Elaine could speak to, and the best advice she could give was to show up at the fact-finding hearing in January. Elaine hung up feeling uncommonly deflated. She'd always prided herself on her ability to navigate up a chain of command to get things done. Now, facing a legal challenge that was personal rather than professional, she'd gotten stuck behind a wall of bureaucracy. Did they really expect Elaine to wait two whole months to find out what was going on while her granddaughters languished in the care of a flighty babysitter?

Absolutely not. She'd figure out another way to get those records.

Elaine picked up her laptop and settled into the red velvet wingback next to her hotel window. Since arriving in Seattle, she'd been staying in this rather shabby downtown suite because she couldn't bring herself to set foot in the Four Seasons, where she'd stayed with Steve on previous trips—too many memories of eating alone in the hotel restaurant, working while Steve went to visit Hannah, or times when he'd asked her to tour the city but she'd stayed behind to finish a brief. Here at the Rainy City Hotel, the cheap mattress made her hips ache and the detachable showerhead refused to detach, but at least she wasn't haunted by all the ways life had passed her by.

A burning in Elaine's chest sent her hobbling to the bathroom, where she washed down four antacids with a glass of water. Glancing at her reflection, she grimaced. Who was this wrinkled old lady in the mirror? Her once piercing blue eyes looked dull and almost cloudy. She dabbed some cold cream on the puffy purple half moons below her eyes, but nothing changed. No beauty cream could turn back time. No wonder they'd asked her to leave the firm.

"Oh, posh," Elaine said out loud. "They didn't kick you out because your looks went south, but because your brain did." Yesterday she'd spent ten minutes searching for her reading glasses, only to find two pairs stacked on the crown of her head. And her coworkers didn't know the half of it: even her stately, unemotional demeanor was crumbling. These days she read *romance* novels, for God's sake. And not the dignified kind, but the kind with covers featuring half-dressed young men who could have modeled for Michelangelo. What started as a simple three-letter mistake—typing *exposed* instead of *exposure* when she ordered her latest Cold War spy thriller—had developed into a perverse compulsion she couldn't stop. Every time the heroine rode off into the sunset, Elaine had to wipe away tears.

She squared her shoulders and walked out of the bathroom. Sentimental ninny or not, she had to find a way to get that case file. Sinking once again into the velvet chair, she opened her computer and was temporarily distracted by the spreadsheet on her desktop: a list of possible wrongful termination attorneys for her case against Greenbaum & Sons. She itched to dive in and start making calls, but instead she closed the spreadsheet with an emphatic click. "Priorities, Elaine," she said, opening a blank document to brainstorm next steps.

The cursor blinked as she recalled her granddaughters in the grocery store—bold, swaggering Wren and sweet, serious Ivy—and suddenly she pictured Hannah. Not the haggard, angry woman of recent years, but the golden-haired princess she'd been as a child. Elaine closed her eyes.

To hear Hannah tell it, Steve had been the only nurturing one, the one who truly raised her, but that was because Hannah couldn't remember the earliest years of her life. Back then, before Elaine made partner and they moved from New York City to Chicago, mother and daughter had been two peas in a pod. Elaine remembered sneaking out of work on Fridays and collecting Hannah early from daycare so they could visit the Central Park Zoo, climb trees, or simply bask in the sunshine.

One afternoon they'd brought drawing pads and markers and sat side by side, leaning against the trunk of a giant oak. "Mommy, I'm going to draw you," young Hannah had said, scrunching up her brows as she studied her mother's face. Ten minutes later when she handed over the portrait, Elaine gasped: far from the simple stick figure you'd expect from a four-year-old, Hannah had drawn detailed features, an accurate hairstyle, even the heart-shaped pendant around her mother's neck. At that moment, Elaine realized her daughter's drawing skill didn't come from a particular knack for holding a pencil, or even a vivid imagination—what set Hannah apart was all she *noticed* in the world.

Later, in elementary school, Hannah would sit for hours in their front yard, sketching the blades of grass beneath her toes or the chickadee perched on a sedan across the street. For a portrait of the neighbors' black Lab, she would use blues and purples and grays to create the impression of blackness, darker and more nuanced than the color itself. When Elaine made partner, she framed Hannah's best drawings to line the walls of her new corner office. How such a strange and talented creature had spawned from her own sober, logical self, Elaine would never understand.

But as Hannah grew older, Elaine expected her to switch to more serious subjects. Creativity and passion were lovely luxuries, but the world rewarded hard work and diligence. "Especially for women," she told Hannah again and again, "it's an uphill climb. To be successful in a man's world, you've got to be smarter than all the suits around you."

Hannah only frowned and shook her head. "Mom, I don't *want* to be like you." She had no interest in Elaine's work, never wanted to visit her office or see the inside of a courtroom. "It's all so vague," Hannah complained, idolizing instead her father's work building houses to supplement the family income. "Dad uses his hands to create beauty you can live in." Elaine would shake her head and wave her checkbook in Hannah's face.

"Beauty doesn't pay the bills, sweetheart."

Then Elaine would guide Hannah into a chair at the dining room table to finish her long division, applying just the slightest pressure with her nails to indicate getting up wasn't an option until she finished the work. Did she enjoy these power struggles with her daughter? Of course not. But she did it out of love.

When Hannah became a teenager, their shaky relationship exploded. She started bringing home report cards littered with Cs and Ds and choosing boyfriends to maximize shock value—the more heavily inked and pierced, the better. Elaine hated her daughter's new style of art: instead of watercolor landscapes, Hannah splashed oil paints across her canvases with angry abandon. Or she'd start a classic portrait of a nude woman, lying on a sofa with her back to the artist, only to add bloody slash marks across her back. Hannah's anger seeped out her pores and infected them all, and no amount of reasoning could calm her down. What, pray tell, did Hannah have to be so angry about? Elaine could never understand. She and Steve did everything for their daughter, gave her anything she could possibly want, yet Hannah insisted on being miserable. Worse, the frequent shouting matches triggered Elaine's migraines, which sometimes became so fierce even Imitrex couldn't touch them.

When Hannah left for college, some part of Elaine was relieved; the other part worried they'd never see her again, that maybe she'd drop out of Illinois State and take a bus to California to live on the streets. But instead, she met Alex, got married, and poured her artistic soul into photography and mothering. Elaine would be forever grateful to her son-in-law, the cheerful, kind computer scientist who'd tamed her wayward daughter.

At the thought of Alex, Elaine stood abruptly, sending the computer sliding off her lap and thudding to the carpet. She bit her lip, wondering again if Hannah would be better off knowing the truth. But no, she'd hashed it out with Steve over and over. This way, Hannah couldn't blame Elaine for Alex's death, and Hannah was spared any of her own guilt. Steve's words echoed in her mind: *I've got to know my girls will stick together.*

Even without spilling her shameful secret, Elaine had let her husband down.

Without thinking, she grabbed her phone and dialed Hannah's number one more time. Hannah must have cleaned out her voicemail because, for once, her voice came through, smooth and strong, asking Elaine to leave a message. Elaine opened her mouth, ready to apologize—to say she missed her daughter the way she'd miss her right arm if it was severed from her body—but a lifetime of emotional wall-building had poorly trained her tongue. She gagged on the words, and after a strangled pause, her voice came out harsh and strident.

"Hannah. What can I say? You've screwed up royally this time. Stop pretending you can handle this on your own and call your mother."

Nineteen

After they got back from the library, Julie cobbled together a quick dinner of fruit salad and macaroni and cheese. Not from scratch—she wasn't that adventurous yet—but the box boasted 98.8 percent organic ingredients, and she added frozen peas and carrots for color. Her goal was healthy but manageable, as she eased herself from nightly takeout to preparing the girls three square meals a day. Bumping around the kitchen, she kept tripping over Ivy and Popsicle, splayed out side by side on the floor.

"Ivy, why don't you help your big sister set the table?" Mostly Julie wanted to get her out from underfoot, but also, she'd just started reading *We Belong Together: Fostering a Sense of Family for Your Foster Kids*. The third chapter stressed the importance of daily chores. Julie put Wren in charge of everything breakable, while Ivy handled the silverware and napkins. But even after they sat down, and after she lit a candle to set a calm yet festive mood ("Chapter Two: Creating Rituals"), she kept glancing at her phone. Jake wouldn't text so soon, would he? She stashed the brick in her jeans pocket, only to snatch it back out thirty seconds later.

"You're acting funny," Wren said, carefully sorting the peas and carrots out of her macaroni. "Is it because we're going to school tomorrow?"

"No, sweetie, I'm just waiting for a friend to call." Wren kept reminding Julie that tomorrow was their first day at Green Harbor. Even though they'd picked out glow-in-the-dark galaxy backpacks and filled each one with No. 2 pencils, a box of thirty-six jumbo crayons, and a wide-ruled notebook with fluffy puppies on the front, Wren worried she wouldn't be prepared.

"What about markers? What if I'm supposed to have markers?"

"Not on the checklist. Look." Julie plucked the Green Harbor welcome letter off the countertop. For the fourteenth time, she showed Wren the list, each item checked off in thick red Sharpie. Wren studied the letter, and they ate in silence for several minutes. Ivy gargled her water as she drank, a wet gurgle that drove Julie batty, but she bit her lip to keep from snapping. She hadn't yet read "Chapter Ten: Choose Your Battles," but she could guess its content.

"What if I don't like what they have for lunch?" Wren asked.

Julie checked her phone again. No Jake. "I'm packing your lunch. As long as you like peanut butter and jelly with the crusts cut off, you're all good."

Wren sat in silence for a moment, stirring the pile of peas and carrots she hadn't eaten at the bottom of her bowl. "But what if I have to go to the bathroom?"

"Schools have bathrooms. Just raise your hand and ask."

"The teacher might say no."

Julie sighed. They'd been going in circles all day, and nothing she said could blunt Wren's anxiety. "You're always allowed to go to the bathroom. The teacher wouldn't want you to pee in your pants, would she?"

Wren frowned, considering this logic. "But what if I get a mean teacher, and she says no anyway?"

"She won't."

"But what if she does?"

Wren's constant badgering had stretched Julie's patience as thin as crepe paper, and now she felt it rip. *"She won't."* Julie banged her glass down on the table, harder than she meant to, and their pasta dishes rattled. Wren's lower lip trembled. "Oh, honey." Julie went over to Wren, crouching down and draping her arms around the girl's shoulders. "I know you're nervous, but school will be fun. You'll love it." She kept her voice bright, careful to hide any whisper of her own reservations.

School had been no picnic for Julie herself. Even before cystic acne made her the social pariah of middle school, kids had teased her for the triple sins of being chubby, short, and shy. Her own second-grade teacher had been elderly and hard of hearing, and she was forever asking Julie to speak up in class. On the playground, kids turned the teacher's polite appeals into jeering taunts: sticking out their two front teeth and cupping their hands like rodent paws, they'd sneer, "Squeak, squeak, Julie-mouse, we can't hear you."

But school would be different for savvy, confident Wren. "You'll get to be with friends all day," Julie said, "and learn cool new stuff. Besides, you're so smart, the teacher's going to love you."

Wren glared at Julie. "You can't make me go. Mom didn't make me. She said school was . . . soul stomping? No. Soul crushing." Wren's brows furrowed, her forehead a field of worry. "What does that mean, to crush your soul?"

Before Julie could answer, the doorbell rang. She fled from the table, grateful for whatever package delivery had saved her from this conversation. Upon opening the door, she was shocked to find Rhonda, looking rather sheepish and holding out a very ratty, very purple Batgirl stuffie, along with a slightly less tattered Belle doll.

"Wow, your timing is perfect." Julie had to stop herself from throwing her arms around Rhonda—and she wasn't the sort of person who generally inspired hugs. "Wren is *super* nervous about starting school tomorrow."

"Maybe these'll help." Rhonda handed over the dolls. "Sorry to barge in on you, but I realized I was driving right by your house on my way to the next home visit."

"No, this is great." Julie traced her finger over Batgirl's embroidered nose, which had been loved so much the threads were torn. Maybe a superhero could give Wren the extra dose of bravery she needed. After waving goodbye to Rhonda, Julie went back into the kitchen, clutching the dolls behind her back.

"Hey, girls, look who showed up on our doorstep."

At the sight of Batgirl, Wren's eyes filled with tears. She snatched the stuffie out of Julie's arms and raced into the guest room.

—⁓—

At 7:55 the following morning, when two smiling teachers met them at the front desk of Green Harbor, Wren stayed silent. White-faced and resolute, she shouldered her backpack and marched obediently to room five, not even looking back to wave.

Ivy, on the other hand, began to sob.

"There, there," crooned the room-two teacher, patting Ivy's trembling back as Julie held her tight. "Just hand her to me, Mom. Trust me, they're always fine once the parents are gone." Julie gripped Ivy tighter.

"You know, right?" Julie surprised herself with the sharpness in her voice. "What they've been through in the past couple of weeks? I'm their foster mom."

"Yes, I'm aware." The teacher made a conspicuous adjustment to her ID badge so Julie could see the long title below her name: CLARA DAYTON, MS, NCC, LPS, HEAD TEACHER AND BEHAVIORAL INTERVENTION SPECIALIST. "Believe me, we're equipped to handle children like Ivy."

Children like Ivy? Julie narrowed her eyes. This woman made her sweet, scared three-year-old sound like a disobedient pit bull. Ivy shrank farther into Julie's armpit, but the teacher looked nonplussed. "Here we go," she said cheerfully, and tried to wrench a shaking Ivy from Julie's arms. Ivy grabbed fistfuls of Julie's wool cardigan and began to wail.

"She'll be fine," the teacher said again, prying clumps of sweater from Ivy's fingers.

Julie opened her mouth to protest but stopped, cowed by the woman's authoritative tone. She was a behavioral intervention specialist, after all, and Julie was—what? A wannabe mother, playing house.

Ivy's shrieks echoed down the hall, even after the duo disappeared into the preschool room. As Julie headed back to the front desk, she pondered the parade of children's artwork lining the walls—bright-yellow suns, pink-and-purple houses with smoke-puffing chimneys, smiling stick figures holding hands. Awfully sanguine for a center specializing in traumatized children. Somewhere, hidden in a dark closet perhaps, Julie imagined a messy stack of a different kind of art—moms drawn with fuming eyebrows and gaping mouths; crumbling houses with garbage-strewn lawns; a solitary, disembodied face with a lonely tear slipping down its cheek. Or perhaps the teachers stuffed those drawings in the recycling bin straightaway, before they could taint the perky assurance of a place like Green Harbor.

Julie stumbled out the glass doors into a fine gray mist. The bleak weather matched her mood: churned up inside, as raw and emotional as if she herself faced a mob of taunting second graders. She checked her phone. Finally, a text from Jake: Two more shifts to go. Beer Thursday evening? Julie grinned, grateful no one was around to see the goofy smile on her face.

Would love to, she typed, then quickly hit delete. What was she thinking? Thursday was Thanksgiving, the girls' first chance to meet the extended Abbott clan. Up in Lynnwood, her mom would already be whirling around the kitchen, apron tied over her jeans and flour up to her forearms, whipping up a pecan pie. Can't, Julie typed, Thursday is Thanksgiving with the fam. She hesitated, realizing that if she could have bowed out of the meal without hurting anyone's feelings, she might have chosen beer with Jake over her favorite holiday of the year. Friday, please? she added, and pressed send. The girls had their first visit with their mother on Friday afternoon, so Julie would be free.

She clutched her phone, willing it to ping again. Did *please* sound too desperate? *You're overthinking*, she chided herself. She and Jake were hardly dating. He didn't think of her that way. They were nothing more than two old friends grabbing a casual beer. For all she knew, he had a girlfriend.

The phone buzzed three times, and Julie almost dropped it.

"Julie, hey." Her stomach turned cartwheels at the way he said her name, intimate and breezy as if they'd never lost touch. "Can't believe I forgot about Thanksgiving. Usually I fly out to Ohio with Eva and Sam, but this year I'm stuck with the holiday shift, so it's Chinese takeout for me. Any chance you can slip away after the family dinner?"

Julie brushed the damp bangs from her face. "Wish I could. But I'd need to get someone to watch the girls, and finding a babysitter, on Thanksgiving . . . ?"

"Right, not going to happen. What's the story with the girls, though? You said they're staying with you?"

"I'm their foster mom."

"Wow, really?" Jake paused, and Julie wasn't sure what else to say. "Actually, I'm not surprised—I remember how good you always were with my sisters."

Julie smiled. Jake had complained whenever they tagged along, but she'd loved those four little stair-step girls. Now she tried to imagine them all grown up, even the youngest old enough to be married with a toddler.

"Anyhow," Jake said, "sounds like we have a lot to catch up on. But the timing couldn't be worse. A colleague had a family emergency, so now I'm headed to Ann Arbor on Friday for a weeklong conference. Beer when I get back?"

Julie hung up feeling deflated. Then again, she'd gone fifteen years without seeing Jake—what was another ten days?

—⁓—

"You did it, foster mama!" With a sheepish grin, Julie's office mate Sally pulled two Mylar balloons from beneath her desk. IT'S A GIRL, the shiny globes proclaimed, in blinding shades of neon pink and purple. "Sorry, couldn't help myself."

Sally had been Julie's cheerleader during the long and sometimes disheartening foster-application process. After Sally's mom died of breast cancer when she was eight, she'd spent two years in the foster system herself, bouncing from family to family until a single mom adopted her. Then Sally and her partner, Gwen, chose fostering to start their own family, and their four-year-old became Julie's poster child for foster-to-adoption success.

Now, Sally clutched her in an exuberant hug, but Julie had a hard time returning the enthusiasm. All she wanted to do was bury her nose in a spreadsheet of dull, reassuring ICD-10 codes. Sally held her friend at arm's length, studying Julie's face. "Not so easy, eh?" Her eyes radiated part concern, part *I told you so*. "Those girls running you ragged?"

"No, no." Julie tried to keep an unexpected wave of sadness from flooding her voice. "I had to drop them at school for the first time this morning, and they didn't want to go. After two weeks of nonstop togetherness, they're finally starting to trust me. I feel like a traitor, leaving them there."

Sally squeezed her shoulder. "It's going to be hard for a while, but it'll get easier."

Another coworker popped his head over the cubicle partition. "We're all proud of you. You're a hero for doing this."

Julie smiled, but inside she wilted. A true hero wouldn't consider hiring a babysitter on Thanksgiving. "Thanks. But I better get to all this." She motioned to her overflowing desk.

"Okay, but later we're taking you out to celebrate." Sally tied the balloons to Julie's chair. "Friday happy hour wasn't the same without you."

Putting on her noise-canceling headphones and cranking up the Beatles, Julie hoped "Here Comes the Sun" would clear the fog from her mind. But she couldn't stay focused on work—her thoughts kept drifting back to Jake. As soon as Sally went on lunch break, she dialed

Anitha. "Don't kill me, but I have another giant favor to ask. Remember when you told me Jake Lankowski moved back . . ."

Anitha squealed when she heard about their chance encounter at the library. "Fate brought you together, before I could even get involved. Is he single?"

Julie groaned. "Of course that's the first thing you'd ask. But yeah, I think so. He wasn't wearing a ring, and if he has a girlfriend, why would he spend Thanksgiving alone?"

"Good point," Anitha said. "And you bumped into him yesterday, right? A waxing moon in Gemini, that could be good."

"Now you're so desperate to marry me off you've resorted to astrology?"

"You need all the help you can get, sister."

But as much as Anitha wanted to play matchmaker, she couldn't babysit Thursday night—her husband's family was in town for the holiday, and festivities with his Irish Catholic parents inevitably lasted into the wee hours of the morning.

"But Jules," she said, "why not invite him to your parents'? They'd love to see him again, and then you can woo him with your mom's garlic-butter potatoes."

Julie could hear the smirk in Anitha's voice, but her friend had a point. She'd never dare bring a regular date to Thanksgiving—her family's overexuberance would scare the poor man off before dessert—but Jake had eaten dinner at her house practically every third night during sixth and seventh grade. He and Drew shared a mutual adoration of the Green Lantern. And if she told her mom Jake Lankowski would be spending Thanksgiving alone in his apartment, she'd be the first to extend an invitation.

"Strange idea for a first date, but you're brilliant. I think I'll do it."

Julie hung up and dialed Jake before she lost her nerve. He answered on the fifth ring, and as soon as she heard his raspy, sleep-caked voice, she knew she should have texted. After a night shift at the hospital, of course he'd be sleeping. But he sounded genuinely thrilled at the invitation to Thanksgiving.

"You're sure I won't be intruding?" he asked. "I'd love to see your parents again, and Drew. God, Drew, and all those games of *GoldenEye* we played in your basement. Is the man still obsessed with video games?"

"A programmer on Xbox. So yeah, a little obsessed." Julie laughed. "But you can get all the details from him on Thursday. Go back to bed."

"Me, asleep at noon on a Monday? Never."

"You were totally sleeping, don't try to pretend." Without meaning to, Julie had conjured an image of Jake lying in bed, wearing plaid boxers and the faded yellow Bee Gees tee he'd loved in junior high. But it was clearly not sixth-grade Jake: his pale sinewy frame was only half covered by a balled-up sheet, and the calves sticking out of the bedclothes were tight and muscular. Sally bustled back into the office with an armload of take-out boxes, and Julie blushed.

"Gotta run, sleepyhead," she said. "See you at four on Thursday. I'll text you my parents' address."

Jake laughed. "No need. If I get lost, I'll just close my eyes and imagine myself twelve again, riding my ancient ten-speed."

As Julie hung up, she hoped Sally wouldn't notice her flaming cheeks.

"Hard at work, I see." Sally raised her eyebrows but didn't pry. Checking her watch, Julie frowned. For the girls' first day, she'd promised to pick them up at three thirty instead of sending them to aftercare, which meant she had less than three hours left to finish a week's worth of chart reviews. She replaced her headphones and cranked up the volume, but even the Beatles couldn't block the scenes replaying in her mind: Wren's small dark head disappearing down the hall at Green Harbor; Jake ruffling his nephew's curls at the library; Ivy sobbing and clinging to her sweater as chilly Ms. Dayton tore her away. Two more days, she told herself, and the girls would get a vacation from school. And she'd get to spend Thanksgiving Day with Jake.

Twenty

For two days Hannah brooded over how to prove her mother's incompetence as a caregiver. The answer lay just out of reach, a hazy swirl of half-baked ideas, until the primordial soup of her mind crystallized into a plan so obvious, it startled her awake at 3:00 a.m. Hannah's eyes flew open and she sat up with a jolt, confused by the silvery-green light bathing her face. Morning already? No, just a full moon, and she'd forgotten to close the curtains.

Hannah had been dreaming about the cottage on Whidbey Island, and in the magical wanderings of her mind, her father was alive and well. They'd been tiling the shower in the main bathroom, alternating ceramic squares of gray and turquoise as they chatted about the pros and cons of a telephoto lens for photographing children. Even as the details of the dream began to float away, a sense of comfort and camaraderie remained.

In the dream, Hannah had been trying to reach the top corner of the shower, teetering on a giant cardboard box labeled "Photos, etc."

"Watch out," her dad said. "You're standing on my memories."

Now, as she pulled the comforter up to her chin, Hannah clung to his words. On their final trip to Whidbey together, he'd given her a collection of old letters, not in the cardboard box she'd seen in her dream but in a giant accordion folder, ripped on one side and nearly falling apart. The mementos inside might provide the evidence she needed. "You'll have to sort through all this," he'd told her, "but I saved every drawing you sent me in August of '92." Hannah was fourteen that summer, and her dad had taken a lucrative but soul-sucking job building high-rises in Springfield. He might have stayed on through the fall if she hadn't written him so many pitiful letters, detailing her mother's faults and begging him to come home.

Her dad had saved the pages not for the words she'd written but to preserve the elaborate pencil sketches in the margins. Hannah's fairy obsession had peaked that summer, and sprinkled through the letters were drawings of wide-eyed elfin sprites, tiny winged women with lustrous hair and dainty bare feet. But if she remembered correctly, the letters also gave a detailed account of Elaine's more egregious maternal failings.

Some of Hannah's complaints that summer could be chalked up to hormonal drama, the typical mother-daughter spats everyone experiences during their teenage years. But she doubted a judge would look kindly on Elaine's more shocking episodes—for instance, the time she got so fed up with Hannah's poor school performance that she pushed her onto the front porch and locked the dead bolt. No matter how loudly Hannah hollered or pounded on the door, Elaine refused to let her in, not even when it got dark and a steady rain began to fall. Eventually, Hannah had walked, in shirtsleeves and stocking feet, to a nearby friend's house, where she'd begged to stay the night. The incident convinced her dad to quit his job and come home, and if Hannah could find the evidence now, perhaps it would also convince a judge that such a hot-tempered woman would not make a fit guardian for Wren and Ivy.

When she'd first gotten the packet of letters, Hannah had been too devastated by her father's diagnosis to care about fairies, and she'd stashed the folder among the growing detritus from the remodeling project. Now, she wanted to drive straight to the cabin to look for it, but her calendar was already full: before she could get out to the island, she'd have to endure her first day of outpatient therapy, five miserable hours of baring her soul to strangers.

—⁓—

The moment she walked through the double doors, Hannah felt uncomfortable—Presley had the same antiseptic smell she associated with the nursing home where her dad died. And the maze of beige walls and gray tile floors did little to alleviate the sick-person atmosphere. Despite the directions of the cheerful greeter who handed her a "Personalized Treatment Packet"—including a master schedule of all the torture sessions she'd have to endure over the next twelve weeks—Hannah struggled to locate room 1309B. By the time she found the right door and peeked through the tiny glass window, all twelve folding chairs in the circle were occupied.

Each participant held a clipboard, and they appeared to be madly scribbling on some kind of checklist. One woman, ironically wearing a turquoise hoodie that said **POSITIVITY** across the front, sobbed in her chair, fat droplets of devastation splattering her paper. Hannah scanned the room for Dr. Banning and checked her schedule—nope, this session was run by a Ms. Kimberly Perrera, who Hannah figured must be the one wearing three ID badges around her neck. She also appeared to be in charge of the tissue box, which had just made its way around the circle to the crying woman. She pressed the box against her chest but made no move toward damming her tears. Apparently, unlike Hannah, this lady had zero reservations about falling apart in front of an audience. Hannah shuddered. Perhaps tearful public outbursts were routine in this strange new world of therapy.

Just as she'd gathered her courage to go inside, the group set down their pencils. Ms. Kleenex Box finally pulled out a tissue, but still didn't bother to wipe away the rivers on her face. With extreme reluctance, Hannah turned the handle and eased open the door.

The therapist's effervescent voice made her feel instantly exhausted. "Thank you for filling out your thought inventories, everyone. Today we're going to talk about how thoughts can trigger feelings, and how changing those thoughts can in turn change how we feel. Because depression is all about feelings, right?"

The entire room nodded, and the crying woman blew her nose into a tissue. Hannah felt like an intruder, hovering by the door, but there were no empty chairs and the therapist still hadn't noticed her. Stealthily, she inched along the wall and found a spot in the corner to lean against—perhaps her presence alone would fulfill the requirements of the program, and she could stay below the radar, not participating.

A blond man raised his hand. "Kim, we seem to have a visitor."

Kimberly turned in her chair and gave Hannah a wide smile. "Excellent. Dr. Banning told me we might have a new person today, but he wasn't sure if you'd come. I'm so glad you did." She walked over to the stack of folding chairs leaning against the wall. "Can we make our circle a bit wider, folks? And why don't you introduce yourself? Maybe tell us your name, one interesting thing you'd like to share about yourself, and what you're hoping to get out of these group sessions."

Twelve pairs of eyes focused on Hannah, and her thoughts turned into static fuzz. She'd never been a social butterfly, even before Alex's death, but after two years of isolating herself with only the girls, this cluster of strangers might as well have been a full auditorium. Taking the chair from Kimberly, she unfolded it as slowly as possible, stalling an extra few seconds by pretending it got stuck halfway. "My name's Hannah," she finally said, her voice rusty. "I used to be a photographer, and I'm here because . . ." She paused. The truth—that she was only here to get her girls back—would lead to more questions. Hannah couldn't trust herself to talk about Wren and Ivy without breaking down, and she had no desire to end up like the blubbering woman with the Kleenex box. She glanced at the packet Kimberly had just handed her, with its "Negative Thought Inventory" right on top. There would be no checkbox for *The state stole my daughters* or *I accidentally killed my husband* or even *My mother's selfishness meant I never got to say goodbye to my dad.*

Everyone continued staring at her, waiting for an answer. She blurted out the first lie that popped into her head: "I'm here because ever since my sister died, I've been too sad to pick up a camera."

The therapist beamed. "Very perceptive, Hannah. I hope the thought work we're about to do will help you find a way back to your art." All around the room, her fellow group members offered encouraging smiles. Hannah felt relieved—maybe she could bear therapy after all. She could give the doctors what they wanted and check the "treatment" box on the state's requirement list, without divulging any of her secrets. Besides, part of her answer was true—someday, after she got Wren and Ivy back, she would love to return to photography.

—※—

By the time Hannah made it onto the highway, commuter traffic had already clogged I-5, and she didn't arrive at the ferry until the line of waiting cars snaked more than a half mile from shore.

All day, through that first group session, a mindful yoga class, and two hours of art therapy, Hannah had managed to distract herself from thoughts of Wren and Ivy. Unexpectedly, she half enjoyed talking with her group mates, so long as she asked the questions. It wasn't hard to deflect the conversation from her own problems—people liked to talk about themselves. But when a question did come her way, Hannah expanded on the tale of her lost sister: the same imaginary sibling she'd longed for as a girl, the one she might have had if her mother hadn't hated children. "Before Abigail got sick, we did everything together," Hannah told a new friend. "She was the one person I could count on."

Now, in the ferry line, she had no one to lie to, nothing to keep the words *preponderance of evidence, danger to her children,* and *unfit mother* from playing in her head. She reached for her phone to distract herself with the news, but she'd already lost signal. Finally the driver behind her laid on his horn, and she jerked the gear shift into drive, relieved to be moving forward.

On the ferry, she left the car and trudged up three flights of concrete stairs to the boat's upper deck. The only passenger brave enough to face the bracing November wind, Hannah stood alone at the bow of the ship. Breathing in the salty air of the Puget Sound, she watched the army of Douglas firs on the beaches of Whidbey Island grow closer. Fifteen months ago she'd crossed this same water with her dad by her side, already knowing the trip would be his last. He'd been so infuriatingly cheerful, refusing to let a terminal diagnosis dampen his spirits for their final construction hurrah. Her dad could no longer climb a ladder or handle power tools, but he'd hired contractors to do the heavy lifting. While the crew worked, he taught Hannah the fine art of drywall installation, and together they finished most of the downstairs.

It wasn't raining, but a fine silver mist coated Hannah's eyelashes and hair, and by the end of the twenty-minute ride, the late-autumn sun had disappeared from the sky. The boat lurched as it collided with the buoys of the Clinton ferry dock, and she smiled despite herself. She loved this place, had loved it ever since she and Alex had brought toddler Wren to picnic on Double Bluff Beach. After she and her dad had rebuilt the cottage together, creating their final set of memories, she only loved the island more.

As she drove down the long dirt road to the cottage, the familiar shapes of her favorite trees seemed to welcome her home—the big-leaf maples had fewer leaves than the last time she'd visited, but the western hemlocks were as green as ever and the pale bark of the alders glowed in the reflection of her headlights. The moment she stepped out of the car and felt the mossy ground squish beneath her feet, her blood pressure dropped. Something about the island air was cleaner, fresher, than the air in Seattle—she could release the tightness in her chest and gulp it down as greedily as she wanted. Using the flashlight on her phone, she made her way up the fern-lined path to the cottage, where she stopped short.

The property looked somehow neater than she'd left it a week ago. When had she stacked that pile of firewood by the side door or cleared the paint cans off the porch? The smell of latex enamel seared her nostrils as she opened the front door, and when she shone a flashlight around the main room, all four walls seemed to glow, white with the barest hint of sun-kissed cream.

Goose bumps shivered down her spine. Hannah could've sworn she'd painted only half the room. For a second, she almost believed her father's ghost had returned to finish the job. Pressing her thumb to the wall and pulling away, she half expected to find a crescent of wet paint. Nothing. Shaking her head, Hannah walked into the master bedroom. Losing the girls had sent her mind into a tailspin, and now this new medication from Dr. Banning must be further scrambling her brain. He'd promised it would even out her moods and help her sleep—not to mention add *compliant with medication* to her case record—but Hannah was still reluctant. If the pills were summoning ghosts, maybe she should start splitting the capsules in half.

It took forty-five minutes of searching by flashlight, but finally she unearthed the crucial folder under a pile of plastic sheeting. Dear Dad, read the first letter in boxy cursive, on a page torn from a yellow memo pad dated August 2, 1992. Mom hates me. Worse, she ignores me. The letter went on to describe boycotted meals, verbal boxing matches, and slammed doors followed by hours of the silent treatment. Hannah cringed at the petulant tone of her younger self: She's refusing to pay me for washing the car. So what if the windows have streaks? That wasn't in the job description. Hannah tried to imagine Wren seven years in the future, sloppily performing her chores but demanding to be paid anyway. These were hardly the kind of letters she could read to a judge. To prove Elaine's negligence, she needed to find the account of the night her mother locked her out.

As Hannah flipped through the stack, a typed envelope with the return address of Elaine's law office caught her eye. The letter inside was written on thick ecru stationary, and even before she recognized the loopy scrawl, Hannah knew she'd struck gold. She read quickly, skimming to find the parts where Elaine would surely complain about her incorrigible daughter, the biggest mistake of her life.

Dear Steve, Elaine had written, Hannah keeps telling me everything would be better if only you'd come home. For once, I agree with her. I'd hoped this would be a summer of mother-daughter bonding, a time of togetherness to finally bring us closer. Hannah's eyes narrowed. She was surprised Elaine had taken the time to contemplate the state of their relationship, as she'd always felt like nothing more than a fly in her mother's otherwise spotless ointment.

She kept reading, slower this time.

I've tried so hard to teach her diligence, patience, poise—the qualities she'll need to succeed in life. But everything I do infuriates her, everything I say is wrong, and amid her hormonal tantrums, I'm not even modeling good behavior. I've yelled; I've threatened; I nearly slapped her yesterday, and I'm afraid I can't hold out much longer.

I miss our sweet, wide-eyed Hannah-banana the way she used to be—remember those beautiful portraits she used to draw? I'm afraid I've lost that girl forever. Please come home; she looks at you with a respect I can only dream of. Even if you're only back for the weekend, it'll be long enough to repair the hinges on our bedroom door. I've slammed it so many times in the last month, the bolts are coming loose. And while you're in the bedroom, darling . . .

Blushing, Hannah crammed the letter back into its envelope. In all the years she'd seen her parents together, they'd never given each other more than a chaste peck on the cheek. Yet here was her mother, acting coquettish and silly in a letter.

This wasn't the kind of evidence Hannah had hoped to find, but she felt strangely pleased. Elaine could have written about Hannah's bad grades and missed curfews, or how she'd dyed her hair a forbidden pink. But instead of a litany of grievances, she'd written about how she missed Hannah's younger self and how she struggled to be the mother she wanted to be: *I nearly slapped her yesterday.* To her credit, Elaine had reached out for help when she'd gotten to the end of her rope. Hannah stuffed the envelope into her pocket, wishing she could say the same about herself.

She scrolled through the contacts on her phone and paused on the thumbnail photo of her mother, cropped from a portrait she'd taken years ago, a few months after Wren was born. A reluctant grandmother, Elaine had sat primly on the edge of the sofa, staring directly into the camera lens instead of at the wriggling baby in her lap. What was going on behind those icy blue eyes and serenely upturned lips? Hannah had always assumed her mother's smile was too calculated to be real, but perhaps her deliberate expression was simply a sign of how hard she was trying at a relationship that didn't come naturally. On a whim, Hannah pressed the image and dialed her mother.

She held her breath, waiting for a ring, but nothing happened. No service, dammit. She'd finally mustered up the courage to reach out, and the universe said no. Hannah gathered up the contents of the folder, relocked the cabin, and used a flashlight to guide herself down the rocky path to the car. Inky clouds blocked the moon and stars, and she dreaded the long trip back across the water. She hated taking the ferry at night, especially without a moon. No matter, she'd stay in the car, away from the observation deck and churning water.

Halfway across the Sound, Hannah's purse vibrated. Cell signal was restored, at least for now, and she'd missed a call from Rhonda reminding her of the supervised visit on Friday. As if Hannah didn't already have a countdown set on her phone: thirty-seven hours, twenty-five minutes, and nineteen seconds until she could hug her daughters.

She studied her recent call list, wondering if she should try Elaine again. Part of her felt stubborn—once her mother had found out about the girls, shouldn't *she* have been the one to call? Then with a shock, Hannah remembered: she'd blocked her mother's number months ago, which meant Elaine's calls would've gone straight to voicemail without triggering a notification. Feeling shaky, Hannah opened her call settings and unblocked the number. Instantly, twelve missed calls appeared—and one voicemail.

Her finger hovered over the play button. Digging through those old letters, she'd hoped to unearth a skeleton. What she'd found instead was . . . well, she wasn't quite sure. Fragments of compassion, maybe, or bits of hope like uncut gemstones, dirty and rough around the edges. She held her breath and pressed play.

Elaine's smooth, polished voice purred in her ear: "You've screwed up royally this time. Stop pretending you can handle this on your own and call your mother."

The click as Elaine hung up sounded far too loud, an exploding grenade that shattered any warm feelings Hannah had just been having. *This time*, as if screwing up was Hannah's specialty. *Call your mother*, as if Elaine could fix all of Hannah's mistakes with a wave of her expert wand. Hannah played the message over and over, each time becoming more furious. By the time the ferry docked in Seattle, she felt angry at everyone—including the driver in front of her, who'd arrived late to her car, stumbling under the weight of a giant gift bag with a shiny orange turkey on the front.

Tomorrow was Thanksgiving, Hannah realized with a bitter laugh. No matter what tragedy had just befallen her—Alex's fatal accident, her dad's cancer, now the theft of her children—the obstinate calendar marched forward, forcing the insistent, mocking cheer of Thanksgiving! Christmas! New Year's! on all who continued living. Turkey be damned; she'd eat chocolate for dinner and spend the rest of the night recleaning the house. When Rhonda showed up with the girls on Friday, the sinks would shine bright enough to blind her.

Twenty-One

Elaine couldn't erase that disastrous voicemail—not without tracking down Hannah and stealing her phone. But now there was no chance in hell Hannah would call back, let alone sign a form granting access to her case file. The more Elaine thought about it, the more she wanted those records: not only to save Wren and Ivy from foster care but also because solving Hannah's legal troubles might be the only way to win her back. Once Elaine knew the details of the case, she'd devise a brilliant strategy to prove Hannah's innocence. She imagined bringing the girls home herself, ringing the doorbell and watching Hannah break down in happy tears. She'd have no choice but to be grateful. After all those years of disdaining her mother's profession, Hannah would finally see why a good lawyer was so important.

Unfortunately, CPS seemed awfully protective of their records. Elaine groaned as she read the website: all requests must be made in writing and include express authorization from the party under investigation. Besides, Elaine knew all too well how slowly the wheels turned in these large bureaucratic organizations; even if she had Hannah's permission, going the official route could take weeks.

Elaine didn't have weeks. After pacing her hotel room for two days, trying to think of a way to help Wren and Ivy, she'd given in and started calling attorneys about her lawsuit against Greenbaum & Sons. She could work on two cases at once, after all. Most had politely declined, but yesterday she spoke to an old friend who seemed interested—and he owed her a favor. "But this is a sensitive subject," he said. "I'd rather discuss it in person. How soon can you come to my office?" Elaine explained she was stuck in Seattle at the moment, due to a family emergency, but she'd call him as soon as she got back. "The sooner, the better," he'd told her. "My schedule is filling up."

So she'd gone back to studying every website she could find related to CPS records. Finally, an article from the attorney general provided the hint she needed: "In accordance with state law, a copy of all records to be used in the proceeding shall be provided to you or your designated attorney." Elaine fixated on the words *your designated attorney*. Rhonda would never be fooled, but Rhonda wasn't in the office today. It was the day before Thanksgiving, and according to a very friendly receptionist who'd answered the phone at the DSHS office, Rhonda was already on her way to eat mashed potatoes in Spokane.

When Elaine checked the address for the office, she discovered it was only blocks away from where she'd bumped into Wren and Ivy at the grocery store, less than ten minutes from her hotel. Clearly, an in-person visit was in order. As Elaine tugged on her shapewear and blow-dried her hair in the tiny hotel bathroom, her confidence grew. It felt good to wear a suit again, and by the time she'd applied her signature mauve lipstick, she'd hatched a plan. Sure, a records request could take weeks . . . but what if she'd already filed it?

Elaine pulled into the parking lot of the white concrete building and took a deep breath. Her plan required winning the trust of the front desk staff while telling several outright lies—then again, she hadn't become senior partner at the best law firm in Chicago without being willing to get her hands dirty. Summoning all her most compelling and imperious energy, she opened the glass door and strode into the waiting room, pleased to find it empty except for a twentysomething receptionist, partially blocked from view by a giant bouquet of sunflowers and baby's breath on her desk. Elaine peeked around the flowers, but the woman didn't look up from her bridal magazine.

Elaine cleared her throat. "Good morning—" She checked the lanyard hanging around the woman's neck. "Tiffany. I'm Elaine Montgomery, attorney-at-law, and I'm here to pick up my client's records." She held out her photo ID, trying to prove she had nothing to hide.

Tiffany pulled out her earbuds but didn't glance at the driver's license. "What's that again?"

Elaine repeated her introduction, inwardly cheering. If Tiffany spent her downtime planning her wedding and listening to music, perhaps she wasn't particularly invested in her job. "I filled out all the necessary paperwork last time I came in. So, if you'll just print out the records I need—" She gestured to the large printer along the wall behind the desk.

"Oh, that's not how it works." Tiffany frowned. "Once we get the appropriate documentation, we send all our records through the mail. What did you say your case number was again?"

"One moment, let me see . . ." Elaine hefted her briefcase onto the desk, popped open the brass hinges, and began to sort through papers that had absolutely nothing to do with Hannah's case.

"Never mind. If you give me the name, I can look it up." Tiffany's manicured fingers tapped loudly against the keyboard. "Okay, I see the case, but no pending records request. You're sure you filled out both the case information request and the authorization form?"

"Ages ago," Elaine fudged. "I expected the records to arrive last week, but perhaps they got lost in the mail. Rhonda told me I could pick them up today if I came in person."

Tiffany's posture straightened at the mention of Rhonda. "Rhonda's not in the office today. Actually, none of our caseworkers are here right now, and we're about to close for the holiday. You should come back next week."

"Not possible. Our hearing starts on Monday." As soon as the words were out, Elaine wanted to kick herself; the actual court date was probably right there on the screen. But she continued in her smoothest possible voice, hoping Tiffany wouldn't double-check. "As I'm sure you're aware, state law requires CPS to provide the defense attorney—that's me—with a copy of all documents to be used in court proceedings. If I don't get those documents today, I'll have to file a motion to delay the trial. And you know how much Rhonda hates delays."

"You can say that again." Tiffany clacked away on her keyboard a few more seconds, and for a moment Elaine thought she'd won her over. Then Tiffany shook her head. "Nope, I still can't find your authorization form. And the only thing Rhonda hates more than a delay is a breach in protocol." She shrugged. "You'll just have to come back next week."

"Wait." Elaine scrambled for another idea, anything to keep from leaving the office empty handed. "Could Rhonda have left my paperwork on her desk? Maybe there's an envelope somewhere with my name on it."

Tiffany looked doubtful. "She would've told me if she was leaving documents for someone to pick up."

"It's easy to forget things during the holidays. You know, I was defending a case last Thanksgiving, and I forgot to file the discovery motion . . ." Elaine began babbling, trying to think of a way to gain her trust. Scanning the room for inspiration, her eyes landed on the bridal magazine, now face down next to the oversize vase. "Are the sunflowers from your fiancé? They're gorgeous."

"Oh, these?" Tiffany moved the vase a bit to her left, giving Elaine a better view of the desk. "No, they came yesterday from one of our foster families, as a thank-you after their daughter's adoption went through. Caseworkers can't accept gifts, though, so I'm the lucky gal who gets to take them home."

"You know, my wedding bouquet had sunflowers in it," Elaine said. The story was random, but at least it was true. "We were married at city hall, so I hadn't bothered with a florist, but my dashing groom picked a whole bouquet from the botanical gardens across the street." She chuckled, and to her surprise, Tiffany laughed too. "I'm sure it wasn't legal, but he never got in trouble. We were married fifty-six years, before he passed last year."

"Fifty-six years, wow. So sorry for your loss." Tiffany looked genuinely sad.

"He was something special, that's for sure." To her shock, Elaine felt herself tearing up. Real tears, not manufactured ones in service of her ulterior motive. What was with her these days, constantly getting emotional with strangers? First the bedraggled mother on the plane, now here in the CPS office. She grabbed a Kleenex from the box on Tiffany's desk and blew her nose.

Tiffany was silent for a beat, then brightened. "I love the idea of sunflowers for a bridal bouquet. Bold choice." She picked up a tiny memo pad from her desk and scribbled down a note. When she looked up, she was smiling. "Let me just take a peek in Rhonda's office and see what I can find."

"Thank you," Elaine gushed, realizing this might be her chance. "I really appreciate it."

The moment Tiffany disappeared into the back, Elaine leaned over the desk to peek at the computer. If Hannah's file was still open on the screen, maybe she could hit the print button herself and make a copy of the records before Tiffany got back. Alas, the screen was black, except for a screen saver of the DSHS logo bouncing between the corners. Elaine swore under her breath, but before she could make a new plan, Tiffany had returned, bearing a two-foot stack of papers.

"Here, the entire pile from Rhonda's desk. If you can wait a moment, I'll sort through it and see if there's anything in here for you." Elaine felt hopeful, until she remembered there could be no envelope with her name on it because she'd fabricated the entire story. Somehow she'd managed to fool not only Tiffany but herself too. She sighed, feeling guilty for making this very helpful receptionist scavenge through a mountain of paperwork. Besides, the overhead fluorescents were starting to make her head ache; perhaps it was time to call it a day and go home.

Except—Elaine's heart started beating faster—there, on one of the manila folders at the bottom of the stack, was a familiar name: **WREN SAWYER—MEDICAL RECORDS**. Oversize photocopies of what looked like x-rays stuck out the bottom. Elaine's mind spun through the possibilities. Wren had seemed perfectly fine in the grocery store, but maybe this meant Hannah's case had something to do with an injury. Elaine was desperate to get her hands on that manila envelope, but her time was running out.

Tiffany flipped through the last of the stack and shook her head. "Sorry, I don't see anything with your name on it, not even the authorization paperwork." She held up her hands. "I've tried my best."

"You certainly have, and I really appreciate it." Elaine smiled. "Looks like I'll just have to come back next week. If the trial gets delayed, I'll be sure to tell Rhonda it wasn't your fault." With a wave, she turned to go—and very deliberately swung her briefcase right into the bouquet of sunflowers. The vase flipped off the desk, and Tiffany shrieked. Elaine managed to grab the glass container just before it hit the ground and shattered—but not before the entire bouquet and several cups of water went sloshing all over the floor. Tiffany leaped up, snatching a wad of tissues from the box on her desk.

"Oh goodness, I'm so sorry." Elaine arranged her face to look appropriately horrified. "Me and my clumsy briefcase."

"At least the water didn't go all over Rhonda's paperwork." Tiffany bent down and began to blot fruitlessly at the puddle. "She'd have cooked me alive."

"I feel terrible." Elaine said. "And Kleenex isn't going to cut it. If you have a mop or some rags I could borrow, I'm happy to clean up my own mess." Wren's medical folder was right there on the desk, calling to her, if she could just get Tiffany to leave the room for a moment.

"That's nice of you, but I've got this." Tiffany gave up on blotting and piled the soggy tissues in a heap. "You go on with your day."

"No, I insist. Help an old lady feel needed." Ignoring her protesting back, Elaine bent down to help collect the sunflowers—a few stems were cracked, but most had survived the fall. "It's bad enough I've turned into a klutz these days. If you let me mop up the water, I won't feel completely useless."

"Oh, you're hardly useless." Tiffany gave her a sympathetic smile, apparently swayed more by the old-lady excuse than by Elaine as a high-powered lawyer. "I'll get you a mop." She disappeared into the back room, and Elaine snatched Wren's folder from the bottom of the pile.

Eagerly flipping it open, she found photocopied x-rays documenting the perfectly whole, unremarkable skeleton of her granddaughter's ribs and spine. But across the top of the paper in red Sharpie was a scribbled note: EVIDENCE OF MATERNAL ABUSE. Confused, Elaine flipped to the next page and gasped. The photos told a very different story. Covered in bruises of multiple shades, some fading and others clearly fresh, Wren's torso looked like a page from a textbook on child abuse. Elaine couldn't bear to look. She slapped the folder closed.

"Good God, Hannah. What have you done?" Her voice sounded out of place in the empty waiting room, an echoing reminder that Tiffany would be back any minute. Her left temple began to throb as she tried to reconcile the horrible photos with what she knew about her daughter: Hannah did have a temper, but she'd never been able to hurt so much as a house spider, invariably swooping in with a Tupperware to ferry the eight-legged critter outside. Grief must have transformed her daughter into someone else entirely.

But she had no time to stop and process this shocking new information, and certainly not enough time to read the whole file. As Tiffany walked back into the room with a mop, Elaine stuffed the manila envelope under her suit coat. Rhonda would just have to get along without it.

"Here, if you really want to help—" Tiffany started to hand Elaine the mop, then stopped. "What happened? Are you feeling okay?"

She wasn't, actually. Bright spots danced in front of Elaine's eyes, and a vein pulsed on her forehead. But she nodded, trying to make her expression neutral. In this state, and with a file of x-rays stuck under her armpit, there was no way she could mop the floor. "Maybe I just need some food." Elaine glanced at the clock.

"Right. It's almost noon. You go get some lunch, and I'll clean this up." Tiffany was really quite a dear; hopefully she wouldn't get blamed for losing the file. But Elaine had far bigger problems to consider. She'd come to the DSHS office hoping to gather information for Hannah's defense, but those bruises weren't defensible. Her stomach turned as she imagined Wren cowering beneath the wrath of her mother, Hannah's gentle self somehow twisted into the kind of monster who could hurt a child.

Elaine staggered out of the building, feeling nauseous but determined: if Hannah didn't have an airtight explanation for those bruises, she'd have no choice but to take custody herself.

Twenty-Two

Julie made sure to arrive at her parents' house an hour before she expected Jake, to give the girls time to settle into the noisy bustle of an Abbott family holiday. Julie's mom, the oldest of four siblings who all still lived nearby, had crowned herself queen of their oversize Thanksgivings a decade ago. Every fall, usually well before Halloween, Barbara assigned each relative a specific dish along with the requisite two pies per family. Last year, she'd boasted on social media that their dessert buffet had included twelve flavors of pie.

As Wren and Ivy splashed in and out of the puddles lining the front walk, Julie noted how abruptly the landscape had changed from fall to winter. Three weeks ago, when she'd last visited Lynnwood, the maples and oaks had been awash in color, a backdrop of deep aubergine with vibrant bursts of orange and yellow. Now the trees stood black and bare, and the only evidence of the fallen rainbow sat at the curb, two enormous compost bags filled with soggy leaves.

Julie's mom met them at the door in a velvet A-line dress and knee-high boots. She'd coiled her shiny dark hair, highlighted with streaks of silver white, into a loose bun at the crown of her head, and a pair of chunky silver teardrops dangled from her earlobes. Julie felt instantly self-conscious about her own damp hair and uninspired outfit. She'd hoped to at least put on a skirt—especially since Jake was coming—but during the hour she'd planned to get ready, the girls had insisted on baking turkey-shaped cookies, turning the kitchen into a floury mess.

She'd had time to shower but not shave her legs, so jeans and a sweater were the best she could manage.

"You look beautiful," Barbara said, kissing Julie on both cheeks. "Now where are those sweet girls hiding?" Looking left and right, she pretended not to see Wren and Ivy, who'd shrunk behind Julie's legs in an effort to become invisible. They'd met Barbara twice before, but at Julie's apartment. A new house full of strange relatives was bound to make them shy. "How disappointing," Julie's mom said with an exaggerated sigh. "I was so hoping they'd be here today. I have this brand-new coloring book I just don't know what to do with." She pulled Spider-Man from behind her back.

Wren emerged slowly from behind Julie's legs. "Thank you," she said in a whisper-voice, taking the outstretched coloring book. "Here, Ivy, we can share it."

"Nope." Barbara smiled. "There's one for each of you. Let me show you where to find the crayons." She led the girls inside, through the living room where Julie's dad was serving up his signature cranberry bourbon cocktails to an eager swarm of aunts and uncles and cousins, and past the kitchen where Julie's grandmother bustled over the stove, to a back room set up with a small table and kid-size chairs. A bin of LEGO bricks sat in the corner, along with a cardboard box filled with some rather ancient plastic toys. "You three can stay in here as long as you like. And—" She leaned over to whisper in Julie's ear. "I've instructed all the relatives to visit one at a time." As Barbara disappeared into the kitchen, she winked, as if to brag, *Look how well I followed your instructions: "reserved yet welcoming" to a T.*

Her mom had gone to a lot of trouble to make the girls feel comfortable. Now if only the rest of her family would follow suit.

Not two minutes into coloring, Julie heard a booming voice from the doorway: Uncle Frank, the most exuberant of her many exuberant relatives. She jumped up from her chair, determined to greet him in the hallway. He grabbed her hand and pumped furiously. "You've grown six inches since I've seen you last." She laughed and made a face. He'd delivered this same line every Thanksgiving since she could remember. She was never sure if he was making fun of her short stature or of his own ridiculous, repetitive humor. Either way, she sort of loved him for it, the way you love a hideous old sweatshirt that somehow fits just right.

"Quite the little girls you've got yourself," he said, motioning into the room. "Awful cute for foster kids."

Ugh. Julie glanced at the girls, heads down over their coloring books, and hoped they weren't listening. Why would being in foster care make them any less cute? Uncle Frank was seeming less like a faded sweatshirt and more like smelly old socks.

Julie's mom appeared behind him. "Frank, what did I tell you?"

"Oh, right." Uncle Frank chuckled. "Barbie here thinks I'm too overwhelming."

Julie's mom glared at her little brother, the way she always did when he called her Barbie. "You can talk to them all you like, once they settle in." She pushed a glass of red wine into Julie's hands. "Go on, say hi to the rest of the family. I'll stay with Wren and Ivy for a bit." Julie hesitated, but the moment her mom sat down, Ivy climbed into her lap and Wren started telling her about a drawing. The girls were in capable hands, so Julie led her uncle down the hall, where his thoughtless comments couldn't do any damage.

In the living room, he followed her over to the spread of fruit, crackers, and gourmet cheeses laid out across the sideboard. "How old is the little one? Your mom says she can't talk yet."

"Not to me. But she talks to her sister, in some sort of gibberish language." Julie spread a dollop of brie on a raisin cracker. "And sometimes I see her talking under her breath, almost like she's counting."

Uncle Frank picked up an apple and tossed it from hand to hand. "Seems a little old not to be talking."

Julie shrugged, mouth full of cracker. To her dismay, they'd gained an audience—four cousins and an aunt, all waiting for her to swallow her bite. "I really think her speech is all there, but somehow neglect made it go underground. The social worker says that happens some-times and can take a while to resolve."

"So this is your new career, then?" Frank asked. "Raising orphans? Won't that be a lot of work, all on your own?"

Suddenly this Thanksgiving felt like all the others, when her family had grilled her about dropping out of law school, quitting teaching, or her broken engagement with Seth. "It's not a new career. I'm still at Virginia Mason." Julie thrust out her chin, daring them to mention any of her previous dead-end plans. Fostering would be different. She wasn't going to quit on Wren and Ivy.

"You're keeping them, then?" one of the cousins asked.

Julie took a gulp of wine—too big of a sip, and the tannins burned her throat. Saved by a coughing fit, she dove into the kitchen.

Alone at the sink, she sipped water and considered splashing some on her burning cheeks. She'd underestimated the challenge of bringing Wren and Ivy to Thanksgiving, and Jake wasn't even here yet. The last thing she wanted was to let her relatives' prying curiosity mess things up, especially after last night. Jake had called her from the hospital, and they'd talked for almost two hours.

"Aren't you supposed to be working?" she'd asked, not even trying to hide the smile in her voice. The girls were already in bed, and Julie was sitting on the floor, surrounded by a sea of polka dot leggings and glittery T-shirts, still warm from the dryer.

"I am working," Jake said. "But it's a slow night, so I'm here in the call room, writing up notes and waiting for my pager to go off. I can multitask."

While Julie sorted socks, they rehashed escapades from middle school, running through the list of their mutual acquaintances and guessing where everyone had ended up. Then they switched to favorite movies, and Julie finally screwed up the courage to ask the question burning in her mind since the library.

"No girlfriend to watch with?" Her heart pounded.

"One hundred percent single." Jake sighed. "As of last year."

Julie felt like cheering, except she picked up on a note of sadness in his voice. She sensed he had a story to tell, but at that moment his pager started buzzing.

Now she wished their first date didn't involve every member of her extended family. On the phone, she could keep up the relaxed, playful banter that had always characterized their friendship. But here, with all her relatives? And the chances of escaping without at least one comment about the two of them ending up together were close to nil. She checked her watch. Impossible to uninvite him now.

"Better get that relish made before your friend gets here." Julie's grandmother appeared at her elbow, holding a bag of frozen cranberries. "Don't worry about the girls; your mom took them out to explore the clubhouse."

Julie glanced out the kitchen window at the small shed across the patio.

"You'll have to go see it," her grandma said. "Yesterday we set up your old toy kitchen out there, since we've finally got some girls around to play house."

Julie considered voicing her usual argument that her nephews could play house, too, but decided the cause was hopeless. "Speaking of houses . . . do you know how Mom's open house went yesterday? Any bites?"

Her grandmother's face lit up. "Six offers, all above list price." While Julie diced an apple and zested lemon, her grandmother gushed about Barbara's success and then moved on to other family news. As the minutes ticked by, Julie grew more and more nervous about Jake's imminent arrival. When the doorbell finally chimed, she jumped and her knife slipped, almost lopping off her thumb.

Her grandma laughed. "Bit anxious about your gentleman caller? Better go answer the door before Frank gets to him."

Julie weaved through the crowded dining room and reached the front hall just as Aunt Judy swung the door wide, revealing a somewhat rumpled Jake carrying a windswept bouquet of orange Peruvian lilies and lavender carnations. He held out the flowers.

"Sorry they're crumpled. Made the mistake of opening the windows on the highway."

"Aunt Judy, meet my friend Jake." Julie wished her voice didn't sound so eager and high pitched.

Aunt Judy looked charmed by the flowers, no matter how bent. "Lovely, thank you. I'll go find a vase and leave you young people to say hello." She gave Julie a conspicuous wink but wandered off without further comment.

Ushering Jake through the door, Julie battled a wave of shyness. *Stop being ridiculous,* she told herself. *It's only Jake.* At one point he'd known his way around this house almost as well as she did. But as he gave her a hello peck on the cheek, her face brushed against his now-trimmed beard. Hardly her twelve-year-old buddy. Dressed in a white button-down and fitted black jeans, he looked every bit the distinguished physician. Her aunts would gobble him up like a thirteenth flavor of pie.

Julie swallowed hard, looping her arm through Jake's. "Come with me for a second to check on the girls, then I'll introduce you to everyone." She hustled him through the kitchen toward the back room before he could get engulfed by a horde of relatives. "Glad you made it in one piece. Thanksgiving traffic can be brutal."

"Worth it, to have dinner at your house again." Julie's stomach did a flip-flop—was he flirting or simply complimenting her mom's cooking? She stole a sideways glance, but Jake was looking away, admiring a tower of plates on the marble countertop. "You Abbotts sure go big for the holidays. How many are coming?"

"Last count I heard was forty-two, including babies. Since my cousins started getting married and breeding like bunnies, our Thanksgivings have ballooned out of control. Just wait—after we stuff ourselves, Uncle Frank will set up a Ping-Pong table on the patio, and we'll battle for the title of Top Table Tennis Turkey." Jake snickered. "You can thank Drew for the dorky alliteration."

They'd made it to the back room, but the girls hadn't returned; no doubt Julie's mom was helping them cook up a storm of plastic food in the playhouse. Jake wandered over to the kids' table and picked up a sheet of paper. "Impressive. Did one of your girls do this?"

Julie gaped at the drawing in his hands. "Sheesh. Wren's got talent." Instead of coloring Spider-Man, she'd ripped out a page and folded it into nine squares, then used the blank side to draw what looked like a comic sequence. Each panel depicted the same caped supergirl in various poses—jumping, flying, running, sleeping. "Look at that shading," Julie said. "And the expressions." Wren had even started to add talk bubbles, but it looked like she'd gotten frustrated and crossed out all the words. Julie took the paper and held it up to the light, trying to read beneath the scribble. "She told me her mom was teaching her to draw, but I didn't expect *this*." Yet again, this mother surprised her. What kind of abusive parent gave art lessons?

Jake grinned. "A foster daughter after your own heart. I seem to remember a certain other young girl who loved comics."

"Reading them, not drawing them." Julie made a face. "You might also recall, every character I ever created looked like a hamster."

"That's not how I remember it." Jake took a step forward, close enough for Julie to admire the indigo flecks in his pale blue eyes. "I've thought about calling you so many times. Don't know why I never did."

Julie glanced away, pretending to be captivated by a lone swing out the window, swaying in the November wind. Jake was acting like—no, too much to hope for. He'd never thought of her like that, not even back in middle school. She forced a laugh. "Maybe you never called because your girl Melody couldn't wait to see the back of me." Jake's high school girlfriend had been a gifted guitarist but snooty as heck. And not a fan of Julie. "I figured you guys would be married by now, with three rock star babies."

Jake laughed. "Oh, Mel. Always destined for greatness. She married a dentist and works as his hygienist now."

Julie smirked, trying not to let her elation show. She had rather despised Mel, all punk rock attitude and perfect skin. "Do you still play?"

"Nah, I was terrible. And thirteen years of medical training pretty much drained the musical aspirations from my system. Now when I have free time, I'd rather watch *Daredevil* on Netflix or hit the gym."

"Fair enough." Julie felt relieved. Superheroes had brought her and Jake together in sixth grade; music—and distance—had torn them apart. "Sign me up for a *Daredevil* marathon anytime."

Jake raised one eyebrow, a trick she'd always envied. "Anytime, eh? You don't know how often I might take you up on that. Binging on Netflix alone is pathetic, but with company, it's a perfectly respectable way to spend the weekend."

Julie flushed, imagining a whole weekend with Jake on the couch. As she tried to find the words to reply, her mom and the girls appeared in the doorway. She almost didn't recognize Ivy, disguised by a pirate's hat and eye patch, swimming in a striped costume two sizes too big.

"Ahoy there, Captain Ivy." Julie feigned a naval salute. "I see my mom introduced you to the costume stash."

"Yarr," Ivy hollered, waving a plastic sword. Julie couldn't help but grin—*yarr* wasn't a proper word, but it was close.

"She learned that from Henry," Barbara said. "I know you worried they might be nervous around the other kids, but Ivy's quite the little extrovert. And did you see the comic Wren started?"

"This one?" Jake held up the drawing, and Barbara's face lit up.

"Jake! You made it." She pulled him into a hug, then took a step back to look him up and down. "Seeing you all grown up makes me feel simply ancient. How's your mom, and all those sisters of yours?"

Knowing her mother wouldn't let Jake loose until she'd dragged out every detail, Julie took the girls by the hand. "C'mon, let's go look through the costumes again. I think I need one too."

For the rest of the evening, Julie wore a pirate hat and reveled in her role as the girls' mother, wiping noses and washing hands alongside her cousins and their prolific offspring. She'd always felt a bit left out at these gatherings, the only one without a partner to complain about or a baby to cuddle in her lap. But this year, Wren and Ivy joined the raucous kids' table in the kitchen, laughing at potty jokes until their sides burst, while Jake sat next to her at the crowded table in the dining room. He regaled the aunts and uncles with tales from his intern nights in the ER, and then after the meal, he and Drew took all the kids outside for a rousing game of tag. Jake even tied with her dad for second place in the Ping-Pong tournament. Except for a few meaningful glances from Aunt Judy, they survived the gathering without any embarrassing innuendo.

Best of all, Julie kept catching Jake staring at her when he thought no one was looking. She kept telling herself maybe she was misreading the situation, but when she passed him the dinner rolls, Jake let his fingers linger over hers for three electric seconds. Later, he promised to take her to the new Marvel exhibit at the MoPop and said he'd found a great wine bar they just had to try. By the end of the night, Julie was bursting with not only mashed potatoes and pumpkin pie but also with a sense of well-being that felt too perfect to last.

As she bundled the girls into their mittens and hats to drive home, Jake stood a few feet away, laughing with Uncle Frank. Struggling with the sticky zipper on Ivy's coat, she eavesdropped on their conversation.

"Julie's a saint for taking them in," Uncle Frank said, nodding toward the girls. "Raising my own two kids nearly killed me. Don't know if I'd have the stamina to parent someone else's."

"I hear you," Jake said. "After my dad left us, my mom had to work all the time, so I practically raised my four little sisters. All those meals and baths and help with homework was enough parenting to last a lifetime. Now I can't imagine having *any* kids, foster or otherwise." Julie's head snapped up. "No doubt, she's a saint."

Julie stared at the man with whom she'd just been spinning a fairy-tale future. Jake was still focused on Uncle Frank, so he didn't register the dismay on her face. She searched his expression for some hint of humor—was he joking? Exaggerating perhaps, for Uncle Frank's benefit? But no, his tight lips and set jaw looked quite serious. Julie felt overheated in her puffy winter parka, desperate to escape the stuffy house. Sure, Jake Lankowski was sweet and sexy and possibly falling for her. Perfect, except for one crucial, unavoidable detail: he didn't want kids.

As Julie lifted Ivy onto her hip, she buried her nose in the toddler's curls. Heading out the door, she grabbed Wren's hand, squeezing maybe just a little tighter than necessary.

Twenty-Three

Hannah had scrubbed the toilets and swept the floors and even baked brownies so the house would smell like chocolate when Rhonda arrived. But when she answered the door on Friday afternoon, she didn't find her caseworker. On the stoop stood a young woman with silky straight black hair and a thick fringe of bangs, wringing her hands and shifting from foot to foot.

"I'm Irena." She stuck out her hand, flashing an impressive array of flower-painted fingernails. "The CASA for your girls."

Hannah gave her a blank look.

"Court Appointed Special Advocate. Didn't anyone tell you?" The woman cleared her throat and started again. "I'm here solely on behalf of your daughters, to advocate for their best interests in this challenging situation." She'd clearly practiced her pep talk in the mirror. Ignoring the woman's outstretched hand, Hannah peered at the empty space behind her.

"You've got to be kidding. Where's Rhonda? And more importantly, where are my kids?" Hannah had waited too long for this visit to let them put it off, even for another hour.

"Um, well—" Irena turned and glanced at the street behind her.

"Do you realize, Ms.—" Hannah squinted at the ID badge swinging from Irena's neck. "Ms. Perez, that the court mandated biweekly visits? Yet it's been more than two weeks, and I haven't seen my girls once." Technically, that wasn't true. She'd seen them at the library, but spying didn't count.

Irena gave a vigorous nod. "And I apologize for the delay. Our department's been hit by a bout of flu, so we're short staffed. But I know you're eager to see them, and that's why I combined my first home assessment with a supervised visit. It's a little unusual to do parent visits in the home, but in this case I thought it made sense. I'll go get the girls in just a minute." Irena motioned to the red hatchback parked on the street.

"Wait, you—you left them in the *car*?" Hannah wasn't sure whether to laugh or cry.

The CASA worker looked bewildered, oblivious to the irony. She took a step back and almost toppled off the porch before grabbing the railing for support. "I wanted to make sure we had the right house, and to warn you. Wren's a little bit . . . upset."

Hannah stiffened. Of course Wren was upset; she'd been snatched from her home and forced to live with a complete stranger. "She's my daughter. I can handle her big feelings."

"Great." Irena flashed another nervous smile. "I'll just go get them, then."

Hannah followed Irena down the steps and out to the street. Rocking back and forth on her heels, she waited as Irena struggled with the booster seat buckles. Ivy came shooting out like a rubber-band rocket, hitting her mother's knees full force.

"Mama! Mama!" Her frantic exuberance was a salve for Hannah's bruised mother-ego. At least Ivy had missed her. Hoisting her daughter into the air, Hannah twirled in a circle, laughing even as her eyes stung. Around and around they went, Hannah's arms aching with the heft of her baby, so much heavier than she remembered. Then, too dizzy to spin anymore, she collapsed on the damp grass and cuddled Ivy in her lap.

"I've missed you so much, Ivy-bean." Hannah started to bury her nose in Ivy's curls, but another whiff of Julie's horrid grape shampoo made her gulp for fresh air instead. She looked around. "Where's your sister?"

Wren, oddly enough, had not appeared. Hannah reluctantly plucked Ivy from her lap, set her on the grass, and approached the car. "Wren, honey? Aren't you getting out?" No answer. "Come see what I did with your room."

Ivy had still been a baby when Alex died and their lives began to unravel, so until that morning, the girls' room had looked like it belonged to an infant, with a toy bin filled with rattles and pacifiers and a baby bouncer gathering cobwebs in the corner. Needing an outlet for her nervous energy before the visit, Hannah had decided to redecorate. She'd wandered through T.J.Maxx, dodging Black Friday shoppers and feeling normal for the first time in weeks. When she saw the giant bean-bag chairs shaped like teddy bears, she couldn't help but throw them into the already burgeoning pile in her cart.

Twenty minutes later, as she watched the number on the register grow, Hannah realized she'd been foolish. She was fast approaching the credit limit on her last card, and besides, how could she spend a hundred dollars decorating a home she was about to lose to the bank? Stammering excuses to the saleslady, she fled from the counter to put most of the items back. But she splurged on the giant teddies—buy one, get one free—just to see Wren and Ivy squeal as they leaped into those plush arms.

Except now, Wren wasn't racing inside to see her surprise. She wasn't even getting out of the car. Irena stood awkwardly in the street, holding the door open and making coaxing sounds.

"Let me." Brushing aside the CASA lady, Hannah leaned into the back seat. She caught a glimpse of Wren's red-rimmed eyes and tight-set lips before she turned to the window, glaring determinedly at nothing. But even the back of her seven-year-old's head filled Hannah with joy. She reached out to touch the sleek brown bob she'd missed so much, and Wren's head pressed ever so lightly against her hand, like a standoffish cat who nevertheless wants to be stroked. In that almost imperceptible movement, Hannah knew they'd be all right. "Baby," she said gently. "Come inside."

—◊—

It didn't take long for the girls to get excited about being home. Wren was clearly punishing Hannah for the trauma she'd suffered the past few weeks, but as soon as she saw her stuffed animals all lined up in the living room window, the LEGOs now organized in bins, and especially the new teddy bear chairs, she forgot to stay angry.

Wren tugged on Hannah's arm and whispered in her ear. "Mom, you're back." She paused, her next words so soft Hannah almost didn't hear them. "I was scared."

The look in Wren's eyes cut Hannah to the core. She wanted to defend herself, to say she'd never left, but deep down, Hannah wasn't sure if that was true. Cringing, she remembered the stacks of food-crusted dishes she'd only recently washed, the piles of shopping bags filled with purchases she couldn't remember making, and worst of all, the row of empty wine bottles lined up like soldiers along the kitchen counter. She wanted to explain to Wren that depression was a sickness, but one you could often recover from, like a cold or the flu. But Irena's round black eyes watched their every move, and Hannah didn't want to risk uttering words that might come back to haunt her at the hearing.

Instead, she cooked the girls' favorite alphabet pasta and let them smear their brownies with generous dollops of homemade vanilla frosting. After the snack, she brought out craft supplies so they could all make beaded necklaces. Sifting through a hodgepodge of letter beads, Hannah eventually found what she needed: two hearts, four letter *M*s, and two *O*s. She tied the **LOVE, MOM** chains around her daughters' tiny necks and hoped it would be enough for now. Then she let Irena put away the craft supplies so the CASA worker could fish around in her newly organized shelves. See, you meddling snoop? No skeletons in this mama's closet.

She'd planned to put on this Carol Brady routine for Rhonda, but after spending two hours with Irena, Hannah felt almost giddy. No matter how much the house sparkled, one pleasant afternoon would never have changed Rhonda's mind, not when she was so focused on those bruises. Irena, on the other hand, seemed highly impressionable. She declined the offer of a brownie—"Sorry, departmental policy"— but had no reservations about building her own ice cream shop out of LEGOs or stringing necklaces with Wren and Ivy. By the end of the visit, Irena seemed to hold a new view of the girls' "best interest." If Hannah kept up this rather ostentatious display of mothering prowess, she hoped Irena would share her favorable impressions with the judge come January.

As Hannah knelt to tie Ivy's shoes, the little girl's lip began to quiver. Hannah wrapped her arms around Ivy's small body as she began to wail, big racking sobs that ripped Hannah's heart in two.

"No," Ivy screamed. "I doh wanna go! Stay wif Mama!" She dug her tiny nails into Hannah's arm, and Hannah scooped her up, squeezing tight.

Hannah glared at Irena, who looked like she might cry too. But Wren gave her sister a quizzical look. "Ivy. You're talking."

"What do you mean?" Hannah asked, as Ivy's nose burrowed into her armpit. "Of course she's talking."

"Not when we're with Julie."

"What? She doesn't talk? Not at all?" Hannah found this difficult to believe. Ivy had always been quieter than Wren, but she'd started babbling at ten months and could string words together by age two. All the usual milestones.

"Nope. She jabbers to me in that old baby talk language we used to use, but she never says a word to Julie. They're going to take her to the doctor, I think. For some kind of artistic evaluation."

"Artistic . . . ? Oh, you mean an *autistic* evaluation." Hannah looked at Irena, who nodded in confirmation. Hannah shook her head. Perhaps she should have been concerned, but instead she felt a swell of pride

179

for her spunky three-year-old, loyal and silent. Hannah turned to Irena, with ice in her voice. "Well, you can see she talks when she's at home with me. Perhaps you can communicate this to Rhonda and Julie, so they can skip the unnecessary testing."

Irena nodded again and pried a still-wailing Ivy out of Hannah's arms. "Come on, sweetie. I'll take you back home."

Wren glowered at the CASA worker. "*This* is our home. Julie's house is just where we sleep." She dove into her mother's arms, and Hannah counted out three exaggerated kisses. Wren clung to her on the last kiss, but when Hannah finally let go, Wren turned and dashed out the door.

From the front window, Hannah watched Irena load her daughters back into the car. Ivy had quit crying before they made it down the front walk, and Wren hardly glanced back as she climbed into her seat. But the tears kept rolling down Hannah's cheeks. Sixty-two more days until the fact-finding hearing and the end of this impossible nightmare.

Twenty-Four

Two days went by before Elaine could bring herself to open Wren's file a second time. On the drive back from the CPS office, the pounding in her head had bloomed into a full-blown migraine, a crushing ache that forced her into bed with an ice pack, shades drawn and lamps off. None of her medications helped, and she couldn't stand the light from her phone, let alone her laptop.

But on Friday afternoon, when the pain finally eased and her thoughts no longer throbbed, she poured herself a glass of brandy from the minibar and collapsed into the red velvet wingback, clutching the manila folder.

Along with the x-rays and photographs—which she could hardly bear to look at—Elaine found physical exam notes, lab results, and statements from several doctors. Everyone had come to the same conclusion: the bruises were consistent with nonaccidental trauma, a.k.a. child abuse. But as she flipped the pages, something about Rhonda's margin notes felt off. Sure, *no alternative explanation for bruising* made sense, next to lab results ruling out hemophilia and vitamin K deficiency. And she had to agree with Rhonda that Wren's inconsistent story was *highly suspicious*. Wren wasn't a child who easily forgot things, after all.

But next to *sparse past medical history*, Rhonda had written not again, and beneath the doctor's concluding statement, she'd scribbled what looked like reminds me of OC. Or maybe DC? Elaine got out her reading glasses and tried again. Okay, definitely *DC*, but what did that mean? She kept flipping pages, hoping for an explanation.

On the back of the final sheet, Elaine found an unexpected gold mine: what looked like the messy draft of a letter from Rhonda to her supervisor, first detailing the basics of the charges against Hannah and then giving her opinion on the case plan. Elaine's eyes widened at *abandoned in a motor vehicle* and *positive for methamphetamines*. At least now she knew what they were dealing with. If this is really child abuse, Rhonda had written, and that's certainly what it looks like, how can we be sure these interventions will be enough? We need to learn from our past mistakes.

Past mistakes had been underlined twice. Elaine closed the file and reached for her laptop, wondering what exactly those mistakes might be. Five minutes of googling and she had her answer.

She sucked in her breath as she scrolled through the search results, scanning headline after gruesome headline: "Child Burns to Death in House Fire," "After Seven CPS Citations, Child Dies of Neglect," "Relatives Beg for Mercy for Mother of Dead Son," and finally, "Caseworker Speaks Out in Dylan Cooper Case." This last article was the only one Elaine could stomach. Bracing herself, she clicked on the link.

Rhonda hadn't been the caseworker who'd visited the squalor of the Cooper home; she hadn't seen the diapers piled in corners or the three-year-old picking through the trash to lick the sticky insides of a peanut butter jar. Worse. She'd been the supervisor who signed off on all seven times the state prioritized keeping the family together over the safety of Dylan Cooper and his four siblings. Month after month, a caseworker had arrived to offer in-home services: therapy for mom, rehab for the always-drunk stepdad, food stamps, and help with budgeting to keep the family afloat. And yet, month after month, nothing changed. Calls came in from concerned citizens: the teacher who noticed burn marks on Dylan's torso; neighbors who'd watched three kids running in the yard after dark, no adult in sight, no car in the driveway. Seven times CPS had cited the family for various forms of neglect, and seven times authorities had chosen to keep the children in the home, arguing that Emily Cooper's motivation to become a better parent outweighed her clear incompetence at doing so.

Three years after the initial CPS complaint—which, incidentally, had been for leaving her kids unattended in the car—Ms. Cooper locked her youngest son in a bedroom while the other children were at school. She left the house with a stick of incense still burning on the kitchen table. Later, Emily claimed she locked her son in the bedroom so she could attend a job interview; but at the moment her house erupted into flames, police determined she was at a convenience store, buying cigarettes.

Six-year-old Dylan Cooper lost his life, and Rhonda Thompson resigned from her supervisor role. "We strive to both protect children and keep families together," read Rhonda's quote, "but it's a tough balance. If we focus only on child safety, we end up taking too many children from their families; if we focus only on preserving families, we fail children who are truly in danger." The article went on to describe all the ways the system was set up to flounder: a severe shortage of foster homes, a constantly revolving door of social workers, and a major funding crisis following recent budget cuts.

Elaine closed the laptop and massaged her temples, trying to fight off the return of her migraine. No wonder Rhonda was against sending the girls back to Hannah; the last time the caseworker trusted a mother who'd left her kids in the car, a little boy died.

But Hannah wasn't anything like that other mother. Was she?

Elaine grabbed the manila folder and flipped back to page one. Wren's hospital intake form had contact info for both Hannah and the foster mom, with Hannah's old street number still listed as her current address. The information might be old, but it was the best chance Elaine had of finding her daughter. She snatched up her purse, took the elevator to the parking garage, and climbed into her rental Cadillac. Costing her a hundred dollars a day, that damn car, yet another reason she needed to hurry up and get back to Chicago. Except, depending on what Hannah had to say about those bruises, maybe she wasn't going back at all.

As Elaine drove the twenty minutes south to Beacon Hill, she channeled her outrage into a fiery speech, full of probing questions and demands for the truth. But when she turned onto Hannah's street, she found the house as dark and silent as before. Since her last visit, someone had dragged an overflowing trash bin to the curb, but again, no one answered the doorbell.

So be it. She'd camp on the lawn if she had to; she wasn't returning to her hotel room until she'd spoken with her daughter. Dusk was already beginning to fall, and she wished she'd thought to bring a sandwich. Yet again, the bright lights from the remodeled house next door reminded her of Alex. As she adjusted the back of her seat, trying to get comfortable for a long wait, the memories of his death came flooding back. For once, she didn't fight them.

—⁓—

Elaine had been reading the latest Elizabeth George novel in bed—back when she still preferred mysteries to romance—and was immersed in the misty moors of England, about to discover the murder weapon, when a buzzing noise broke the silence. She jumped, convinced the villain was coming for her with a power saw. From his spot on the neighboring pillow, Steve laughed.

"Book's got you spooked, huh?"

Elaine made a face. Steve was presently engaged in flinging banana peels at digital opponents while racing around a giant cupcake, so he had no right to laugh. The man was seventy-four, same age as Elaine, yet he'd bought himself a portable video game device like the kids used. She patted the covers around her, still searching for the source of the sound.

"Your *phone*, Elaine." Steve smirked. "On the bedside."

Snatching it up, she was surprised to see her son-in-law's face grinning back at her. She answered immediately.

"I've got a favor to ask." Alex sounded a bit breathless.

"Anything for you, darling. You know that."

Steve rolled his eyes, and Elaine elbowed him in the ribs. Even if Alex didn't help enough around the house, he was the best thing that had ever happened to Hannah. Every time they chatted, Elaine felt grateful for his presence in their lives.

"Well, it's just . . ." Static drowned out Alex's voice, but not before Elaine picked up a hint of nervousness.

"What's that? I can't hear you."

"I *said*—" He raised his voice. "Hannah and I are on the rocks."

Oh, God. All those "business trips" he'd been taking . . . if Alex was about to tell her he was having an affair, Elaine didn't want to hear it. "I may be a coldhearted lawyer, but I refuse to give divorce advice to my son-in-law."

Alex laughed, or at least Elaine thought he did. With all the background noise, she couldn't quite tell.

"Hang on," he said. "My Bluetooth is acting up."

Three clunks and some more buzzing, then Alex came in clear as day. "I'm not calling for divorce advice, Elaine. Jeez, you always think the worst."

Whew. Elaine stopped clutching her book and dropped it into her lap.

"But—" Alex's voice caught. "We had a fight."

"How bad?"

"Our worst in a long time, maybe ever. Hannah's exhausted; I work all the time. We're drifting apart."

"Hannah said as much on the phone today." Elaine clucked her tongue, remembering those blurry days of early parenting, when she and Steve had been little more than coparents who happened to share adjacent sides of the bed.

"I want to make it up to her," Alex continued. "Thought maybe we could take a weekend out on Whidbey; do that hike she loves so much. Could you and Steve fly out to watch the girls?"

"Absolutely." Elaine grabbed her laptop from the side of the bed and popped it open, bringing up her calendar. "But I've got three cases coming up, and you know how my schedule gets. Which weekend?"

"Hadn't got that far. Hang on." Elaine heard shuffling, and a smooth, toneless female voice.

"Alex?" Elaine frowned. "Somebody there with you?"

"No, that was GPS. I'm driving. Let me call you back about dates. Can't get to my calendar at the moment."

"Right. Don't you dare text and drive." Now the Bluetooth made sense. But if Alex wanted babysitting, Elaine needed to know soon. Her weekends were already booked up for the next three months, so she'd have to shift everything around. "Hmm . . . the weekend of the fifth could work."

"Hang on." Alex sounded flustered. "I think I took a wrong turn."

"Or I could do the seventeenth. Could you just pull over quick and check so I can pencil it in?"

More rustling on Alex's end. Good, maybe he was pulling over.

"I'm going to have to call you—" Alex was interrupted by a loud thunk, and then the line went dead.

"Alex? Alex?" Damn connection. "Well, text me some dates, then." But Alex was already gone.

—⁓—

Elaine shook her head, trying to clear the memory. Why hadn't she let Alex hang up, instead of badgering him about her precious calendar? The other driver happened to be a drunk teenager, and with a perfectly good explanation for the crash, the cops hadn't bothered with cell phone histories. Except for Steve—now also dead—not another soul knew Alex had been on the phone that night, distracted by his type A mother-in-law at the moment of his death.

Elaine's eyes burned as she studied the house where her daughter now lived alone. She frowned at the thought of Hannah making dinner for one—a loneliness Elaine knew all too well. Maybe the angry speech she'd prepared was the wrong approach, a sledgehammer when what she needed was an ice pick. Better to start gently with Hannah and coax out the truth. But for now, she had to wait.

Elaine sighed, sinking deeper into her seat and closing her eyes. Her back would kill her for this tomorrow.

The next thing she knew, a bright light shone in her eyes and someone was banging on the window. Elaine wiped a trickle of drool from the corner of her lips, trying to remember why she was napping in a dark car and who might be pounding on the glass. Hannah. Of course. Elaine rolled down the window.

"Well, Mother. I figured you'd show up at some point, but I didn't expect to find you sleeping in my driveway at ten p.m." After all this time, Hannah's voice sounded breezy and careless, like they were any normal mother-daughter pair, with weekly phone calls and birthday presents and gosh-I've-missed-you brunches. She stepped away from the car and started up the path to the house. "Come on," she said, turning back and motioning to Elaine. "You might as well come inside."

Elaine heaved herself out of the car—slowly, her stiff joints still half-asleep—and followed Hannah up the walkway, analyzing the contours of her back: too thin, even in a heavy winter jacket. Hovering in the doorway, Elaine braced herself for piles of garbage and layers of dust. But once her eyes adjusted, she breathed a sigh of relief. No dirty diapers here. The hardwood floors looked freshly swept and the whole place smelled of lemons. Wandering into the kitchen, Elaine noticed a dozen beaded bracelets lined up on the counter, each threaded with a different color of neon pipe cleaner. Either Hannah had gone into business selling hideously ugly children's jewelry or the girls had been here recently.

Hannah floated up behind her. "What are you doing here, Mother? I thought I made it clear: I don't need your help."

Turning to face her daughter, Elaine took in Hannah's hollow eyes and lifeless, greasy hair; she must have lost fifteen pounds in the past year. The hell she didn't need help. Elaine felt her muscles tense, and the gentle overtures she'd wanted to make—*it's been so long, how are you holding up, please tell me what happened*—died on her lips. "I've seen the photographs of Wren's bruises."

Instead of meeting her mother's eyes, Hannah examined her own bare feet, one crossed over the other, fidgeting against a cracked tile on the kitchen floor. Elaine followed her gaze, fixating on the specks of forgotten polish dotting Hannah's uneven toenails. Like everything else she'd let go in her life, Hannah had given up on her feet.

Elaine waited for her daughter to speak, or at least look up. Whatever Elaine could see in those clear blue eyes would tell her what she needed to know.

Silence. More staring at the floor.

"I read the whole medical file," Elaine finally said. "It doesn't look good."

"What do you mean, you read the file?" Hannah's head snapped up, but all Elaine could see in her eyes was an angry blaze. "So now CPS is sharing my personal information?"

"You need help, Hannah."

Those were the wrong words. Hannah turned away and began furiously sorting a stack of envelopes on the counter, flinging magazines and junk mail into one pile, bills into another. "What a surprise. Here comes Supermom to swoop in and save poor little Hannah." A toy catalog skidded off the counter and landed at Elaine's feet.

She picked it up, wishing she could use it to whack her daughter upside the head. "Your girls are in foster care. Wren was covered in bruises when the police took her in, but she won't tell anyone how she got them. Rhonda's got an entire file of doctors agreeing it was child abuse. Sounds like you've got it all under control."

Hannah gave an angry snort. "The girls will be coming home right after the fact-finding hearing, just you wait. See those bracelets?" She motioned to the pipe cleaner creations. "Wren and Ivy made those with Irena, their CASA worker. It's Irena's job to tell the court what's in the girls' best interest, and she made her opinion quite clear today: the girls should come home."

"That's not what Rhonda thinks. And unless you can tell me the truth about those bruises—"

"Here's the truth, Mom: if you think I'd hurt my daughters, you don't know me at all." As Hannah snatched up the mail and stalked upstairs, three sheets of paper fluttered to the floor behind her.

Elaine scooped up the letters and trailed her daughter up the stairs. She'd let Hannah walk out of her life once before—she wouldn't make the same mistake today. Not bothering to knock, Elaine flung open the door to Hannah's bedroom and found her lying face down on the unmade bed, a pillow clutched over her head.

"How did Wren get all those bruises, then?" Elaine paused, waiting for her daughter to respond. But Hannah's body lay rigid in the darkened shadows, more still than if she were asleep. Ignoring her better instincts, Elaine forged ahead. "And why in God's name didn't you call me when you first fell apart, instead of forcing your seven-year-old to take over the parenting of her baby sister?" That part of Rhonda's note—describing how Wren had cooked for Ivy, bathed her, dressed her, and watched her all day long—had been almost harder to stomach than the medical reports.

With her face still buried in pillows, Hannah stuck out her hand and flipped Elaine a middle finger.

"Mature, sweetie, real mature. But fine: if you won't talk to me, I can't be sure my granddaughters are safe. I have no choice but to take custody myself."

At this, Hannah rolled over and sat up, facing the wall. "Isn't that what you were planning all along, Mother? To rush in here and steal the granddaughters I've been keeping from you?" The familiar defiance of

Hannah's shoulder blades made Elaine feel like she was in a time warp, back to fighting with her sullen teenager about AP tests and driving privileges. "Although I can't understand why you want to mother them," Hannah said, still refusing to turn around, "when you never wanted to mother me."

"That's unfair, and you know it."

"Is it? What would you have done if Dad hadn't been there to take care of me all those years? At least Wren and Ivy have each other."

"I never neglected you." Elaine's voice trembled, the anger in her chest like an animal threatening to pounce. On her own, Elaine had changed, softened; with Hannah, she was the same hothead she'd always been. "Turn on that light and look at me when I say this: you pushed me away, but I never abandoned you. Not the way you've abandoned Wren and Ivy."

Hannah moved then, reaching toward the bedside lamp, an ugly contraption shaped like a wine bottle. But instead of flipping on the switch, her fingers curled around its ceramic neck. Before Elaine could register what was happening, Hannah had seized the lamp and yanked its cord from the outlet. Something heavy and olive green whizzed past Elaine's right ear, hit the wall, and shattered.

Elaine stared at the shards of ceramic, a jagged mosaic of her daughter's fury. No wonder the state thought Hannah guilty of abuse: she'd come unhinged. As Elaine flew out the door and into the starless night, she knew there was no turning back. Taking Wren and Ivy against Hannah's wishes was the nuclear option—after that, there would be no repairing their relationship. But she pictured the bruising on Wren's torso and winced. Hannah had left her with no choice.

Twenty-Five

Julie's first official date with Jake turned out to be a disaster, in the sense that it was the best night of her life.

She'd postponed the date twice—they could never have a serious relationship, not if Jake didn't want children—but eventually Julie convinced herself it was still okay to go to the pop-culture museum. She couldn't very well break up with a guy before their first date. Besides, once they'd spent a bit more time together, things would surely go the way of all her previous relationships. Either Jake would turn out to be completely wrong for her or he'd give her the line she'd heard more than once: "You're a really sweet girl, but there's just . . . something . . . missing." Julie always blamed that *something* on her doughy calves and bad skin, her limp hair that even a whole bottle of volumizer couldn't fix. She felt guilty for even thinking these kinds of thoughts—looks weren't supposed to matter, not to a confident, empowered woman like herself. And yet. Getting ready for the date, she spent forty-five minutes in front of the mirror before she found a pair of jeans that didn't inspire hatred of her hips.

But as Jake drove Julie to the museum, he didn't seem to be considering her so-called flaws. His hand kept drifting across the gear shift to brush against her leg, and he insisted on paying for her museum ticket. Twice during the intro film, Julie caught him gazing at her instead of the screen.

She was finding it similarly hard to focus. Jake had been charming and funny with her relatives at Thanksgiving, but he was even more adorable surrounded by comic book characters. How could she not fall for a guy who looked so at home in Tony Stark's fake laboratory, mixing pretend chemicals like a kid in a candy shop? For every quiz question the exhibit threw at them, Jake knew the answer and more. Who was Tony Stark's father? Howard Stark, modeled after Howard Hughes. How many Iron Man suits did he make in the comic books? Fifty-three, plus a rescue suit for Pepper Potts. By the time Jake busted out the silly acronym behind Iron Man's artificial intelligence—Just A Rather Very Intelligent System—Julie howled with laughter.

"Do you know how much of a dork you are?" She poked him in the ribs. "But wait until we get to the Black Widow exhibit. I'll show you what's up."

"Uh-huh." Jake looped an arm around Julie's waist and pulled her close, planting a soft kiss on her forehead. By the time they separated, she was floating three feet off the ground. This was not going well.

After the Marvel exhibit, as Jake drove them to the promised wine bar, Julie considered asking him more about his thoughts on kids. Maybe she'd misunderstood his comment to her uncle. After all, he'd seemed entirely smitten with his nephew at the library. Then again, she'd scared off so many men by bringing up the future too soon. There would be time to talk about kids later—in the meantime, she could let herself enjoy this one perfect night.

At the restaurant, they shared appetizers while squeezed into the same side of a booth. Jake raised his eyebrows when Julie suggested a flatbread with roasted pears and port-braised figs, but after scarfing down a third slice, he vowed to put fruit on all his pizza forevermore. Emboldened by the buzz from her second glass of pinot grigio, Julie asked jokingly how a man so charming could still be single at thirty-six.

"Divorced, actually."

Julie paused midbite, her slice of flatbread hovering in the air. "That sucks. I'm sorry."

"Don't be. It was for the best. Turns out I'm a rotten judge of character." As Jake fiddled with his butter knife and studied the dessert menu, Julie waited to see if he'd say more. She was dying to hear the story, but they'd reunited only a few weeks ago—she hadn't earned the right to ask.

"Decaf cappuccino?" she finally suggested, holding up her menu.

He gave her a wry smile. "Nope. This woeful tale deserves ice cream. Want the short version or the long one?"

Over raspberry gelato, Jake described how he'd fallen for Alexandra on the day they met, the first day of their third year in med school. He was just coming back to medicine after finishing his PhD thesis, and the smart, stunning redhead from Atlanta was the first of his new class-mates to say hello. Through month after month of 5:00 a.m. rounds and sleepless overnight calls, they kept each other going with kisses and coffee. By the time they'd matched together for residency in Ann Arbor, Jake had bought a ring and popped the question. For three blissful years he thought he'd hit the marital jackpot—until the afternoon he came home early and found Alexandra in bed with her chief resident.

One betrayal would have been crushing, but over the following weeks, Jake learned Alexandra had cheated not once but three times. Apparently the entire derm department, perhaps even the whole University of Michigan medical complex, had known of her infidel-ity: four months earlier, she'd been cited for improper relations with a patient. They'd separated, of course, but Alexandra's duplicity had confirmed what he'd always feared: Jake Lankowski was a dupe of the worst kind.

"Sorry for the sob story," he said, spooning up the last pink droplets of his gelato. "More than you bargained for, eh?"

Julie shook her head, a parade of her own failed relationships march-ing through her mind. "I hope they kicked her out of the program."

"Far from it. She's about to join the most successful derm practice in the city." He drained his wineglass. "And I hear she's engaged again."

"But in bed with her boss, most likely."

Jake laughed, but his eyes looked sad. "It wasn't all her fault. Before I found out about the affairs, she asked if we could try couples' counseling. I watched her break down crying on the therapist's couch, telling him how lonely she was. But even after that, I kept working extreme hours, prioritizing my research over our relationship. No one wants to play second fiddle to a petri dish."

Julie shook her head. "You can't take responsibility for her bad behavior." She imagined taking Jake's hands between her own and promising she'd never hurt him, no matter how many hours he spent in the lab. Not even after they were old and gray and celebrating their thirtieth wedding anniversary. She bit her lip—too soon, way too soon.

"Maybe Alexandra and I just wanted different things," Jake said, picking his spoon back up and twirling it between his fingers. "She wanted to practice medicine, sure, but she also wanted a white picket fence, fancy vacations, and two point five perfect children—I was never going to be able to give her that."

Julie sucked in her breath, trying to hide her horrified expression. So the comment to her uncle hadn't been a one-off—Jake absolutely didn't want kids, and his feelings ran so deep they'd led to his divorce. She felt like crying, but instead she sipped the last of her coffee and pictured Wren and Ivy. Why was she even on this date? The girls were the ones who needed her.

Ivy had been inconsolable when Julie dropped her off at Anitha's house four hours earlier. Originally Julie had planned to use the state-provided respite-care service—free babysitting for foster kids through another licensed provider—but at the first number she called, she could barely hear the lady's voice over the screaming in the background. The woman's shouts of "Shut up, everybody" did little to quiet the chaos, and her angry tone convinced Julie not to trust her—or any other stranger—with Wren and Ivy, not even for the evening. Julie almost canceled the date, until Anitha begged to take the girls instead. "Motherhood's not martyrdom," she'd said. "You deserve a break." Eventually Julie had relented, mostly because Wren was having mean-girl trouble at school, and Julie thought an overnight with Anitha's friendly, extroverted boys might do her good.

The girls had been with Julie for over a month now, and each passing day made it clearer how ill prepared she'd been for fostering. She envied the mothers who'd started with their children as newborns. If she'd raised Wren from birth, maybe she'd know how to comfort her when she came home from school with a tearstained face, ripped backpack, and two skinned knees. Or what to do when the teacher called to report how, in the middle of a spelling quiz, Wren had reached across her desk and yanked the ponytail of the girl in front of her. As it was, Julie felt like she was flying a rocket ship with no instruction manual. The girls had suffered major trauma, losing their mom and getting taken into custody, not to mention whatever neglect and abuse predated CPS. Julie wished she had more to offer them—a degree in child psychology, maybe, instead of a dumb weekend training course.

At least she and Wren had bonded over superheroes. Julie had started reading *Batgirl* aloud every night at bedtime, and on Tuesday, she'd discovered several more hand-drawn comics in Wren's backpack, all featuring the same supergirl as the drawing she'd found at Thanksgiving. A lot like Batgirl, but with an orange suit and cat ears. Again, it looked like Wren had tried to make word bubbles but scribbled them out.

"Wren, this is so cool. Are you writing your own comic book?"

She snatched the pages back. "Very funny. Haven't you noticed? My handwriting stinks."

"That doesn't matter. The way your character looks three-dimensional, and all the poses you can draw? Your mom must be some art teacher."

"Too bad she never taught me how to write. My teacher doesn't care about drawing. She says my letters look like a kindergartner's."

Julie clenched her teeth. Didn't that teacher remember that Wren had never been in school before? She forced herself to swallow the few choice adjectives coming to mind. "Nonsense. You write beautifully; you just need more practice. Besides, talk bubbles are tiny. No wonder you can't fit in everything you want the characters to say." She pulled out a chair at the dining room table and sat down, motioning Wren to do the same. "How about we do it together? You draw the pictures, and then tell me what to write."

Julie expected Wren to shake her head and walk away. Instead, she plopped down in the chair and smoothed the pages in front of her. "You'd really write all the words for me? It might be a long book."

"I'd be honored. I'll get to be the first one to hear your story."

Wren leaped up to get a pencil, and Julie thanked the universe for superheroes, coming to the rescue as always.

Now, in the wine bar, Jake put his finger lightly on Julie's chin and tilted her face toward him. "Hey. You look a million miles away."

"Sorry, just thinking about . . . bad boyfriends." Julie couldn't bring herself to say what she was really thinking, not when he was gazing into her eyes with such a sweet, concerned expression.

"Yeah?" Jake raised his eyebrows. "Got a story to match mine?"

Oh, brother. She hadn't meant to open *that* can of worms. She didn't want to talk about Seth. Not tonight, and if she was honest, not ever.

"Not much of a story. I dated an asshole." Julie made a face. "I guess we're both rotten judges of character."

Jake squeezed her hand. "One more thing we've got in common." The hopeful sparkle in his eyes made Julie cringe.

On the drive back home, she promised herself she'd break things off before getting out of the car. Staring out the window, she mulled over which words would set her free but inflict the least pain on her old friend. But then he grabbed her hand and held it the whole way home, stroking his thumb along the inside of her wrist. She kept glancing at his profile and marveling at his perfect lips—she'd never wanted to kiss someone so much, and the unfairness of it all made her chest burn. She couldn't tell Jake the truth, that his position on kids was a deal-breaker, because it just seemed so presumptive—he'd taken her on one date, not asked her to marry him. But neither could she lie and say, "I'm just not ready for a relationship"—not when every fiber of her being ached for exactly that.

When Jake pulled up alongside her town house and flipped on his hazards, Julie opened her mouth to tell him they could only be friends. Before she could speak, Jake touched a single, silent finger to her parted lips. A shock of heat tingled down her spine, scorching the words she'd been about to say. Julie closed her eyes and leaned in, tasting the salty texture of his fingertip. As they became a blaze of lips and hands and bodies, her good intentions sprinkled like ashes to the floorboards.

—⁂—

"That good, eh?" Anitha flashed a conspiratorial grin as she shut the car door behind Wren and Ivy.

"Good and bad." Julie's cheeks flushed.

"Bad because it was so good?"

"You know me too well." Julie made a face and changed the subject. "How did the sleepover go?"

"Fabulous." Anitha hefted a backpack and two sleeping bags into Julie's front seat. "Your girls are amazing. They sit still. Chew with their mouths closed, color on paper instead of walls, pee *in* the toilet, and then, wonder of all wonders—they flush! *A whole new world . . .*" Anitha delivered her last line in singsong, sounding exactly like a Disney princess. "Now tell me everything."

Julie laughed. "Gotta run, details later. But I owe you one."

Anitha's brown eyes twinkled. "Marry Jake, and all debts will be forgiven."

Julie stuck out her tongue. But at the same moment, her phone bleeped from inside her pocket, and she felt a sharp thrill, hoping it might be a text from Jake. Anitha laughed. "You're in deep, girl, whether you like it or not."

"It's not that simple." She pulled out her phone, unable to resist.

Anitha was reading over her shoulder, but she was too excited to care. **Miss you already,** Jake had written. **Free tonight?**

Anitha whistled. "Uh-huh, whatever you say. But it looks pretty simple to me."

—⁓—

Of course Julie wasn't free that night, or any of the nights that followed. She'd traded the freedom—and loneliness—of life as a single thirty-something for the sweet but exhausting predictability of parenthood. For at least the next six weeks, her days would revolve around the girls: picking them up from school, cooking their dinner, baths and books at bedtime. Exactly how Julie had always wanted it, until Jake had come along.

Now she was also caught up in the blustery whirlwind of a new relationship, made all the more intoxicating because she knew she shouldn't be dating Jake at all—they had no future. But every night after she'd gotten the girls to sleep, Julie would rush downstairs and dial his cell. On call nights, Jake would say a quick hi from the emergency room; otherwise, he'd drive over and sneak up the fire escape to her bedroom balcony. Julie tiptoed around like a teenager hiding from her parents, jumping at the slightest cough or bump from the girls' room, and always ready to shove Jake into a closet if Ivy or Wren woke up.

Jake laughed at her paranoia, but Julie dreaded the girls finding him in the house at night. They knew Jake, of course, and squealed with excitement when he rang the doorbell—mostly because he always had something hidden behind his back, maybe a pack of stickers or cookies from the bakery across from the hospital. But Julie had worked hard to gain Wren's trust, and she worried the nighttime presence of a boyfriend might make her feel anxious, or betrayed. Besides, she didn't want Wren mentioning the midnight visits to Rhonda. Julie knew the rules, of course—her training had been very specific—any adult who spent more than twelve nights in the home needed to submit to a background check and TB test. Jake was only on night number three, as long as you didn't count the nights he drove home at 3:00 a.m. (Julie didn't count them). If needed, he'd surely jump through the necessary hoops, but asking him to do a background check would force the issue she was trying to ignore.

If—when?—she had to decide between Jake and the girls, Julie knew she'd pick Wren and Ivy a hundred times over. Together, she and Wren had made fast headway on the first issue of *Kitty Girl*, with a giant striped tiger named Popsicle featuring prominently as sidekick. As they spent hours plotting villains and sketching heroes at the kitchen table, Julie realized Wren was a lot like she'd been as a girl, losing herself in an imaginary world of superpowers to forget her own unhappiness. Granted, Wren's problems were way bigger than the schoolyard bullying Julie had endured, but Kitty Girl could take on anything. And Ivy—well, Ivy was a cuddle bug in the extreme, and it was hard not to bond with a child so willing to snuggle and laugh and play. The girls needed her, and as the weeks went by, Julie's love gained a ferocity she hadn't thought possible.

Meanwhile, Jake never mentioned his thoughts on kids or their future together, and the upcoming holidays offered plenty of distraction. On one of his days off, Jake helped roll out dough for dozens of Christmas cookies. The girls cut out shapes, whipped up frosting, and doused them with so many colored sprinkles it looked more like Easter than Christmas. Jake and Julie went shopping together and bought matching LEGO kits for the girls and Jake's nephew Sam. They never ran out of things to talk about—from *Guardians of the Galaxy* and the bizarre antilogic of billing codes to their shared hatred of Coach Ballesteros from sixth-grade PE—so there was no need to bring up anything uncomfortable. As long as they stayed in this unofficial limbo, desperate to be together but never discussing the future, Julie hoped she'd never have to choose.

Twenty-Six

Ten weeks, six days, five hours, and approximately twenty-three minutes after the police stole away her daughters, Hannah sat on a wooden pew outside the King County dependency courtroom. She'd been sitting there for almost an hour, waiting for hearings to restart after the lunch break, so she'd had plenty of time for useless calculations.

No matter which way she shifted, her butt bones hurt. She tried not to think about how much weight she'd lost since this ordeal began, or how her gaunt figure might appear to the judge. Good mothers had apple cheeks and childbearing hips, but these days even the thought of food made Hannah's stomach turn—a side effect of her new meds, maybe, or just one more piece of collateral damage caused by CPS. Once she got the girls back, she'd give up her diet of club soda and ramen noodles and start cooking healthy meals again.

Once she got the girls back . . . this refrain had kept Hannah going through a lonely Christmas and miserable New Year's, and past the annual trauma of Alex's birthday. She never knew what to do on that day of mourning-celebration. Pull out the photo album from his final year, and cry over the grinning forty-one-year-old who didn't know those candles would be his last? Wrap him a gift and burn it in the fireplace? Or just hide under the covers and pretend January sixth was a day like any other? This year, she had convinced Irena to bring the girls for an extra visit. As galling as it was to need "supervision" during such an intimate family moment, Hannah didn't have a choice. On that day, they needed to be together.

After looking at photos and talking about how much they missed Daddy, Wren had pulled out construction paper and crayons to make him a birthday card, like she'd done every year since Alex's death. This was the first year Ivy made one, too, scribbling on the front and then dictating a short message to the father she'd never remember. After Hannah finished writing, Ivy grabbed the card again and crayoned three wobbly letters. Hannah choked back a sob. Who had taught Ivy to write her name? And how many more milestones would Hannah miss before the State of Washington set her daughters free?

Her case was one of the last on the docket, and she'd spent all morning listening to other families' pain, alternating between sympathy for the parents and outrage at what had happened to some of these children. Addictions, sexual assault, abuse victims growing up to hurt their own. Every inch of Hannah's skin felt flayed and raw, split open by emotions she didn't have the strength to absorb.

She checked her watch. The judge said hearings would resume at 1:00 p.m. sharp, but at nine minutes past, neither the judge nor her public defender had appeared. Each time the heavy wooden door labeled **DEFENSE** swung open across the hall, Hannah expected to see her lawyer. Each time it was some other suit and tie, bearing a thick stack of papers and bustling with self-importance.

The door opened again, and finally Mr. Gorman appeared. Hannah had spent all morning staring at the slope of his shoulders and the pattern of gray flecks in his hair, so she expected his rumpled brown suit, thick glasses, and apologetic frown. She did not expect him to be dragging her mother by the arm.

"I'm sorry, ma'am, you can't be in here. This room is for defense attorneys only." Mr. Gorman let go of Elaine's arm, but she leaned closer.

"I *am* a defense attorney. What, just because I'm a woman, you think I don't belong?" Elaine's chin jutted forward, every fiber of her compact, all-business frame buzzing with energy. Her shrill voice echoed down the hall, obliging everyone waiting on the benches to turn and stare. Hannah almost laughed. Her mother, always happy to turn her own misconduct into somebody else's crime. The poor lawyer blushed and stammered an apology.

Hannah stood up and stepped toward them. "Mom, I think you're supposed to be on *this* side of the hall." She motioned to the door behind her, marked **DSHS/CPS**. "That's the room for child stealers."

The public defender looked shocked, his already buggy eyes bulging out until Hannah worried they'd pop out of their sockets. "This is your mother? And she's a lawyer?"

Elaine thrust out her hand. "Ms. Elaine Montgomery, attorney for Greenbaum & Sons, at your service." She grinned, revealing a mouthful of shiny, perfect teeth.

"But she's not defending me," Hannah added, straightening her shoulders and giving Elaine the most intimidating glare she could muster. "She's trying to get custody herself."

Mr. Gorman had cautiously given Elaine his hand, which she pumped aggressively. His attempt at a smile came out a grimace. As soon as Elaine let go, he grabbed Hannah by the elbow and gave her a small push toward a side hallway. "Ms. Montgomery," he said, turning back over his shoulder. "We'll see you momentarily. In the courtroom."

Once they were in an alcove, safely out of earshot, Mr. Gorman began to pace. "This is the kind of thing you need to tell your lawyer *before* the day of your fact-finding hearing. On the phone last week, when I asked if there were any new developments, you might have said, 'My mother'—" He glared at Hannah. "Whom until now, I might add, you haven't even bothered to mention." Another withering glare. "You might have said, 'My mother is a high-powered attorney trying to gain custody of my children.'"

If the situation hadn't felt so serious, Hannah would have laughed. Her lawyer's eyeballs protruded from his pale face, and his nostrils flared. All he needed was a nose ring and some billowing steam: Hannah would wave a red flag in front of the judge, and Gorman would bore right through him.

"Are you even *listening* to me?" The lawyer flapped his hand in front of Hannah's face. She forced herself to focus.

"I didn't mention Elaine because I've got it taken care of." Hannah patted her bulging handbag, filled with the letters she'd finally sorted through from Whidbey. "That woman was a far more neglectful mother than I've ever been, and I've got all the evidence right here."

"Evidence?" Mr. Gorman spluttered. "What do you think this is, *Judge Judy*? Your mom's not the one on trial here. Besides, you can't just present new 'evidence' to the judge; we exchanged discovery at 8:00 this morning." He took a deep breath, like he might be counting to three. "How can I speak for you in court if I have no idea what's going on?"

Hannah forced her features into an expression of contrition. "Sorry. I should have mentioned the Elaine issue. But I've done my reading too. The State of Washington grants parents input on who they want their kids to live with while they're in out-of-home care. In the unlikely chance my girls aren't coming home with me today, I want them to stay with Julie."

Mr. Gorman nodded, still frowning. "I'll communicate your wishes to the judge. But the state also prioritizes kinship over foster care. If there's a suitable relative who wants to take your children, that opens foster beds for other needy families. Regardless—" He paused for emphasis. "A dependency hearing is the last place you want to engage in do-it-yourself legal representation. If you're serious about getting your kids back, you've got to trust me. And tell me every detail—I mean *everything*—that might be relevant to your case."

Hannah sighed. No matter how many details she'd given him these past weeks, he still seemed convinced she was hiding the truth. She'd been honest with him about how she'd once left purple splotches on

Wren's arm after pulling her back from the street, and another time bruised her torso lifting her out of the tub, but these confessions only made him ask more questions. Questions that scared her, like, "Is there any way you could have inflicted the bruises this time, maybe without realizing it?"

Now an impatient-looking woman in a forest green sweater tapped on Mr. Gorman's shoulder. "Hearings are starting again. Please take your seats in the courtroom."

"Come on, then." Mr. Gorman gripped Hannah's elbow tighter than she thought necessary. "Let's not keep the good judge waiting."

—⁊⁊—

"Do you solemnly swear to tell the truth, the whole truth, and nothing but the truth, so help you God?"

So help me God. The truth was harder to tell than Hannah expected. Did she know how Wren got those bruises on her back? No, she couldn't remember. Had she ever left bruises on her daughter before? Not on purpose, of course, but her lawyer said she had to be honest about those accidental times. And had she been angry that day, when she yanked Wren back from the street and left fingerprints? Hannah could no longer be sure. The more questions the court asked, the more she questioned her own reality.

Did she provide nutritious, balanced meals three times a day? Sometimes. Other times, when she got depressed, she provided Twinkies and orange juice. Had she allowed her seven-year-old access to unsafe conditions involving the illegal remodel of a house that didn't belong to her? Yes, but thank God the court didn't ask about that. None of them believed Wren's bruises came from a fall, anyway.

Not once did they ask about the things that mattered—whether Hannah loved her daughters more than breath itself, whether she'd risk everything to keep them with her. She wanted to tell them about the kind of parent she used to be, the one who breastfed her babies to bolster their immune systems, who read her children a dozen picture books before bed, who taught them to draw and plant flowers. But with each pointed question, the assistant district attorney stripped away another layer of her self-defense. Hannah's shoulders slumped, remembering all the days she'd wallowed in bed, leaving Wren to cook and care for her baby sister; all the times she'd stormed off to be alone, telling the girls she couldn't take another minute of their squabbling. When she finally stepped down from the witness stand, she collapsed into her seat.

"Thank you for your testimony, Ms. Sawyer," the judge said. "I appreciate your honesty." So far, Judge Nakamura had been the most surprising element of the trial. Hannah had expected him to be brusque and businesslike. Morally superior. Judgmental. Instead, he seemed professional but friendly, a man of few words who listened intently, his deep brown eyes taking in every detail of the proceedings before him.

As the prosecution began calling witnesses to the stand, Mr. Gorman's voice echoed in her head, reminding her that if she just signed the dependency agreement and agreed to give the state custody, she could be done with this nightmare trial. Maybe she deserved to lose her babies for a while, so she could emerge on the other side a better mother.

No. Hannah shook her head to clear the dark thoughts threatening to pull her under. If the document actually told the truth, the whole truth, and nothing but the truth, she would have signed it. But the whole truth was that she'd neglected her girls because she'd been grieving and depressed, a depression for which she'd taken some pills and gotten over. And the document blamed her not only for neglect but also for physical abuse. Like she'd told Mr. Gorman: no matter how fuzzy her memories were, she never would've hit her daughter.

DSHS didn't understand that Wren was born black and blue—literally, her whole face purple from being squished against Hannah's tailbone during labor. For all seven years of Wren's life, she'd bruised at the slightest bump of shin or knee or chin: Hannah's peach, sweet but fragile. If the judge had asked the Sawyers' family doctor in Chicago, she could have told them how many times Hannah had brought Wren in for bruising as a toddler, only to be told her iron levels came back normal. "Kids fall down, mothers fret, kids are fine. That's just life," the kind doctor had always said, patting Hannah's hand.

She'd asked for a referral to a specialist, but the doctor assured her it wasn't necessary. That's part of why Hannah had quit trusting the medical system: doctors never seemed to listen. Once Alex died and they lost their health insurance, she gave up taking the girls for their yearly physicals. As babies, they'd been vaccinated for every possible disease. As long as they stayed healthy, what did she need with a pediatrician?

Apparently, Hannah now learned, she needed an official stamp of approval from the medical industrial complex. CPS considered the girls' blank medical histories another sign of Hannah's inadequate mothering—medical neglect, Rhonda called it—and now she brought forward a tall, skinny doctor to testify. Young and nervous, she spoke too loudly and kept brushing strands of dark hair out of her eyes.

"The paucity of the girls' prior medical history, and the lack of a primary care physician to give us longitudinal data regarding family safety, makes it difficult to assess the level of risk. Regardless, the bruising we witnessed went far beyond what one would expect, even in an active, ambulatory seven-year-old." She took a gulp of air before continuing. "The pattern of injury, combined with the presence of ecchymoses at multiple stages of healing, is suggestive of nonaccidental trauma." Hannah glanced at Rhonda as the doctor spoke this mouthful of jargon, but the caseworker seemed to have no trouble understanding. Her head bounced like a fishing bobber as she scribbled furiously on a stack of papers.

As the doctor continued to speak, Hannah conducted a silent cross-examination. Sure, Ms. Doogie Howser, you've got a medical degree, but have you spent any time with seven-year-olds? Do you know how they shimmy up trees and scale fences and balance on towers of tippy rocks? This doctor had clearly never met a child like Wren, brave and foolhardy but with skin that bruised purple and green at the merest provocation.

"We tested for all the regular bleeding disorders," she continued. "Prothrombin time, platelet count, and fibrinogen levels all came back normal."

"Thank you," the judge said. "Now, in English please: In your professional opinion, has this child been abused?"

"I can't say for certain, Your Honor, and I'm only a pediatric resident, not an expert in child abuse. But yes, I think it's likely."

As the pediatrician stepped down from the stand, Judge Nakamura frowned. "Why didn't we get an abuse specialist to review this case?"

"We did, Your Honor," Rhonda said, sounding embarrassed. "But I'm sorry to say, I can't read their statement."

Judge Nakamura adjusted his glasses. "Can't read it?"

"Wren's medical file was—misplaced, somehow." Rhonda's cheeks darkened. "And we're still trying to get a new copy of the official report. But the gist was that yes, the pattern of bruising is highly indicative of abuse."

"Objection," Mr. Gorman broke in. "Without the actual statement, that's hearsay."

"Sustained," the judge said. "Strike that from the record." He turned to Rhonda. "But please have that report available before the next hearing. I've never known you to lose things."

"Yes, Your Honor. Thank you." Rhonda sat down with a look of extreme displeasure, bordering on fury. Hannah felt sorry for whichever poor secretary had lost the file.

The assistant DA began reading a series of statements from various adults involved with Wren and Ivy's care. First, a psychologist from Green Harbor called Hannah out for not sending them to school. "Educational neglect," she'd labeled it, claiming Wren lacked proper socialization because she'd never been to kindergarten. Never mind that Hannah had kept Wren home for her own good, after seeing how basic the curriculum was, numbers and letters Wren had known for years.

Sure, Hannah's elaborate plans for "project-based homeschooling" had never materialized, but unschooling seemed to be working just fine for her bright, self-motivated daughter.

Next they read a statement from an alleged neighbor, a woman whose name Hannah didn't recognize, but who claimed to have witnessed—horrors!—the girls playing alone in their yard. "Even in winter," the note read, "and even after dark, when children ought to be in bed." Except that during winter in Seattle, Hannah thought bitterly, it got dark around four in the afternoon. She wanted to hand every member of the court a copy of Richard Louv's *Last Child in the Woods* and call in her own expert to explain the importance of outdoor play for proper development. Didn't any of these people remember their own childhoods? But those were the good old days, when everybody's children played outside and nobody's neighbor called the cops.

Hannah breathed a sigh of relief when Irena took the stand. As the one who'd gotten to know the girls best, her recommendations would hold strong sway. Stepping up to the witness stand, she smiled straight at Hannah, one ray of warmth in the ice world of the courtroom.

"Wren and Ivy appear closely bonded with their mother, and they've told me in no uncertain terms—once Hannah has recovered from her depression, they want to go home." Irena's voice was a soothing balm for Hannah's frayed nerves. "On multiple occasions, Hannah has welcomed me into her home for supervised visits, always providing healthy snacks and craft activities for the girls. At every visit, her home has been clean and well appointed . . ."

Hannah's mind wandered as Irena described the girls' *child-friendly* house. Perhaps she wouldn't speak so kindly if she knew that same house was in foreclosure, that just this week Hannah had been given final notice: thirty days to move before the cops barged in and dragged her out. Hannah had been so focused on the upcoming hearing and getting the girls back, she hadn't made plans for where they'd go after she lost the house. As long as Wren and Ivy were with her, they could sleep in the car, for all she cared.

With Irena's vote of confidence, maybe the girls would come home sooner than expected. "If you saw how their faces light up when they see their mother," Irena told the judge, "or their tears when it's time to go home—well, it's not what you'd expect from an abusive relationship." Hannah imagined driving to Julie's straight after the hearing, ringing the doorbell and hearing the pitter-patter of little feet as Wren and Ivy raced to the door. Their faces would really light up when she told them they were coming home for good.

Mr. Gorman elbowed Hannah and brought her back to reality. Irena had stopped talking, and a nervous shuffling rippled across the room. Hannah stifled a groan. Elaine had left her seat and was striding toward the judge. "Permission to approach the bench, Your Honor?"

Judge Nakamura peered over his glasses. "And you are . . . ?"

"Elaine Montgomery, Your Honor. Mother of Hannah, and grandmother of Wren and Ivy." She paused. "Also, senior partner at Greenbaum & Sons." Hannah shook her head. This far from Chicago, Elaine's fancy firm didn't elicit the collective gasp she'd likely hoped for.

Judge Nakamura looked unimpressed. "Something you'd like to say to the court?"

"Yes, Your Honor. I fear my daughter has not been honest with her CASA worker." Hannah froze as Elaine stepped forward and handed the judge a single sheet of pink paper. But—she'd stuffed all those heinous notices into the third drawer of her desk in the bedroom. How could Elaine have gotten ahold of one? The judge took his time reading, and as his eyes shifted down the page, his frown deepened. Under the table, Hannah dug the nails of one hand into the flesh of the other, stopping only when her skin felt about to give way. Self-inflicted wounds wouldn't help her case.

"Your Honor," Elaine said again. "Given that my daughter is clearly not in a situation to provide appropriate care or housing for her offspring, I'd like to officially petition the court for custody of my granddaughters."

Hannah's breath caught, and she plunged her hand into her purse to finger the old letters. She'd known this custody grab was coming, but facing her mother in court still felt surreal. At least she'd brought the proof she needed.

"Hannah." The judge finally looked up. "This document is indeed a foreclosure notice, but it's dated in November. I assume you've straightened all this out with your caseworker?"

Elaine butted in before Hannah could reply. "I called the bank, Your Honor. My daughter has until February twenty-second to vacate her home, or she faces forcible eviction."

Beside Hannah, Mr. Gorman sprang to life. "Your Honor, I object. All new evidence should have been exchanged in discovery this morning."

"Overruled." Judge Nakamura waved the pink slip. "This new information is highly relevant to the girls' well-being."

Elaine cleared her throat. "Also, just so you know, my daughter's anger-management classes do not appear to be working. During our last encounter, she threw a lamp at my head."

Mr. Gorman swore under his breath, and Rhonda and the assistant DA bent their heads together, whispering fiercely. As the judge banged his gavel for order, Hannah caught Elaine's gaze. Her thin lips curled at the corners, and she lifted her shoulders ever so slightly—whether in apology or satisfaction, Hannah couldn't tell. Then Elaine turned away, leaving Hannah to stare at the back of her mother's white head, perched prim and straight on her neck like a haughty swan.

Twenty-Seven

Elaine hadn't meant to take the foreclosure notice, not at first. She'd planned to hand it back, along with the other three envelopes that had fluttered to the floor when Hannah retreated up the stairs. But a flying ceramic projectile will make anyone forgetful, and by the time Elaine realized she was still clutching Hannah's mail, she was already in the car. For weeks, that wrinkled pink paper stayed crammed in her handbag—until she cleaned out her purse and discovered she held a custody trump card, right there in Hannah's forgotten mail.

Now, as Elaine returned to her seat, her limbs felt shaky. She normally savored the buzzy feeling that came from turning a courtroom upside down with a startling revelation, but today the thrill of adrenaline felt more like nausea. She tried not to look at Hannah, who, despite the bustling chaos around her, had gone completely still; her face placid, as if her mind had already floated out of the courtroom to some peaceful beach or forest or hidden universe where no mother could be accused of failing her children.

Elaine shook her head, trying to clear the tendrils of guilt winding through her thoughts. But the way that Irena lady had been carrying on, the judge might have sent her granddaughters home any minute.

"To offer just one example," Irena had said, before Elaine interrupted the cheerleading routine, "Ivy has been completely nonverbal at her foster mother's house. At first I thought this might be a symptom of developmental delay, or perhaps a result of neglect, but at the end of her first visit with her mother, Ivy *spoke*." On the last word, Irena's voice took on a note of reverence, as if getting a three-year-old to talk had been a miracle. "Ivy's words were, and I quote, 'No, I don't want to go. Please let me stay with Mama.'"

Elaine doubted this was a direct quote from Ivy. Even before the recent trauma, she hadn't been a particularly articulate child. But Judge Nakamura leaned forward in his chair, hanging on Irena's every word. A Google search of the judge's name had turned up videos from every Family Reunification Day for the past decade—the man was a sucker for happy endings. He made the same speech in every video, claiming nothing made him prouder than handing a parent their "graduation certificate" and watching them walk out the door of dependency court, hand in hand with their children.

Knowing the judge was a softie, and listening to Irena wax lyrical about sweet little Hannah Homemaker, Elaine knew she had to act fast. And indeed, her revelation quickly shifted focus from the girls' strong maternal attachment to how Hannah had misled the court.

"Are you aware that during a CPS investigation, you're legally required to notify DSHS as soon as any changes are made to your living arrangements?" The judge frowned and held up the pink paper. "Changes, for example, like losing your house to foreclosure."

Hannah whispered to her lawyer, who repeated his request for a temporary adjournment of the trial. The judge looked about to agree when Rhonda intervened.

"Before a recess, Your Honor, I have one more witness who's been waiting to speak." The judge nodded, and Rhonda motioned to a fresh-faced young man seated at the back. Thin but muscular, he practically bounded to the witness stand, white coat flapping behind him. Rhonda's lawyer introduced him as Dr. Eric Banning, attending psychiatrist at the Presley Center for Positive Mental Health. Hardly old enough to attend to himself, Elaine observed, let alone anyone else.

He spoke with a booming, made-for-Hollywood voice. "Technically, Ms. Sawyer has complied with the requirements of her outpatient treatment, in that she's been physically present at every therapy session." His Adam's apple bobbed as he swallowed. "However, as her supervising physician, I must admit I have some concerns." He sent a significant glance in Hannah's direction. "One of the most important factors for success is what we call *buy-in*, or a basic trust in the therapy process. Despite filling her prescriptions and showing up for appointments, Hannah appears to have little faith in her own recovery. She rarely speaks up in our group therapy sessions, and when she does, she seems not entirely sure of her own story."

"You mean she's lying?" the judge asked, frowning. Elaine wasn't surprised. Apparently her daughter had been lying to everyone.

"More like telling stories to cover up her true pain. It's as if she's afraid to get better, perhaps, or thinks she doesn't deserve—"

The judge interrupted again, tapping his pen against the bench. "All we need to know is whether Ms. Sawyer is stable enough to care for young children on her own."

Elaine's mind flashed to some of her own moments as a young mother, those rare weekend afternoons when Steve had to work and she was left alone with toddler Hannah: always squirming, always touching, always begging for one more game or one more story. Hannah was right: something about that unrelenting neediness triggered Elaine's headaches, in a way the courtroom never did. *What would you have done,* Hannah had asked, *if Dad hadn't been there to take care of me all those years?* Elaine pushed the question from her thoughts: she would have risen to the occasion, stepped up to do whatever needed to be done—just like she was about to do for Wren and Ivy.

"No. She's not stable enough. Not yet," the doctor said, shaking his head. "I would strongly caution against adding additional stress to Hannah's life by returning the girls home. But perhaps after another three months of outpatient therapy . . ."

Judge Nakamura wiped his brow. His brown eyes now looked sunken instead of shiny. "Very well, I don't think we need to spend any more time on this one." He turned to Hannah. "Ms. Sawyer, the preponderance of professional opinion suggests you are not ready for custody of your children." Elaine should have felt victorious, but her heart wrenched as she watched her daughter slump forward, pressing her face into her hands. "At a minimum, you need to start cooperating with therapy and find somewhere to live. I recommend checking out our affordable housing program."

Turning to face the courtroom, he continued in a flat voice. "I hereby declare Ivy Elizabeth Sawyer and Wren Abigail Sawyer to be dependents of the State of Washington, to remain in out-of-home care until the dependency review hearing in six months' time."

Once again, Elaine stood up from her seat. "Permission to speak, Your Honor?"

The judge nodded.

"As I said previously, I am the girls' grandmother, and as their closest—and only—living kin, I would like them transferred from foster care into my custody immediately."

Hannah's head shot up, and she leaped to her feet, whirling around to face Elaine. "No. The state gives me the right to decide where my children stay, and under no circumstances do I want them living with you."

"Not the right to decide," Elaine said. She'd expected this onslaught, but hearing Hannah say those words in a courtroom still felt like a gut punch. "The right to provide input. Isn't that right, Your Honor?"

The judge sighed. He looked poised to say something, but Hannah spoke first. "Perhaps my maternal failings are genetic, Your Honor, because my mother is about the last person who should be raising children." Looking alarmed, Hannah's lawyer began tugging on her sleeve to sit down. She ignored him and waved a stack of wrinkled papers in the air. "If you're interested, I have dozens of letters from my own childhood, describing just exactly how negligent and abusive my mother can be. Want the one where she forgot me at school until 9:00 p.m., or the one where she locked me out of the house, barefoot, in the rain? Or the one—"

A vein on Elaine's forehead began to twitch, but she kept her voice calm. "My daughter is angry with me right now, Your Honor, and she's clearly letting that anger cloud her judgment about what's best for Wren and Ivy."

"Here, try this one," Hannah said. "*August 12, 1992. Tonight my mother splashed soapy water in my face because I refused—*"

The bailiff took a step toward Hannah, and the judge banged his gavel. "Stop. This is a courtroom, not a mother-daughter free-for-all." He turned to Rhonda. "Do you have any concerns about Ms. Montgomery's suitability as a caregiver?"

The caseworker shrugged. "My understanding is that she lives in Chicago."

"Wait, you're hoping to take them out of state?" The judge peered over his glasses at Elaine.

Elaine shook her head. "Obviously, that's not possible during a CPS case. I'm fully prepared to move to Washington, and I've just started my required kinship care training course. As soon as I get custody, I'll move the girls into my home on Whidbey Island." Elaine chose not to mention how this home still needed flooring in half the rooms, but she made a mental note to move construction to the top of her to-do list.

The judge looked pleased by this answer. "Whidbey Island is gorgeous. Spent some time out there with my own kids last summer." He turned to Rhonda. "Let's keep the girls in foster care for now, but schedule weekly visits for Ms. Montgomery and her granddaughters. That will give Irena the chance to assess what's truly in the girls' best interest."

This was not the immediate custody transfer Elaine had been hoping for, but visits were a step in the right direction. As she filed out of the courtroom, she avoided looking at Hannah's sagging shoulders and instead beelined straight for Irena—the next one she needed to win over. Pasting on her most friendly smile, Elaine trailed the CASA worker down the hall.

But just as she was about to follow Irena into the elevator, a hand gripped her shoulder. Elaine turned to find a stony-faced Hannah, who shoved a pile of letters into her hands. "These weren't nearly as useful as I'd hoped, but maybe they'll give you something to chew over while you plot to steal my children."

Elaine fumbled with the letters, dropping half a dozen on her feet. Startled, she recognized Steve's handwriting on one of the envelopes and bent down to snatch it up. "Wait, Irena—" But the elevator doors had closed, and when she turned back to Hannah, the hallway was empty.

Twenty-Eight

When the phone rang at seven thirty the following morning, Julie wasn't entirely happy to hear Rhonda's voice on the other end of the line. It had been a rough night, following a rough week, and the girls had already been up for two hours. They were fighting again, this time over which cartoon to watch. As they tugged back and forth on the remote, their voices fast escalated from hollers to shrieks, until Wren abruptly let go, sending Ivy flying into the two bowls of soggy Cheerios beside them on the floor. Milk sploshed first onto Ivy's pajamas, then all over Julie's brand-new ivory shag carpet.

"Augghh! Wet, Mama Julie! All wet!"

Wren leaped up and started blotting the milk with a throw pillow, glaring at her sister. "It's your fault, Ivy. You're the one who tried to grab the remote."

"No! No-no-no-no! Wenny fault. Wenny did it."

Part of Julie felt like screaming too. Ivy's verbal skills had returned full force, and now Julie was subject to nonstop chatter and bickering, an auditory onslaught slowly driving her bananas. But even with Ivy screeching at the top of her lungs and a milk stain spreading across the floor, Julie had to hold back a smile. Midfight, the girls reminded her of angry anime characters: Wren with her exaggerated pout and arms held akimbo, and Ivy's messy ponytail that had migrated from the back of her head and now stuck out behind her left ear, like a palm tree sprouted sideways. Julie would miss these sibling squabbles if they were gone.

"Wren, leave the poor couch pillow out of this." Julie grabbed a rag from the kitchen and tossed it onto the spill. As she began to peel away Ivy's sticky pajama top, her cell phone buzzed.

She knew the hearing had been scheduled for sometime last week, and she'd worked hard not to think about the call that would come any day now. When she'd first started fostering, she'd planned to go to all the hearings, but now she couldn't imagine sitting through a trial to decide their futures. She'd tear up the minute they showed those photos of Wren's bruises, and she didn't trust herself around the girls' mother, the one-woman explosive who'd inflicted all this damage. Not just physical damage either—the emotional wounds were perhaps worse.

Wren's school troubles had multiplied, and the twice-a-week play therapy they drove across town for didn't seem to be helping. While Julie flipped through three years' worth of *Prevention* magazine in the waiting area, the therapist took Wren into a special room with dolls and toys, where she supposedly acted out her emotions through play. Gave voice to her fears and released her anger, or something like that. The therapist kept assuring Julie that the sessions were going well, despite Wren's worsening aggression at school and increasing obstinance at home. But the only specifics the therapist could offer were things Julie already knew: Wren had abandonment issues and thought it was all her fault she'd lost her mother. Obviously. Without an adult taking care of her, the poor girl had been forced to carry all the weight of the grown-up world on her seven-year-old shoulders.

If the judge somehow decided to return the girls to their neglectful, abusive mother—well, Julie didn't know what she would do. But she didn't trust herself anywhere near that courtroom.

With a shaking hand, Julie picked up her cell. A pause, and then Rhonda's voice blared loud and staticky into her ear. "Sorry, didn't get a chance to call you last night because we had to race over to another emergency removal. But the hearing's done, and they're yours for another six months, at least. They're going to start visits with their grandmother, though . . ."

Rhonda kept talking, but Julie struggled to focus on her words. *Another six months.* Ivy was still clinging to her hip and whimpering, and after doing a halfhearted job of blotting up the milk, Wren had stormed upstairs. Julie didn't know how they'd get through the next six hours, let alone six months. But the girls she loved were safe, and they were one step closer to adoption.

When Julie hung up, all she could think about was Jake. The way he carried Ivy like a football and pretended to score touchdowns with her at the park, or how he always asked Wren what was happening in her current chapter book. How could he be so sweet with them, yet not want kids of his own? A tiny part of her wondered if, after spending two months with Wren and Ivy, he might have changed his mind. But then she remembered their first date, the conviction on his face when he said his ex-wife wanted something he could never give her: children.

Julie took a deep breath. She was both madly in love with Jake and desperately attached to her foster daughters. Now that she knew the girls weren't going home anytime soon, she had to stop avoiding the issue.

They needed to get out of the house anyhow—too much indoor time on Saturdays inevitably led to an explosion—so she called Jake and asked him to meet her at the new park on Yesler, the one with the big Astroturf hill the girls had been dying to slide down.

When they arrived, they found the playground deserted and messy. A light drizzle had soaked the sea of flattened boxes littered around the park—every kid brought a sheet of cardboard to ride down the hill, but not every kid remembered to take it home. Bathed in a cold gray fog, the park resembled a recycling center, but Wren and Ivy didn't care. Racing up the hill, they whooped as if Julie had brought them to Disneyland. Wren grabbed two of the soggy makeshift sleds and positioned them at the top.

Off to the side, Julie hopped from one foot to the other, keeping warm while burning off the nervous energy buzzing through her limbs. She kept scanning the parking lot for Jake's navy Prius, wondering what to say when he arrived. She'd tell him the results of the hearing, of course, but the conversation needed to go deeper than that. She needed to know where all this was going, whether he still saw a place for himself in her life, if that life might always include Wren and Ivy. Julie glanced back up at the girls, still negotiating on top of the hill. The wind carried their voices down to where she stood.

"Here, Ivy, sit on this." Wren held the scrap of cardboard still as her sister maneuvered onto it, encumbered by her oversize puffy coat and fuzzy mittens. Ivy plopped down twice on the fake grass, missing the cardboard altogether. But when she finally planted her tiny bottom in the very center of the cardboard sled, she lost her nerve.

"I go tummy." Ivy flopped onto her belly like a penguin, except feet first.

"No, on your bum. Like this." Wren sat down on her own corrugated square, gripped the sides tightly, and gave herself a push. She squealed as she picked up speed, the ends of her scarf flapping behind. Halfway down, the cardboard slid out from under her, and she tumbled to the bottom without it, laughing. "C'mon, Ivy, try it."

Still hesitant, Ivy lay on her belly at the top of the hill, ready to slide but unwilling—or unable—to loosen her hold on the fake grass. Wren scrambled up to help.

"Just. Let. Go," she said, trying to pry her sister's fingers loose.

"Wren, leave her be," Julie called. "If she's scared, she doesn't have to do it." If Wren pushed her sister past her comfort zone, Ivy would end up sobbing at the bottom, scared to death and wailing to go home.

But the wind had picked up, and Wren either didn't hear Julie or chose to ignore her. Lifting both of Ivy's hands at once, she gave a gentle push.

"Auuuuggghhh!" Ivy howled as she flew down the hill, and Julie sprinted to meet her, bracing for waterworks. At the bottom, Ivy stayed face down, completely still. So still Julie's heart skipped a beat. "Are you okay?"

Ivy sat up, cheeks red and windswept, eyes aglow. "Again, again!"

Julie laughed with relief as the girls scrambled up the hill once more. Turning her back on them for a moment, she took in the breathtaking view: to the left, the arches of the Seahawks stadium, and to the right, the jagged skyline of downtown. Across the glassy, gunmetal depths of the Puget Sound, Julie could just make out the snowcapped peaks of the Cascade Mountains. She took a deep breath, wishing she could stay in this moment forever.

When she glanced back at the girls, Jake had joined them. His tall lanky frame was silhouetted against the sky, feet spread apart and hands outstretched, poised to surf down the hill on his own cardboard scrap. Julie smirked—nothing more than an overgrown kid, that one.

"You're going to break your neck," she yelled into the wind, but Jake had already pushed off. Only a few feet down the hill, he hit a bump and began to wobble. He frantically windmilled his arms to regain balance, but it was no use: Jake's feet slid out from under him, and he crashed onto his tailbone, sending his makeshift surfboard shooting down the hill alone.

Laughing, Julie ran up the hill and held out her hand. "Nice moves, Lankowski."

Jake's pale blue eyes sparkled, and he clutched Julie's hand. But instead of trying to stand up, he pulled her down on top of him. "Anything to impress you," he said, his breath warm and fuzzy in her ear. Suddenly two hard thumps landed against Julie's back, as the girls leaped on top of her to join the family dogpile.

Family. Whether Jake liked it or not, the word felt right, and it warmed Julie from the inside, like a steaming mug of cocoa on a freezing winter's day.

—m—

The girls hardly left Jake's side at the playground, and a part of Julie felt relieved—maybe they wouldn't get a chance to talk today, after all. Then Jake suggested tacos for lunch, and he left his Prius parked on the street so they could ride together. By the time they arrived at the restaurant and peeked into the back seat, both girls had fallen asleep.

"They really can sleep anywhere, can't they?" Jake motioned to Wren, whose head lolled to the side. "What do you say we leave them here and go have a quiet lunch?"

Julie gaped at him, aghast and indignant, until she saw laughter at the corners of his mouth. "You jerk," she said. "You know that's how their mom lost them."

His smile faded. "Shouldn't joke about it. Sorry. Any updates?"

Julie nodded. "Rhonda called this morning with good news. They're with me for six more months, at least. Their mom's about to lose her house to foreclosure, and she hasn't been doing well in therapy. And—" Julie lowered her voice. "The judge thinks she's the one who gave Wren those bruises."

Jake let out a long whistle. "Jeez, that's intense. Poor lady."

"Poor girls, you mean. Their mother made her bed; now she gets to lie in it." Julie was surprised at the venom in her voice, but she'd been struggling to muster sympathy for this woman who'd abused and neglected the girls she loved. "If Hannah keeps screwing up, it won't be long until they terminate her rights."

They didn't talk for several moments, Jake staring out the window and Julie fiddling with the toggles on her wool coat. This was her moment, the perfect opportunity to ask what part he wanted to play in their fragile little family. But Julie's tongue turned thick and fuzzy, and she couldn't bring herself to break the silence.

Finally, with a sigh, Jake turned away from the window and took Julie's hand. The intensity of his expression scared her. "You know I love hanging out with you and the girls, right?" Julie focused intently on scraping a fleck of dirt from her jeans. "Wren and Ivy are the best, and the last two months have been amazing. It's just that—" Julie sucked in her breath and bit her lip to keep from crying. She recognized this scene, because she'd watched it play out so many times before, with Seth and all the others. This was the part where he'd call her a lovely person and say that never in a million years would he want to hurt her, but there was no use pretending to feel something he didn't. Jake was about to set her down gently but firmly and walk out of her life.

"They still belong to their mother."

Julie's head snapped up. These were not at all the words she'd expected, and for a second she didn't understand.

"They still need her," Jake continued. "They're not *yours*. You forget that sometimes."

Looking into Jake's eyes, Julie saw a mix of sadness, hesitation, even a bit of fear. She hated what he said, but she felt like laughing with relief: he was afraid to tell her what she didn't want to hear. Because he cared.

"I know they're not mine." The words caught in Julie's throat. "Or not yet, anyway. But their mother is a hot mess, and their grandmother is terrifying, so I'm all they've got right now." She turned and looked into the back seat. Ivy's head slumped at a painful-looking angle, and tiny snores escaped from her parted lips. Julie's voice wavered. "How am I supposed to love them the way they need to be loved without starting to think of them as mine?"

Jake turned back to the window. Outside the wind had picked up, bending the bare branches of the oaks lining the sidewalk and sending little twisters of brittle leaves into the air. "I don't know, Jules. But vilifying their mom isn't going to help. She has problems, no doubt, but obviously she did something right."

Julie cocked her head to the side, not following.

"The girls. They're awesome. Wren is the smartest, most self-reliant seven-year-old I've ever met, despite never going to school before now. I've seen her drawings, and the way she takes care of Ivy. You think she figured out how to read recipes and add quarter cups of flour all on her own?"

Julie frowned. She hadn't thought of it that way. "But Wren shouldn't need to know how to cook at her age. She shouldn't have to take care of her baby sister. That's her mom's job."

Jake's lips were pressed into a thin line, and there was a crease in his brow she'd never seen before. "And that's why the girls aren't back home yet. But their mom was depressed when all that happened, right? At some point the doctors are going to find the right blend of therapy and medication to make her better, and then don't you think she deserves to get her daughters back?"

Julie's eyes filled with tears. "Not if there's a chance she'll do it all over again. You didn't see those bruises." How could Jake be siding against her on this? "Wren is a great kid, sure, but she's got problems. She's hitting other kids at school, lashing out for no reason at all. Clearly her mom did the same thing to her."

Jake stayed silent for a second, then shook his head. "Maybe. Or maybe Wren's acting out because she misses her mom and feels abandoned. I don't want to fight about this, Jules, I really don't. But I'm not going to celebrate when some poor woman loses her kids."

"When did I say we were celebrating? You're twisting my—" Julie stopped, aware of her rising volume. Wren and Ivy stirred in the back seat, and she turned to face them. "Good afternoon, sleepyheads." Her voice sounded far sunnier than she felt. "Want to get some lunch?"

As usual, Ivy woke up grumpy from her nap, and now she kicked hard enough to send her Velcro shoes flying across the car. While Julie tried to calm her, Jake went around to unbuckle Wren's booster seat.

"Jesus, Wren." Jake sounded angry, and Julie froze. He never talked to the girls that way. "Were your straps too tight?"

Wren shrugged.

Leaving Ivy in her seat, Julie walked around the car to investigate. Jake's face looked even whiter than usual, and he was peering intently at Wren's shoulder. Beneath where the left booster strap had been, barely peeking out from her baggy sweatshirt, was an angry-looking welt. Jake gently pulled her sweatshirt aside, revealing a thick streak of reddish purple, like someone had swiped her shoulder with a paintbrush. The other side had a matching stripe of color, darker than the first. "Does it hurt?" Julie asked, touching one finger to Wren's bruised skin.

"It's nothing." Wren scowled and pulled the neck of her sweatshirt back up. "I always get bruises, didn't I tell you that?"

"But honey, just from your booster straps?" Julie had never heard of a child getting injured from sleeping in a car seat. "Maybe you bumped your shoulders sledding down the hill. Jake, do you think she could have?"

"Sure. Must've been the hill." Standing up, he made an exaggerated gesture with his hands, brushing one palm against the other to say "Case closed," subject no longer up for discussion. "Let's go get some lunch, then."

Julie opened her mouth to ask more questions, but Jake waggled his eyebrows and mouthed a silent "Not now."

As they crossed the street to the taco joint, Julie grabbed Ivy's hand. A neon sign flashed **WELCOME** in three colors, and a bell tinkled merrily as the door closed behind them. After the windy park, the warmth of the restaurant should have felt cozy, but somehow the scent of corn tortillas made Julie's stomach turn. Those bruises had left her rattled, and she didn't like the strange new tightness in Jake's jaw.

The waitress led them to a paper-lined table for four in the back. Once the girls were a safe distance ahead, Jake leaned over and whispered in her ear. "Abusive mom, my ass. That girl needs to see a hematologist. She's got some kind of bleeding disorder."

Twenty-Nine

Steve's letter pulsed against Elaine's chest as she hurried to the underground parking garage next to the courthouse. She propped it carefully on the passenger seat for the drive back to her hotel. Each time she glanced over, seeing *Hannah Montgomery* written in her husband's slanting scrawl sent her on a merry-go-round of emotions—excitement, then grief, then a bizarre gratitude toward Hannah for sharing this unexpected treasure.

But by the time she made it to her room, Elaine wasn't sure she wanted to read the letter after all. As long as she kept Steve's words tucked inside the envelope, a moment with her husband still waited for her in the future, instead of all their moments being frozen in the past. She leaned Steve's note against a fake fern on the dresser and carefully sorted through the rest of the letters, all written by teenage Hannah to her father. A collection of screeds detailing Elaine's dreadful parenting, somehow both neglectful and suffocating at once. Looking back, she wished she'd taken Hannah's volatile moods more seriously.

When she could stand no more emotional flogging, Elaine checked her voicemail—nothing from Rhonda about visits yet, but there was a polite decline from a law firm she'd contacted weeks ago. Pulling out her planner and a thick red pen, she started to cross another name off her to-do list, then stopped and laughed out loud. Fighting for her job didn't make sense anymore—like she'd told Judge Nakamura, she wasn't going back to Chicago. She ripped the entire page from her notebook, crumpled the list of lawyers into a ball, and tossed it in the trash.

More important things concerned her now, like getting the cabin ready for Wren and Ivy. She opened her laptop and pulled up the website for the construction company Steve had hired after he got sick. Remote forest living had never been on Elaine's bucket list, but now she found the idea appealing—making a home with her granddaughters in the last place Steve had worked and been happy. She imagined the look of surprise on his face, learning that she'd willingly moved to the woods. Except, no. Steve wouldn't be proud of her—he'd be appalled she'd taken the girls from Hannah.

Elaine's knees cracked as she stood up from the desk. Time to get outside—if she spent another day alone in this hotel, she'd think herself in circles.

—⁓—

The bell above the door of the construction office tinkled like a wind chime, its relaxed, beachy sound a sharp contrast to the horrid weather outside. The rain had stopped briefly while Elaine was on the ferry, but the wind had picked up so much she was afraid to venture onto the outer decks for fear of getting blown off the boat and into the choppy whitecaps below. She was one of about six passengers onboard—even the car decks were empty—and Langley had felt all but abandoned as she wandered the soggy streets. Such a change from the bustling springtime traffic of two years ago, when Steve had first brought her here, proselytizing about the healing properties of island life, on a mission to convince her to let him buy the cottage for Hannah and the girls.

As they'd driven down a narrow dirt road into the forest, tangles of blackberry bushes scraped the sides of their car. "She needs a project," Steve had insisted. "Something tangible that will get her out of the house and out of her head." Hopelessly optimistic, like most of Steve's plans, but even before she saw the house, Elaine wondered if he might be right. When her own thoughts turned dark and sour, the only thing that saved her was a tough case, the stickier and more complicated the better.

So, when the path finally opened into a clearing and Elaine spotted the crumbling cottage, it hadn't taken much convincing. Sure, the wraparound porch was half detached and two windows were broken on the second floor, but that was the point: the required work would help Hannah pull herself out of the abyss of grief.

Now, Elaine wandered the front office of Whidbey Design & Build, admiring their framed photos of sunset beach châteaus and glossy log cabins. "It would have worked, Steve," she muttered. "I know it would have."

"May I help you?" A buttery voice cut through her thoughts, and Elaine looked up to see a woman in violet cashmere stepping out from the back room. Not much younger than Elaine herself, judging from the deep wrinkles around the woman's eyes and mouth, but her easygoing charm seemed to epitomize island living. "Elizabeth Waters, office manager," she said, extending her hand. "Call me Bess. How can I help you?"

Elaine explained how she'd left messages but hadn't heard back. "I'm looking for a contractor to finish a project my husband started about eighteen months ago, a fixer-upper cottage off Lone Lake Road. He mentioned he'd gotten some help from you all on the roof and said you did quality work."

"Lone Lake Road." The woman cocked her head, as if scrolling back through past clients, then snapped her fingers. "Think I remember him—Sean, was it, or Sam?"

"Steve. But only a few months into the project, he was diagnosed with metastatic pancreatic cancer."

"Dear me." Bess's lined face crumpled in concern.

"Now I'm stuck with the unfinished cottage. My daughter and I have tried to spruce up bits and pieces—" It was true. Since arriving in Seattle, Elaine had snuck out to the island several times, and one afternoon she found paint cans stacked in the living room. On a whim, she'd picked up a brush. After a lifetime of working at a desk, watching the walls transform from dull gray plaster to a glimmering off-white had felt somehow miraculous. Not for the first time, Elaine wished she'd said yes to one of the hundred times Steve had asked if she wanted to help with his restoration projects. "But now I'm thinking of moving there, and I'm wondering how quickly a good contractor could get it ready."

Bess pursed her lips. "Construction can be slow this time of year, given the weather." She swept her hand toward the window, where rivulets of water cascaded down the glass, smudging out what should have been a majestic view of Puget Sound. "Want me to schedule one of the guys to come take a look?"

Elaine frowned. "Any chance someone is available today? I've got to get back to Seattle for my granddaughters." Elaine lowered her voice to a whisper. "They're in foster care right now, because my daughter is having some trouble. I flew in from Chicago to help, but I need the cabin finished quickly so the state will let the girls move in there with me."

Bess's eyes widened. "I mean, all of our contractors are busy, but my afternoon appointment canceled—suppose I could take a look myself." After locking the door of the office, Bess followed Elaine out to her rental car.

"It's really detail work at this point," Elaine told Bess as they climbed into the car. "Besides the kitchen, I'd say it's almost done."

But when they pulled up to the cottage, the property looked shabbier than Elaine remembered. A windstorm had uprooted two of the new saplings out front and blown over the pile of firewood she'd so carefully stacked against the western wall. Elaine's confidence flagged as they walked from room to room—the kitchen needed cabinets, the bathrooms needed sinks, and even her beloved paint job looked spotty in the gray light. She tried to imagine the cottage come summertime, with furniture in place and sunshine streaming through the windows. She could picture a grandmother here, puttering in the garden, baking blackberry pies, poring over jigsaw puzzles with the girls at the kitchen table.

But the woman in her imagination was plump and gray haired, smiling. Soft in all the ways she herself was sharp. Even after Bess pronounced the cabin "six weeks away from finished," Elaine felt deflated. Hard as she tried, she couldn't place herself in that idyllic island scene.

Thirty

Hannah went straight home from the hearing and flushed her new meds down the toilet. For the past ten weeks she'd done everything exactly according to their instructions—taken every mind-numbing pill, attended every worthless jabbering session they called therapy, visited her daughters on all the appropriately prescribed days under the appropriately prescribed supervision. She'd scrubbed her house until it shined and baked the CASA worker fricking brownies. But none of it mattered. Elaine had waved a single sheet of stolen pink paper in front of the judge, and he'd snatched her girls away for another six months.

"We have services to help you find housing," the judge had said, "but we can't help if you aren't honest about your needs." He still seemed irritated she'd kept her impending foreclosure under wraps, maybe because it showed she hadn't bought into the *just trust us* fairy tale everyone kept repeating ad nauseam. It was what Officer Perry had said on the morning of her arrest—"Calm down, miss. We're only trying to help"—and what every do-gooder in the system had echoed since: "We all have the same goal, we're here to help your family." Yeah, right. If the state wanted to help single, widowed mothers like herself, they could offer free universal childcare, or health insurance that didn't cost more than the monthly food bill— services that might have kept her daughters out of foster care in the first place. Now the state had added *find child-friendly apartment* and *get a job* to the list of things she needed to do before they'd even consider reunification.

Enough. Hannah wasn't going to follow their orders anymore; she'd find her own way to get her children back.

She longed to return to the mental state she'd been in before the girls were taken, when she'd had goals and plans and felt on top of the world. Right now her brain was too fuzzy to plan tonight's dinner, let alone figure out a strategy for fighting the system. To get clearheaded, she needed to ditch the mood stabilizers, and probably all those anger classes too. Instead of managing her anger, Hannah wanted to give it wings—wings that would propel the three of them to a new and better place where the Washington State authorities would never find them. Maybe Canada, or Fiji.

The day after the hearing, she showered and dressed like usual. For more than eight weeks, Friday mornings had meant group therapy at Presley. Because she didn't yet have any idea what to do instead, she pulled on leggings, wrapped a scarf around her hair, and took the bus south to Tukwila.

Perhaps if she'd been honest with the doctors, had shared even a fragment of her real feelings, the parade of cognitive behavioral therapy, interpersonal therapy, and mindfulness therapy might have done some good. As it was, the only sessions that felt remotely healing were the art therapy ones, where she saw a faint glimmer of her former self reflected in the colors she splashed across a canvas. In the other meetings, her initial half truths to Dr. Banning—coupled with the secrets she kept from Rhonda and the police—begat more and more lies, until Hannah could no longer keep straight what she'd told to whom. Was this the session in which she'd invented a kind older sister, who protected her all throughout childhood, only to die from breast cancer? Or the class when she'd ratted on her abusive cousin, a fictitious teenage menace lurking in dark closets and abandoned garages? Keeping track of her lies was exhausting, but it kept her mind off the freight train of real guilt weighing on her heart.

Today, same as always, an interminable gray drizzle accompanied Hannah from the bus stop to the hospital. By now she could find her way through the maze of corridors with her eyes closed, but she walked slowly, placing one foot in front of the other, in no hurry to start the two-hour snore session that always felt like four.

With each footfall, Dr. Banning's words from the hearing echoed in her head . . . *seems not entirely sure of her own story . . . telling stories to cover up her true pain.* What would it feel like to tell the truth for once, to bare her soft, wounded underbelly to a roomful of strangers? Well, not so much strangers anymore, after all they'd told her about their lives.

As her fingers hovered over the handle of 1309B, an old memory of her mother flashed in her head. "Gotta give the world what it wants to see," Elaine had said.

Four or maybe five years old, little Hannah had been watching in the bathroom mirror as Elaine squeezed her long black eyelashes between the silver pads of what appeared to be a Byzantine torture device. "Doesn't that hurt, Mommy?" No reply, so Hannah pressed further. "Why are you doing that?"

"Just putting on my face, sweetie. Every day before I step out this door—makeup, hair, and a smile. Gotta give the world what it wants to see."

Elaine's edict went far beyond eyelashes: what the world *didn't* want to see was young Hannah's tears or tantrums or whining. By grade school, Hannah had become an expert at burying her feelings, and even now, she found it hard to excise the core beliefs that lay beneath Elaine's perfect mask. Despite losing her husband, her father, and now her girls, Hannah still tried to give the world what it wanted to see: a clean house, artfully designed craft projects, homemade brownies.

Now, whipping open the door and storming into the room, she wanted to cram those brownies in Dr. Banning's face—of course he had to be the therapist in charge of today's session. She dropped herself into the one remaining seat with enough force to make the metal rungs clatter. Heads snapped up around the room, and Dr. Banning raised his eyebrows.

"So glad you could make it."

Hannah glared at him, but he gave her a placid smile.

"We've been going around the room, each naming a feeling that's come up for us in the past week, and how we've handled it. Why don't you go next?"

Before she could stop herself, Hannah blurted out the truth. "I'm angry."

Dr. Banning beamed, as if her simple words represented a breakthrough. "Good. Very good. And tell us, how have you been handling this emotion?"

She ignored his follow-up question. "I'm angry at people who demand the truth, yet don't tell the truth themselves." A knot tightened in her belly as she recalled his calm, clear voice from the witness stand, pronouncing her *not stable enough.*

"Do you want to say more?" Dr. Banning glanced at the curious faces around the room.

Hannah took the bait. "Yes, Doctor, I want to say more. More about how you betrayed my confidence and testified against me yesterday. More about how you pretend to know exactly what's going on inside my head, and now I can't get my girls back. More about how you violated the promise you made to all of us when we started here, to keep everything in this room *confidential.*" She spat out the last word, relishing the surprise on the faces of her therapy mates.

"Hannah." Dr. Banning's voice was infuriatingly calm. "By law I'm required to disclose medical information to the court when—"

"Whatever. I'm angry. Next person."

The doctor frowned, then forced his face back to its usual mask of tranquility. "Wait. Let's go deeper into this anger, find out what it's trying to tell us." A wave of nods traveled around the room. Hannah stared at her lap, hoping silence would convince Dr. Banning to move on. "Hannah, try closing your eyes and letting yourself *feel* the anger, really feel it. What color is it? Now, dive deeper, way down into the center of the anger, and tell us what you find."

She rolled her eyes. Once Dr. Banning got started, there was nothing to do but play along. "Fine," she said, keeping her eyes wide open. "Let's dive deep. How about we dive straight down to fathers who promise to be there, always, right before they go and fucking *die*?" Hannah glared around the room, her rage feeding on all the kind, concerned expressions reflecting back at her. "Or even deeper, to husbands who don't do shit around the house, ever, but then complain about dishes piling up in the sink. Husbands who fly into a rage when you ask for a little help, who get angry enough to speed straight into a drunk driver, sentencing you to a lifetime of guilt." Admitting the truth felt reckless and thrilling, like skiing downhill wearing a blindfold. Her voice rose with each sentence, and once she got going, she found she couldn't stop.

"Yeah, Doctor. Let's dive deep. Down, down, down, to where the real dirt lies, to mothers who care more about themselves than their children, to a mother who can't stop telling her little girl she isn't good enough, smart enough, *driven* enough, until no one needs to tell her anymore. Because now she tells herself every damned day." Hannah took a gulp of air, and in the momentary silence, one woman started to clap. Others joined in, and Hannah felt a strange sense of freedom as she studied the faces around her, people she'd looked at for months but never really seen.

"You go, girl," the woman said. "That's the first real thing you've said to us. But—" She turned to Dr. Banning. "What's all this crap about confidentiality?"

The group veered off in a new direction, and Hannah sat stunned and silent. Where had all that garbage about Elaine come from? Hannah was livid about the foreclosure notice, sure, but why had she gone off on a tangent about her childhood? She'd buried those hurts years ago. But in the midst of her rant, Hannah realized something important: Alex and her father had *died*, yet she was still mad as hell they'd abandoned her. No doubt it would be the same for Wren and Ivy, regardless of how hard she fought to get them back. Years from now, they wouldn't blame CPS or Rhonda or Julie for this mess. In their minds, it would all boil down to one thing: Mommy left me.

Hannah couldn't afford to waste more time waiting on the court. No matter what it took, she had to get them back, and soon.

—॥—

The minute she got home, Hannah began throwing clothes into a bag and gathering up the girls' favorite toys. She considered googling "best place to hide from CPS," but anything she searched would show up later when the detectives started looking. If only they could hide out at the Whidbey cottage, safe among the trees and tucked away from the world—but the cops would find them there in minutes. And flying wasn't an option: they'd trace the airline records and come whisk the girls away before she finished unpacking. In the end, Hannah decided on La Paz, Mexico. Sunny, cheap, and two thousand miles away—and accessible by Volvo.

The biggest hurdle would be figuring out how to sneak off with the girls quietly to give themselves at least a few hours' head start before the authorities started looking. A tricky challenge, given that the judge had refused to lift the supervision order and she had no way to see the girls by herself.

As Hannah racked her brain for a plan, she scribbled checklists of everything she needed to do: change the oil and put air in the tires; get the girls' passports out of the safe deposit box; learn Spanish. Earn Julie's trust. Hannah kept the lists in her pocket at all times, lest she accidentally leave one behind and give a clue to their whereabouts. Perhaps she should have felt terrified as she contemplated becoming a fugitive, but each day that Hannah skipped her pills, she felt better by degrees. Even her mother couldn't dampen her spirits: sure, Elaine had enrolled in the kinship care training program and was about to start weekly visits, but what did it matter? Hannah and the girls would be long gone before she had time to finish the program or find a place to live.

By midweek, Hannah's mood had lifted, her mind cleared, and the thousand miles of I-5 south sparkled like the yellow brick road.

Thirty-One

Julie pushed the refried beans around on her plate with the back of a spoon, mashing them against mounds of tomato-orange rice, shredded lettuce, and pico de gallo until her salad became an unidentifiable brown mush. Every few seconds she glanced at Jake, searching for clues to what might be going on behind those ice-blue eyes. His jaw still held a curious tightness, but he smiled at the girls as they chattered away, devouring their crispy tacos and blissfully unaware of the tension. Ivy had somehow covered herself in refried beans, and Julie dabbed a napkin into her water glass to wipe the toddler's face. "You've even got beans on your forehead," she said, forcing a laugh.

Julie longed to ask Jake more questions, and his fierce whisper still burned in her ear: *She's got some kind of bleeding disorder.* What if the dramatic purple splotches signaled some mysterious virus or nutritional deficiency, or God forbid, cancer? But Wren had been so nonchalant, saying she'd bruised like this her whole life, nothing special, and Jake would have rushed her to the hospital if he thought the marks required urgent care.

The alternative scared Julie almost as much: if something as minor as tight booster seat straps had left strangle marks on Wren's neck, then the ghastly bruises on her back might have come from an equally innocuous situation. Like slipping off a stepladder—what Wren had been telling them all along.

Julie pulled out her phone and held it in her lap, staring at the blank screen. Part of her wanted to duck into a bathroom stall and call Rhonda for reassurance. "Impossible," the caseworker would say, in the same brash, confident tone she always used. "The doctors ran all the tests." But what if they hadn't? What if this new information changed everything and meant the girls should be returned to their mother immediately?

Jake might be wrong, though; she might take Wren to a hematologist only to discover her blood clotted just fine. Besides, last time she'd frantically called Rhonda with a problem—bumping into Elaine in the grocery store—the caseworker had bitten her head off. Julie squared her shoulders and slid the phone back into her pocket.

—⁂—

Later, after they'd parked the girls in front of a movie and were cleaning the kitchen, Julie asked Jake to help get Wren an appointment. "Just to check it out," she said, stacking clean bowls from the dishwasher onto the counter. "You know better than anyone who to contact."

"I can make a few calls, but shouldn't you be coordinating this with Rhonda and DSHS?" She hated the sympathetic, knowing look in Jake's eyes—as if he could see into her head and already knew how much the fear of losing the girls was driving her decisions.

"No sense bothering Rhonda unnecessarily." Julie kept her voice light and airy as she sorted spoons into the drawer. "Not until we know what's going on."

Jake stopped unloading dishes and turned to face her. "What's going on is that Wren's blood isn't clotting right, and she's bleeding into her soft tissues with even minimal trauma. Those bruises aren't normal."

"Right. You're the expert." Julie dropped a pile of forks into the drawer with a clatter.

"Well, yeah. I'm a pathologist; I spend all day looking at tissues and—"

"*Dead* tissues." Julie slammed the butter knives one by one into their slot. "I may not have medical training, but don't forget, I'm the one who's been her mom for the past eleven weeks—" Her eyes filled with tears, and she had to gulp down a lump in her throat to keep going. "I've driven her a hundred times in that booster seat. If there was a problem with her blood, I would've noticed more bruises by now."

Even as Julie said it, she wasn't sure it was true. Wren had been guarded from the moment she arrived, never wanting to bathe or change clothes with Julie in the room. If Wren had been getting new bruises all along, she could have missed them.

"Jules." Jake's tone sounded conciliatory, and as he wrapped his arms around her, Julie leaned into the hug, assuming he was about to apologize.

"I know this is hard, but you've got to call Rhonda. This could change everything."

His arms felt suddenly heavy, a lead blanket dragging her down. Julie shrugged out of his embrace and took a step backward. "Probably suits you just fine, this new development."

Jake gave her a blank look, which Julie found infuriating. How could he pretend he hadn't noticed what they'd been avoiding all these months? "I know you don't want kids, so if Wren and Ivy go back to their mom, you're thinking maybe this will solve our little dilemma." She turned back to the silverware so she wouldn't have to see his face. "You'd get to have a *normal* girlfriend, one who can stay out late and have movie marathons and take weekend ski trips to the mountains."

"What are you talking about? I never said I wanted—"

"But you're wrong. Losing Wren and Ivy won't solve anything between us." A fat tear rolled down Julie's cheek and into the corner of her mouth, spreading salt across her tongue. "Being a mom is hard and messy and nothing like I expected—but it's still what I want. If fostering has taught me anything, it's that I'm done changing who I am for other people. For once in my dismal, disappointing life, I'm doing something that matters. And I won't give it up just because my workaholic boyfriend doesn't want kids."

Julie took a shaky breath, waiting for Jake to respond. But when she finally glanced up, he had turned his back on her and was calmly stacking glasses in the sink. For the first time since they'd been dating, he reminded her of Seth, stonewalling instead of talking through a problem. "If you have nothing else to say," she snapped, "maybe you should go."

Jake froze, his fingers clutching a wineglass in midair over the sink. She held her breath, waiting for him to contradict her, to say their relationship was worth saving no matter what it took. To say he loved the girls as much as she did, and that he'd be devastated to lose them, if it came to that in the end.

But he only said two words: "Call Rhonda." Then, wiping his hands on his jeans, he walked past her out of the kitchen. Seconds later, the quiet click of the front door confirmed he'd left, without so much as a word to Wren and Ivy in the living room.

Julie held back an angry sob. Perhaps she was being unfair, punishing Jake for something that wasn't his fault, but at this point she didn't care. He no longer seemed like her dear, sweet childhood friend, or the hot new boyfriend she couldn't keep her hands off. He'd become a slippery snake, trying to force her to take a bite of knowledge that would tear apart her world. Wiping away her tears, she resolved to make a doctor's appointment for Wren—with her regular pediatrician, in case she was really sick. But she wouldn't call Rhonda. Not until she had concrete news to share.

—⁓—

Julie didn't hear from Jake for the rest of the weekend. Monday she left a message for the pediatrician, but the doctor didn't call back. Probably too busy dealing with real emergencies—they'd get back to her eventually.

A hundred times that week she considered calling Jake, but each time she stopped herself. His words looped over and over in her mind—*abusive mom, my ass*—but Julie couldn't agree. She remembered the way Wren took care of Ivy when they first arrived, more mother than sister, and how they'd never had a proper bedtime or set foot in school. Wren had regularly wandered off in the neighborhood, not understanding why it was a problem, completely oblivious to the notion that a seven-year-old could rely on adults to help her navigate the world. Whether she'd been physically abused was almost beside the point; nothing could change the fact that the girls had been taken into custody for severe neglect.

But she couldn't believe Jake hadn't called to apologize. On Thursday, when the doorbell rang unexpectedly during dinner, she knew it had to be him. Her heart beat furiously as she glanced at her unshowered reflection in the hallway mirror. She tugged out her ponytail elastic and tried to fluff her hair. But Jake wouldn't care; on the other side of that door he was probably in scrubs himself, straight from the hospital and carrying conciliatory flowers. Julie took a deep breath and told herself to be strong. Before diving into his arms, she needed to make sure he understood her point of view.

Except when the door swung open, it wasn't Jake, but a stranger: a tall thin woman with giant aqua sunglasses and a checkered scarf wrapped twice around her honey-colored hair. She pulled off the glasses to reveal blue-gray eyes that were achingly familiar. "You must be Julie."

Julie's hand flew to her chest. "Hannah?" There was no one else this woman could be, not with those eyes, but she looked nothing like the struggling, beleaguered mother Julie had imagined. Instead of greasy-haired and twitchy, with bags under her eyes and dirty fingernails, this woman looked like she'd just stepped off the set of *Thelma & Louise*. As Julie was trying to recover enough to say something, Ivy burst out of the kitchen and ran straight to her mother, burying her face in Hannah's bony thighs.

"Hi there, love bug." Even Hannah's voice was a surprise: low and scratchy, but comforting like the purr of a cat. She stroked Ivy's head and waved to Wren, hanging back in the kitchen doorway.

"How did you—I mean—did Rhonda—?" Julie couldn't think straight; there was no protocol for when a biological mother randomly showed up on a foster parent's doorstep, because it wasn't supposed to happen. The social workers had promised to keep Julie's contact information, especially her address, strictly confidential.

"Yeah, Mommy, what are you doing here? It's not a visit day." Wren came to stand next to Julie, eyeing her mother suspiciously. Hannah had picked up Ivy and was nuzzling her hair.

"Sorry to interrupt your evening. I happened to be driving through the neighborhood and saw Wren's scooter out front. Of course I recognized the basket—what are the chances of another little girl painting the exact same *Batgirl* logo on a shoebox? And then . . ." Hannah trailed off, looking sheepish. She set Ivy back down on the stoop.

Julie didn't want to appear unwelcoming, but this story seemed far-fetched. "Girls, why don't you go inside for a minute? If we leave the door open like this, Popsicle will get out." Against their protests, Julie herded Wren and Ivy into the house, then stepped back outside and closed the door—unsure whether to let Hannah in or ask her to go away until she could discuss this bizarre situation with Rhonda.

But then Hannah pressed her hands to her cheeks and started over. "Okay, wait. None of that was true." She took a deep breath. "The truth is, I overheard Rhonda say your name on the phone, in the courthouse bathroom after the very first hearing. I tracked down your address months ago."

Julie's eyes widened, imagining Hannah peeking out from behind bushes and darting down alleyways, stalking their every move for the past three months.

"Don't worry," Hannah said quickly. "I only came here once, in the beginning, because I needed to know—" Her voice caught. "I needed to know my girls were okay. But as soon as I saw how good you are with them, I stopped following you. I swear."

Julie swallowed hard. Hannah had no right to come to her house, but Julie might have done the same thing in her position. And she couldn't help feeling touched by the compliment. "Why are you here now?"

"I need to talk to you about something that happened at the hearing, with my mother."

Before Hannah could elaborate, Wren poked her head out the door. "Can Mom come inside and see my *Kitty Girl* book?" She stepped onto the porch, then squealed as her bare toes hit the icy concrete.

"I mean, I don't want to intrude—" Hannah said.

But what choice did Julie have? It was February, and Hannah's lips had already turned blue from the cold. Of course she should come in, and once she was inside, of course she should visit the girls' bedroom and see their artwork and help them climb into their pajamas. Julie didn't know how to be anything but welcoming.

As Wren and Ivy led their mother through the house, Julie cringed at the mess. Hannah was the one being monitored by CPS, but tonight, with her inquisitive eyes traveling over every surface of the unprepped house, it was Julie's mothering on trial. Hannah stepped over a pair of Ivy's dirty underpants, and Julie snatched them up. "Oh, gosh, sorry."

Hannah smiled. "No apology necessary. I know exactly how it goes." Her gaze landed on the cluster of family photos on the hallway table, young Julie and Drew with their parents. She picked up a frame, wiped a finger along the dusty top edge, and replaced it. "Did the girls tell you I used to be a family photographer? Until my husband died. Then I couldn't stand all those happy families."

"Um, no. They didn't mention it." Julie knew Wren and Ivy had lost their father a few years back, but she'd never considered what that must have been like for Hannah.

Despite Julie's best intentions, she found it hard to hate this woman. The girls dragged their mother into the bedroom, excited to show off their matching comforters and the dollhouse Anitha had given them for Christmas. As Julie watched the three of them cuddle together on Ivy's bed, flipping through the sixteen pages of Wren's comic-in-progress, they looked so similar she wanted to cry. Hannah's snub nose matched Ivy's, and Wren had clearly inherited her mother's olive undertones. But looking alike didn't mean they belonged together, did it? Not if Hannah couldn't take care of them properly.

Julie checked her watch, ready for this surprise visit to be over. She was relieved when the girls were finally tucked into bed, and Hannah suggested she get going. "I'll see you this weekend," she told Wren and Ivy, planting a kiss on each of their foreheads before turning out the lights. "For our zoo trip."

Back downstairs in the entryway, Hannah seemed nervous. "Sorry again for barging in like this. But I wanted to warn you, in case Rhonda hasn't said anything—my mother is trying to get custody."

Julie clutched the sippy cup she'd carried down from the girls' bedroom. Rhonda had mentioned the girls' grandmother would be starting weekly visits, but she hadn't said anything about wanting permanent custody. "Wait, isn't she just visiting? I thought she lived in Chicago."

"Yes, but Elaine is a force of nature. She gets what she wants." Hannah looked Julie straight in the eyes, her blue-gray irises rimmed with red. "Look, Rhonda has probably convinced you that I'm a terrible parent, but the truth is, I want what's best for Wren and Ivy. Given that my mother had no interest in parenting me when I was a kid, I have no idea why she's desperate for granddaughters now. If the choice is between you or Elaine, I'd rather have the girls with you. They seem happy here." Hannah grabbed Julie's hand and pressed a slip of paper between her fingers. "My phone number. If you hear anything about Elaine, or if there's anything I can do to help, call me."

Before Julie could respond, Hannah had let go of her hand and darted out the door. Halfway down the sidewalk, she turned back. "Tell the girls I love them and I'll see them Saturday."

Julie stood on the doorstep and watched her drive away, struggling to reconcile the Hannah she'd imagined with the Hannah she'd just met. *If the choice is between you or Elaine, I'd rather have the girls with you.* Julie hated to admit it, but Jake was right—Hannah seemed less like an abusive monster and more like a loving mom who'd been through a tremendously tough time. As Julie typed Hannah's number into her phone, she decided maybe Hannah deserved a bit more credit. Maybe they were on the same side after all.

Thirty-Two

As Elaine pulled into the Family First Visitation Center, tucked into a strip mall off Aurora Avenue, her clammy hands left prints on the steering wheel.

Steve used to claim that no matter how big of a case she was prosecuting—no matter what big-name newspaper interviewed her, or which steel-spined judge she had to face—Elaine never sweated a drop. "You should be an antiperspirant ad," he'd tease. It wasn't that anxious thoughts never popped into her mind; she was just an expert at blocking them out. Before a trial, she'd let herself envision all the possible outcomes, good and bad. Then, one by one, she'd take each negative scenario and snuff it out in her mind—poof, fade to black, not going to happen.

But today, facing the prospect of two hours with Wren and Ivy, all those visualization techniques failed her. She'd wanted to take the girls somewhere educational, like the flight museum or the Museum of History and Industry, but apparently the girls' foster mom had objected, saying it might be "too much" for a first visit, and Rhonda had agreed. "It's been a while since you've spent time with them, right?" she'd asked.

Elaine knew exactly how long it had been, because it was the same amount of time Steve had been gone, and despite her best efforts, she couldn't seem to stop counting. To Rhonda, she only shrugged. "About a year, maybe. Not that long." But a year was half a lifetime for a toddler, and in the grocery store, Ivy hadn't even seemed to remember her.

The visitation center looked incredibly boring, sandwiched between a dry cleaner and a diagnostic radiology center whose banner advertised affordable colonoscopies. What would Elaine do with the girls here, for two whole hours? Rhonda had assured her the center would have toys, but Elaine cringed at the thought of grubby, germ-covered plastic. A colonoscopy might be preferable.

Inside, a receptionist guided Elaine down a long hallway and into a brightly lit room. Wren sat on a striped couch, looking forlorn, while Ivy played with a dollhouse—ugly and plastic, as expected, but so clean it looked practically new. From the acidic sting in her nose, Elaine guessed they scrubbed the whole place down with antiseptic wipes between each visit. She felt relieved, until she saw the mousy woman from the grocery store crouched on the floor next to Ivy. When she saw Elaine, she leaped up and stuck out her hand.

"I didn't know you'd be here," Elaine said. "I thought my visits were unsupervised." She glanced toward a large mirrored window, likely one-way glass. The whole room had a big-brother feel, and she glared at the receptionist. For the next visit, she'd insist on a museum.

"Julie wanted to wait until you arrived and the girls got comfortable," the receptionist said, "and don't worry about the mirror. Your visits are indeed unsupervised, although we're always here to help." Elaine couldn't imagine what kind of help she'd need from a receptionist, and she was eager to get Julie out the door so she could be alone with the girls.

"Here, I brought you a little something." After meeting with Bess at the construction office again yesterday, she'd stopped in downtown Langley. Unfortunately the toy store had closed by then, and the only open shop sold handblown glass. Even Elaine knew buying glass for a three-year-old was a bad idea, but the paperweights were smooth and sturdy, with ribbons of color reminiscent of seagrass in a tide pool. She'd picked up stone after stone, wishing she knew the girls' favorite colors and debating whether to get two of the same color, so they couldn't fight, or different ones, so each one felt special. This was why she'd never been good at parenting—too many choices, too many ways to go wrong.

Now Ivy seemed more excited by the tissue paper than by the gift, and once Wren offered a polite "Thank you," there wasn't much more to say about a clear glass stone. Elaine noticed Wren kept holding hers, though, flipping it over and over in her hands. Once Julie left the room, she turned directly to her grandmother.

"You're not trying to take us, are you?"

Elaine suppressed a smile. Exactly why Wren had always been her favorite: she didn't beat around the bush. "I'm not trying to 'take' you. I'm just trying to figure out the best place for you to live. Under the circumstances, that best place might be with me."

"But you live in Chicago." Wren slid forward on the couch and picked up a box of Jenga blocks from the table. She set the paperweight aside and dumped out the wooden pieces with a clatter.

"Not anymore," Elaine said, picking up a block and twirling it between her fingers. "I might move to Grandpa's cabin on Whidbey Island. Would you like that?"

Instead of answering, Wren snatched back Elaine's Jenga piece and added it to her quickly growing tower. When she'd used up all the blocks, she picked up the paperweight and carefully balanced it on top. "It's not Grandpa's cabin anymore. It's Mom's, and we were helping—"

The tower began to lean precariously, and Elaine rescued the paperweight just before the blocks fell, scattering across the floor and table. At the sound of the crash, Ivy leaped up from her dollhouse, tripped over a truck on the floor, and catapulted into Elaine's lap. Instead of scrambling away, she sat there for a moment, eyeing the glasses on a string around Elaine's neck.

"Me wear?" She reached out a tentative finger and gave the glasses a tap.

Elaine's first instinct was to push Ivy away—her glasses cost hundreds of dollars, and wire frames bent so easily—but it had been a long time since she'd had a child in her lap, all warm and wiggly. "Sure, try them on." Pulling the string over her head, she positioned the glasses on Ivy's nose. "Just be careful."

The lenses made Ivy's round blue eyes look even rounder, and Wren giggled. "You look like a bug." Which of course made Ivy leap up from Elaine's lap and start flying herself around the room, buzzing and flapping. Elaine wanted to chase after her and snatch the glasses away, but she heard Steve's voice in her head, from a hundred years ago when Hannah was small: "Let her play, Elaine. It's like you see a child having fun and instantly assume they're about to break something."

Elaine stood up from the couch and tentatively lifted her own arms. She could do this, really she could. Steve wasn't here to be the fun grandparent, so she'd have to take on his role, winning over Wren and Ivy's hearts the way she'd never been able to win Hannah's. Stretching her arms wide, she began to flap, first slowly and then with vigor. "Bzz, bzz," she tried. "Watch out for Grandma bug." Still waving her arms, she began to chase Ivy around the room, sidestepping the plastic land mines strewn across the floor. "Wren, join us. I can't be out here looking ridiculous by myself." She held out her hand, and although Wren took it reluctantly, in only a minute all three of them were zooming around the room, buzzing and flapping and laughing.

"Grandma bug is a tickle bug!" Elaine cried, reaching out just as both girls ran past in opposite directions. Wren swerved right as Ivy swerved left—and they collided with a sickening crunch. Elaine was devastated at the state of her reading glasses, until she saw Wren's hand clapped across her face, blood oozing between her fingers.

"My loof toof," Wren said, hardly understandable through her mouthful of blood. Panicking, Elaine snatched up her handbag and dug frantically for tissues but came up empty. "Help," she hollered at the one-way mirror. "Tooth emergency!" More blood dribbled down Wren's chin, and Elaine backed away, feeling faint. Wren grabbed the only absorbent material in sight, which unfortunately happened to be her grandmother's cardigan, thrown over the arm of the couch.

"Wait, that's cashmere—"

Wren stuffed the pale-yellow sweater into her mouth, just as Julie came charging into the room with ice and towels.

So much for the unsupervised visit. Apparently the foster mom had been watching through the window the entire time, despite her promise to leave them be. Elaine glared at Julie, who held a small white tooth and pressed a towel firmly into the new gap in Wren's smile.

"That tooth had been loose for weeks," Julie said. "I should have warned you."

Elaine sighed, holding up the ruined cashmere, destined for the same garbage can as her broken glasses. She checked the clock and shook her head. Somehow less than thirty minutes had gone by, and already she wanted a break. Of course, she'd never admit that to perky Julie, who must have witnessed the entire ridiculous buzzing bee routine and now got to jump in and play rescuer. "Wren," Elaine asked, nudging Julie aside so she could stroke her granddaughter's hair. "Is this your first lost tooth?"

Wren nodded, unable to talk through a mouthful of terry cloth.

"Ooh," Julie said. "Then it's the first time you'll get a visit from the tooth fairy."

Wren rolled her eyes and temporarily removed her gag. "Uh-huh. Except I hear she's busy these days, helping the Easter Bunny."

"Stop talking," Julie said, grabbing a new towel and reapplying pressure. "You're making the bleeding worse."

A fresh red trickle down Wren's chin sent Elaine's blood pressure tanking a second time, but even as she slumped onto the couch, she had to grin: of course Wren was too sensible to believe in the tooth fairy. Hannah hadn't believed in that nonsense either.

—⁓—

That night, Elaine couldn't fall asleep. She'd finished one romance and started another, but the words kept swimming in front of her eyes as her mind drifted back to her disastrous visit with the girls. Sure, they'd had some moments of silliness and bonding, but if Elaine was completely honest with herself, the girls had exhausted her—and she hadn't even spent the full two hours with them. Decades ago, Elaine had found parenting one child a challenge, even with help from her stay-at-home husband. Now she somehow expected to manage—alone—with two? Hannah's words again echoed in her mind: *What would you have done if Dad hadn't been there to take care of me all those years?*

With a grunt, Elaine threw off the covers and hobbled over to find Steve's letter in her briefcase, right next to Wren's stolen file and all her notes about the case. She felt stuck at some kind of crossroads, a densely wooded one where every path forward was blocked from view. Before she could stop herself, Elaine slid the faded lined paper from its envelope, hoping this decades-old letter could somehow guide her. As she scanned down the page, her throat tightened. Steve had been writing to teenaged Hannah, but his words seemed aimed straight at Elaine.

You have no idea how similar you two are, and maybe that's why you fight so much. I've never met a pair more unwilling to compromise, nor so uncompromisingly passionate about their work. You see your art and your mother's legal profession as polar opposites, but I look at the way you approach your canvas and can't think of anything except your mom's intensity and drive. Someday, Hannah, after you've matured enough to see your mother's strengths, and she's learned to let go of trying to control your life, maybe you'll finally see each other the way I do.

The last line was the hardest to bear: Just you wait. Years from now, you'll become each other's fiercest friend. Elaine's mind flashed back to the courtroom scene, Hannah's angry outbursts and her own calm betrayal, marching that foreclosure notice up to the judge. Wherever Steve was now, she hoped he hadn't been watching.

Thirty-Three

It took almost an hour for Wren's gums to stop bleeding, and each time Julie pulled the towel away to find more bright-red blood, her jaw clenched tighter. Lost teeth shouldn't bleed this much. She'd almost decided to take Wren to urgent care when the rag finally came away clean. By that point, most of the allotted visit time had been used up, and Elaine seemed annoyed by Julie's presence. By the end she became downright hostile, snapping at Ivy for bouncing too close to Wren and griping about her ruined glasses. Honestly, what did Elaine expect, letting a three-year-old play with wire frames? Hannah was right—Elaine hardly seemed prepared to parent little girls.

As the receptionist sealed Wren's tooth in a clear plastic baggie for her to take home, Julie brainstormed possible prizes she could scrounge up on short notice. Wren might not believe in the tooth fairy, but Julie didn't believe in ignoring a big milestone like losing your first tooth. Wren looked so different with her new gap-toothed smile—Hannah would be shocked at her next visit. Which, Julie realized, was tomorrow. Now that both Elaine and Hannah had weekly visits, plus the mandated play therapy and school five days a week, the girls' schedule was entirely too crowded. Tomorrow, while Wren and Ivy were gone, Julie would call Rhonda to ask if they could scale back Elaine's visits—and maybe casually mention the tooth that wouldn't stop bleeding.

Saturday morning, the girls were cranky and sluggish as Julie dressed them for the zoo. Wren refused to brush her teeth for fear of making her gums bleed again, and Ivy insisted on wearing shorts and a tank top despite the forty-degree weather. Julie eventually caved and let her wear the summer clothes, but only if she'd layer fleece leggings and a sweater underneath.

Irena was supposed to pick up the girls at ten o'clock sharp, but by 10:10 she still hadn't arrived. Julie opened the shades on the front window so the girls could keep watch, and as they pressed their noses to the glass, fat raindrops began to fall. Then it was 10:15, and 10:20, and still no Irena. Julie checked her phone—one missed call and a text: Car trouble. Should probably cancel the visit. Julie sighed. This wasn't the first time Irena had changed plans last minute. "It's not the end of the world," Julie told the girls, gesturing toward the window. "You'd have gotten soaked." Ivy groaned, but Wren seemed relieved to stay indoors, especially when Julie suggested a Guess Who? marathon.

Halfway through the second game, the doorbell rang. "Zoo, zoo, zoo!" Ivy squealed.

"No, Ivy," Julie said. "Irena's car isn't working today, remember?"

But when Julie answered the door, she found Hannah on the stoop, grinning broadly. Despite the same checkered scarf around her hair, she looked far less glamorous today. She clutched a windbreaker over her head like a makeshift umbrella, and wet strands of blonde hair clung to her forehead. "Who's ready for the zoo?" she asked, and the girls cheered. "Irena asked me to pick them up—she got a flat tire, but she's putting on a spare and said she'll meet us at the zoo as soon as she can."

"That's strange," Julie said, ushering Hannah inside. "I thought Irena said we were canceling. She sent me a text." Julie checked her phone but found only the same message from before: Should probably cancel . . . Well, Irena didn't say they were *definitely* canceling.

"She sent me one too," Hannah said, "but I told her I couldn't bear to miss my visit, and I'd be happy to pick up the girls. Didn't she tell you?"

Julie shook her head.

Hannah shrugged. "Maybe her phone died or something."

Indeed, missed communications seemed to be the norm in social services. Reluctantly, Julie collected the girls' coats and the backpacks she'd loaded up with water bottles, trail mix, packs of tissue, and even a ten-dollar bill zipped into each front pocket, in case Hannah hadn't budgeted for the entrance fee. But as she handed over the packs, a little alarm bell began to ding inside her head—was she really allowed to let the girls go unsupervised with Hannah? She didn't want to seem paranoid, especially when Hannah had just started to trust her, but she also didn't want to get in trouble. "Are you sure it's even worth going in this weather?" Julie asked. "You wouldn't rather stay here and join our board game tournament?"

Hannah held up her phone. "Rain's supposed to clear in thirty minutes. By the time we get there and buy our tickets, the sun will be shining." Ivy and Wren were already dancing around their mother, too excited to put on their shoes.

"Why don't I drive the girls to the zoo, then, and you can follow in your car," Julie suggested. Hannah gave her a blank look. "I mean, that way they'll be in their proper car seats."

Hannah's face turned red, and Julie instantly regretted her awkward phrasing. "I'm their mother," Hannah said. "Obviously I have 'proper' car seats for them."

"Right. Of course." There was no graceful way to explain. "It's just—I mean—in training, they said we're always supposed to supervise, and—"

"Wren-baby, your tooth!" Hannah had apparently just noticed the gap in her daughter's smile, and Julie was grateful for the interruption.

Wren gave her mother a wide snaggletoothed grin. "It fell out yesterday, during our visit with Nana."

Hannah laughed. "Of course it did. Did she faint from the shock? Like I told you, Julie—my mother has never been one for hands-on parenting."

"No fainting," Julie said. "But some blood got on her sweater. And Ivy broke her glasses. Maybe not the best visit."

"Sounds like it wasn't." Hannah looked practically gleeful, and Julie appreciated being on the same side again, united against Elaine.

"Wait, that reminds me." Julie ducked into the kitchen and returned with Wren's baby tooth, a tiny pearl inside the plastic Ziploc. "Wren didn't want to put it under her pillow last night, so I thought you should have it."

Hannah's eyes grew shiny as she took the bag, and instead of stepping away, she grabbed Julie's hand and gave an unexpected squeeze. "Thank you."

Julie had almost kept the tooth for herself, but now she was glad she'd been generous. This was the right thing for the girls, seeing their two mothers being kind to each other. Hannah's thin fingers contained a surprising strength, and up close she smelled like a cozy attic, all candle wax and cardboard boxes. The moment they stepped apart, Hannah picked up the backpacks and opened the door. "Come on girls, let's go. If we hurry, we can still make the falcon show."

Julie opened her mouth to protest, then stopped. She didn't want to ruin the bonding moment they'd just had, and it was all of five minutes to the zoo, where Irena would be waiting. Besides, the girls were already scampering down the sidewalk toward the gray Volvo. The rain had almost stopped, and now that their mother was here, they seemed happy to be leaving Julie behind. Her heart lurched as she watched them skip toward the car.

"Girls," Hannah called, "don't forget to say goodbye. Give Julie a hug before we go."

Wren and Ivy came racing back up the stairs, and Julie felt irrationally grateful to Hannah for this moment of reprieve. Burying her face in Ivy's frizzy topknot, she relished the scent of baby shampoo for a few more seconds. She wondered how Hannah had guessed she needed those extra hugs, until she realized: Hannah understood in a way no one else could, because she'd had to say goodbye so many times herself.

"Be careful," Julie called as they trotted down the sidewalk. "See you soon!"

Thirty-Four

Hannah wanted to laugh. All that time she'd spent trying to figure out how to sneak the girls away, and then the perfect opportunity landed in her lap: Irena, canceling the visit because of car trouble; Julie, perfectly gullible, believing Hannah's lie about a change in plans.

The extra goodbye hugs were a stroke of genius. The more Julie liked and trusted her, the longer it would take for her to call Rhonda or Irena or the cops. Even so, Hannah felt an unexpected stab of sympathy as she watched Julie wave goodbye, looking crushed. Obviously this woman had taken good care of Wren and Ivy, and for that Hannah was grateful. But in the end, they were *her* daughters. It wasn't her fault Julie had let herself get attached.

As soon as they rounded the corner on Phinney Avenue, Hannah broke the news.

"Julie was right. Too wet for the zoo, don't you think?"

"No way." Wren sounded indignant. "You said the sun is about to come out. And Mama Julie says the animals are more active when it's cold, to keep themselves warm."

Hannah's skin prickled at the mention of "Mama" Julie. "Maybe your foster mom doesn't mind freezing her butt off, but I, for one, would rather go to the beach." Hannah glanced in the rearview mirror, relishing the looks of surprise on the girls' faces. Then Wren rolled her eyes.

"Super funny, Mom. It'll be colder at the beach. And you hate wet sand."

Hannah flipped on her turn signal and changed lanes as they cruised down Aurora. They needed to make a quick stop at home before hitting the highway—she'd been afraid to pack too much into the station wagon, in case Julie noticed the boxes. "Thought we'd take a little vacation. Drive to a new beach, somewhere warm and sunny."

"Sunny! Yay, sunny beach!" Always the easy sell, Ivy kicked her feet and shrieked with glee. Wren stared out the window and said nothing.

"Mom," Wren said after a pause. "Are you still taking your medicine?"

Hannah gave a hollow laugh. "What's medicine got to do with it? I just want to take you on a vacation. I thought you'd be thrilled."

"Mama Ju—Miss Julie told me you're getting better because you're taking some medicine to help your brain work right again. And that when you're all better, we might get to live with you again."

Heat rose in Hannah's face. Any sympathy she'd developed for Julie dissolved. "Miss Julie has no idea what she's talking about." Her voice came out sharper than she'd intended, and she tried again, forcing herself to stay calm. "My brain works just fine, honey, no medicine necessary. We're heading home to get our things, and then we're driving to the beach. You're my daughters, and I'm taking you on a fun little vacation."

This time when Hannah glanced in the mirror, Wren's eyes were wide and shiny. Ever-cheerful Ivy kept kicking her feet against the back of the passenger seat. "Come on. I'll buy you new sand toys and swimsuits when we get there." Hannah began to sing. *"We're going to the beach, beach, beach . . ."* She hoped the catchy tune would distract Wren from thinking too much about the details.

"Julie won't like it if we're gone for too long." Wren chewed on her lip. "It's against the rules."

Of course. She should have guessed her clever, rule-oriented daughter would smell a rat and make their escape difficult. It would've been smarter to wait until they'd crossed state lines before telling Wren the truth. "I'm your mom," she said, smiling with more confidence than she felt. "I make the rules." She stuck out her tongue in the mirror and waited for Wren to make a silly face back, the way she always did. Instead, Wren plastered her nose against the window, staying that way until they'd pulled into the driveway at home.

—⁓—

Hannah had managed to cram all their necessary belongings into six small cardboard boxes. Their craftsman was overflowing with *stuff*, but as she'd begun to pack, she realized how little any of it mattered. What good was a wedding dress shrouded in layers of tissue, a stack of heirloom china from her traitorous mother, or the umbrella stroller that once carried her daughters, now spackled with black mold? Relics couldn't bring back the past. And next week the repo men would just transfer it all into a dumpster.

Hannah had left the boxes they needed just inside the front door; loading them into the Volvo wouldn't take more than a few minutes. Glancing around the car for something the girls could play with, she spotted the perky little backpacks Julie had assembled: one a smiling polka-dotted ladybug, the other a cheerful yellow bumblebee. A snack would keep the girls occupied. She handed them each a baggie of Julie's trail mix and told them to stay buckled in their seats.

As she headed up the front walk, an admonishing voice echoed in her head: *Never leave a child unattended in a vehicle.* For a moment Hannah saw flashing red and blue lights, but she pushed the image out of her mind. *Shut up,* she told the voice. They were in their own driveway, for heaven's sake, and she'd be right inside the front door.

Hannah lugged the first few boxes to the car: two filled with clothes and a third packed to the brim with the girls' dolls and stuffed animals. "Hey, Wren," she said, knocking on the back window. "Want Pinkie Pie for the car ride?" Hannah held up the beloved stuffie, a plush My Little Pony doll second only to Batgirl among Wren's favorites.

Wren shook her head and stared at her lap. Hannah turned away, cursing Rhonda and DSHS and this whole ridiculous ordeal. In just three months, they'd transformed her sweet, exuberant seven-year-old into a sullen teen. Hannah tossed Pinkie Pie into the back of the wagon and trudged up the porch steps for the last three cartons.

Grimacing, she maneuvered the heaviest box onto her knee and then into her arms, but as soon as she took her hand off the bottom, it ripped. Books spilled out the underside, and a hardcover copy of *When Things Fall Apart* landed on her toes, followed by a folder labeled "bank statements and tax returns." Hannah sank to the floor, dropping the box. Why had she bothered to pack tax returns? She was about to abscond to Mexico with her stolen daughters—the IRS was the least of her worries.

After dumping both the folder and the book into the kitchen garbage, she grabbed a roll of packaging tape and began patching up the box. This time she remembered the fold-up dolly Alex kept in the basement and wheeled the last three cartons out to the curb. From the sidewalk, Hannah took one last look at the house that had sheltered them for the past five years: Ivy's birthplace, and the last home she would ever share with Alex.

"That's it, girls." She tossed the final items into the back of the station wagon. "Ready to hit the road." Climbing into the front seat, Hannah felt better than she had in months. Almost as good as she'd felt on that sunny morning in November, before the cops stole away her daughters.

She glanced in the rearview mirror to make sure the girls were still buckled in. Ivy gazed back, placidly munching raisins. But in Wren's booster seat—nothing but an empty sandwich baggie, upside down with a few peanut crumbs clinging to the clear plastic. Hannah whipped around, frantically scanning the front yard and down the street. No Wren. "Where's your sister?" she asked, trying to keep the panic out of her voice. Ivy shrugged and kept eating trail mix. Don't be silly, Hannah told herself, this is Wren's house, her neighborhood; she wouldn't get lost around here. She must have gotten tired of waiting and gone to climb the Japanese maple in the backyard, or maybe she'd slipped inside to use the bathroom before Hannah locked the house. "Ivy," she asked again, "do you have any idea where your sister is?"

Ivy smiled, revealing bits of peanut and raisin stuck in her teeth. "Joo-ey?"

"No, not Julie. *Wren.*" Hannah didn't mean to snap, but it annoyed her that Ivy would think of Julie as a sister. "Why did Wren get out of the car?" Ivy shrugged again, and for once Hannah found the cheerful bobbing of her daughter's curls infuriating. "Well, now we've got to go find her."

Ivy pouted. "No beach?"

"Yes, beach, but we've got to find Wren first." Hannah stormed out of the car and around to Ivy's side to unbuckle her. She'd learned her lesson—this time she wouldn't let Ivy out of her sight.

But she didn't find Wren scaling the Japanese maple, or hiding in the camellia bushes, or inside using any of the bathrooms. Upstairs in the girls' room, Hannah peeked under blankets, opened the closet door to peer behind dresses and coats, and even pulled out the storage boxes under the bed to make sure Wren hadn't wriggled in behind. She must be hiding on purpose, Hannah decided, punishing her for veering off script and not taking them to the zoo as planned.

"Wren, come out," she called. "I'm sorry. We can skip the beach today and just go see the falcon show." Straining her ears against the silence, she listened for giggles or the reassuring rustle of a small body crawling out from a hiding place. "Olly olly oxen free," she tried. "You win!" More silence.

With Ivy jostling on her hip, Hannah raced downstairs and into the living room, where she tore open cabinets and flung aside couch cushions. Running through the list of her daughter's favorite hiding places, Hannah tried to pit logic against her rising fear. She couldn't very well escape to Mexico without Wren, but if they delayed any longer, Julie would report the girls missing before they even got out of Seattle.

Then Ivy let out a high-pitched squeal, right in Hannah's ear. "Wenny's sparkle shoes!" Squirming with excitement, she pointed a sticky raisin finger toward the front hall. Sure enough, a pair of glittery purple ballet flats—the shoes Wren had been wearing in the car—stuck out from the overflowing rack, squished between a pair of Hannah's brown leather boots and one of Alex's old gym trainers. Somehow, more than two years later, bits of Alex still popped up everywhere. But Hannah picked up Wren's shoes with a sigh of relief.

"If her shoes are here, she must be inside," she told Ivy, and they set off on a second circumnavigation of the house. This time she even checked behind the washer-dryer and climbed on a stool to see above the giant bookcase in the upstairs hall. "Wren, this isn't funny any-more," she called. "Come out or you're going to be in big trouble. I'll—" Hannah tried to think of a punishment with maximum impact. "I'll break your colored pencils in half."

She listened to the silence for several seconds, then collapsed against the wall. She wanted to pound her fists against the plaster and tear at her hair, but Ivy's round eyes tracked her every move. Why had she been so stupid to tell Wren about her plan? Hannah's eyes filled with tears. She'd told her because she expected Wren would be excited, thrilled even, to be reunited with her mother. To never have to go back to Julie. But maybe Hannah had misunderstood everything—maybe over the past few months she'd become such a stranger to Wren that now her daughter felt safer with her foster mom.

Hannah glanced at the wall clock: 11:55 a.m. Somehow, nearly an hour had passed since she'd last seen Wren. Shoes or no shoes, it was time to search outside. Grabbing Ivy by the hand, Hannah dragged her to the front hall. As she threw on a pair of sneakers and pulled on Ivy's pink slip-ons, Hannah noticed an empty space on the otherwise crowded rack. She scanned the rows of footwear, searching for Wren's black boots.

Shit. Wren had gone outside after all. Ever the practical child, she must have slipped inside to switch her ballet flats for boots before taking off on foot. Hannah felt a wave of nausea as she realized how far Wren could have walked by now. She raced out the door and plunked a protesting Ivy into the umbrella stroller she'd so recently discarded.

"Stop struggling. We've got to find your sister."

"Joo-ey?" Ivy said again, in a hopeful tone that split Hannah's heart like an orange slice. But how could she blame her daughter for missing the woman who'd taken care of her for the past three months? At Ivy's age, three months must have felt like a year. With the stroller bumping ahead, Hannah jogged down the street, hollering Wren's name as loudly as she could.

Halfway down the block, a gray-haired woman in pajamas stepped onto her porch. "Hannah?"

Hannah's heart sank: Mrs. Li, the same neighbor who'd given her the pills so long ago. Part of Hannah wanted to turn and flee, while the other part wanted to stay and rant about all the damage that medicine had done. Sure, Mrs. Li had been trying to help, and Hannah should have known better. But still.

"Lost your girl again?"

Hannah nodded, shame flooding her cheeks. "Stalked off about an hour ago, after I refused to take her to the zoo."

Without a word, Mrs. Li disappeared inside her house and reappeared seconds later, keys in hand. "I'll help you search. Called the police yet?"

"No, no." Hannah backed away from the porch, hoping her face didn't betray the horror she felt at the idea of involving police. "No need for that. No need to drive around looking for her either. I just—" She pulled out her phone. "I just got a text from her friend's mom. They found her."

Mrs. Li raised her eyebrows, two gray crescents above disbelieving eyes. "Been wondering about you all. Haven't seen the girls for weeks now. Hoped it meant you were doing better."

The words Hannah could have said lined up on her tongue—*Of course you haven't seen them, because CPS stole them away, thanks to the pills you gave me*—but instead she plastered a smile on her face. "We're great, now that Wren's been found." Hannah turned and took off at a run, Ivy's stroller still jostling in front. As she huffed down the sidewalk, she called over her shoulder, "Thanks anyway!"

Safely around the next corner and out of sight, Hannah doubled over, panting. The trapped, pounding sensation in her chest brought back memories of one terrible night when she was a teenager. On a dare, she'd broken into a corn maze after dark with some friends, and then got hopelessly turned around and lost the group. Racing blindly through the tall stalks, she'd smacked into one prickly dead end after another, but even when she made it back to the farm and found a pay phone, she couldn't bring herself to call her dad. Hannah's fear of disappointing people had always eclipsed her terror of the dark.

But now her dad was dead. Alex was dead. Any neighbor she asked for help would surely call the police, and then, even if they found Wren, the cops would load the girls into a squad car and drive them away. She imagined watching Rhonda on the witness stand at the next hearing, accusing her not just of abuse and neglect but kidnapping.

Hannah kept walking, this time calling more quietly so she didn't attract attention. Over and over they circled the neighborhood—no sign of Wren. The rain returned, a soft drizzle, and Ivy started to fuss.

"All wet, Mama! Go home."

"We're not going home without Wren. We've got to find her."

"Wenny go Joo-ey."

"What?" Hannah stopped short and whirled the stroller around so she could see Ivy's face. "Wren went back to Julie's?" Ivy shrugged, and Hannah wanted to shake her. Upside down, like a piggy bank, to loosen information. "Are you sure? Did she tell you that's where she was going?"

"Wenny not tell. I jus tink."

Hannah studied Ivy's pale frame, shivering beneath her thin cotton sweater and leggings. A good mother would have at least grabbed Ivy's coat. Suddenly her plan to whisk the girls off to Mexico seemed downright ridiculous, not to mention hopeless. How had she thought this would end, except with more flashing lights and another ride in a police car? Stealing children, even her own children, surely counted as a felony; after a stunt like that, she'd never get the girls back. No wonder Wren had gotten one whiff of her plan and run away.

Pressing her fingertips against her soggy forehead, Hannah forced herself to think. Walking back to Fremont from Beacon Hill would take hours, even if Wren knew where to go. But she'd always loved riding the bus, and she knew how to take the 36 downtown to Westlake Center. They'd done it together so many times . . . would Wren try to get on a bus by herself? Not possible, Hannah decided. No decent driver would let a seven-year-old board a bus alone, not even a smart, savvy one like Wren. Besides, she didn't have any money. Except—with a sinking feeling, Hannah remembered those blasted backpacks. Did Julie put money in those?

Grabbing the stroller handle, she took off at a run. "Ivy, let's go back to the Volvo. If we look for Wren from the car, at least we'll stay dry."

Sure enough, Wren's bumblebee backpack was missing. And inside the front pocket of Ivy's ladybug was a crisp ten-dollar bill.

For the next half hour, they circled the neighborhood in ever-widening circles, until Hannah felt out of her mind with worry, so desperate to spot Wren that she started seeing brown-haired little girls everywhere. Too much time had passed. Wren could be anywhere by now, especially if she'd gotten on a bus. Hands shaking, Hannah finally broke down and dialed the one person in her life who, no matter how dire the situation, always knew what to do.

Thirty-Five

As Elaine flew through yellow lights and swerved in and out of traffic on her way to Beacon Hill, she tried to convince herself it couldn't be that bad. Hannah had sounded downright hysterical on the phone, but most likely Wren was tucked away in the house somewhere; she'd always played a mean game of hide-and-seek.

Ten minutes earlier, Elaine had been shocked to see Hannah's number light up her phone, and even more shocked at her first breathless words: "Mom, I need you—" Hannah gulped for air, and Elaine felt a warm glow spread through her chest. When was the last time her daughter needed her for anything? But her next words were like a bucket of ice: "To come to the house right away. Wren is missing."

"Missing? From Julie's?" Elaine couldn't wrap her head around why the girls would be with Hannah in the first place.

"No time to explain. Just get here as fast as you can." Hannah had hung up before she could ask more questions. Now, as Elaine pulled into the driveway, she took one look at the boxes jammed into the back of Hannah's station wagon and knew they were in deep trouble. "Where in the devil's name were you going?"

Hannah slumped against the hood of Elaine's rental car, idling behind the Volvo. She looked too distraught to hold herself up. "La Paz, Mexico."

"Mexico?" Now Elaine was the hysterical one. "You were taking my granddaughters to *Mexico*?"

"Can you really blame me? The state was never going to give them back, and I needed Wren and Ivy to know—" Hannah gulped, her next words half a sob. "I'd give up everything to get them back."

Elaine rubbed her temples, glad she'd popped a migraine pill on the drive over. Hannah was giving up everything, all right, and she'd find herself a new home in a prison cell if she wasn't careful. "Let me get this straight. You told Wren you were taking her to Mexico, and then she disappeared?"

"I didn't tell her the Mexico part. Just said we were going to the beach."

"In this nasty weather?" Elaine waved her hands around her head, wondering if her daughter even noticed the wind and rain. Water dripped from Hannah's nose and chin, and her eyes blazed. The kerchief around her head had come mostly undone and flapped behind her like a kite tail. No wonder Wren had gotten spooked and flown the coop. Elaine vowed that after she rescued the girls, she'd make sure Hannah checked herself into a residential program and got some real help.

"Yes, Mom, I get it. I screwed up. But there's no time to explain." Hannah's lips trembled, and her eyes kept darting from Elaine to the back windows of the Volvo, where Ivy had fallen asleep. "I can't report Wren missing, I can't. Help me find her and get the girls back to Julie. Then you can lay into me all you want."

Elaine opened the driver's side door and ushered Hannah into the Volvo, then climbed into the passenger seat herself. At least in the car, they'd stay dry.

"We should split up," Hannah continued, her teeth chattering. "I'll keep circling the neighborhood, and you call the Metro. If Wren tried to get on a bus alone, one of the drivers might have filed a report, and—"

Elaine shook her head. "First thing the bus company will do is call the police. They're going to end up involved either way; we might as well call them now so it looks like you did the right thing."

Hannah moaned, all the color draining from her face. "If the cops get involved again, I'll never get my girls back. We've got to find her ourselves."

Elaine slammed her fist against the center console. "Jesus, Hannah, listen to yourself. What's more important, that you get custody back or that we find Wren and make sure she's safe? What if she's been kidnapped, or she's out there hurt somewhere? You're being selfish."

Hannah recoiled as if she'd been slapped. Burying her face in her hands, she began crying harder, until tears gave way to silent sobs. Elaine reached out a tentative finger and placed it on her daughter's heaving shoulder. Wonder of all wonders, Hannah leaned into the touch. Without thinking, Elaine wrapped her arms around Hannah's shaking body and began rocking back and forth, the gear shift poking awkwardly between them. The scent of Hannah's rain-soaked skin brought back memories of plastic slickers and tiny rubber boots, stomping in every puddle, and somehow Elaine's impending headache melted away. She could have sat there for hours, cradling this daughter she thought she'd lost for good. Instead, she pulled away. As long as Wren was still missing, sentimentality would have to wait.

"You've got one hour." Elaine checked her watch. "If we don't find her by then, I'm calling the police no matter what. In the meantime, I'm starting a search party." She pulled a notebook and ballpoint pen from her purse. "Give me phone numbers for all your friends and neighbors. Anyone who might be able to help."

Hannah's shoulders slumped. "I don't really do friends anymore. You wouldn't understand, but after Alex's accident—"

Elaine held up her hand. Since Steve died, she hadn't been to a single party or symphony or lecture. Without him by her side, even her favorite plays had lost their charm. "I get it. I'm a widow too." Elaine's eyes welled up. All this time, instead of fighting, she and Hannah should've been comforting one another. "Now that your dad's gone, no one knows what to say to me anymore."

"Exactly." Hannah looked up, blinking at Elaine like she'd never seen her before. Then her eyes narrowed. "But I bet I know one social butterfly who could help us."

Thirty-Six

Watching the girls skip down the block with their mother made Julie's stomach lurch, but the moment Hannah's car disappeared around the corner, she felt an odd sense of lightness: a three-hour reprieve from parenting, and on a Saturday, no less. For months she'd said yes to every endless round of hide-and-seek and craft project and make-believe game; now, underneath her bubbly veneer, Julie felt depleted. Not just tired but sucked dry of energy and personality and joie de vivre.

Without anyone tugging at her arm for juice or begging her to split apart stuck-together LEGOs, Julie hardly knew what to do with herself. Wandering into the living room, she cringed at the wreckage of Guess Who? cards, picture books, and stuffed animals. Her town house had been messy before, but never quite like this. She spotted the tip of an unfamiliar black leather glove sticking out between two couch cushions. Slipping it on, she wiggled her fingers—at least an inch of room at the end of each fingertip. A lump formed in her throat. This could only be Jake's glove, left behind a week ago when he stormed out after the argument over Wren's bruises.

She traced a guilty finger along the cracks in the leather. Since their fight, she hadn't spoken to Jake, and she'd never bothered to call Wren's doctor a second time. No more excuses, she promised herself—she'd dial Dr. Stanley first thing Monday morning.

Julie drifted into the kitchen and began clearing the girls' cream-cheese-crusted breakfast dishes off the kitchen table. Ivy had only eaten a third of her onion bagel; instead of tossing the remnants in the compost, Julie took a big bite, now gummy and stale.

"You know you're a mom when lunch means eating crusts off a kid's plate."

The voice seemed to come from nowhere, and Julie jumped, nearly dropping the dish. She whirled around to find Anitha standing at the kitchen entrance, grinning broadly and wagging her finger. "But moms usually remember to lock the front door."

"Good grief, you scared me." Julie laughed, shaking off the adrenaline still tingling on her skin. "What are you doing here?"

"You haven't returned any of my calls or texts this week, so I figured I'd better track you down and find out what's wrong." Anitha helped herself to a clementine from the hanging fruit basket, and as she sank a manicured fingernail into the bumpy orange peel, a spray of juice splattered her nose. "Judging from the state of the living room, it's been a rough few days."

Julie didn't know where to start. Usually Anitha knew all the tiny details of her life, but Julie hadn't said a word about her fight with Jake or the resulting week of silence between them. She told herself it was because she'd been too busy to chat, but truthfully, she was afraid of what Anitha might say when she heard what they'd fought about.

"Everything's fine. Just busy with the girls and all."

Anitha paused midpeel, eyeing Julie with suspicion. "You look positively miserable, and you're as jumpy as a mouse on Ritalin. Clearly everything isn't fine."

Most of the time she loved that Anitha knew her well enough to read her mind, but today she wished she could wrap a blindfold around those x-ray emotion goggles. No use pretending; Anitha would drag the whole story out of her eventually. Julie started with Jake's surfboard antics at the park. By the time she got to the part in the car—the moment she was sure Jake was about to break up with her—Anitha had covered her eyes. "Don't tell me he dumped you." One brown eye peeked out from between her fingers. "It's not possible—Jake's been in love with you since we were twelve."

"Nope, didn't break up with me. Almost worse. He took Hannah's side over mine."

"The bio mom?" Anitha uncovered her face. "What's she got to do with anything?"

"Jake thinks I'm judging her too harshly, that she deserves to get the girls back if she can clean up her act."

"Well, doesn't she?"

Julie frowned. Apparently, for all Anitha's experience as a mom, she didn't understand the complex emotions tangled up in fostering or the subtle scars left by neglect. "Wren keeps hitting other girls at school. She's violent and angry, and maybe even depressed. The therapist says it's all coming out now because she finally feels safe—for the first time in her life, she knows she can rely on an adult. Going back to her mom now would be a huge blow."

"But they're not going back now, not for a minimum of six more months, right?" Anitha's skeptical expression made Julie want to scream, until she remembered what the foster parent liaison had said: sometimes you've got to reach out to another foster parent, because nobody else can understand. On the other hand, another foster parent would surely give Julie a tongue-lashing for waiting to report Wren's new bruises. How many times had the instructor stressed the importance of notifying DSHS immediately about all medical concerns? Not only for the kids' safety but also for legal protection. Julie stared out the window over the kitchen sink, watching raindrops trickle down the glass. She really should have made that doctor's appointment already.

Anitha's voice broke into her guilt spiral. "Can we get back to the part where Jake walks out on you, and you guys don't talk for a week? That's what I don't get."

Julie's eyes burned. "It doesn't matter anyway. Jake doesn't want kids, and I do." Despite her efforts to sound strong, her voice wobbled. "Not a solvable problem."

Anitha hopped up on the countertop, perching her butt on the edge. "But do you *know* he doesn't want kids? Like have you actually talked to him about it, not just overheard some dumb conversation with your uncle?" She patted the counter next to her, inviting Julie to sit.

Julie shook her head. She'd rather pace. "I don't have to ask. It makes perfect sense, after what he went through with his sisters. And I told you—he divorced his ex-wife because they wanted different things. She wanted kids, he didn't."

"Um, no," Anitha said. "He divorced his ex because she was sleeping around."

"Well, that too."

"Jules. Don't take this the wrong way. But are you sure you're not hiding behind this whole *Jake doesn't want kids* thing?"

Julie gave her a blank look. Anitha, more than anyone, knew how much she wanted to be a mom, knew about the sperm bank and the miscarriages and everything she'd gone through. How could her best friend not see this was a deal-breaker? "I'm not following."

Anitha sighed, slid off the counter, and walked over so they stood eye to eye. "Think about it. You won't even *ask* Jake where he's at on the kids issue. Maybe that's because if you end things now, there's no chance you'll get your heart broken again."

Stalking over to the sink, Julie splashed water on her burning cheeks. Anitha was wrong. She wasn't "hiding" behind the kids issue; she just didn't want to hear Jake confirm what she already knew.

"Sorry to bring up Mr. Shit-Face," Anitha continued, "but you've given me no choice. When Seth broke off your engagement—"

Julie groaned. "Don't even start." Once Anitha got into therapist mode, there was no stopping her.

"Shush, Julie, and hear me out. Three years with Seth deluded you into thinking you don't deserve to be loved. Now you've fallen for the perfect guy, but instead of jumping in with both feet, you've convinced yourself there's something irreparably wrong with the relationship. So wrong you can't even ask him whether it's true."

Julie's cell phone buzzed from its charging cradle, and Anitha paused her tirade to pick it up. "Somebody named Hannah? Is that the bio mom?"

Julie grabbed for the phone, wondering if they'd surrendered to the bad weather and were coming home early. But the clipped, gravelly voice on the other end didn't sound anything like Hannah, and Julie froze when she realized she was talking to none other than grouchy grandma Elaine. But her words didn't make sense—something about Wren, and buses, and a disappearance. Julie's stomach clenched.

"What are you talking about? Wren isn't missing. She and Ivy are with Irena, at the zoo."

"There was a change in plans," Elaine said firmly. "And now we need your help."

Anitha waved her arms, mouthing "Speakerphone" while frantically punching her finger against an imaginary brick.

Julie obliged, desperate to share this disturbing news and hoping Anitha might have a clearer head. For her part, Julie couldn't think of anything but the purple bruises across Wren's shoulders that she'd failed to report to the doctor. Elaine kept talking about bus routes, and cash, and Wren's bumblebee backpack, but Julie had trouble focusing—until Elaine said Wren might be on her way back to Julie's apartment.

Aha. Julie's heart seized on this detail and clung to it: Wren *did* feel safer with her than with Hannah. But why hadn't Wren just waited a few hours, until Irena brought her back? Now Elaine was talking about a search party, and Anitha began scribbling names on a scrap of paper. "Wait, where did you say you are again?" Julie couldn't work out how the girls had ended up in Beacon Hill. "Irena is there with you, right?"

"Long story," Elaine said. "But it'll have to wait. The important thing now is to get as many people as possible looking for Wren. You better stay where you are, in case Wren is on a bus, headed your way. But if there's anyone you could ask to help us . . ."

"Of course." Julie began listing off the members of her vast support network: Anitha, obviously; her parents and cousins and brother; Sally and Gwen, and everyone from work. Her best friend was already racing for the door.

"You've called the police, right?" Julie asked. "And Rhonda?"

"We're calling everyone we know," Elaine said. "Hannah just thought you might have a wider circle."

Julie hung up feeling disoriented, and as she watched the taillights of Anitha's silver SUV disappear down the street, she regretted staying behind. Pushing aside stuffed animals and plastic dishes, she collapsed onto the couch. Popsicle jumped on her thighs and circled twice before settling into her lap, but Julie hardly noticed. Her limbs twitched, and she sat for only a moment before springing up and dumping the cat to the floor. She never should've agreed to wait at home. Even the most precocious seven-year-old couldn't navigate from Beacon Hill to Fremont on her own. The longer Julie waited, the bigger the pit of dread grew in her stomach.

Thirty-Seven

Elaine had to hand it to Julie—quite a popular girl, to have so many friends willing to drop everything at a moment's notice and come search for a missing foster kid. Car after car pulled up in front of Hannah's house, each vehicle disgorging two or three more of Julie's friends for the search party, until there was no street parking left and a whole crowd tramped about on the soaking wet grass.

Julie's best friend showed up first, dragging three young sons eager for a detective case. "The boys will make flyers for the neighborhood, and we brought photos of Wren from last weekend at Sam's birthday. And—" Anitha held up a stack of pamphlets. "Extra bus maps."

"Where'd you get those?" Elaine asked. Julie herself might be a flutterbudget, but she apparently had competent, take-charge friends.

"They're free on all the buses, and my nine-year-old is obsessed with maps and timetables. I've got a drawer full." The rain still hadn't let up, so Anitha sent her sons inside with her laptop. "Give them ten minutes, and they'll have designed the flyers. They're wizards with Photoshop."

Elaine frowned. If Wren was gone long enough to need missing child signs, they'd really be in trouble. She checked her watch: two minutes until Hannah's deadline, but Hannah had already disappeared into the neighborhood on foot, vowing to search every yard, tree, and sidewalk one more time. Elaine pulled out her phone and called 911, wishing she'd done it sooner.

"I'd like to report a missing child." Her voice shook as she gave the emergency operator Wren's name and address. Until now, the situation had felt more like a strange dream than reality, and she still half believed Wren would pop out from the bushes any minute now, irritated at her grown-ups for making a fuss.

The dispatcher said the police were already investigating two gunshot wounds and a motor vehicle accident, but they'd be there as soon as they could. While she waited, Elaine divided the recruits into groups of two, giving each pair a map to one of Wren's possible bus routes, along with a photo. Hannah had been out of printer paper, of course, but Anitha's clever boys combed through the recycling bin for anything with a blank side. Elaine cringed when she saw Wren's face printed on the back of a threatening notice from a credit agency. Oh well. Before Wren disappeared, Hannah had been planning to abduct her own children and run from the law to Mexico; airing dirty laundry to the neighborhood was the least of her troubles.

Climbing to the top of the porch steps, Elaine hollered out directions. "Follow your route and check every possible stop, especially Westlake Station. That's where Wren might transfer buses. And be on the lookout for a yellow bumblebee—"

She whirled around at the sound of shouts coming down the street. An elderly woman in a silk bathrobe puffed toward her, moving at a rather shocking clip. "Don't just stand there," the woman yelled. "She's hurt!"

Thirty-Eight

Hannah had walked past the half-finished house a dozen times on her frantic laps around the block, but the boxy four-square had been under construction so long she'd ceased to notice the mounds of dirt and crushed rock in the front yard. Each face of the neighborhood eyesore bore a different color of metal siding—mottled caramel on the front, mahogany wood grain on the north side, and solid black on the south— as if the builders had run out of money and used whatever scraps they happened to find lying around. For unknown reasons (Drainage? Electrical wiring? A twisted desire to maximize hazards to passersby?), a broad ditch, two feet wide and more than five feet deep, snaked along the walkway from the street up to the side door. On a whim, in case Wren happened to be hiding in the abandoned house, Hannah took a few steps down the concrete path and called for her daughter.

Later, she'd wonder if the faint whimper she heard had been real or imagined. But something—a sound, a hunch, or mother's intuition— made her run down the length of the walkway, scanning the trench. A flash of yellow caught her eye, and her heart stopped.

What at first glance looked like a pile of rags was actually Wren, curled on her side in a pool of mud, unnaturally still. For one dreadful second Hannah thought she wasn't breathing. Then the shape twitched and gave a small moan, and Hannah shuddered in relief.

"Wren!" Hannah threw herself on the wet concrete and reached down the muddy sides of the ditch. Her arms weren't nearly long enough. "Help," she called. "I found her!" She squinted through the mist, hoping to see a figure sprinting down the sidewalk. Nothing.

Without thinking, Hannah flipped to her belly and slipped down the trench wall, careful not to land on Wren. Close up, she looked even worse. Her left foot stuck out at an odd angle and her forehead sported a massive purple goose egg. Hannah placed a tentative hand on Wren's clammy cheek, but her eyelids fluttered only a second before closing again.

"Wake up," Hannah pleaded, her voice hoarse. "Please wake up." Wren needed to get to a hospital, and fast. But reaching into her back pocket, Hannah gasped. She'd handed her phone to Elaine to call Julie and hadn't remembered to get it back. The top of the ditch came to just above eye level, and Hannah jumped, clawing at the soggy edges. Mud dissolved between her fingers; the sides were too slick to climb back up.

As Hannah crouched beside her daughter's crumpled body, a memory flashed in her mind: Wren's round, frightened eyes as Hannah whirled around the house, painting walls and baking cookies and buying toys. During those chaotic weeks before the girls were taken, she hadn't been *super mommy* but *scary mommy*. And now her big selfish plans had left her daughter broken.

"It's all my fault," Hannah whispered into the tangle of Wren's hair. "I'm so sorry." What kind of a mother would steal her daughters and take them to Mexico, when what those daughters truly needed was some semblance of stability and routine, a regular life with a regular mom? All this time, Julie had been giving them what Hannah could not.

She began to scream in earnest, no longer bothering with words.

Just when she thought her voice would give out, Mrs. Li's round face appeared over the side of the ditch. Her brown eyes widened at the sight of Hannah and Wren, but she didn't say a word.

"Get help, please." Hannah's voice cracked. "She's hurt."

Mrs. Li nodded and disappeared once more. Moments later, Hannah heard loud footsteps and voices, the herd of Julie's friends stumbling over one another to help. Time sped up then, and everything happened at once: a redheaded EMT lowering his ropy arms and hoisting her up; the ambulance arriving with a stretcher; a dozen policemen pulling up in their cruisers to interrogate everyone with meaningless questions. Another EMT grabbed Hannah by the shoulder and shoved her up into the ambulance after Wren. For a second she felt relieved to escape the chaos, until she discovered she'd entered an even more frantic nightmare.

A dark-haired woman in a black uniform held a mask against Wren's mouth and nose, frowning at a beeping line on her monitor. "Pressure's dropping, and she's got a sluggish left pupil. Radio to get the OR ready, and make sure neurosurgery is standing by."

"Neuro—?" Hannah's knees buckled, and another EMT grabbed her by the elbow.

"Here, sit." He guided her to a metal seat that folded down from the wall, facing center. "Buckle up."

"She won't need brain surgery, will she? It's just a goose egg . . ."

Hannah was still fumbling with the seat belt when the back doors slammed shut and they lurched forward, sirens blaring. She asked two more times whether Wren would be okay, but the EMTs ignored her as they tended to their patient, poking and prodding and connecting various tubes and wires. They tucked a bright-silver warming blanket around Wren's tiny frame. In any other context, Hannah would have joked she looked like a foil-wrapped burrito, and Wren would have laughed—that half-giggling, half-choking sound she always made. If only. Hannah leaned closer to her daughter's heart-shaped face, now putty gray and distorted by the swelling on her forehead. Wren lay within arm's reach but felt as distant as the moon.

"Go ahead and talk to her, Mom." The dark-haired EMT hooked a bag of clear fluid on the wall beside Wren's stretcher. "She'll feel better if she knows you're here."

Hannah cringed, wondering if that was really true, but she leaned over and began whispering into Wren's ear, murmuring the same three phrases over and over: "I love you. I'm here. You'll be okay. I love you." Whether or not Wren could hear, the mantra calmed Hannah's nerves.

Over the steady bleep-bleep of the monitors, she made a bargain—with God, or love, or Mother Nature; she'd take any form of higher power who was listening. If only Wren would be okay, Hannah promised, she'd stop being selfish and proud, stop pretending she could do it all on her own. She'd commit to therapy, take the meds—heck, she'd even beg Elaine for legal help.

The ambulance screeched to a halt in front of Harborview, sending Hannah's stomach somersaulting into her throat. The EMTs leaped to their feet and opened the back gate, revealing a team in scrubs already assembled to ferry Wren into the hospital. A dozen hands gripped the wheeled stretcher as they lowered her to the ground. Almost before the gurney touched down, they began running, racing her through a side door and out of sight.

Stunned, Hannah stood at the back of the open ambulance and watched the rain pour down, pooling in the terra-cotta planters that lined the walkway to the ER and drenching the steady stream of colorful puffy coats traipsing in and out of the double glass doors.

Hannah's brain felt thick and sticky, her thoughts like swirling glue. She ought to go inside and register, find a seat in the waiting room where she could tap her feet and pull out her hair and chew her fingernails down to the quick, but she felt too unsteady for the two-foot jump to the ground. Fighting the urge to vomit, she collapsed onto the chrome bumper of the ambulance and closed her eyes. Maybe the icy raindrops would clear her head.

"Ma'am, you need to get down. I need to prep the ambulance for our next call." Hannah's eyes flew open to find the dark-haired EMT, who'd apparently stayed behind to clean up.

"Will she be okay?" Hannah asked. Blood pounded in her ears as she waited for the answer.

The woman fiddled with a latch on the back of the ambulance gate, not meeting Hannah's gaze. "She's inside now, with the doctors.

They're doing everything they can to get her stable." She offered an arm as Hannah slid off the bumper. "Need me to walk you inside?" Shaking her head, Hannah hurried away. Her legs felt wobbly, and she didn't trust herself to speak.

Halfway to the sliding doors, a desperate voice called Hannah's name. She whirled around to see a small sobbing figure sprinting toward her. Without a second's hesitation, the woman threw her arms around Hannah's shoulders and enveloped her in a rather suffocating bubble-gum-scented hug. Of course. Julie.

She was crying so hard Hannah could hardly make out her words, and none of them made sense. "This is all my fault," Julie blubbered. "I'm so, so sorry."

Apparently Elaine hadn't told Julie about the Mexico plan. Hannah tried to squirm out of her embrace, but Julie held tight and continued to blather nonsense, something about a guy named Jake with weird bruises who hadn't called the doctor.

"Stop." Hannah grabbed Julie's shoulders and held her at arm's length. "None of this is your fault." *It's all my fault.* But Hannah wasn't ready to say those words out loud, not yet. Julie took a ragged breath, and for a second Hannah thought she'd gotten herself under control, until she dissolved into another fit of sobbing.

"Going to pieces isn't going to help." Hannah dropped Julie's shoulders and grabbed her hand. "Wren needs us. Let's go inside and figure out what's happening." Before Julie showed up, Hannah had felt ready to fall apart herself, but somehow this emotional outburst had snapped her into take-charge mode.

Julie gulped and nodded, wiping a trail of snot and tears from her nose with the back of her hand. Hannah reached for her purse to grab a tissue, then realized with a groan she had no idea where her bag had ended up. Maybe back at the house, or still lying in the ditch at the construction site—at this point it hardly mattered.

"Come on," she said, taking Julie's arm. "Let's go inside."

Thirty-Nine

Elaine watched as Hannah and Julie staggered through the ER doors together, both ashen faced and soaked from rain, each leaning heavily on the other's arm. Hannah's blonde hair had transformed into a tornado of damp curls, and Julie's skin looked even more blotchy than usual. Once inside, Hannah headed straight for the clerk's desk and cut in front of three people standing obediently behind the wait-here-for-the-next-available-representative sign. When she demanded information about Wren Abigail Sawyer in an unexpectedly loud and commanding voice, Elaine couldn't help feeling proud.

After stashing a bewildered Ivy with one of Julie's friends, Elaine had followed the ambulance to the hospital, parked illegally at the curb, and raced through a door marked **EMERGENCY PERSONNEL ONLY**, just as the doctors were wheeling Wren down the hall. Only one person frowned at her as she trailed behind the gurney, through the big double doors and past another bright-red sign forbidding visitors. She managed to stay under the radar for all of sixty seconds before a fuming charge nurse took her by the arm and marched her back to the waiting room. But Elaine had been back there long enough to hear the words *hypovolemic shock* and *intracranial bleeding* and to understand that her granddaughter was in serious trouble.

As was her daughter. Elaine glanced toward the reception desk, where Hannah seemed on the verge of fisticuffs with the triage nurse.

She hurried over to defuse the situation before Hannah got them all kicked out of the waiting room.

"I don't care who the records show as her legal guardian. I'm her *mother*, and I demand to know what's going on back there. Right now."

"Hannah, darling." Elaine stepped between her daughter and the nurse, who had a face like a bulldog and at least a hundred pounds on either of them. "I just came from the back. They've got Wren in a private treatment room, and everything's going well. I overheard the doctor say she might need surgery, but after that, she's going to be fine." She invented the last bit—no one had given a prognosis—but Elaine felt certain Wren would be okay. She was a fighter, like her grandmother.

Elaine patted Hannah's shoulder. "Why don't you take Julie and go find a seat?" The foster mom leaned against a nearby wall, her face still the color of leftover oatmeal. "Looks like she needs to sit down." Hannah gave her mother a withering look but dragged Julie to a row of vinyl chairs.

By the time Elaine got through the line and received the requisite clipboard of forms—which apparently only the legal guardian was allowed to sign—Julie had disappeared outside. Elaine spotted her on the other side of the glass doors, pacing in front of the vending machine like a tiger in a cage. She'd lost her bewildered look and was in some sort of heated conversation on her cell phone.

Elaine gasped. She must be talking with Rhonda. If the caseworker heard even a whisper of the Mexico scheme, Hannah could end up in jail for attempted kidnapping. Squeezing her eyes shut, Elaine rewound her conversations from the past two hours. No, she realized with relief: Julie had been too distraught to ask questions, and she doubted Hannah had mentioned her absurd plans. At least for now, they were safe.

Elaine's knees groaned in protest as she collapsed into the chair next to Hannah, who let out a small sob. "Did you see Wren's head? She looked so tiny in the ambulance, under all those tubes and wires. I almost couldn't believe it was her."

Elaine ached to hold her daughter again, the way she'd done earlier in the car. "They told me she's dehydrated," she said, fudging *hypovolemic shock* to sound more palatable. "She'll perk up with fluids. The real trouble will be when Rhonda gets here. Whatever happens, we can't let her find out you tried to run off with the girls."

"Shit. Rhonda." Hannah groaned and buried her face in her hands.

Elaine reached out again, her fingers hovering awkwardly above Hannah's left shoulder. But before she could decide what sort of touch might be interpreted as comforting rather than condescending, Hannah sat back up, wiped her cheeks, and looked Elaine straight in the eye. "You know what, it doesn't matter. As long as Wren gets better, I don't care what Rhonda charges me with."

This was an alarming turn of events. "Don't say that, honey. Of course you care. But maybe there's a way we can work this out, just the three of us, without involving Rhonda."

Hannah scoffed. "Without CPS, you mean? In case you forgot, that ship sailed back at the fact-finding hearing, when a certain someone presented the judge with a foreclosure notice." Hannah's eyes flashed, and Elaine cringed. Her daughter was right—so far her brilliant schemes had done nothing but muck things up.

"Sorry, sorry, a thousand times sorry. But maybe there's another way."

At that moment Julie came bursting through the sliding glass doors, practically leaping over chairs to reach them. "He's coming, he's on his way. They won't listen to me, but they'll listen to him."

Elaine turned to Hannah, who looked equally befuddled.

"Won't listen to what?" Elaine asked, at the same time Hannah said, "Who's coming?" Julie looked from one to the other and took a deep breath.

"I should have told you earlier. But we think Wren's got some kind of problem with her blood, that keeps it from clotting. Jake—he's my boyfriend, or was my boyfriend, rather, until we had a—"

"We don't care about your boyfriend," Elaine snapped. "What's going on with Wren's blood?" She gave Julie a contemptuous look, wondering if wrapping her fingers around Julie's neck might squeeze out information faster.

"Sorry. He's a pathologist here at Harborview, and he started suspecting last week, when she got bruises from the straps on her booster seat. I think that's why she's hurt so badly now." The blood drained from Elaine's face, and Hannah's mouth dropped open, a gaping question mark on her lips.

"Good lord, Julie, you've got to tell the doctors. Is that why her tooth bled so much?" All Elaine's frustration with Julie came flooding back, for her Mickey Mouse clothes and wishy-washy attitude and spineless approach to discipline. "What on God's green earth are you waiting for?"

"They're not going to listen to me. I don't have proof, and I'm just the foster mom."

"Doctors don't care if you're an alien from Mars if you've got critical information about a patient who's crashing." Elaine grabbed Julie's hand and dragged her toward the front desk.

"Crashing?" Hannah trailed after them. "Mom, I thought you said—"

"She'll be fine, honey." Elaine bulldozed her way through the line and stepped up to the clerk, who looked none too happy to see them again. She still refused to let them into the treatment rooms, but the words *undiagnosed bleeding disorder* seemed to get her attention, and she promised to page the charge nurse.

"Someone will be out to talk with you shortly," she said, glaring at Elaine. "Now, if you'll step aside, there's folks behind you who've been waiting patiently. For their *turn*." Inwardly seething, Elaine offered the politest smile she could muster. The patients behind her looked fine— they had sore throats, maybe, or a bad case of indigestion—whereas Wren might be bleeding out on an operating table somewhere in the back. Elaine was about to explain the definition of triage to this infuriating gatekeeper, when Julie gasped.

"Jake!" She flew across the room and collapsed into the arms of a very tall, very pale man in a long white coat. They hugged for a moment that struck Elaine as inappropriately long, given the urgency of the situation, but she was willing to forgive anything if this man could help Wren. When he finally let go of Julie, strode to the locked double doors, and swiped his badge, Elaine let out a small whoop. A green light flickered on the card reader, and the doors swung open.

"Hannah, Elaine," he said, waving them over. "Let's go see about your girl."

—⁂—

As it turned out, Jake and Julie were right. But it took the doctors several days to figure out just what kind of bleeding disorder had made Wren's broken ankle swell to the size of a softball and caused the bump on her head to keep bleeding and bleeding, until neurosurgeons had to bore into her skull to relieve the pressure.

Elaine shuddered at the idea of a hole in her granddaughter's head, but Jake told her not to worry. He promised craniectomy was the gold standard for reducing intracranial pressure after traumatic brain injury.

"Great, but what does that *mean*?" Elaine demanded.

"It means any further swelling won't press on Wren's brain, while the doctors pump her full of platelets and clotting factors and a medicine called desmopressin to stop the bleed." Jake smiled. "But never fear. They'll pop that skull flap right back on once the inflammation goes down."

Elaine shuddered again.

Three days later, after the doctors stopped the sedation drugs and Wren woke up smiling and chatty, they all nearly died of relief. Then the test results came back, proving Wren's lifelong history of black-and-blue marks had a name: von Willebrand disease, type I. The most common bleeding disorder in the US, though none of them had ever heard of it. Wren had likely inherited it from Alex, the doctor said, since neither Hannah nor Elaine had ever shown symptoms.

Hannah nodded, looking thoughtful. "He used to go through a box of Kleenex every time he had a bloody nose. Never thought to mention it to a doctor. But why wasn't—" Hannah's voice broke.

Elaine finished her sentence. "Why wasn't it discovered after his accident?"

Jake explained as delicately as he could: Alex had died from a head-on collision, so liters of blood loss seemed nothing out of the ordinary. No one runs coagulation studies on a dead guy.

For a second, Elaine felt relieved. Maybe she hadn't killed her son-in-law with a phone call; maybe he'd died of a bleeding disorder. But Jake took one look at Hannah's stricken face and quickly added: von Willebrand had nothing to do with Alex's death, not if he'd died on impact. Alex was gone before clotting became an issue. "And don't beat yourself up for not catching Wren's case either," Jake said. "It's a tricky diagnosis, because the standard bleeding tests often come back normal."

Later that afternoon, Hannah nearly cried when the doctor handed her the lab report. Right there on paper, in all caps and highlighted in neon yellow, was the word that set her free: **ABNORMAL**. Wren's blood contained only 6 percent of the usual amount of von Willebrand factor. Without enough of this critical "glue," even mild injuries like bumping her knee on a table—or too-tight booster straps—gave Wren puffy, tender bruises. Falling into a five-foot ditch and hitting her head on a rock had almost killed her.

The hematologist misinterpreted Hannah's tears. "Oh, don't worry." She picked up a box of Kleenex from the silver tray beside Wren's bed. "It's always scary when a child is diagnosed with a bleeding disorder. But armed with knowledge of her condition and a medical bracelet, Wren will go on to live a perfectly normal life." Hannah nodded and dutifully blew her nose, but fat tears kept rolling down her cheeks. Elaine suspected they were tears not of fear but of relief. With this single sheet of lab results, the doctor had absolved Hannah of the abuse charges and flipped the CPS case on its head—so long as Rhonda didn't find out about Hannah's attempted kidnapping.

Elaine felt more relieved by the diagnosis than she wanted to admit but also guilty for doubting her daughter in the first place. Hannah swore she hadn't physically abused Wren; why had Elaine needed a doctor's proof? Perhaps because the rest of the case seemed so damning. The basic facts hadn't changed: Hannah had still neglected the girls, was still unstable and refusing to take her medicine, was still about to lose her house. And each day Elaine spent with her in the neurosurgery ward, she became more convinced Hannah wasn't ready for solo parenting. One minute she'd bury her face in Ivy's curls and refuse to set her down, and the next she'd be staring into space with vacant eyes, oblivious to her preschooler disappearing around a corner down the hall. In the cafeteria line, she handed Ivy a carton of cow's milk before Julie swooped in to snatch it back.

"Allergic, right." Hannah smacked her forehead. "How could I forget?"

But a few hours alone with Ivy forced Elaine to give up on taking custody herself. As adorable as the three-year-old's antics were, she ran circles around her grandmother. One afternoon in the step-down unit, after Wren had been transferred out of the ICU, Elaine reached the end of her rope. A red crayon had snapped in half, resulting in Ivy's fourth tantrum of the hour.

"Oh for heaven's sake, quit whining." Elaine lifted Ivy's squirming body off the floor and dumped her at the foot of Wren's bed. "Fussing isn't going to put the crayon back together, and the floor's filthy. You'll make yourself sick."

But Ivy's wriggling jostled Wren's ankle, and soon the girls were hollering at each other.

"Stop!" Elaine raised her voice above the din. "You'll have the nurses in here with all that racket, and then Ivy and I will get kicked out. Is that what you want?" She glared at the girls. "Be quiet, or I'll unplug the TV." The girls glanced at the screen above Wren's bed, playing a cartoon on mute.

The threat worked for about two minutes. When the girls started in on each other again, Elaine collapsed into a chair—she'd done all she could. Let them suffer the wrath of the charge nurse.

But when the door swung open, it wasn't angry Nurse Megan; it was Julie, with a giant stack of construction paper, markers, and the idea to make Valentine cards for every patient in the step-down unit. Surprised, Elaine checked the date on her cell—in all the chaos, she'd forgotten tomorrow was Valentine's Day.

"The nurse gave me a list of names. And when we're done making cards, we can wheel you around to deliver them." Julie's enthusiasm was contagious, and soon Wren and Ivy were happily engaged in cutting out paper hearts, all animosity forgotten.

Over the tops of the girls' busy heads, Elaine caught Julie's eye. "Thank you," she mouthed, and Julie smiled back. Stable, energetic, and 100 percent sane: maybe Julie was exactly what they needed.

—∙∙∙—

"Mom, what *is* this?"

Wren was off with the physical therapist, and Julie had taken Ivy home, so Elaine found herself in a rare moment alone in Wren's hospital room with her daughter. Hannah was leaning over and peering into Elaine's handbag, and the incredulity in her voice made Elaine blush. Only one thing she could have found.

"What's what?"

"This *book*. It's like—there's a naked man on the front." Hannah held up *The Knight of Secrets* by the corner.

Elaine snatched the paperback and tucked it under her armpit. "Just a little light reading I picked up at the gift shop. And he's not naked—he's wearing breeches. It's historical fiction."

"That's not historical fiction, that's a bodice ripper. And I'm pretty sure they don't sell *that* at the gift shop." Hannah pressed her fingers to her lips, clearly trying to hold back laughter. "I mean, it's great—nothing to be ashamed of, of course. I just never thought—"

Elaine made a huffing sound. "There's a lot about me you don't know. So what if I'm embracing my emotional side these days—isn't that what you've complained about all these years? That I'm too cold and unfeeling?" The truth was, Elaine *had* bought the book in the hospital gift shop. She'd been surprised to find it there, but in a way it made sense—if you were stuck in a waiting room, counting the minutes until you found out if your beloved made it through surgery, you'd need the most gripping, most escapist book possible. And just the way hunky lords could distract folks in waiting rooms—well, they could distract her from the fact she was a lonely seventy-six-year-old widow, sans job and with a daughter who despised her.

She almost hadn't bought the book for fear someone might find it. Steamy romance on your Kindle was one thing, steamy romance in your purse quite another. But then she'd remembered the feel of Hannah's head on her shoulder in the car and the sound of Wren's raspy laughter after she woke up from surgery to find Nana by her bedside, cuddling that purple bat doll. Maybe it was time to stop hiding.

"*Cold and unfeeling* may have been overly harsh," Hannah said. "More like we're on opposite sides of the spectrum: lawyer and artist, never the two shall meet."

Elaine cocked her head and squinted at Hannah. "You know, your dad said the exact same thing, in that letter he sent you way back when."

"Wait, now you're reading the letters Dad wrote me too?" Hannah picked up the duffel bag Julie had brought over that morning, crammed with Wren's clothes, and began sorting leggings into piles on the hospital bed.

"You gave them to me," Elaine said, "in the courtroom after the hearing. And I'm glad you did, because the whole time we've been in the hospital together, I've had your dad's voice in my head. He wanted us to stick together, you know." She grabbed a pile of wrinkled T-shirts and started to help. "Steve always knew the right words. Me, the only way I knew how to show my love was to hold you to the highest possible standard. Demand your best, in the hopes it would bring you the life you want."

Hannah gave a sour laugh. "At this point, I think we can both agree I'm pretty far from the life I want."

Elaine hated the resignation in her daughter's voice. Her impulse was to change the subject or invent an excuse to flee the room—go in search of coffee, maybe, or an impenetrable steel suit to protect her from all these wretched *feelings*. Instead, she placed a hand on Hannah's shoulder. "We're all doing the best we can, right? If I could, I'd change a thousand things about the way I mothered you."

There, she'd said it out loud. And instead of looking angry, Hannah seemed thoughtful as she added another pair of fuzzy black leggings to the stack. "I don't know, Mom. All these years I blamed you for putting your work first, but now I'm realizing you also took care of yourself, by keeping your goals alive. That's not easy to do as a mom."

"You're being kind. We both know I went overboard in that direction." Four decades ago, when Elaine first discovered—feared—she was pregnant, she'd been terrified of ending up like her own mother, a miserable 1950s housewife. After Steve took over most of the parenting duties, she'd prided herself on their modern, egalitarian relationship and thought she'd been setting the best possible example for her daughter. But now she saw how Hannah had lost herself by going in the other direction, determined to be the opposite of her mother. A generational pendulum, decades of women swinging between one extreme and the other—all desperate for that elusive, impossible balance.

Elaine had run out of shirts, but her hands needed something to do. Without thinking, she plucked the black leggings off the top of Hannah's pile and refolded them, tighter and straighter than Hannah had.

"And here I was, thinking you'd changed," Hannah said, shaking her head at the refolded leggings. "You're just as controlling as always." But her eyes sparkled, and Elaine could tell she wasn't mad.

She patted her daughter's hand. "Me and my controlling self are going to make sure you get healthy, and make sure you get those girls back." In all the chaos of Wren's surgery, Rhonda hadn't questioned what they'd told her about the car trouble and missed text messages—at the moment, it was all a big misunderstanding. They just had to keep it that way until the hearing.

Forty

"Mama Julie, these puzzles are way too easy." Wren added *Highlights* to the assortment of rejected magazines, books, and board games strewn across her hospital bed and gave Julie an exaggerated pout. "There's nothing to *do* here. Can't we just go home?"

Home. The word bounced around in Julie's mind like a Ping-Pong ball. For almost two weeks now, she'd managed to pretend life in the hospital was all there was, that she might go on forever trading shifts with Hannah and Elaine. None of them wanted to leave Wren by herself, so during the day they switched off between keeping Wren company and minding Ivy as she cavorted around the hallways and nursing stations, collecting stickers for Wren as if her sister's life depended on them. At night Julie took Ivy home, while Hannah and Elaine took turns in the creaky metal cot beside Wren's bed. But how much longer could the three of them go on ignoring the obvious: Now that a blood test had proved Hannah innocent of abuse, did the girls even need a foster mom?

Julie took a deep breath. For now, she was still Wren's guardian. And at the moment, Hannah had taken a bus to therapy across town, and Elaine was off at the park with Ivy, leaving Julie to help Wren wade through an afternoon of boredom.

She perched on the end of Wren's bed. "Why don't we finish *Kitty Girl?*"

For weeks, Wren had been stuck on the ending. Every time Julie asked if she wanted to keep working on it, she shrugged and changed the subject. Julie tried not to feel disappointed—sure, it was their bonding project, but the whims of a seven-year-old changed daily.

This time, Wren surprised her. "I think I finally thought of an ending. But my book's not here, so how can we work on it?"

Grinning, Julie went to riffle through her purse. After a moment, she pulled out the stapled-together pages, sandwiched between two pieces of cardboard. "I brought it to read in the waiting room while you were in surgery. Seemed like good luck. Ivy and I read it over and over, and she kept bugging me to know how the story ended."

After the first few pages, during which Kitty Girl learned she had the powers of invisibility and superjumping, the story had taken a sci-fi turn: Kitty Girl was actually an alien, stranded on Earth after her parents accidentally dropped her from their spaceship. Now Kitty Girl had discovered a portal back to her home planet, but she'd been having so much fun fighting crime—and adored her new Earth-bound sidekick, Popsicle—that Kitty Girl wasn't sure she wanted to jump through the portal and go home after all.

Julie handed Wren the book and her box of colored pencils. "What's she going to choose? I'm dying to find out."

Wren flipped to the back and stared at the blank pages. "She's not going to decide. It's too hard of a choice."

"But isn't the portal going to close? I thought she only had twenty-four hours or she'd never be able to get back home."

"That's what Kitty Girl *thought*." Wren grinned. "But then Popsicle chases a mouse through the hole, and Kitty Girl has to go after, because of course regular cats can't breathe on Planet KG. And Kitty Girl is crying because she thinks Popsicle will suffocate, until . . ." Wren made a *bum-bum-bum* sound, waiting for Julie to look properly aghast. "Turns out it's a two-way portal. Kitty Girl can go back and forth anytime she wants."

Julie clapped. "Perfect ending." Wren looked adorably pleased with herself, and Julie reached out to ruffle her brown bob, then stopped short, inches from the bandage taped across Wren's half-shaved head. Julie tapped her lightly on the nose instead, then pushed the colored pencils closer. "You draw, and tell me what to write."

While Wren got to work on Kitty Girl's final scene, Julie chewed her lip. Questions had been swirling in her mind since the accident, but she'd been waiting for the right moment. "Wrenny-bird, can I ask you something?"

Wren nodded without looking up, her forehead furrowed with concentration as she began to sketch.

"Back in November," Julie said, "after you first came to my house and we found those bruises on your back—why did you lie about where you'd gotten them? First you said you fell off a ladder, then out of a tree."

Wren dug through her pencil box, refusing to meet Julie's eyes. "I didn't want Mom to get in trouble."

A chill ran down Julie's spine. "But if your mom didn't make the bruises, why—?"

"We weren't supposed to be at the cabin. Mom said if Nana found out, she'd put us in jail for sure." The pieces began to click together in Julie's mind. No wonder Wren had been terrified to bump into her grandmother at the grocery store.

"So the ladder you fell off—that was at the Whidbey cabin?"

Wren nodded, and Julie's heart broke a little. Poor Wren, caught in the web of her mother's deception. "Okay, another question—how'd you end up in that ditch, anyway? Trying to superjump like Kitty Girl?" Julie flashed what she hoped was a lighthearted grin. Instead of answering, Wren grabbed an eraser and began rubbing furiously at the paper. "Were you trying to explore the construction site? Or maybe you just like extra-muddy slides?"

Wren finally looked up. "The ten-dollar bill. You know, the one you put in my backpack."

"The money I gave you made you fall in a ditch?"

"Yep," Wren said, as if this explanation made perfect sense. Julie futzed with a bouquet of flowers on the bedside, waiting to see if she'd continue. For Wren, apparently that was the end of the story.

"Sorry, not following."

Wren let out an exasperated breath, a sound Julie had come to know well—the sigh of a seven-year-old whose mind was ten steps ahead of her grown-up's. "I couldn't get back to Fremont without taking the bus, and you said you'd given us money just in case, so I was unzipping my pouch to check. I took out the money and tried to put it in my pocket."

Julie could imagine where this story was headed, and she felt herself sinking under a brand-new layer of guilt. Looking back, putting money in the girls' backpacks seemed awfully passive aggressive. Why hadn't she trusted Hannah to take care of the zoo tickets?

"But then there was this giant whoosh of wind." Wren waved her hands in the air. "And it blew the money into that big ditch. I thought if I just leaned over the edge with a long stick, I might be able to pull it out. But the sides were all squooshy, and somehow I fell and hit my head on something at the bottom."

"A rock." Julie shook her head, remembering the terror of that day. "Good thing your mom found you when she did."

Wren nodded, but a small crease appeared between her brows.

That wrinkle felt significant—what was Wren not saying?—and it gave Julie the courage to voice the question she'd been working up to all this time. "But why did you run away in the first place? Your mom said that when Irena didn't show up at the zoo, it was your idea to head back to her house in Beacon Hill."

Wren snatched up *Kitty Girl* and shoved it into Julie's hands. "Here, time for you to write the word bubbles."

"It's okay if you don't want to talk about it," Julie said gently. "But if there's something you need to tell me—"

"Never mind, let's do Kitty Girl later." Wren grabbed the comic and returned it to the cardboard sheath. "I want to watch TV." Plucking the remote from the bedside, she began rapidly changing channels. Clearly Julie's opportunity had passed.

Three episodes of *The Magic School Bus* later, Wren had forgotten about the probing questions and was back to bored and cranky. The swelling in her brain had temporarily affected her balance, and the doctors wanted her to wait a few more days before trying crutches. But even stuck in bed, Wren hardly sat still—she wiggled and fidgeted enough to make lying in bed look like an exercise program. Julie had never been so thrilled to see a child bored.

Wren flipped off the TV and snapped her fingers. "Wait, I know. Maybe you could get me something from the *gift shop*." Her voice trilled up on the last two words, as if the existence of a hospital gift shop was a question rather than a certainty.

Julie couldn't help but laugh. Wren had been dropping hints about the gift shop ever since Irena came by yesterday, lugging a giant bag from Harborview Gifts, full of salty snacks and random plastic trinkets. The light on the blinky unicorn key chain had already died, and windup somersaulting Yoda didn't land on his feet anymore, but Wren didn't seem to care—the grown-ups could always buy replacements at this magical place called the gift shop.

"Okay, kiddo, I'll go find something. How about a magazine? Or I saw they have Super Slime."

"Surprise me," Wren said, scratching at the oversize cast that swallowed up her foot and half her lower leg.

Julie didn't want to be one of those pushover moms who got her kids a toy every time they set foot in a grocery store, but in this case, she felt safe. As long as she only bought Wren toys every time she was hospitalized for a near-fatal head injury, it probably wouldn't break the bank.

—⁓—

"Wren seems more like a Mowgli than a Belle."

Jake's voice made Julie jump; he'd snuck up behind her in the coloring book section and stood so close that her nose brushed his chest when she whirled around. Taking a step back, she couldn't help but smile at the way his powder blue scrubs perfectly matched his eyes. Heat rushed into her cheeks. Something about his tousled hair and baggy pants reminded her of just-woken-up Jake, which reminded her of all the nights he'd spent in her bedroom.

"Surprised to see me?" he asked, grinning. "Wren told me you were here when I stopped by the room."

"No. You just—" Julie paused, willing herself to stop acting like a lovestruck teenager. "I never see you in scrubs, that's all."

Jake smoothed the front of his smock. "I almost always change when I come up from the basement. Cuts down on the formaldehyde stench and all. But I wanted to catch you before you take Ivy home for the night." He placed a hand on her forearm. "You've been a hard one to pin down lately."

"I know, I'm sorry." Julie sighed, staring at his hand. "It's just . . ."

"Stop. You don't have to explain a thing. Your foster daughter just got out of the ICU. But as soon as you're ready, we need to talk." He dropped his hand and stared at his shoes. In the awkward silence, Julie wondered how far down the rabbit hole this conversation would go.

When Jake looked up, his eyes were shiny. "I've been miserable these past two weeks. You're right. I'm a workaholic, and I never thought I wanted kids. I'm honestly terrified to be a father, given what a disappointment my own dad was. But I love you—" His voice wobbled, and Julie could see his Adam's apple dipping as he swallowed. It was all she could do not to leap into his arms and smother his words with kisses. Except she desperately wanted to hear the rest of what he had to say. "No matter what happens with the girls, you need to know how much I want to make this work."

Julie grabbed Jake's hands, fighting back tears of her own. "That's all I want, for us to try—"

"Julie!" A shrill voice called her name from the entrance of the gift shop.

She dropped Jake's hands and groaned: Rhonda, all tight smiles and fire red lipstick, hurried toward them as fast as her two-inch heels could go. In a black pantsuit and crimson silk scarf, she looked fancier than usual. "How perfect to bump into you." She gave Julie an awkward side hug, apparently oblivious to what she'd interrupted. "I was just buying a gift for Wren. Would've visited sooner, except I came down with the flu, and it's been nonstop emergencies all week."

"Wren's much better." Julie took a step back. "A few more days of observation and IV antibiotics, and the doctors say she'll be able to go home." That word again, sticking in Julie's throat.

"Wonderful." Rhonda clapped her hands together, then frowned. "But I'm going to have to write up a full report on how all this happened—Irena said she canceled the visit, but somehow the girls ended up leaving unsupervised with their mother? That's a real safety violation."

The stern tone in Rhonda's voice made Julie want to crawl into a hole. "It must have been a miscommunication," she said, trying to sound confident. "Hannah told me Irena was meeting them at the zoo."

Rhonda raised her eyebrows. "And you believed her? If you haven't noticed, that woman seems to have a shaky relationship with the truth."

Julie's jaw tightened. She didn't think of Hannah as *that woman* anymore, not after the two of them had bonded during their twelve days together in the hospital. Julie now knew Hannah's coffee order by heart, had given her tampons, and had even asked her advice about the Jake situation. "I don't blame Hannah for wanting to make the visit happen," Julie said, "especially since Irena had canceled several times before. Besides, won't the judge lift the supervision order anyway, now that we know Hannah had nothing to do with those bruises?"

Rhonda pursed her lips. "But do we know that for certain? It's tragic, but as a twenty-year veteran of CPS, I can tell you: it's possible for bleeding disorders and abuse to coexist. Even with the von-whatever-it's-called, we're still dealing with serious neglect, noncompliance with the treatment program, and lying about foreclosure. Not to mention Hannah has neither a house nor a job. Honestly, I'm not sure this diagnosis changes anything."

"Of course it changes things." Julie suddenly felt hopping mad. "All this time, everyone's been assuming Hannah beat her children, when really, she's just a struggling mom with no support system. Mental health problems aren't a reason to take someone's kids away." Julie glanced over at Jake and realized she was repeating essentially the same argument he'd made to her a few weeks ago. Frowning at Rhonda, he put an arm around Julie's shoulders.

"Why don't we have this conversation later," he said, "when both Hannah and Elaine can be present?"

"I'm sorry," Rhonda said, peering at his ID badge. "Who are you again?"

"Dr. Lankowski, pathology." Jake extended his hand. "Nice to meet you."

Rhonda looked from Jake to Julie and back again, clearly trying to discern their relationship. Julie didn't feel the need to explain. "Let's go upstairs," she said. "We can find the others and sort this out properly."

—m—

Wren's hospital room was crowded when they returned: Elaine and Ivy had come back from the park, noses pink with cold, and Hannah had returned from her therapy session. Julie watched the color drain from Hannah's face as Rhonda slipped in behind Jake.

"Wren, my dear, how are you?" Despite her airy tone, Rhonda's voice sent a chill through the room.

Ignoring the caseworker, Wren sat up taller in bed and tried to peer around Julie's back. "Whadja bring me, Miss Julie?" When they were alone, Wren always said "Mama Julie," but in Hannah's presence, Julie became "Miss." She understood, of course, but it still stung.

"Sorry, hon." Julie held up her empty hands. "Couldn't decide between two coloring books, so I came back to ask. Belle, or Mowgli?"

Wren wrinkled her nose and said, "Mowgli, of course," at the same time Ivy started jumping up and down, chanting, "Belle, Belle, Belle!"

"I'll get both," Julie said, laughing. Elaine gave her the evil eye—spoiling them rotten—but Julie didn't care. If she had only a few days left as their foster mom, she was going to buy the girls as many coloring books as she damn well pleased.

Rhonda cleared her throat. "Wren, I'm glad to see you looking so healthy. Would you let me borrow your grown-ups for a minute? We've got some important information to discuss."

Hannah's face turned pale, and her hands trembled as she collected her purse. Taking a step closer to her daughter, Elaine stuck out her chin. "There's a family meeting room down the hall," she said, glaring at Rhonda. "Let's use that."

Jake offered to stay with Wren and Ivy, so Elaine led them past the nurse's station and into a small windowless room, empty except for a gray plastic conference table flanked by a dozen metal chairs. Julie picked the seat next to Hannah.

"I'll stand," Elaine said gruffly. "Better for my knees."

"Then I'll stand too," Rhonda said, pulling Wren's file from her briefcase. "Folding chairs are a nightmare for my back." Julie wasn't fooled—neither woman wanted to cede the higher ground.

No one spoke for a moment, and then everyone started talking at once. "Of course, we'll conduct a full investigation," Rhonda said, at the same moment Elaine piped up with, "The abuse charges will need to be wiped from Hannah's record."

"You can't possibly think this was Hannah's fault?" Elaine asked, her arms folded tightly across her chest. "Wren made the stupid decision to run off by herself, then slipped on some mud. Kids trip all the time; it's nobody's fault."

Rhonda looked unmoved. "What I really want to know is how Wren and Ivy ended up in Beacon Hill in the first place, unsupervised with their mother?"

Elaine continued as if she hadn't heard the question. "Haven't you been reading the reports from the doctors? All this time you've been accusing my daughter of abuse, comparing her to that monstrous mother Emily Cooper, when it turns out Wren has a bleeding disorder."

Rhonda narrowed her eyes. "Comparing her to Emily—wait, how do you even know about that? I never . . . I only wrote about that in my private notes." Rhonda's skin went blotchy as recognition dawned on her face. "*You* were the one who took Wren's medical file? That's tampering with evidence." Rhonda dropped the thick manila envelope on the table with a smack, and Julie's mouth dropped open. She knew Elaine was a force of nature, but she had no idea she'd stolen a file.

"I'd press charges if I weren't up to my ears in paperwork already," Rhonda said, jabbing her finger toward Elaine. "*You* were the reason I looked ridiculous in front of the judge, and why we had no statement from the abuse expert."

"Good thing, because that abuse expert would have been wrong," Elaine said, not missing a beat. "Again, we need to get those charges wiped from my daughter's record."

Rhonda glared at Elaine, still obviously furious. "Like I told Julie, I'm not sure this diagnosis will make much of a difference. Children who are properly supervised can't run off, or if they do, their grown-up runs right after. I understand that's not what happened in this case. Wren was gone—what, about two hours?—before anyone called the police. That's negligence no matter how you look at it."

Rhonda's certainty irked Julie to no end, and before she could think it through, words came tumbling from her mouth. "Elaine's right. It wasn't Hannah's fault; Wren's slippery like that. I lost her myself once, in downtown Target, no less."

The social worker flipped open Wren's file. "Wait, you never reported—"

"I turned my back on her for a second to look at a sweater. And poof! When I turned around again, she was gone."

Rhonda clucked her tongue. "Not the same thing at all. You were right next to her."

Julie glanced at Hannah, who looked back with something like gratitude radiating from her clear blue eyes. Julie took a deep breath. "Rhonda, if you want someone to blame, you might as well pin this accident on me. Jake noticed unusual bruising around Wren's collarbone two weeks ago, and I never called to tell you."

Elaine inhaled sharply and bugged her eyes at Julie—*close your damn mouth,* her expression seemed to say. She stepped around the table to stand next to Julie. "That's neither here nor there. You called Wren's pediatrician, right? But the doctor's office never called you back. That's on them."

Julie felt confused. Elaine seemed to be playing from both sides of the chess game, trying to defend Hannah but also wanting Julie to look good in front of the caseworker.

Rhonda glared at the trio of women, now all together on the opposite side of the table. "Julie, I'm not sure why you're coming to Hannah's defense here. I'll be as glad as anyone if we can prove Wren's bruises weren't caused by abuse, but the truth is, the one time Wren ended up alone with her mother, she almost *died.* That's a clear and present danger if I ever heard one." Rhonda fixed her eyes on Julie. "But if you can't protect Wren either, we'll find a foster parent who can."

Julie gasped, and for once Elaine was speechless. Hannah, who'd been silent the entire meeting thus far, scraped back her chair and stood up.

"No." Her voice was barely a whisper but filled with calm authority. "You will not blame this accident on Julie. Wren took off and ended up in that ditch because I told her we were running away. To Mexico."

Elaine groaned and covered her face with her hands. It took Julie a moment to process Hannah's words, and then her mouth dropped open. A moment ago, Hannah would've had a good chance of getting the girls back, but she'd just blown it. On purpose, to protect the foster mom she'd known for only a few weeks. Julie wasn't sure whether to be grateful for the confession or furious that Hannah had planned an escape in the first place. She gaped at Hannah, who returned her gaze with eyes that looked neither sorry nor scared.

"To *Mexico*?" Rhonda's tanned face deepened to a dusky red. "That's felony child abduction, you know."

Apparently recovered enough to argue, Elaine held up her hand. "Not exactly. *Taking* the girls to Mexico would have been a felony. But Hannah didn't even start driving."

"Fine. Attempted felony child abduction, then." Rhonda scowled at them. "Still a crime."

"Attempt requires not only intent but direct action toward completing the crime," Elaine said. "Let's leave it to the judge to decide what constitutes—"

"Mom, I'd packed the Volvo," Hannah said. "Believe me, I had every intention of stealing my daughters. If Wren hadn't gotten hurt, the three of us would be lounging on a beach in Baja, sipping cold Cokes in the sunshine." A small smile crossed her lips, as if she were imagining white sand and foam-tipped waves. Then she shook her head and became deadly serious.

"I'm done pretending. The girls need to stay with Julie, for the next two months or six months or however long it takes me to get better. I can't—" Hannah wavered slightly, and Elaine placed a bony hand on her shoulder. "For so long, I've been trying to parent completely on my own—to stuff down my grief, be both mom and dad to the girls, pretend my depression is something simple I can toss off like a blanket when I need to. Well, if there's one thing I learned from Wren's accident, it's that I can't do it alone. For now, I'm not sure I can do it at all." She gave another small, sad smile. "And if someone else is going to mother my girls for a while, it's got to be Julie."

Julie couldn't help it. She burst into sobs, and the three of them became one big huddle, Hannah's tears blending with Julie's as Elaine squeezed them both in a hug so tight they started laughing, a release of all the pent-up tension and fear and grief from their time in the hospital. For a moment they forgot all about Rhonda, until she made another grumpy throat-clearing sound. They reluctantly pulled away.

"This is a highly unusual situation, for the biological family and the foster family to suddenly band together." Rhonda shook her head, clutching Wren's file against her chest. "All I'm trying to do is find a safe placement for these girls, yet you three seem hell bent on making that difficult." She glowered at Elaine. "I want that medical file back in my office, first thing tomorrow morning. As for the rest of you, I'll see you at the hearing." She stormed out of the room, and together they listened to the dagger-click of her heels, a shower of angry sparks fading down the hall.

"Well, that went well," Elaine said, and Julie gave a guilty snicker. She'd landed herself on Rhonda's shit list, but at least she had company.

"Come on," she said, taking Hannah's arm. "Let's get back to Wren."

Forty-One

Hannah's life didn't become all sunshine and rainbows the minute the three of them decided to work together. At first, not much changed, except she began to grieve all over again, this time mourning the loss of false hope that had sustained her for months—the thought that any minute her daughters would be coming home. In the days following her confession, Hannah suffered waves of regret, what-the-hell-did-I-just-do moments when she wished she could take back her words and crawl into the comfortable cocoon of denial once more. But in that ambulance, watching Wren's blood pressure plummet and her skin turn ash white, she'd made a promise: from now on, her pride and fear meant nothing compared to the well-being of her daughters.

Two weeks after the accident, the doctors said Wren could go home. After they'd filled out the last of the discharge paperwork, Elaine wheeled her down to the curb, while Hannah carried her crutches and a bouquet of Mylar balloons. As they waited for Julie to pull the car around, Elaine turned to Hannah with a stern look.

"I keep meaning to tell you, that off-white has too much yellow."

Hannah glanced down at her black sweater. "White?"

"On the living room walls. At the Whidbey cottage. Evidently you've been violating our agreement."

Hannah scanned her mother's impassive face. Surely Elaine wasn't about to chew her out for working on the remodel now. Over the past two weeks, her mother had been kinder and more emotionally available than Hannah could ever remember. Still, this was Elaine.

"I told you not to set foot on the property." Elaine gave Hannah another long glare, then broke into a grin. "And you went and picked butter for the walls. Criminal."

Hannah swatted at her mother, who jumped out of the way with a laugh. "But don't worry, I've got a plan to fix it. Maybe once you've finished therapy and found a job, you can come help me on the weekends."

Hannah nodded, relieved Elaine wasn't going to serve her a lawsuit. But after they'd loaded Wren into Julie's car and kissed the girls goodbye, she started feeling angry. After all they'd been through, her mother was still going to claim the cabin? It didn't help when Elaine insisted on driving Hannah home, then pretended she needed to use the bathroom. Even with the water running, Hannah could hear her rifling through the medicine cabinet above the sink. She barged in.

"Just stop."

"Stop what?" The mirrored door still swung on its hinges.

"Come off it, Mom. You're digging through my medicine cabinet to check my pill supply."

Elaine scratched her chin. "I needed . . . a Band-Aid."

Hannah rolled her eyes. "My meds are none of your business. But if you must know, why not ask? Instead of sneaking around behind my back, making secret plans to solve everything." The more Hannah had thought about the confrontation with Rhonda in the hospital conference room, the more she wondered whether Elaine had orchestrated the whole thing. "My whole life, you've treated me like I'm incompetent, one step away from abject failure. And like you said, I screwed up—"

Elaine frowned. "I never said—"

Hannah held up her hand. "Mom, I've got it on voicemail. Screwed up *royally*, I think it was. If you want to help me get better, you've got to stop protecting me from the truth."

At the word *truth*, Elaine's eyes grew wide. To Hannah's surprise, they filled with tears, and Elaine slipped past her out of the bathroom.

Hannah watched her mother walk to the window and stare out at the backyard for a long moment. When Elaine finally turned around, shiny rivulets streaked her face. "I should have said something years ago. It's just, your dad thought—I felt so guilty—"

In all her thirty-nine years, Hannah had never seen her mother cry, let alone shake with heaving sobs. Watching Elaine fall apart felt wrong, like spotting an actor in costume coming out of a bathroom stall. Hannah turned away to give her privacy, but Elaine reached out and clung to her daughter's shoulders.

"It's my fault, not yours. He wanted to do something nice for you." Elaine gave an undignified hiccup. "I'm the one who made him stay on the phone. Me and my big plans."

Now Hannah was thoroughly confused. "Who wanted to do something nice?"

"Alex." Elaine took a step away, leaning heavily against the back of the couch. "He called me the night he died." With shaky breaths, Elaine spilled the secret she'd kept for more than two years. As Hannah listened to this extra, hidden chapter of her husband's death, a mix of emotions churned in her gut.

"How could you have kept this from me?"

"I thought—your dad and I both thought—you'd blame yourself if you knew he died trying to plan you a weekend getaway. And your dad thought you might never speak to me again."

Hannah let out a bitter snort. "How could I blame myself any more than I already have? All this time I thought Alex died furious with me."

Elaine sniffed and wiped her nose on her sleeve, the same gesture she'd snapped at the girls for a hundred times. "No. Alex told me you'd fought, but he was over it already."

Hannah choked down a sob. That was one of the things she loved best, how Alex never could hold a grudge. "Mom, you should go. I need to lie down." She longed to be alone, for time to filter all her memories through this new reality and let them settle again, like silt in a riverbed.

For once, Elaine did as Hannah asked, but not before making her a pot of tea and promising to return in a few hours.

When Hannah woke up, the room was dark. Elaine had come and gone again, leaving a manila envelope on the entry hall table. Your dad would have wanted you to have this, she'd written. A peace offering: You decide what to do with it.

Inside, Hannah found the deed to the Whidbey cottage.

—⚡—

As promised, Rhonda moved the next hearing up from July to mid-March. The new court date was scheduled a few days after the doctors had sawed Wren's cast in two, revealing a better-than-ever ankle—a bit stiff, with pasty, wrinkled skin smelling faintly of old fish—but whole and functional. Elaine baked a chocolate cake to celebrate, and Hannah fought with a stubborn tube of red icing to trace the outline of a foot and ankle on top. A miserable failure, because when they rang Julie's doorbell to deliver dessert, Ivy met them at the door and asked why Mommy had decorated the cake with a headless duck.

"It's supposed to be my ankle, silly," Wren said, hobbling up behind her sister. By then her balance had mostly recovered, and Julie had pulled her short brown hair into a side ponytail, making the dark peach fuzz on the other side look more like a fashion statement than a battle scar. Hannah beamed at her healthy daughters. They made all the sacrifices of the past few weeks more than worth it.

Despite the dry mouth, cloudy brain, and shaky hands she hated, Hannah had gone back on her medication. But she'd switched psychiatrists, and her new doctor was a single mom herself, who understood that Hannah's challenges lay as much in her circumstances as her brain chemistry. "No wonder you were drowning," the doctor said, after listening to Hannah's honest account of the past few years. "Trying to do everything and be everything for your girls, all while stuffing down your grief—that's too much to ask of anyone."

Indeed, now that Julie and Elaine shared the parenting load, Hannah had more energy than she'd had in years, and enough free hours to take on a part-time job while she wasn't in therapy. Selling used photography gear at the neighborhood camera shop netted barely more than minimum wage, but chatting with customers about lens types and fill lights, exposure bracketing and depth of field felt invigorating, like rescuing part of her brain from a chest of mothballs. The store also offered photography lessons and had a small darkroom in the back where Hannah could develop her own film—baby steps toward returning to her art. Her monthly income wasn't nearly enough to pay down their overdue mortgage, but she'd made peace with losing the house. The twin ghosts of grief and guilt hid in every corner and closet of that old place, and Hannah breathed easier once she'd settled into a spare white-walled efficiency in Capitol Hill.

She kept her lease month to month—the girls would never fit into 450 square feet—but Elaine's gift meant they had options. They'd finish the renovations together, and once the girls came home for good, Hannah could move them all to the island, or sell the cottage and use the proceeds for a home in Seattle.

So sure, she was making progress, but the road felt long and slow. And Hannah was painfully aware that none of it could have happened if she'd had sole custody. She missed her daughters every hour of every day, and Julie's chipper sweetness still got on her nerves. But Julie wasn't her adversary anymore—she was a lifeline, the one making Hannah's recovery possible.

On the morning of the hearing, the five of them met at Julie's to take the bus downtown together. Elaine suggested they bring the girls along this time to let the judge see for himself how well they'd adjusted to having their three caregivers working as a team. Hannah had been reluctant to bring them at first—what if Rhonda or the judge said something upsetting?—but Elaine insisted. With the girls right in front of him, the judge would be less likely to fixate on the details of who'd kept what secret from whom. He'd stay focused on what mattered: the girls' best interest. And clearly, living with Julie while Hannah continued her recovery would be the least disruptive option, especially with Elaine around to help. In the weeks since Wren's accident, she'd officially retired from Greenbaum & Sons and devoted all her copious mental energy to preparing for the hearing.

After running the whole plan by Hannah's lawyer, Elaine called it virtually foolproof. Shared parenting was the latest movement in progressive child services, and according to this new model, the more collaboration between bio and foster parents, the better. The judge would approve their arrangement, Elaine promised, regardless of what stories Rhonda told about escape plans, unsupervised visits, or stolen files. Sure, they'd each made a few mistakes, but only with the best of intentions.

As the five of them exited the bus in front of the courthouse, Hannah stepped down first, gripping Wren's sweaty palm in her own. Julie got off next, with Ivy clinging to her hip like a baby monkey. Elaine brought up the rear, a determined expression on her face and a thick file folder tucked under one arm, filled with Wren's medical records, journal articles about von Willebrand disease, and past court cases she'd assembled for ammunition.

After a long cold February from hell—including multiple snowstorms, which shut down Seattle but delighted the girls—the temperature had finally shot up into the sixties. The balmy spring air was thick against Hannah's bare forearms, and she felt surprisingly calm.

Maybe it was her new routine of daily meditation, or the breathing exercises she'd learned from her therapist, or simply the strength of five strong females marching in step, but even the long line at the courthouse metal detectors didn't upset her. She smiled at the tight-lipped security guard, whose holstered gun jiggled at his hip as he waved a wand across her body. Ivy and Wren both jumped when their grandmother's artificial knee set off the alarm, but they relaxed once they'd left security behind and wandered into the main foyer. With its high ceilings, gleaming brass elevator doors, and colorful medallions set into a marble floor, the space felt more reminiscent of an upscale hotel than a place to sentence criminals. In front of the elevators, they stepped around a pair of lovebirds taking selfies; both wore jeans, but the woman had flowers in her hair and a gauzy veil trailing down her back.

"Look," Hannah said, squeezing Wren's hand. "Those two are getting married here." *See,* she was telling her daughter, *this isn't a scary place. I am keeping you safe, even if I won't be taking you home today.*

The atmosphere felt a bit gloomier on the second floor, where they had to navigate a maze of small, dark hallways to find east 201, the same courtroom where Hannah had faced off against her mother three months ago at the fact-finding hearing. The wooden benches hadn't gotten any softer, and just as many self-important suits bustled through the fluorescent-lit corridor, but it all seemed friendlier with Wren and Ivy by her side. One caseworker stopped to give the girls crayons and coloring books, and when she offered Hannah a sympathetic smile— the same look she used to find so patronizing—Hannah let herself smile back.

Her confident mood evaporated, however, when Rhonda rounded the corner and strode down the hall, deep in conversation with a ruddy-faced, white-haired man Hannah recognized as the district attorney. Rhonda took one look at Julie and the girls seated next to Hannah on the bench and began whispering furiously in the man's ear. He studied them for a moment, frowning, before he turned on his heels and guided Rhonda back through the door of the DSHS/CPS room.

"She still seems upset," Julie whispered in Hannah's ear.

"More like furious," Hannah said. "But I feel like she's been biased against me from the beginning."

"I wouldn't take it personally," Elaine said, leaning across the girls so she could keep her voice low. "She's just a stickler for safety, and after the cases she's been through, I can't say I blame her. I told you about Dylan Cooper, right?"

Hannah tipped her head toward Wren and Ivy, silently begging her mother not to go into details. "It'll be fine. The judge will see that letting the girls stay with Julie for a while, with near-daily visits from me, will be best for everyone." Hannah's voice sounded more certain than she felt. Wren began coloring harder, gripping her crayon with white knuckles and pressing down with fast, forceful strokes. "Are you okay, honey?" Hannah touched Wren's shoulder.

Shrugging off her mother's hand, Wren kept coloring.

Julie stood up. "Think I'll go for a little walk down the hall, see if there's a vending machine. Ivy, Elaine—want to join me?" Hannah gave her a grateful look as they sauntered off, then turned back to Wren.

She took a deep breath, hoping she could find the right words. "None of this is easy, and you have every right to be mad at me. In a perfect world, your dad would never have died, and I would never have gotten sick." Wren sniffled without looking up, and two dark splotches splattered her paper. "The idea of being separated from you, even for a short time, tears my heart in two. But you know this doesn't mean I'm giving up, right?" Gently cupping Wren's chin, Hannah tilted her face so she could look into her daughter's eyes. "It means I'm finally taking steps to get better."

Wren nodded, but the wrinkle between her brows didn't fade. How could it? Hannah could hardly expect her seven-year-old to grasp what she herself had only recently begun to understand. For now, the best she could do was let the waves of Wren's anger and grief roll over them both, and hope that someday, maybe in the far-off future when Wren cradled a baby of her own, Hannah would have the chance to explain.

Motherhood demands pieces of yourself, Hannah would say. *Your body, your solitude, at worst your mental health. All that giving and giving and giving away can come at a cost, and one morning you might wake up to realize you've lost yourself and can no longer mother at all. Then,* Hannah would tell her dear grown-up daughter, *you must make a different kind of sacrifice, by letting go of being the giver and the caretaker, and learning to ask for help.*

—☙—

In the end, the hearing took less than an hour. With Elaine and Mr. Gorman waltzing together in perfect time, and the girls snuggling on Julie's lap at the back of the courtroom, Rhonda's objections fell flat. At one point Elaine even raised the ghost of little Dylan Cooper, saying if more families embraced shared parenting, maybe there'd be more resources to go around, and fewer children would fall—tragically—through the cracks. Rhonda nodded at that line, and at one point, she even smiled. As long as the girls were safe, she said, CPS had done its job.

Sunlight streamed through the courtroom windows, and the temperature climbed as they plodded through the necessary details. Hannah pledged to file a parental consent agreement at the superior court, giving Julie temporary guardianship of the girls while she finished her therapy. In return, Judge Nakamura agreed to dismiss the dependency petition: with the abuse charges resolved and a solid parenting plan in place, CPS could take a step back. Instead of the state paying Julie for foster services, Elaine would provide her with a monthly stipend to cover the girls' expenses.

After the last minutiae had been ironed out, Hannah expected Judge Nakamura to adjourn the court, but instead he claimed to have one more order of official business. In a voice suddenly booming and serious, he said, "By the power bestowed upon me by the State of Washington, I hereby order you, this very afternoon . . ." His face broke into a grin. "To take these girls out for ice cream sundaes."

Mr. Gorman, Irena, and the district attorney began to clap, and even Rhonda joined in. By the time Judge Nakamura dismissed them, they were all flushed and giddy. Ever-stately Elaine looked both delighted and disheveled, her white bangs a feathered mess from all the times she'd run her fingers through her hair. Julie beamed from ear to ear, especially when Jake joined them in the hallway and high-fived the girls. Wren and Ivy had gone wiggly, already riding a sugar high from the prospect of ice cream.

Hannah alone felt the loss, an ache both sharp and dull, of all the moments she would now miss. Admitting she needed help didn't make it easier to share her daughters. But watching the girls exit the courthouse into the sunshine—Wren with her fuzzy half-shaved head, holding her grandmother's hand, and Ivy, braided pigtails swinging as she twirled in circles around Julie's finger—Hannah couldn't help but smile. For a moment, she closed her eyes, letting the sunlight bathe her lids and dissolve the tightness in her forehead.

She hadn't lost her girls. She'd gained a village.

Author's Note

While this book is entirely fictional, I have done my best to keep the details of the child welfare system accurate. Of note, this story takes place in 2017–2018, when foster care and child protective services in Washington State were run by the Department of Social and Health Services. Since that time, in recognition of the need to better protect at-risk youth and families, the Washington State legislature transitioned control of foster care and CPS to the newly created Department for Children, Youth, and Families, which has launched a variety of campaigns aimed at reducing the number of children taken into state custody.

One such bill, the Keeping Families Together Act (HB 1227, effective July 2023), raised the threshold for removing children from their homes, specifically mandating that poverty, mental illness, and/or substance abuse can no longer be used as justification for separating children from their parents.

ACKNOWLEDGMENTS

I began writing this book while homeschooling my three children, after nearly a decade of being either pregnant or nursing, during a time when intensive parenting had swallowed me whole. I could no longer remember who I'd been before I birthed my babies, nor imagine who I might be when motherhood ceased to claim my every waking hour. Writing this book brought me back from that dark place, not only because it helped me rediscover my long-buried creative spark, but also because it introduced me to an amazing community of writers and writer-parents who reminded me I wasn't alone.

To all the people who helped me on this journey, I cannot thank you enough. I am so grateful to the social workers and foster parents who spoke with me about their experiences, including Nancy Prostak, Maia Anderson, Joey Gaines, and Isabel Tan; and for my anonymous beta readers from Spun Yarn who offered their perspective as parents who'd been through a CPS investigation. Thank you to Kimere Kimball and Kelli Bynum for their legal expertise; Jennifer Lycette for her perspective as a hematologist; and to my community police officer, Corey George, for explaining what might happen when children are found alone in a car in Seattle. Special thanks to Seattle foster mom extraordinaire Christy Krispin, who read the entire manuscript and offered so many helpful corrections. Any remaining errors are mine alone.

This book wouldn't have happened without my spectacular agent, Serene Hakim, who believed in me and my story even when I'd lost the faith myself. I'll also be eternally grateful to Chantelle Aimée Osman for plucking my manuscript from her submissions pile and having the perfect vision to bring it to life. Thanks to the entire team at Lake Union, including the brilliant Jodi Warshaw, whose insightful edits gave my book the final tightening it needed; my sharp-eyed copyeditors Jenna and Stephanie, who saved me from many a misplaced modifier; and my production manager, Angela Elson, who kept everything moving smoothly.

Thank you to all the friends and family who kindly read my early drafts, including Margery Muench, Eric Bahuaud, Laura Jean King, Elizabeth Gillman, Jennifer Jabaley, Genoveva Dimova, Caitlin Cross, Brittney Moraski, Lyn Liao Butler, Nicole Comforto, Adrienne Wiley, and Meghan Nishinaga, who also offered her helpful expertise as a pediatrician. I could not have made it this far without my fabulous mentors: Peter Mountford, Amanda Niehaus, and Joan F. Smith, who each taught me so much about the process of writing and publishing a novel. Huge thanks also to Jackie Cangro, whose generous edit of my first draft help me see a path forward, and Camille Pagán, whose mindset coaching kept me sane amid the roller coaster of publishing.

To all my writer friends from Author Mentor Match and the Women's Fiction Writers Association—your encouragement and companionship have meant the world to me. Thanks especially to Michele Montgomery for introducing me to the wonderful group of Write InMates who keep my butt in the chair.

To Amy Neff, Lauren Parvizi, and Erin Quinn-Kong—you are hands-down the best writing group anyone could ask for. I cannot believe how far we've come in the last few years, and I can't wait to see where we go next. Still Writing, always.

To my family: I am so grateful for your unwavering support. Thanks to my dad, Carl Myers, for showing me what it means to be a voracious reader (no matter how many books I read, I'll never catch up!); and to my mom, Jean Myers, for teaching me to write, to mother, and most importantly, to be kind to myself. All my love and gratitude to my very first reader, my husband Michael Leggett, who cried at the end and told me to keep going—if not for you, I surely would've run screaming from the checkout line long ago.

Finally, to my three wonderful children: you are my everything. Thank you for cheering me on and for giving me the space to write when I needed it. I am honored to be your mother.

About the Author

Photo © 2023 Ian Grant

Hadley Leggett is a novelist and science writer whose winding career path has included degrees in medicine, biochemistry, Spanish, and journalism. After moving all over the United States during her childhood, she now lives in Seattle with her husband and three children, as well as her parents, three cats, and an ever-rotating troop of foster kittens. *All They Ask Is Everything* is her first novel. Visit Hadley online at https://hadley.ink.